THE DEEPEST WOUND
"Reed gives the reader a genre story worth every minute and every penny spent."
—*Book Reporter*

"Whew! The murders are brutal and nonstop. Det. Jack Murphy tracks killers through a political maze of lies, deception, and dishonor that leads to a violent, pulse-pounding climax."
—**Robert S. Levinson**

"The things Reed has seen as a police officer have to make for a great book."
—*Suspense Magazine*

THE COLDEST FEAR
"Everything you want in a thriller: strong characters, plenty of gory story, witty dialogue, and a narrative that demands you keep turning those pages."
—**BookReporter.com**

THE CRUELEST CUT
"Rick Reed, retired homicide detective and author of *Blood Trail,* the true-crime story of serial killer Joe Brown, brings his impressive writing skills to the world of fiction with *The Cruelest Cut.* This is as authentic and scary as crime thrillers get, written as only a cop can write who's lived this drama in real life.... A very good and fast read."
—**Nelson DeMille**

Also by Rick Reed

The Jack Murphy Thrillers

The Cruelest Cut

The Coldest Fear

The Deepest Wound

The Highest Stakes

Nonfiction

Blood Trail (with Steven Walker)

Available from Kensington

The Darkest Night

A Jack Murphy Thriller

RICK REED

KENSINGTON PUBLISHING CORP.
www.kensingtonbooks.com

LYRICAL UNDERGROUND BOOKS are published by

Kensington Publishing Corp.
119 West 40th Street
New York, NY 10018

All Kensington titles, imprints, and distributed lines are available at special quantity discounts for bulk purchases for sales promotions, premiums, fund-raising, educational, or institutional use. Special book excerpts or customized printings can also be created to fit specific needs. For details, write or phone the office of the Kensington sales manager: Kensington Publishing Corp., 119 West 40th Street, New York, NY 10018, attn: Sales Department; phone 1-800-221-2647.

PUBLISHER'S NOTE
This book is a work of fiction. Names, characters, businesses, organizations, places, events, and incidents either are the product of the author's imagination or are used fictitiously. Any resemblance to actual persons, living or dead, events, or locales is entirely coincidental.

First Lyrical Underground edition: April 2017

ISBN-13: 978-1-60183-642-7
ISBN-10: 1-60183-642-2

First trade paperback edition: April 2017

ISBN-13: 978-1-60183-643-4
ISBN-10: 1-60183-643-0

*This novel is dedicated to the brave law enforcement officers of
the Iberville Parish Sheriff Department
and Plaquemine Police Department in Louisiana.*

*Being a career officer, I am saddened by the cynicism and criticism
that are heaped on law enforcement today, when so little
appreciation is shown.*
*As a citizen, you won't find the protection or assistance you need
by posting on Facebook.*

*When duty calls, your officers will always answer. Count on it.
Times may be bad, but police officers are not.*

Chapter One

She regained consciousness, choking and gagging on the rum that was being forced down her throat. She sputtered and sucked in air, and the glass lip of a bottle was forced between her lips and deep into her throat. The bottle was yanked out, chipping her teeth, and her tortured lungs struggled to expel the liquid fire.

A man's voice seemed to come from far down a tunnel. "Who else knows?"

She had been stripped naked, tied in a chair, and beaten unconscious several times. She was drowning sitting up, and the lack of oxygen made her thoughts fuzzy. She knew this voice belonged to the man-mountain, but she couldn't think. His big fist struck the side of her head, and pain exploded behind her eyes.

"Who else knows?" the man asked again.

She wanted to answer, but she just coughed and sucked air into her burning lungs.

A palm that dwarfed her face stung her cheek and blurred her already-fuzzy vision.

"Who have you talked to?" the voice demanded.

She felt the words forming, but her throat was so damaged she rasped out nonsense and expected another blow. None came.

She swallowed saliva and what tasted like blood and lifted her head. Through the slits of swollen eyes, she watched the giant open the door to the room and speak to the two men. They came in and the door was closed.

These were the two men who had brought her here and beat her before the giant came. One man was tall, thin, balding, and muddy brown. This one stood beside the door watching her. The other man was short, almost as short as her five foot, three inches. He was *muscular, with almost black skin, maybe pushing twenty years old and buzzing with energy. He enjoyed hurting her.*

Neither man had spoken to her, or asked her who she was or what she was doing there. They had just grabbed her, hit her, and she came to here. The tall man had beaten her in the face and bare breasts with his fists. She remembered thinking that using his bare knuckles was stupid because it was a good way to break your hand. His hand hadn't broken, but she was sure he had broken her nose and knocked teeth out.

The questioning and beating had come to a halt, and she took deep breaths, clearing her mind, trying to remember if she had told them anything.

She remembered screaming in pain. She remembered the giant asking over and over again. "Who else knows?" But try as she might, she couldn't remember if she had told them the little she knew or what she suspected. Had she told them about her friend's visit? Or his name? She didn't think so, but it was possible.

Blood trickled down her lips into her mouth, and she spit it out.

"You gon' be better soon," a voice said beside her ear and startled her.

She felt a man pushing his crotch against her back in a state of arousal while he massaged her shoulders. His hands moved from her shoulder. One gripped her neck, the other down her bare front, cupping a breast, squeezing until she thought she would scream.

The hand on her breast relaxed and moved down, probing between her legs, rubbing, exploring, burrowing into her most tender spot until he made painful penetration. He moaned in spasms as he ground his hardness into her back.

His breath smelled of decomposing meat. Strong hands gripped her throat until she felt light-headed. Her breaths came in rapid gasps, and black spots gathered in front of her eyes. The hands fell away from her throat, and she heard a soft thud behind her.

As her lungs filled and the world swam back into focus, she heard the smaller man say, "Damn, DeeDee. Why you hit me?" The voice was coming from the floor behind her.

Now she had a name for the tall one. The one who had just saved her from being raped. He was named DeeDee. She intuited that DeeDee was the careful one, but just as capable of dispensing torture or death if the giant commanded it.

"Papa say keep this one alive for now," DeeDee said.

"I wan'..."

"I know what you wan'," DeeDee said. "If Papa catch you he cut your dick off. Papa say watch, no touch. Next time, I kill you myself." DeeDee opened the door and stood still as if he was going to say something, thought better of it, went out and shut the door.

"DeeDee don' wan' fun. He wan' kill you," her abuser said. His rough hands returned to her breasts. Calloused thumbs rubbed her nipples until they responded, and he squeezed until her breath caught in her throat. She fought down a scream as tears ran down her face.

"Don' worry, you. I gon' make de pain go way. My juju make it better."

Now she knew the names of two of her captors. The tall one was DeeDee and the giant was the one called Papa. She had heard of Papa. He was the reason she had come here. Getting caught and tortured was not the way she had expected this little excursion to end.

The small man stepped in front of her and leaned over, his face inches from hers. She could see he wasn't a man at all. He was barely a boy, fifteen or sixteen if that. But what he lacked in size and age he more than made up for in aggression and violence

He lifted her face and smiled at her, showing a piano keyboard of ivory teeth. The expression turned serious. "Don' move, bitch." He pulled a machete from his belt and moved it back and forth in front of her eyes until he was sure he had her attention. He cut through the bindings on her ankles, and her feet tingled like she was standing on a bed of nails. She wiggled her toes, willing the circulation to come back.

He must have read her expression and stood, brandishing the machete. She saw the wood handle of a revolver stuck down in the front of his pants. He sliced at the air with the machete, the smile gone.

"No way out, bitch. Papa no here. DeeDee no here. I here. You here. Dis gun here. And this," he said and held the blade of the machete to her neck. "You be nice, I no hurt you. You move, I cut you deep."

He cut the binding holding her wrists. She let her arms fall to her sides and remained motionless, passive, buying time for the feeling to come back into her arms and hands and feet.

He came up close beside her and put a hand on her face, pulling it toward his crotch.

She lunged out of the chair, grabbed him by the throat, and slammed him into the wall by the door. His hands went to his throat just as she had hoped and she wrapped a hand around the gun's handle, reached down with a finger, and pulled the trigger. His clothing and the proximity to his body muffled the blast, but she didn't know where DeeDee was. Or when Papa might reappear. She leaned into him and ground the barrel into his crotch and pulled the trigger again and again. He went limp, and she let him fall to the floor. A reddish stain blossomed between his legs and spread around him.

She staggered into the wall for support. Her feet felt like swollen lumps of clay, but she thought she could walk. She put her ear against the door to listen, but her ears were still ringing from the gunshots. Even if someone was coming she had to leave this room. Try to get away.

The doorknob turned before she could reach it and the door opened. DeeDee stood in the doorway gaping at her. His hand moved for his waist, but he was too slow. She shot him in the chest twice and kept pulling the trigger, the hammer falling harmlessly on empty chambers.

DeeDee fell up against the wall and slid down to his butt, legs spread out. She could see the blood bubbling around the holes in his chest. He was as good as dead, but his hand groped for his gun. She slapped his hand away and yanked the semiautomatic out of his waistband. She knelt beside him and put the gun against his cheek.

"How do I get out of here?" she asked. She knew she was in a basement or other subterranean place, but when they'd knocked her out, she was outside, in the woods, watching the giant from a distance.

"Shoot, bitch," he said, and she did.

She left the revolver, and went through DeeDee's pockets. He had some paper money, change, a pack of gum, but no keys and no extra ammunition. She dropped the clip from the semiauto and *counted. The clip had six bullets, so she had seven rounds counting the one already chambered.*

DeeDee's body lay slumped in the middle of a long hallway with walls, floors, and ceilings of smooth unpainted concrete. Lights were recessed into the ceiling, and in both directions the hallway appeared to branch into intersecting hallways. On each side of the hallway she saw steel doors, most likely to other rooms like the one she had been in. There were a half dozen doors in this hallway alone. When she had awakened in the room, although tied to the chair, she assumed she was in a basement of a commercial building. But this was no basement.

She got to her feet and headed to her right. It didn't matter what direction she went as long as it took her away from here. It was dark at the end of the hallway. She hesitated, but turned right. As she walked, the overhead lights came on. She crouched, turning, pointing the gun in all directions, and expecting to see Papa or more men coming for her. She was alone. She realized the lights were motion activated.

At the end of this hall she saw concrete steps ascending to a wide landing with two steel doors. Three steel doors were on the left of the hallway and one on the right. She moved toward the stairs and froze when she heard something. It didn't sound like a voice, but it was human and the sound was coming from the other side of a door.

She put her ear against each of the doors, and at the second one she could hear someone crying. A child. The doors were secured with a sliding bolt. She lifted the bolt and opened the door. The light from behind her bled across the threshold and across the figure of a tall disheveled girl staring wide-eyed at the naked woman with the gun. The sobbing stopped.

"Please don't kill us," the girl said.

Tiny heads peeked up from dirty mats scattered on the floor.

"Oh, my God!" she exclaimed. She had hoped to find something, someone, but this was far beyond what she'd imagined.

She heard indistinct talking and a door opening by the staircase. She hurried into the room and pulled the door shut. She listened to the sound of footsteps, two people, coming closer. They would have to walk right past her. She stood beside the girl and whis-

pered, "I'm here to take you all home. Get the other children and keep against the wall."

Without questions the girl ushered the younger children into a corner of the room just as the sounds of steps were right outside the door.

The door opened, and a man's voice asked, "Who's in there?"

She stood in a shooter's stance, two hands on the gun, shoved to the front, eyes level with the top of the slide. The door opened wider, revealing a dark-skinned man with a handlebar mustache. He said, "Oh shit!" before she shot him in the mouth. She heard the other man beat feet toward the stairway and knew she wouldn't catch him.

She turned to the children but spoke to the tall girl. "I can't take you with me. It's too dangerous. Do you understand?"

Tears welled up in the girl's eyes, but she said, "Yes."

"I'll be back for you. I promise. Be brave. Can you do that for me?"

The girl went back to the other children and began comforting them. Her heart ached as she backed out of the room. She kicked the dead man's leg out of the doorway, shut the door, and slid the bolt home. Maybe it would keep them safe until she got help.

She raced up the steps and came to the double set of steel doors. A wooden door was to her right, but she chose to go straight ahead. She pushed one door open and was struck by the heated air of late summer and the smell of dirt and the Mississippi. Nothing ever smelled so good.

She stepped out into the night and ran to her left. She had no idea the direction she was going because the moon was hidden behind thick cloud cover. The gravel bruised and cut her feet as the hue and cry of voices was raised from every direction. Her foot came down in soft dirt and she stumbled into a sugarcane field. Most of the stalks were dried out, dead, and the leaves sliced her skin. She got to her feet and tried to run, but something hard came down on the back of her head and she went face-first into the soft dirt. She lifted her face and spit out dirt as strong hands yanked her to her feet. She couldn't see their faces, but several men, all armed with handguns or rifles or shotguns, surrounded her. The barrel of a pistol was shoved in her mouth, and something hard jammed into her spine.

Another man was on a cell phone. "Papa. We foun' her. She alive."

Her heart sank and all of the fight went out of her. She hoped they would kill her here, right now. She didn't want to go back to that room. Back to that hellhole. She could still see the frightened faces of those poor children. She had promised to save them, and she had let them down.

The man put the phone in his pocket. "Papa say bring her."

Another man came running up. "DeeDee dead. He dead."

The one that had been on the phone laughed, pointed a pistol in her face, and said, "Papa say bring her. He no say alive."

Chapter Two

Detective Jack Murphy felt something wet on his mouth. A tongue. And it was working its way inside. Without opening his eyes, he drew his head back and said, "Hold on, Katie. Let me get awake first." The chuffing sound in his face made him jerk wide awake.

"Oh Christ!" he said and jumped out of bed, spitting and wiping at his mouth.

Katie rolled over, saw Cinderella staring at Jack, and laughed.

"You think that's funny. She put her tongue down my throat."

"She's just hungry, Jack. She needs to be fed," Katie scolded him. To Cinderella she said, "Good girl. Want some food? Want some food? Daddy will feed his baby."

Katie always sounded like she was talking to a two-year-old and not a mangy mutt.

"Are you sure your sister won't keep her?" Jack asked.

Katie's sister, Moira Connelly, first in her class in law school, had come home almost a year ago. She became a deputy prosecutor just days before her boss, the Prosecutor, shot himself in the head.

"Moira's seeing someone, Jack. And he's allergic to dogs. You know that."

"Well, I'm seeing someone too," Jack said with a pout. "Or don't you mind me swapping spit with a dog?" He moved toward Katie, his lips puckered for a kiss. "Come on. Gimme a big wet kiss. It's just the widdle baby's spit."

Katie crawled over Jack and got out of bed. "I'll feed her. You need to use some mouthwash. Both of you."

Cinderella followed Katie out of the bedroom. Jack sat on the side of the bed. His life had changed in the last six months. He and

Katie had been divorced for three years longer than that, but she had always been there for him when he needed her. He'd gotten himself banged up pretty good last year when some asshole tried to rob the Blue Star riverboat casino. Katie had been by his side almost constantly while he was healing. She'd moved into his river cabin, fed him, bathed him, took him to doctor's appointments and the like. He'd always heard that you don't appreciate what you've got until you lose it. Almost dying was his wake-up call. He knew there would never be another woman for him.

He'd dated around after the divorce. Came close to getting engaged once. But Katie was the yardstick he measured other women by. When she'd asked him to move from his cabin back into the house, he didn't have to think about it. He'd said yes. But this was just a house. Katie was his home. They'd had problems—would have more undoubtedly—but he was sure they could weather them, together.

He got up and went to the bedroom window to see into the backyard. When he was in the third grade, he'd broken Bobby Sanders's nose right out there. It was like all fights, silly, full of testosterone and "you take that backs." His mom had insisted that his dad, Jake, punish him for fighting. His dad said he would take care of it, took him out to the garage, hugged him, and called him a chip off the old block. His dad pinched his arm so hard he screamed. "That was for your mother to hear," his dad explained. "You did the right thing breaking that bully's nose. Don't ever take any shit from a bully, son. They never stop if you do."

He didn't know why that particular memory had surfaced, but maybe it was just being back here; being back in the house where he'd grown up. He and Katie had lived here until their divorce. But he tried to put the past away, and make himself be Mr. Positive. He was positive he could smell coffee brewing. He would choke down a cup of coffee and stop at Donut Bank on St. Joseph Avenue to get some real coffee on his way to work. Katie had never seemed to get the knack for brewing a good cup of coffee. She was, however, an excellent cook, which reminded him, he'd have to start watching his weight again and do more exercise.

He stood and examined his naked form in the mirror on the back of the bathroom door. He was a little over six feet tall, medium build, and solid. But he'd lost count of his scars from knives, from shrapnel, from bullets. The scar that stood out the most ran from his neck just beside his ear, and on downward across his chest. It was an ugly red color and sometimes tingled, sometimes hurt, and sometimes felt dead. But the man who had given it to him *was* dead. So it all evened out.

He showered and brushed and rinsed and laid his clothes out on the bed. One of his best suits, dark blue with a muted chalk strike, white button-down shirt straight from the package, red tie, shiny black shoes. He didn't normally dress this way for work, but he had a meeting scheduled this morning with Deputy Chief of Police Richard Dick, aka Double Dick, or simply the Dick. He wanted to show Dick respect by spiffing up a little. He knew that was the reason because Katie had told him that was why. He wanted to get the ass chewing over with so he could go forth and commit mayhem.

Katie came into the bedroom and remarked, "That suit looks nice on you. Sexy. Can I watch you dress?"

He wrapped her in his arms, led her toward the bed, and kissed her passionately. He didn't want his last kiss to be from that damn dog's tongue. "I love you," he said and squeezed her tight.

When he didn't let go, she said, "Well. Where is this coming from?"

"The same place this is coming from," he said with a wry smile.

Jack changed his mind about the suit. He dressed in khakis and a brownish-gold Ben Hogan knit shirt. Katie came back in the bedroom carrying a mug of coffee for him and sat on the edge of the bed looking at his pants.

"You looking at my pants?" Jack asked.

"You shouldn't wear those," she said.

"Damn, girl. Slow down and let me catch my breath."

She slapped his rear. "I mean you shouldn't wear those clothes to the meeting this morning. If you want to get on Richard's good side, you should wear something a little dressier. I liked the suit you laid out."

"It's just Double Dick," he said. Seeing her eyebrows raise, he corrected himself. "I mean Deputy Chief Richard Dick. Sorry. I slipped."

"I don't mean to be critical. It's just that if you were meeting

Liddell those would be more-than-appropriate clothes. But when you've been asked . . ."

"I was ordered," Jack corrected her this time. "The Dick never asks."

"Okay. When you've been ordered to meet with a deputy chief, you should show respect. If not in your own mind, at least in the way you dress."

"I promised to *try*, and I will," he said. He was rewarded with a patient-but-knowing smile.

She took clothes from the closet and laid them across the bed. Dark blue suit, white button-down shirt, red tie with tiny blue boat anchors, lace-up dress shoes.

"That's more like it," she said. "There's your coffee, and if you have time I'll make some breakfast." With that she left him to change clothes.

He took a sip of the light brown liquid and poured the rest down the bathroom sink and ran water. He put the clothes away that she had laid out and snuck out of the house. He felt a little guilty, but with all the fooling around, he didn't have time to go to Donut Bank. And that made him wonder how his partner was making out in Louisiana. Bigfoot had left at the end of their shift yesterday and was driving straight through. He told Jack it was a twelve-hour drive. Jack knew it would be fourteen hours with food and pee stops.

Chapter Three

Plaquemine, Louisiana

While Jack was being tongue raped by Cinderella, Liddell was coming awake to the smell of frying bacon and freshly brewed coffee. He raised his head from the arm of the couch and squinted at the dim light coming through the front windows. The sun was just a promise on the horizon. He had left Evansville around 3 A.M. yesterday and had driven almost straight through to his hometown of Plaquemine (pronounced *plak-a-mun*). He'd stopped once for gas and Twinkies and had gotten in a little after two this morning.

"I got three hours of sleep so I'm rarin' to go," Liddell said.

Landry gave him a hard look. "Get your ass off my couch, baby brother, and come eat," Landry said. "Breakfast. Just like Mom used to make."

"Okay, Mom." Liddell rose and trudged to the kitchen. He was too tired to even undress and had slept in his clothes. His neck and back were stiff from being folded up on the couch.

Landry said, "You look like a puppet with a stick shoved up its ass." He brought two coffee mugs to the table and set them down by a jar of molasses and two spoons.

"Thanks for leaving me a key last night," Liddell said and plopped into a chair at the table. "I hope I didn't wake y'all up."

Landry made Creole coffee. That's made with very strong coffee, two teaspoons of molasses, and a dollop of cream and two shakes of Tabasco. Landry put a spoon in this and shoved it to Liddell. "Drink that. It'll put some hair on your . . . back."

They both laughed. *No one* said anything improper in front of Mom. Even Big Jim.

"Aren't you going to work today?" Liddell asked. As a boy,

Landry was up, dressed, newspaper route finished, homework done, and hurrying Liddell to the school-bus stop. He'd inherited the "early to rise" habit from Big Jim, whom he idolized. Landry had followed in their fathers footsteps as his father had done down the family line. Blanchards came from hearty stock, a long line of hard men working the river and the oil rigs. Big Jim had died on the job when a steel cable snapped. The iron rail it suspended plummeted and took Big Jim to the bottom of the Gulf. His body wasn't found for weeks.

"Drink your coffee," Landry said, and broke half a dozen eggs into an iron skillet sizzling with butter, salt, and pepper.

Liddell said, "I'm glad you took the house after Mom died. She would have liked what you *haven't* done with the place." Landry still had a rotary-dial landline telephone—black of course—attached to an ancient cassette-tape answering machine. The concession he'd made to modern technology was a cheap cell phone that he wore in case Evie, his daughter, needed to reach him in an emergency. He still gave her quarters and dimes for pay phones just in case. Never mind that pay phones had all but disappeared, and the ones that hadn't were vandalized.

Landry rubbed at the corner of his eye with his middle finger. "You could have had the house. Mom left it to you in the will," Landry said. "You could have put all the doodads in you want. You always were a gadget freak."

Liddell laughed. "Yeah. We even have a color television that we don't have to turn a dial to change channels."

Landry laughed. He said, "Remember when Mom wanted one of those Clapper things and kept after Big Jim about it?" The Clapper was a product you attached to the lamp cord to make the lights turn on and off by clapping your hands.

Liddell grinned. "Yeah. Big Jim said he wasn't going to pay someone to get the clap when he could get it down at the docks for free."

"And Mom came unglued and threw his breakfast out the back door."

Liddell noticed the empty seat at the table.

"Where's Evie?" Liddell asked. "Blanchards don't miss a chance to eat."

Landry served up two plates of bacon and eggs, put out silver-ware, and added a roll of paper towels for napkins.

"Evie already gone to school?" Liddell asked.

Landry didn't answer. He instead gave Liddell an unreadable look and asked, "Have you called Bitty yet?"

Bitty was the nickname given to Detective Elizabeth LeBoeuf. She was with the Iberville Parish Sheriff Department and was Liddell's partner on River Patrol before he married Marcie and moved away. She was called Bitty because, at five foot, six inches, she was itty-bitty compared to Liddell's six-foot five, two-hundred-eighty-pound frame. But the nickname wasn't a sign of disrespect. She was a match for any man.

"I left her a voice mail. She hasn't called back." He took his cell from his pocket and dialed her number again. It went directly to voice mail, and he pocketed the phone. "I'm going over there this morning."

Landry said, "Oh, crap! I forgot this." He dug in his back pocket and pulled out a folded piece of lined yellow legal pad paper with Liddell's name printed on the outside. "I found this stuck under the door when I came down this morning."

Liddell unfolded the creased paper. On it, printed in large letters:

DON'T CALL
COME OVER

Landry asked, "Is it from Bitty?"

Liddell pocketed the note. "Maybe. No one else but you knew I was coming."

The note wasn't signed. The handwriting was carefully authored in large letters. Bitty wrote so small Liddell had to squint to make out the words. But it must have been from Bitty.

Landry cocked his head. "What are you up to? This is all Secret Squirrel and shit. You working a case? Is that partner of yours going to show up, guns blazing, bodies piling up n' shit?"

Liddell gave him a look that said Landry had gone crazy. "Yeah. Bitty called me in on a big case. Someone in Evansville is trafficking human organs and I found out they're sending the brains here disguised as Red Cross relief packages. I figured it would be safe to hang out here because you obviously haven't received any."

Landry gave him a single-digit salute and asked, "How's the coffee?"

Liddell held his cup out for a refill. "You haven't answered me. Where's Evie? Doesn't she know her favorite uncle in the whole world is here?"

"Her only uncle," Landry corrected, and his expression turned sober. "She's not here. I was glad you called yesterday because I was getting ready to call you."

Liddell waited while his brother mixed two more coffees and came back. Landry said, "I got some trouble. It's Evie. I've been to the police twice now and they won't do shit. I don't know what to do."

"What kind of trouble?" Liddell asked. Evie was almost fifteen. He couldn't imagine sweet, polite Evie doing anything worthy of police attention.

Landry was struggling with what he was going to say, and a cold feeling crept down Liddell's spine. He'd given so much bad news to people during his career he knew the signs by heart. "Landry? What is it?"

Landry poured himself more coffee and sat down across from Liddell and said, "Evie's missing."

Liddell thought about Landry's past, both painful and joyful. His brother had been through some very hard times. Times that would have broken most men. But Landry was Big Jim's son, and a Blanchard. Blanchards were a hard bunch.

Landry was finishing his senior year of high school when he found out his girlfriend, Sally, was pregnant. They had been careful, but sometimes life asserts itself and things happen. Landry explained the situation to the parents on both sides. They wanted to get married. Sally's parents seemed to be glad to be rid of her. Landry's dad, Big Jim, was angry, and Mom was disappointed but happy to have a grandchild. Liddell hadn't thought getting married would be such a good idea because he'd come to know Sally, and she was kind of a flake. But, being a good brother, he tried to be happy for Landry.

Landry and Sally continued to go to school as if nothing was going on, and after graduation, Landry found a job working on the docks. After he made a little money, he rented a studio apartment, and he and Sally moved in together. A week later they got married at the courthouse. He would support his new family. Just like Big Jim had supported his.

Sally was further along than she'd thought and four months after they married, Evie came along. Sally was a stay-at-home mom, and Landry worked as much overtime as he could get to buy a small house. But life asserted itself once again. Big Jim died. Evie was still a baby. The news hit Landry hard, and he threw himself into his work as a way of dealing with the grief. It was just a few weeks after Big Jim's death that Landry came home after working a four-teen-hour shift and found Evie alone on the floor in the kitchen. Screaming her head off, and wet, soiled, hungry, and abandoned. She was eleven months old.

Landry had been beside himself; at first thinking something bad had happened to Sally. Her clothes and personal things were still there as far as he could tell, but Sally was nowhere to be found. He called all the surrounding hospitals, and they had no new patients matching her description. He called the police, and still nothing. He stayed up all night, waiting for her to return, but the next morning it had sunk in that Sally had left them. No note. No good-bye.

Their mother took care of Evie while Landry worked. When Liddell had gone off to college at LSU in Baton Rouge, Landry was almost too proud to move home. He did because it was the logical thing to do. He had to support Evie, and this was a way to work, spend time with Evie, and keep his mother company.

Liddell remembered their mother had essentially been Evie's mother until she was maybe ten years old. Liddell regretted that Mom passed away before she had a chance to meet Marcie. With Mom's passing, Landry and Evie kept the house. Liddell remem-bered Evie had baked him two dozen homemade cookies for a going-away present, saying, "I made you a snack, Uncle Liddell."

Landry reached the end of this story and said, "Go ahead and ask your questions."

Liddell wondered how best to approach this. As a cop or as a brother and uncle? He tried to take on the tone of both. "I need to take you through all of this again. Bear with me, okay?"

Landry said he would.

"Who all did you talk to about this?" he asked.

Landry had been pacing, but now sat down and turned his attention to his brother. "I talked to a Plaquemine cop and one of their detectives on the telephone the day before yesterday. They said they didn't come out to take missing-person reports, so I went to the police station. I talked to a cop at the station, and he asked if I had a picture of Evie."

Landry stopped pacing. "I forgot to bring my wallet with me, so I didn't have a picture. I told him I'd bring one back after we took the report, and he got kind of shitty about me driving there without a license. Can you believe that shit?"

Liddell could see Landry's fists clench and the muscles in his forearms bunched like steel cables. "Take it easy," Liddell said. "You can get mad after we find Evie. Okay?"

"Yeah. Okay. So I give him all the information and I even talked to the Chief of Police. I took a picture of Evie back there, but that's been two days ago. Two damn days, and I haven't heard anything. Nada!"

Liddell thought it was strange that the police department hadn't made any contact with Landry. Common police practice was a detective or officer would be assigned, come to the house, and do an investigation. The investigators wanted to keep in touch with the family because nine out of ten times the person would come home, or call at least. Every forty seconds a child goes missing in the United States. There are almost a million people, adults and children, reported missing. Indiana and Louisiana have some of the lowest occurrence rates of the United States.

Liddell also knew that missing-person cases received the least attention by law enforcement because they were busy with homicides, rapes, robberies, and a plethora of other immediate crimes. Homicides have the highest rate of being solved, and missing persons the lowest. Seventy-six percent of abducted children are murdered within three hours of being taken. Even given the statistics, it was very strange that Landry hadn't been updated.

"Do you have a copy of the police report?" Liddell asked.

"They didn't give me one."

Liddell asked, "Did they say they were issuing an Amber Alert?"

Landry's jaw clenched. "The policeman didn't tell me shit. He just said, 'She ain't missing. She knows right where she is,' like it was funny. I grabbed his shirt, and he threatened to arrest me. Battery on a policeman. I told him I didn't see a policeman. What I saw was a lazy piece of shit."

That explained why Landry didn't have a copy of the police report, and why no one had followed up with him. But it was still poor police work.

"Sorry I didn't call you sooner, but the detective I talked to last said I had to wait twenty-four hours before the report would go into the system. I kept bugging them but no one would tell me anything. When you called, I thought you could help."

"Of course," Liddell said. He wanted to tell Landry that he should have called him right away. But recriminations would serve no purpose. "Anything else? Something you didn't tell the police?"

"Look. She's not the same Evie as before," Landry said. "She's changed. I can't believe she's run off, but . . . just wait a minute."

Liddell could hear Landry rushing up the stairs two and three at a time. When he returned, he was holding a blue shoulder bag. It was the kind that his wife Marcie called a beach bag.

Landry unzipped the bag and poured the contents on the table. There was the blackened stub of a burnt cigar, bits and pieces of bleached-white bird bones, a tiny bird skull, singed feathers, a red flannel pouch about two inches square, roughly sewn around the edges with burlap twine, and attached to a necklace of colored beads. There was a ball of twine with colored sewing pins stuck in it.

Anyone born and raised in Louisiana knew what this stuff was. The pouch was a *gris-gris*. A gris-gris is an amulet containing personal articles such as hair, nail clippings, colored sand, and such. Worn around the neck or carried in a pocket, a gris-gris was meant to ward off evil or sickness or bring luck or blessings. The bones and bird skull were used in "readings" to see the future or explain the past. The cigar butt was used to blow the spirit into whatever item was being blessed or used to bring about some wish.

The burlap twine and the sewing needles were another matter. They were used to do evil. A doll was made out of burlap wrappings to represent the person targeted, and the pins were inserted into the parts of the body to cause illness or pain—or death.

Liddell had seen all of these types of things in museums or roadside shops that sell to tourists.

"Where did you find this stuff?" Liddell asked.

"I don't snoop in Evie's stuff. But when she went missing . . . I guess I wondered if there was a boy involved. You know?"

Liddell assured him he did know. Evie was at the age.

"Well, I found this hidden in the back of her closet. And I recognize some of this stuff. It was Sally's."

"Sally? Your Sally?" Liddell asked, unable to hide his surprise.

He saw the look of disbelief on Liddell's face and said, "You didn't know Sally was into Voodoo. No one did. Not even Mom. Sally kept it hid pretty good."

"Maybe it was just for fun," Liddell suggested.

"No. She was into it big-time," Landry said. "It was a family thing. Her dad was some kind of Voodoo priest. She took me to a ritual in her parents' house once, but I don't believe in this shit and I told them so. Her dad tried to tell me there wasn't a lot of difference between Voodoo and Catholicism. They had saints, and we had saints. They had a kind of Devil and a hell and we had the same thing. I reminded him that our religion didn't curse people or try to hurt them and he just laughed. It was crazy. So I refused to go to any more of their stuff. But Sally . . . Sally was a true believer."

Landry thought before saying, "I was ashamed to say anything to any of you. I'd already screwed up, according to Big Jim. I didn't want them disappointed in me."

Liddell processed what he'd just been told and asked, "You said some of this stuff was Sally's. How did Evie get it?"

Landry's cheeks reddened. "When Sally left, I didn't know what to do. I loved her. I didn't have the heart to throw all of Sally's stuff away. I kept a box—a high school yearbook, pictures, jewelry I bought her—things like that. I was going to give it to Evie when she got older, but I would have thrown all this shit out first. Tell you the truth, I forgot where I put it. She must have found it."

"Okay. She found the stuff, and so what? She's gone to find Sally."

"That's what I think."

Chapter Four

Bitty's house was on the other side of Plaquemine in an area annexed by the city several years ago because of the Walmart Supercenter that was being built. Liddell had decided he'd do as he had promised his brother, but he would talk to Bitty first. He hoped he could get Bitty's help. When Liddell had moved to Indiana, Bitty was living with her life partner, another detective, named Dusty Parnell. Last he'd heard they had gone their separate ways. They had seemed to remain friends. Or at least he hoped they were still friends because he might need Dusty's help with finding Evie. Dusty was the Missing Persons detective for the Sheriff's Department. He'd have better luck talking to Dusty than going to the Plaquemine PD. Landry had already endeared himself there, and they may not be receptive to another Blanchard.

Liddell gazed in his rearview mirror at the crimson sunrise and felt his heart melt. He had forgotten how the scenery along the Mississippi River was like no other place on Earth. In high school he'd learned the French called the Mississippi River "Messipi." The indigenous Algonquin Indians called it Misi-zibi, or the Great River. It was, or is, the fourth largest river in the world, running from Minnesota, over two thousand miles, through ten states, and draining into the Gulf of Mexico at New Orleans.

Liddell drove through a neighborhood of Plaquemine known as "Old Town." He'd played with other kids in the yards of some of these houses. Cops and robbers. He'd been the cop, of course. He drove past a big house where he'd gotten his first kiss from Bonnie Lutz on the front porch. The two-story was vacant with windows and doors boarded up, but there was no graffiti visible or trash in the yard or at the curbs. He felt proud that his hometown still had pride and hadn't allowed vacant houses to become a beacon for il-legal activity.

The population of Plaquemine hovered around the seven thou-sand mark. Blacks outnumbered whites, but race had never been an issue here like in some of the bigger towns. Half of the residents commuted to work. The city itself was a mere three square miles of land setting at the junction of Bayou Plaquemine and bordered on the east by a sharp bend of the Mississippi River. To the west was farmland that turned to uninhabited swampland. Bitty's house was on the far west side of town, a hastily built shotgun-style house in an area where the dwellings were slowly being replaced by newly built antebellum and Queen Anne–style homes.

This was Bitty's neighborhood. She and the other residents had refused generous offers from builders who wanted to demolish the entire block and build on the land. She had told Liddell that the houses here had their own history, and preserving that was more re-warding than money. She had no husband, no kids, no plans for ei-ther. She had enough to be comfortable, and cherished a simple life. He had been genuinely sorry that she and Dusty had called it quits because she was alone now. She was too vibrant to be alone.

He remembered talking to Bitty after he married Marcie and was struggling with the decision—take the job in Evansville or stay here. He had a job offer from the Evansville Police Department, but he already had a job here. They were crammed into his tiny apart-ment here, and he would have to get a bigger place no matter if they stayed here or moved to Evansville, where Marcie could be nearer her family. It was Bitty who convinced him to take the plunge. She told him he had a new life with Marcie, and he didn't need the old life weighing him down. After all, it wasn't like Evansville was on the far side of the moon. But it may as well have been. He was ashamed to admit that he'd stayed away almost five years. Not in-tentionally, but there always seemed to be something else that needed to be done.

At the corner of Sawmill and Lock Road, Liddell turned right and drove past her house. Her front blinds were closed, and a news-paper lay on the front concrete stoop. He turned down Lock Road and saw a newer cedar privacy fence and at the back of the fence, a garage he didn't know she'd had built. Knowing Bitty, she'd prob-ably done all the work herself.

He'd tried to call several times during his trip and again when he'd arrived at Landry's, but his calls went to her voice mail. He'd left a message saying, "Bitty, it's me. Call me."

He turned into the alley behind Bitty's house where she'd poured gravel and parked beside her Monopoly-orange vintage seventies Camaro. She'd gone to California on vacation one year and came home driving the Camaro. She'd bought it on a whim and driven it four days cross-country. He was surprised she didn't have the car in the garage because that was the primary reason she wanted a garage.

He got out and noticed her car doors were unlocked. He'd have to get on her for being careless. When he opened the gate latch, he touched something sticky and examined his fingers. It was blood. He pushed the gate open and saw drag marks in the pebble path leading to her back door. The door stood open. He instinctively drew his .45 and held it beside him as he cautiously approached the door.

The dead bolt was missing. In its place was the crenelated pattern of a lug-soled boot. The boot print was too big to be Bitty's. He would later wonder why he didn't call 911 at that point, but he was already committed, and his desire to check on Bitty was greater than his sense of self-preservation or doing things by the book. If she was in there and needed medical attention, he couldn't afford to wait for backup to arrive.

He pressed his back against the wall on the left side of the door; the .45 in his right hand, barrel pointing up, and was about to push the door farther open when his eye caught motion. His .45 rose toward the movement. There was an old woman standing by the house next door. Her white hair set on top of her head like a cotton ball. She was scowling at him, which made her toothless lips suck into her mouth.

He took a breath, let it out, and pushed the door the rest of the way open. The smell of death hit him before he saw the body spread-eagled across the kitchen table. It was Bitty. What was left of her. She'd died hard.

His eyes darted around the kitchen, taking everything in. The flies had found her. Two chairs were turned over. Her naked body was draped across the table, face up, legs spread, arms flung out, face smashed into ground hamburger. Her lips had been cut off and something that resembled a dried corn shuck protruded several inches from where the mouth had been. Dried rivulets of blood ran down the sides of the cheeks but hadn't pooled under the head. Her stomach cavity was sliced open; intestines pulled out and spilling to the floor.

Symbols were drawn in blood on the wall nearest the body. Bloody drag marks on the floor ran from the doorway to the kitchen table. She was dragged in here, not carried, and . . . and what? Displayed? The killing, the damage to the body, had taken place somewhere other than here. The lack of blood indicated she was already dead when she was placed on the table. The evisceration and the destruction to the face had taken place after she was brought here. The bits of bone and tissue and teeth bore that out.

He fought the urge to cover her nakedness, and he felt rage and sorrow and guilt as he stumbled outside and fell to his hands and knees and retched into the grass.

"Oh, Bitty," he moaned. "What the . . . ?"

"Stay where you are!"

Before Liddell could lift his head, there was a popping sound and electricity arced through his body and every muscle seemed to lock up. He lost consciousness.

Liddell came to, facedown in his own vomit, handcuffed behind his back. He rolled onto his side and squinted into the sun. He couldn't make out the face of the man in a police uniform, but he could see the Taser in his hand.

"Don't move, asshole!" He kicked Liddell in the face.

Liddell spit blood into the grass. "I'm a cop . . ." he said, and again felt electricity arc through his body. This time it was of shorter duration. This time he didn't pass out.

"I told you not to move, didn't I? If you spit on me again, I'll tear your head off! Do we understand each other?" the officer asked.

Chapter Five

Officer Barbierre tugged down at the notch of his neck where the Kevlar ballistic vest had rubbed a red mark. Rivulets of sweat ran down the man's face, and beads speckled his arms and stained the armpits of his skintight uniform shirt. He had ordered Liddell inside Bitty's house at gunpoint and for the last several minutes neither of them had spoken a word.

"So, tell me this story again. Why are you here?" Barbierre asked.

Liddell sat on the couch, at the front edge of the cushion, trying to keep the pressure from his wrists handcuffed behind his back. He'd tried to tell Barbierre twice in the backyard, and each time he'd received a jolt from the Taser when he spoke.

"Officer Barbierre, my hands are starting to hurt. Can you cuff me in front? You have my gun and you have the Taser. I promise not to try anything," Liddell said. Barbierre had yet to call dispatch to request backup or to tell them he had someone in custody. Maybe Barbierre had already called for assistance before he'd confronted Liddell, but that had been more than fifteen minutes ago and so far, no one had responded.

Liddell watched Barbierre's face for a reaction. The expression remained neutral except for a slight tic under one eye. Barbierre had stayed focused on Liddell, like a shark on a treat. Liddell pegged him as a rookie with delusions of grandeur. Barbierre acted like he had just caught a serial killer or Osama bin Laden. Liddell was glad Barbierre hadn't confused his Taser with his sidearm.

Barbierre was almost as tall as Liddell, but with the physique of a serious weightlifter. The pitch of his voice was consistent with a steroid abuser, but the facial features weren't swollen. Maybe he was just high strung. Maybe it was his normal voice. But his aggressiveness, tight clothes, overmuscular frame, and eagerness to use his Taser leaned more toward some type of drug-induced psychosis.

"How long have you been with Plaquemine PD?" Liddell asked, hoping to begin a conversation.

Barbierre acted as if he didn't hear, but the tic under his eye grew worse.

"So. Who are we waiting for?" Liddell asked. He could feel the Taser burns on his chest and back.

Barbierre gave Liddell a look that said, "Don't push me."

Liddell tried to engage him again. "While we're waiting we may as well talk a little. I used to be with Iberville Sheriff Department."

Still nothing.

"Okay. I'm just trying to have a friendly conversation here. I'm kind of upset. I came in and found her butchered on her kitchen table, and . . ." He trailed off. He didn't want to sound whiney, or like he wanted to file a "use of force" complaint against the officer; which he did. And there was the matter of Barbierre neglecting to read Liddell his Miranda warning and contaminating evidence by forcing Liddell to walk through the murder scene. That was Cop 101: Don't let anyone in the crime scene. But he couldn't say any of that or he risked a violent reprisal from this gorilla.

"Officer Barbierre, you have my credentials. You know I'm a detective. I work the Homicide Unit in Evansville. Maybe I can help with this."

Still no response. The tic had stopped. *Calm before the storm.*

The thought of Bitty, murdered, mutilated, her destroyed face, and just in the other room, boiled up, and he lost his temper. "Okay. I'll go first," Liddell said. "Did you know that using steroids shrinks the testicles and alters your voice?" Liddell watched Barbierre and thought he could detect the slightest tightening of Barbierre's jaw muscles.

Liddell said, "I knew a guy whose testicles shrunk to the size of little marbles. And he talked like Michael Jackson."

Still nothing.

"Eventually his penis shrank too. Not like jumping into a cold swimming pool type shrinkage. I mean 'get the tweezers out' type of."

Barbierre's fist slammed into the side of Liddell's head. He was knocked against the arm of the couch and leaned there trying to clear his head. Barbierre didn't just look strong, he was strong.

Liddell scooched himself upright again and said, "Okay. I'll shut up."

Barbierre stared at him with undisguised hatred.

"It really did disappear," Liddell said. "We called him Double Dick, but that was just a joke. I mean because he didn't have a dick. That was the joke, see?"

Officer Barbierre moved so fast Liddell had no time to react before he was shoved against the back of the couch and shuddered with fifty thousand volts from the Taser racing through his body. His breath was coming in gulps when it was over, and he could taste metal and smell burning flesh. He would have more burn marks if he didn't shut up.

Liddell felt like he was going to vomit again, but fought it back. Barbierre's eyes gave nothing away. The lights were on, but no human was home. It was as if none of this had just happened.

Barbierre squatted and his face was mere inches from Liddell's when he said, "You killed a cop. In my book, you're already dead. I caught you in the act and tried to Taser you. When that didn't work, I had to shoot you. A dozen times. And I can make it look true if you say another word."

"Well, well. Look who have we here, Barbie." The man's voice came from the doorway between the living room and kitchen.

Liddell couldn't believe his eyes.

"I got him, Detective Troup," Barbie said proudly. "He came at me and tried to head-butt me so I Tasered him. Dumb move for a cop."

Barbierre said to Liddell, "Maybe you should just say you blacked out. And when you came to you—you found yourself in here. Is that it? Did you black out after you butchered her?"

Liddell didn't answer.

Barbierre removed the mirrored-lens aviator sunglasses that set atop his severe crew cut and put them in a case on his gun belt. He pulled a pair of black leather gloves from his waistband and pulled them on. His eyes never left Liddell's face.

"I guess I'm going to have to teach him some manners."

"That's not necessary, Barbie," Troup said, glancing at the

gloves in Barbierre's hands. "Me and Blanchard are old buddies. We used to work together. Didn't we, Blanchard?"

"Hello, Bobby," Liddell said.

Bobby Troup was in his early fifties, tall, skeletal, with sunken eyes the color of faded jeans, pale skin stretched across a too-long face. He held a filterless cigarette between nicotine-stained fingers and brushed some imaginary lint from the lapel of a black suit that draped on him like it was on a clothes hanger. The top of his head was balding, sunburned; the rest was white hair, pulled back in a greasy ponytail. He pulled at a diamond stud earring, sucked down the rest of the cigarette. He dropped the burning butt to the kitchen floor and crushed it with the toe of a shiny black wing-tip shoe.

"Whoops," he said and lifted his foot, looking down at the black mark.

"Surprised to see me again, Liddell?" Troup asked. His almost lip-less mouth twisted into a smirk. "I heard you got married and were playing house in some shithole town up north. Where was it . . . oh yeah. Indiana. Evansville, right?"

Liddell said, "I've got nothing against you, Bobby."

Troup raised an eyebrow. "Is that all you've got to say after— what—four, five years?"

"Look. I wasn't resisting. I found her like that and went outside to call the police. You can check. Officer Barbierre Tasered me in the backyard, handcuffed me, and brought me inside a crime scene. Is that the way things are done now?"

Troup said, "Maybe Barbie caught you in here. Or maybe you were just coming outside. He said you tried to 'head-butt' him."

"He did, Detective Troup," Barbie said eagerly. "That's exactly what he did."

Troup said, "Barbie wouldn't know you're some hotshot detective from the big city of Evansville. And even if he knew he would have every right to defend himself."

Liddell said nothing. He'd let Troup have his jollies so that they would remove the handcuffs and he could find out what happened to Bitty.

Troup continued as if he were admonishing a child. "You were handcuffed for the officer's safety and for your own. You're lucky he didn't shoot you."

"I hear ya', Bobby. Now take the handcuffs off and ask your questions," Liddell said. "I've got nothing to hide. But I don't know how much I'll be able to tell you. I was here a couple of minutes before I made Officer Barbierre's acquaintance.

"Like always, Blanchard, you're assuming too much. Old habits die hard, I guess," Troup said sadly.

"So, you're not going to let me go?" Liddell asked. "You can check with the lady next door. She saw me come to the back door. She can tell you I didn't have time to do any of this."

"Any of what?" Troup asked.

Liddell inclined his head toward the kitchen. "What was done to her. Her face is smashed, and she's been eviscerated. Whoever did this took their time."

"So you admit to being near the body?" Troup asked.

Liddell knew he should shut up, but he made the same mistake many criminals make when they're under pressure or emotional. He said, "I told you I found her. I didn't touch the body. I stepped inside the kitchen doorway and went back into the yard. You know me, Bobby. Do you really think I'm capable of that? She was my partner."

"I remember asking that same question of some people I thought were my friends, or if not friends, fellow cops. Grand jury. Fired. Disgraced. So don't tell me what you're not capable of doing. Anyone is capable of anything."

"Look at the Taser burns on my shirt—front *and* back. And there's a Taser burn on my neck. And he kicked me in the face for nothing. He took my duty weapon and frog marched me through the kitchen."

"Is that right, Barbie? You bring him back inside, or was he already inside when you got here?" Troup asked Barbierre.

"That's what you said to . . ." Barbie stammered, and watched Troup for the correct answer.

Troup lit a cigarette and wagged it up and down like he was conducting an orchestra. Barbie said, "He wasn't outside, Detective Troup. He was standing in the living room when I got here. He had a gun in his hand and he tried to head-butt me."

Troup said helpfully, "So you were using that force necessary to apprehend and overcome the force used by the suspect. Isn't that right, Officer Barbierre?"

"Yes sir," Barbie said. "He killed a cop. And . . . he was being an asshole."

Troup's lips curved into what would have been a smile on any other face. "Barbie says you were inside when he found you. Barbie doesn't lie. He's one of Plaquemine's finest. Ain't that right, Barbie?"

Officer Barbierre's chest seemed to swell at the praise.

Liddell's fists clenched behind his back. "I'll try this one more time. I parked in back by Bitty's car. There's blood on the gate latch. I opened the gate and saw her back door was standing open. I drew my weapon and approached the house. I saw the door had been kicked open. The dead bolt was gone. Look at it. There's a boot print on the door. It's a size ten or eleven and I wear size fourteen. I was concerned for Bitty's safety. I opened the door and came just inside the doorway. "

"Wait a minute," Troup said. He dropped the cigarette butt on the floor and kicked it into the kitchen. "You just said the door had been kicked open. And you said you opened the door. Which is it? Did you kick it open? Or maybe you had someone with you?"

Troup pulled a cigarette pack from inside his jacket, shook one out, and lit it with a match. He took a deep drag and let the smoke out slowly and tossed the match into the kitchen.

"Hold on. Hold on," Troup said. "Even if you look at it from your changing perspective, it doesn't make sense." He took another long drag off the cigarette and sucked the smoke deep into his lungs. "So, what you're saying is that you saw your ex-partner dead—and I admit she's pretty messed up—but you didn't check the house to see if there was a suspect, or if anyone else was injured? You didn't call the police. You just go into a crime scene. Did you call out a warning before you went in. 'Police Department. If someone is in here identify yourself'?"

"No. I didn't identify myself. I'm not with the local police," Liddell answered.

"And therein lies the crux of our problem, Blanchard. YOU are not a policeman here in Louisiana. But against all your police training, against all of your experience, you go into a crime scene with a gun in your hand and contaminate everything."

Liddell said, "You got me there, Bobby. I messed up. I should have checked the house. I could have backed off and called the police to report a break-in. I could have done a lot of things different, but she is—was—my partner. She was my friend. I thought she was in trouble. What if she wasn't dead, just hurt, and I wasted time waiting for you? Tell me. What would you have done?" His throat constricted, and he could feel his eyes threatening to tear up. "She was family to me, Bobby."

"If she was family you knew she lived with another woman. That dyke girlfriend of hers, Parnell. What if Parnell was in the house? What if she did this?"

Liddell could feel his face redden with anger. He didn't like Troup and had no respect for him, and this was part of the reason. He was homophobic and a racist and every kind of foul human possible.

"She and Detective Parnell aren't living together. Detective Parnell moved out months ago. Bitty lived by herself," Liddell said.

"Well," Troup said. "You're saying that dyke bitch partner of hers killed her and you didn't. How convenient."

"That's not what I said."

"So you admit you killed her? Where does that leave Parnell?" Troup asked. "You heard him, Barbie. Put that in your report."

Barbierre took a notebook from his back pocket and scribbled something in it.

"For your information, Liddell, I did know that Parnell and Bitty were no longer shacked up doing the nasty. And I happen to know that Parnell is on vacation in Hawaii, so you can't put this on her."

"Maybe he killed her last night. He came back today because he left some evidence behind. I heard killers return to the scene," Barbie said.

Liddell couldn't believe what he was hearing. Barbie had the IQ of a turnip.

Troup smiled at Barbie and said, "I'll make a detective out of you yet, young Master Barbie."

Liddell said, "Well, you'd better arrest Old Lady Martin, next door. According to your theory she could be the killer."

Troup cupped a hand beside Barbie's ear and whispered something. Then Barbie announced, "I'm going next door to talk to Mrs. Martin. Will you be okay here, Detective Troup?"

"I'll be fine, Barbie."

Barbie glared at Liddell. "I'll be right back, Detective Troup."

When Barbie was gone, Troup said, "Let me see where you claim you were Tasered." Liddell leaned forward and Troup jerked the two Taser darts out of the skin of his back and Liddell winced.

"Did that hurt?"

"What do you think?"

Troup rolled the darts between his fingers. "I can put them back," he offered, and when Liddell gave him an incredulous look, he added, "I'm just kidding. I'm not the violent monster you and Bitty made me out to be."

"If you got something to say, Bobby, just spit it out. Did you blame Bitty for getting fired? Is that what this is about?"

"Are you accusing me?" Troup faced Liddell and asked, "You think I had something to do with Bitty's death?"

Barbie came back into the front room. "She doesn't remember anything, Detective Troup. If she called the police, she doesn't remember."

"You got anything else to say?" Troup asked Liddell.

Liddell knew there was nothing he could say that would make a difference. Barbie hadn't been gone long enough to talk to Mrs. Martin, which begged the question, what had Barbie been doing for the few minutes he was out of the room? He thought that whatever he said, Troup would twist it. He obviously wanted Liddell to be the killer. But why?

"Detective Troup, he had a phone in his pocket," Barbie said and held out an iPhone.

Troup took the phone and punched some buttons, bringing up Liddell's contacts. "You should put a passcode on here," he said, and scrolled through screens. "You've got Bitty's phone number and address. And here's your wife's number." Troup continued to scroll through the contacts. "Have you got an attorney in here, Blanchard?"

"Good one, Detective Troup," Barbie said with a smile.

"If I did he would tell you about the need for a search warrant to go through my phone."

Troup said, "You always were smart, Blanchard. Let's see how that works out for you." To Barbie he said, "Take him to headquarters. I'll be along."

"While you're jerking me around, the real killer is getting away, Troup," Liddell said.

Barbierre gave him an open-hand slap across the side of the head, causing his eyes to tear up. "You shouldn't be disrespectful. You call him Detective Troup. He's a better detective than you'll ever be."

Troup said in a feigned admonishing tone, "I appreciate your loyalty, Barbie, but don't abuse the prisoner."

"Sorry, Detective Troup. I just don't like it when someone's disrespectful of the law."

"Apologize to Detective Blanchard," Troup said.

"I'm sorry, sir," Barbie said to Liddell and yanked him to his feet.

"Leave his shoes," Troup said.

Liddell kicked off his shoes and stood in his socks. "I assume I'm under arrest?"

Troup said, "Officer Barbierre, give my old friend a ride."

A look passed between Barbie and Troup as Barbie shoved Liddell to the open back door.

"You're making a mistake, Troup," Liddell said as he was being led away.

"And no phone calls until I get there," Troup yelled after them.

"You got it, Detective Troup."

Chapter Six

Evansville, Indiana

Jack leaned back in his squeaky chair and pushed a pile of papers around his desktop. His spanking by Double Dick had been less painful than he'd expected, but not less irritating. But before Jack had left the office, Dick had said, "I see your wife has taken you back. Try not to screw it up this time, Murphy."

Jack had turned and said, "Yes, sir. I'll give it my best effort. Thank you for your concern for my well-being." How's that for cool? In the hallway, he'd said, "Screw you, Dick. And the politician you rode in on."

Now he sat here at his desk and sorted case folders into piles. He and Liddell had been assigned a home invasion burglary a few weeks ago. After some digging through old unsolved cases they had found several dozen more that may or may not be connected. None of the cases had a suspect or a description of a possible suspect. They were a mixture of thefts from cars, homes, garages, offices, day-care centers, parking lots, and even churches. Jack had talked to several of the victims. The males' driver's licenses and cash were gone but not the billfolds. The women reported missing checks, cash, and jewelry, but their purses were not taken. The suspect would use the men's driver's licenses to cash large checks written from one of the female's accounts.

So Jack had searched police files for thefts matching this pattern and found there were other cases that went back four years. The first year, two; the second year, six. By the third year, the cases were increasing in frequency and the thief no longer limited himself to breaking into vehicles; now he was going inside the homes. Single women occupied the homes, and most had the habit of coming home and putting their purse down on the kitchen table, or just inside the door. The thief would take what they wanted from the purse, and there was no indication a theft had occurred until the bank notified the victim of a problem with their account.

But in the last few months, maybe in half a dozen cases, female victims reported that personal photos had been taken as well. In two of the recent cases, the thief would hang around inside the house and wait to be seen by the victim. If this guy was showing himself, he was working his way up to something more serious than theft. Jack had shown mug shot books to all the victims, but of the ones that saw the thief in their house, all gave differing descriptions. The suspect was a white male, a Hispanic male, even an albino male. Blond hair, brown hair, gray hair, mustache, beard, no facial hair, glasses sometimes. The few things consistent were the height, weight, and age description of the suspect. Over six foot tall, stocky build, late twenties to mid thirties.

Jack was beginning to chart the occurrences when Sgt. Mattingly came into the detective's office and headed straight for him.

"Those thefts and burglaries you asked me to keep an eye out for," Mattingly said.

"Yeah. You got something?"

Sergeant Mattingly may have found the golden egg to break this case. The current home-invasion victim's name was Gladys Tooley. She was in her early sixties, with tightly permed black hair going gray, slightly on the plus side of plump, but she had been very pretty once upon a time. She told Jack she worked as a secretary for a church downtown. She had come home from shopping for groceries, parked in her driveway, came in the side door to the kitchen, and closed the door but left it unlocked to bring the groceries in. She set her purse on the kitchen table and had to use the restroom. When she came back into the kitchen, the door was open, and the man was standing in the doorway looking at her, grinning, not smiling. She stressed that he wasn't smiling, but was giving her the eye, to which she added, "You know what I mean."

"So it was more of a sexual thing?" Jack asked.

Gladys smiled at him. "Yes. And at my age. Can you imagine?" And before he could respond she asked, "Do you think I'm in danger?"

"I really don't think you're in danger, but I'll have an officer come and talk to you about how to make your home more secure. Now I have to ask you some questions," Jack said. They were in her living room. Patches of the surface of her kitchen table and around the doorknobs were black with fingerprint powder. Jack didn't see her purse.

"Would you like some coffee, Detective Murphy?" she asked. "I've just made a fresh pot."

"No. Thanks. I won't take much of your time."

She ignored his answer and went in the kitchen and brought him one. "Please have a seat. You're making me nervous."

Jack sat on the arm of the love seat and waited for her to be seated. When he had her attention, he said, "I want you to think about this man."

She responded quickly. "That's the last thing I want to think about. But if I must."

"I want you to tell me everything you remember about him."

She gazed into her coffee cup as if the answer was there. "He was white. Early thirties. Medium length blond hair combed down in bangs that almost covered his eyebrows." She held a finger across the top of her eyes to demonstrate. "His hair was tapered on the sides and back." She thought some more and said, "He was six foot three inches and about one hundred seventy pounds, give or take."

She opened her eyes and took a sip of her coffee.

"You seem very sure of the height, weight, and age, Mrs. Tooley."

"Gladys. Please," she said.

"Okay. You seem very definite on some of the description. Can you tell me why?"

In answer, she got up and took a framed photo from the top of the television set and handed it to Jack. It was a wedding photo, groom and bride. The groom was in a white tuxedo, white shoes, white tie, and . . .

"This is of you and your husband?" Jack asked.

She took the frame back and touched the man's face, a smile playing across her lips. "My late husband," she said, "It's almost ten years since he left me."

Jack said automatically, "I'm sorry for your loss."

"What?" she asked and her face came up.

"I'm sorry your husband passed away," Jack said and was puzzled when she laughed.

"Oh, he's not dead. I just tell people that when they see my wedding photo." She pointed to the groom again. "He left me ten years ago, and ran off with his secretary. They live in Aruba now. What a jerk."

"Ma'am, Gladys, I guess I don't understand why you're showing me this."

"Because my burglar could be a twin for the lying, cheating bastard that I was married to. Same hair, same size, same weight. Of course we were much younger in this picture."

Jack examined the photo again. The man did resemble the description she had given.

"You can take the picture if you want," Gladys said.

"That's okay. I will have a sketch artist come and you can show this to him, or her. I may need to put the sketch on television, and we wouldn't want anyone that knew your husband to call and tell us it's your husband."

She laughed again. "If he got arrested it would serve him right. You think I'm awful, don't you?"

Before Jack could respond she said, "I tell people that he's my 'late' husband because it's easier than telling them the truth. We were happy once."

Before she could take him down memory lane, Jack stood and said, "I'll be in touch. If you see this man again, call 911. Do not try to follow him or confront him."

She walked him to the door, where a crime scene tech was finished dusting for prints. The tech said there wasn't much luck.

Gladys took Jack's arm at the door and asked, "Are you sure I'm not in danger? I mean, what if he comes back? The way he stared at me . . ."

"I'm sure you're not in danger. But you need to talk to the officer I send out here and listen to what he tells you. Okay?"

She said she would do as he said, and he escaped. Sergeant Mattingly approached him as he got to the street.

"Was she any help?" Mattingly asked.

"I'm getting a sketch artist to come out, but if you would, can you have the CPO—Community Police Officer—come and talk to her about home security? She and every other woman have the same habit of leaving their purse right out in the open and not locking their doors."

"Too inconvenient," Mattingly said.

"She's not wrong doing what's comfortable. But pond scum like the thief take advantage of any vulnerability. I'm sure he's watching these people. Or he can spot them and just strikes. Whatever, it's been working for him. At least until now."

Mattingly got on his portable and called for a CPO to meet with him.

"Oh," Jack said. "Want to hear a good one?"

Mattingly did. Jack told him about Gladys's "late" husband, and they both had a laugh.

During the interview with Gladys Tooley, Jack learned that her bank was Fifth Third Bank. He was parked in the Donut Bank lot with a real cup of coffee when he called the regional security manager at Fifth Third Bank.

"Maleficent," said the cheerful voice. Her real name was Millicent Daniels, and she had been the Vice President of the Fraud Unit for Fifth Third Bank for as long as Jack could remember. She had a reputation among her peers and in the law enforcement community as one very tough hombre if you messed with the bank. That had earned her the nickname of "Maleficent." She was proud of the name.

"I hope you don't answer the phone like that for a client's call," Jack kidded. He knew she didn't.

"They should all fear me," Millicent said. "Hi'ya, Jack. What can I do you for?"

Jack told her about Gladys's checkbook and wasn't surprised the report had already found its way to her desk. She said one check had been cashed at their main branch drive-thru before the report was made, and she had requested the security camera footage. The check was for fifteen hundred dollars. She gave Jack the information and promised to send the video to Sgt. Walker in Crime Scene. She gave an evil laugh for Jack's benefit before they disconnected.

Jack was about to call Sgt. Walker when the phone rang in his hand.

"Jack. I'm glad I caught you," Katie said. "Hang on."

His partner's wife, Marcie, came on the line. "Thank God, Jack. I didn't know who to call."

"What's wrong, Marcie?" He could hear a tremor in her voice.

"It's Liddell," Marcie said.

The first thought that ran through his mind was that Liddell had been in an auto accident. But he was wrong. It was worse.

Jack was in his car and already heading south on Highway 41. He had assured Marcie that he was on his way and would update her when he got there. She put him back on the phone with Katie.

"Make sure Marcie calls Captain Franklin right away. I'll let you go," he said to Katie.

"She's already calling him, Jack," Katie answered. "What are you going to do? Are you going down there?"

"Already on the highway," he said. "I'll give her a few minutes to talk to the Captain before I call to clear my trip with him."

Katie said, "My phone shows it's about a twelve-hour drive. Aren't you going to take another detective with you?"

"I'm not even going downtown," he said. "If I do, it'll take half a day to get past all the red tape and the wringing of hands and gnashing of teeth."

"Jack, you need to do this right." Katie sounded concerned. "You need the department's backing. Maybe you should meet with Charles before you go."

Charles? She and Charles are on a first-name basis now?

"That's good advice, hon'," Jack lied. "Or maybe you should call *Charles,*" he said. "I'm sure he'll speed things up for you."

"Oh, Jack. You can't still be jealous."

"What . . . me? I don't have a jealous bone in my body." Franklin had always had a crush on Katie and took every opportunity to be there for her when she needed a shoulder to cry on. Those times were always when Jack was in the hospital for some injury or whatever, but Jack knew what was on the lech's mind. He reminded himself to kick *Charles* in the nuts. "If I catch him checking you out again, he won't have an unbroken bone in his body."

Marcie was back on the line. "If you catch who checking me out?"

"Sorry, that wasn't for you. Did you talk to the Captain?" he asked Marcie.

"Yes. He said you should come to headquarters right away."

Shit! Shit!

"On my way," he said. It wasn't a total lie. He was on his way, but he was on his way to Louisiana, not to headquarters.

Marcie said, "Thank you, Jack. You're a good man. Please bring him home."

Jack hung up. Marcie knew he wasn't going anywhere near the police station. And *Charles* knew it too. Jack didn't think he could avoid the Captain forever, but maybe he'd make it to Mississippi before they put out an APB—All Points Bulletin—for him for theft of city property, to wit: one police Crown Vic.

He still couldn't believe what Marcie had said. Liddell was arrested for murder and was being held at the police station. Even the thought of it gave him a stomachache.

He crossed the Twin Bridges into Kentucky and tried to drive and find the GPS function on his iPhone. Katie's sister, Moira, had shown him how to use the function, but it had been over a week ago and he hated technology.

He held the button down and said, "Plaquemine, Louisiana." A cheerful female voice answered, "I'm sorry. I don't understand the command."

He'd had to repeat the name of the city he wanted at least six times and each time a woman's voice would say, "I don't understand that command" or "Here is what I found," and, of course, it wouldn't be what he'd asked for. He yelled, "Siri, I just want you to give me directions to Plaquemine, Louisiana, you stupid piece of shit!"

Whoever thought this crap up must be sadists.

Siri said back to him, "I'm sorry you feel that way, Supreme Commander." Moira must have programmed his phone to call him that. She was an unfunny jokester.

He merged onto U.S. Highway 60 and was heading west before he got the damn directions.

Chapter Seven

In 1803, Danforth Laveau, of the Pennsylvania Laveaus, purchased a portion of land along the Mississippi River in what would later be Iberville Parish. The Parish of Iberville was founded in 1807 and named for Pierre Le Moyne d'Iberville, a Frenchman who had founded the colony of Louisiana.

America's wealthy built cotton and sugar plantations with mansions along a one-hundred-mile strip of the Mississippi River from Baton Rouge to New Orleans and on to Slidell. Prior to the Civil War, this area of the Mississippi River Valley grew most of the cotton and half of all the sugar consumed in America.

At that time, over two hundred slaves and freedmen lived on the plantation, along with scores of children who ran and played or worked the fields alongside their parents.

The Laveau Plantation was passed down through the family until 2000, when the owner died intestate. Louisiana law required the estate be put in temporary holding by the Louisiana Department of State, which would attempt to unite the estate with any legal heirs. None were found, and the property reverted to the State of Louisiana. A year ago it was sold to a foreign corporation. Six months ago, a woman named Marie Laveau—not a relative of the original owners—claimed proprietorship and commenced rebuilding the estate to its former glory, minus the schoolhouse and playgrounds.

Today, Papa sat in the office that had been used by the mansion's former slave-owner. It was ironic because Papa was a black man, the descendant of four generations of slaves who had lived a life of servitude on plantations near New Orleans.

The fact that he had come so far from the days of hangings, beatings, rape of their women and having little more value than a pig, gave him little comfort right now. He'd gotten little sleep during the night. Three of his men had died when she had escaped, but he would have killed them if she hadn't. It was interesting that she had made it onto the plantation. Almost into the mansion itself. More interesting still that she had almost gotten away.

She was strong willed. Tough. But given the right amount of pain, in the right regions of the body, everyone would talk. He'd watched the beating, supervised removing her clothes to weaken her will, and he himself had questioned her. He'd watched as she broke—little by little, blow by blow—but he knew she had still held a little back.

She had come up with some story about suspecting Papa was aiding and abetting illegal immigrants. Hell, illegals worked at damn near every physical-labor job in Louisiana. Why would a sheriff's detective be investigating him instead of U.S. Immigration? Or FBI? Of more importance, was she alone?

He had to hand it to her. Even with beating her bloody, humiliating her sexually, and threatening to let his boys have their way with her, she had changed her story only slightly. She had last claimed to be with the Sheriff's Narcotics Unit and then with the DEA—Drug Enforcement Agency—but he didn't believe for a second that she was working for either of them. There were no drugs. No lab. He didn't allow drugs near the plantation. Anyone caught using or possessing them was executed while the other men watched. A score of unmarked graves in the cemetery behind the mansion could attest to that. Replacement workers were easy to find.

She had given him one piece of valuable information, and he didn't know if she was telling the truth about that. Near the end, she'd said several people knew she was there and that they'd come looking for her. He knew she said that to save her life. And it might have worked if he hadn't gone to call a friend to check out her information. He was on his way back to have her put in the cemetery when he'd been informed that she'd killed three of his men. Three armed men! And she had escaped. But in the end, she was captured. How could she not be, with twenty or so armed men surrounding the property? There was nowhere to go.

He'd had misgivings about killing her. Seeing her naked body, the perfect breasts, the smooth skin and long dark hair, he'd found himself pitying marring such a work of art in his need to beat the truth out of her. He considered keeping her. It had been many years since he'd bent a grown woman to his will, to his needs.

When his men said she'd seen his other guests in the bunker, his mind was made up for him. He had killed many people. Women and children even, some of whom were keeping the others company in the cemetery, but he'd never killed a cop. That was guaranteed to bring a shit storm from hell down on you. Every badge in the country would be out for your blood, and he didn't need that kind of attention or that kind of pressure.

But, what she'd done, what she'd seen. He had to maintain some type of order among his men. She would need to be made an example of. And when the body was brought back to the mansion, Papa himself had executed the man who had killed her for running like a coward when she had shot at him.

The woman's cell phone had given up a name. Liddell Blanchard. He was a detective from Evansville, Indiana. He was the last number called. Blanchard had called her phone six times yesterday evening and one of the voice mails said he was in Plaquemine. It was too much of a coincidence. The cop from Indiana was a loose end, but that was being dealt with.

His security manager knocked on the doorframe and came into the office. His name was Luke Perry. He was nothing like the actor. For one thing, he was black as the ace of spades, and he was short and chubby. Luke had explained that just before he was born his momma had been watching a show with Luke Perry in it. She'd always liked Luke Perry.

Papa still thought it was a stupid name. Like naming your kid Richard when his last name was Head. "The cop from Indiana?" he asked Luke.

"Papa, it's done. He arrested, just like you say, Papa."

"Arrested?" Papa leaned back in his chair, and the hinges groaned with his weight. He stared at Luke a long time, but Luke had nothing to add.

"I didn't want him arrested. I wanted him to disappear. Who arrested him?" Papa asked. Luke was one of his brightest employees, and that's why he'd been put in charge of security. But he was dense as clay sometimes. And he'd let the damn woman sneak onto the property in the first place. The reason he hadn't made an example of Luke, not including the fact that they'd been together for quite a while, was that he still needed the man for the more *delicate* parts of this operation.

"Police got him, Papa. He in a cell."

That meant Blanchard was still alive, which wasn't what he'd wanted. When he'd made the arrangements last night he'd had a different understanding of how this would be dealt with. He was disappointed.

Papa made a dismissive motion. Luke left and shut the door.

It's been taken care of. So why does it feel like someone stepped on my grave?

He picked up the desk phone, punched some numbers, and hesitated. So far no one knew about this screw-up except for some of his security people and the ones helping clean up the mess. He'd locked down the grounds last night when those two morons told him they grabbed the woman who was watching him. He'd checked his desk and his safe and nothing was disturbed. When they caught her, she didn't have anything on her person to indicate why she was there. *But* she did have a cell phone.

He didn't trust his crew to keep their mouths shut. They were all expendable, and they knew it.

He had partners and investors. The investors would be the ones pulling the plug on his operation, and pulling the trigger on everyone who was a threat. If the investors heard about this hiccup before he told them he would be dog shit. Even if he told them, he was dog shit anyway, so his partners were in as much trouble as he was.

Sally was the partner who was involved in the day-to-day operations. He'd have to tell her something. How much of it depended on her response. He dialed her number. When the phone was answered, he said, "We had a little problem here last night. I'm coming to you." He hung up. He didn't feel any better.

Jack's phone rang. The screen displayed, "Captain Franklin." He debated not answering. He gave in.

"Captain." Jack said.

"Should I ask where you are?" Captain Franklin asked.

"Kentucky. Am I fired?" Not that it would matter. He was going to Plaquemine.

Franklin chuckled, and for some reason hearing his boss's laugh was scarier than the screams and threats he had expected.

Franklin said, "Chief Pope is still trying to get in touch with the Plaquemine Police Chief. He said to tell you that you can use your department car, and you can help Liddell through this—as a friend. You are not to attempt to use police authority. You are a civilian there, not a policeman. Do you understand?"

"That goes without saying, Captain," Jack said. He would do or say whatever it took to get Liddell released.

"I'm glad we understand each other."

"Can I turn in my gas and meal receipts?" Jack asked.

"Don't push it, Jack. I'll call when I hear something. Be safe. Oh, and Jack. You pay for any traffic tickets."

They disconnected, and Jack slowed from 105 mph to make the 25 mph exit ramp.

Chapter Eight

It was going on ten hours since Liddell had been transported to the Plaquemine Police Department lockup. There were two holding cells used for short-term detention or for non-felons. The usual procedure for booking a prisoner was to take them to the side door that led to the cells and a property room/booking area. Instead, Barbie had marched Liddell through the front doors of the police station. Barbie had put ankle cuffs on Liddell just for this, forcing Liddell to take baby steps to make his way through the room. This is known as a "perp walk." Barbie's purpose was to humiliate Liddell and to show off in front of his coworkers.

Liddell had been taken through a door that he knew led past the detective's office and on to the detention cells. The detective's office was empty, but Liddell could see a desk with a gold-and-black plaque that read, "B. Troup."

He was taken down the hall to a Dutch door where the top half was standing open. This was the Property Room that also doubled as the booking area. An elderly man with a thick white beard and a khaki uniform had appeared in the opening. Without a word, Liddell's property was taken and put in a banker's box with "L. Blanchard" written on the outside. This done, Barbie shoved Liddell toward an old push-button phone that hung on the cinder-block wall. The phone was the same color as the walls, puke green.

Liddell was allowed to make one phone call, but since he was handcuffed behind his back, Barbie asked for the number. Liddell gave him Marcie's cell phone number, and Barbie held the receiver to Liddell's ear. Technically, listening in to a prisoner's phone call was a violation of civil rights and went against every police procedure. But Barbie was on a roll.

Liddell was able to tell Marcie that he was in jail at the Plaquemine Police Department. He had told her Bitty was dead and that he was a suspect. He was telling her to call Jack when Barbie hung the phone up.

Liddell had asked if he could call a lawyer. Barbie had laughed and said, "You don't need a lawyer unless you want to confess." Then Barbie had thankfully taken the handcuffs and ankle cuffs off and put him in a detention cell.

That was ten or eleven hours ago.

The cell he had been put in had two metal benches, one on each side. One bench was occupied with a guy who smelled like a rat dipped in shit and sprayed by a skunk. A pool of vomit had puddled on the floor under the bench. The orange woolen blanket wrapped around him and pulled up like a hoodie was soaked in more vomit.

Liddell had pulled his shirt over his nose and mouth but it was a futile effort. Like trying to scrub gasoline off your hands with water. Liddell watched the shrouded man across from him. The guy was drunk or stoned or both and hadn't stirred from the bench. His uneven snoring was a concern and Liddell had tried to call a jailer several times to tell them the man needed to be seen by medics. They had ignored his calls. He kicked the bars and yelled, "Hey! This man needs help in here!"

The drunk's eyes opened, but he didn't move. He said in a drugged voice, "Ain'no use. Dey ain' comin'."

Liddell felt relieved the man was alive. He was ashamed to admit it, but it would have been very hard for him to bring himself to give mouth-to-mouth to the stinking man if it had come down to that.

"What did you do?" the guy asked. It came out slurred, "Wha' ju' do?"

Liddell hoped the guy would just go back to sleep, but a door opened and a voice yelled, "Blanchard."

"Yo," Liddell said and stood.

The female police sergeant unlocked the cell door and opened it for Liddell. She was dressed in black BDUs; the pant cuffs tucked into shiny black Wolverine boots laced military-style. Her name tag read "L. Lucas." Her dyed-dark hair was short, military cut, and she carried herself like a drill sergeant.

"Hi, Liddell," she said.

It took him a second to place the face. She'd lost half her weight since he saw her last. And she'd been promoted.

"Hi, Lucy. You've changed. Grown stripes and everything."

"Yeah," she said with a hint of a smile. "I know. It's the haircut. And I lost a bunch of weight, and they make us wear this G.I. Joe stuff now. But don't worry, I don't wear it to bed," she said and chuckled. Her expression turned serious. "You don't know how bad I feel about all this. Bitty was a good person."

He was silent and she added, "We've got a new Chief of Police. Since she took over, they've turned me into a mushroom. Kept me in the dark and covered me with shit."

Liddell wasn't surprised a new Police Chief had taken office since he'd left. Their shelf life expired when a new mayor took office. He'd been gone so long he didn't even know who the mayor was.

"I'm glad to see you, Lucy. You're the first person I've talked to since Officer Barbierre threw me in here this morning." He pointed at the man lying on the bench snoring. "I think he needs to be seen by a doctor."

She said, "He's all right. He's a regular. We should charge him rent." She put a hand on Liddell's arm and asked, "How are you doing?"

"What time is it?"

"Almost ten," she said.

"I've been in here longer than I thought. I'll let you know how I'm doing when I find out what's going on," Liddell said.

"Don't worry about it. I think the Chief is kicking you loose."

"I'm being released?" he asked. "Did they catch someone?" He had a million questions.

"Detective Troup said we weren't allowed to discuss any aspect of this case with you."

"Troup?"

"Yeah," Lucy said. "He's tight with everyone that matters around here. Nobody crosses him. So I didn't tell you that you're being released. *Capisce*?" She pulled handcuffs from her gun belt and handcuffed him in front. "Sorry for this. Things are different. I'm supposed to take you to see Chief Whiteside. Rules are that everyone is handcuffed when they are out of the cell." She took his arm and led him through the steel door and into the detective's office. Liddell remembered the Chief's office was at the back of the detective's office.

Detective Troup sat alone at his desk. He said, "In case you didn't notice, Lucas here is hitting for the other team now, too. I think it's catchy." To Lucas he said, "Sorry Sergeant. That just slipped out." He grinned and Liddell felt the blood run up his neck to his cheeks.

"Say that again," Liddell said to him and bunched his fists. Right at that moment he wanted nothing so much as to smash in Troup's face.

Troup formed his forefinger and thumb into the shape of a pistol and pointed it at Liddell.

"Ignore the asshole," Lucas said and led Liddell to a door. Ornate gold lettering on the frosted glass read:

CHIEF OF POLICE
ANNA WHITESIDE

Lucas knocked. A feminine but serious voice said, "Come." Lucas removed the handcuffs and mouthed, "Good luck." She opened the door for Liddell, and he entered.

The Plaquemine PD office was just as he remembered it from the old days when he was with the Iberville Parish Sheriff. In fact, the two agencies' offices were located downtown and were separated by a handful of city blocks. The office was small for a Chief of Police, but the high ceiling and three floor-to-ceiling windows made it feel roomy if not spacious. The same ancient desk, circa World War II, set in the same space in front of the windows with two heavy straight-backed wood chairs in front, and one in a corner by a set of filing cabinets. The woman sitting behind the desk was new. The nameplate identified her as "A. Whiteside."

Chief Whiteside came around the desk, reaching for his hand and giving it a healthy squeeze before indicating that he take a seat.

"Call me Anna," the Chief said. "I've heard a lot about you Detective Blanchard."

"Nothing bad, I hope," Liddell said, not knowing what else to say. He sat down and was aware that his feet were bare, and he wasn't wearing a belt. His shirt was torn and spotted with blood from being beaten and from the "ride" he'd been given by Barbie.

The Chief seemed to take no notice, as if this were an everyday occurrence.

Anna Whiteside was trim and fit and very pretty, with rosy cheeks and dark brown eyes that matched her short dark hair. She was wearing a light blue uniform shirt with five gold stars pinned to the epaulets on each side of the collar. Her gun belt hung over a hall tree in the corner, sans handgun. The handgun was a Colt 1911 model .45 caliber; the kind used in World War II. It was currently disassembled atop a cleaning cloth on the desktop. She pushed it to one side and picked up a manila folder. He could see his name written on the folder in bold black letters.

"I guess you were expecting someone a little more male," the Chief said with a twinkle in her eye as if she had said this many times before.

"After the day I've had, you're a sight for sore eyes. I thought I'd been forgotten. Glad to meet you. I think."

"Of course you are," she said. She came around the desk with the folder and pulled the other chair around to face him. "Have you called your people?"

"As a matter of fact, Chief, they let me call my wife this morning and tell her I was being held by the police. That was about ten or eleven hours ago, and no one's talked to me since."

"I'm confused. Didn't Detective Troup interview you?"

Liddell decided not to mention the treatment he'd received from Troup or Barbie. He also didn't say anything about Troup's treatment of the crime scene. At least, not unless it became necessary. It's always better not to complain.

"I talked to your Chief a couple of times today. I'm sorry for not keeping you better informed of the progress. I assumed you were told that you weren't being charged."

"No, ma'am."

"I apologize for that," she said, but her tone was all business and not apologetic.

Apparently Troup had played things fast and loose before, and she didn't want to get the department involved in a nasty lawsuit for false imprisonment.

"We're not a big department, and we don't have all the resources available that you're used to in Evansville. But you remember what it's like here. You've had quite a career. Your Chief gives you good marks. Some of the older officers around here remember you, too. So I hope you understand why this has taken some time. I'm releasing you."

He didn't understand anything. He didn't understand why he'd been held in that cell for half the day. He didn't understand why he'd been detained in the first place. He didn't understand why he'd been Tasered and taken through the hoops by Barbie. He didn't understand why someone with Troup's background had been hired by a police agency. But he said none of that. Instead he said, "My boss told you I'm a pain in his ass. You can be straight with me." He forced a grin.

She was quiet and stared out of the window for an uncomfortable length of time.

She didn't seem to remember he was in the room. He asked, "If I'm not under arrest, can I leave?"

"Your partner is Jack Murphy, right?" Chief Whiteside asked.

"Is he here," Liddell asked.

"He should be arriving anytime now, if he's not here already. I can have Sergeant Lucas take you to get your car if you like. Or you can wait here for your partner, and he can take you."

Liddell had never been so glad to hear someone's name. *Good old Jack.* He checked the clock on her desk. "Well, it's almost ten o'clock. I think I'll take you up on that ride," he said and got up.

"Just another minute of your time," Whiteside said.

Liddell sat back down and thought, *Here comes the "but."*

"You are free to go . . . but . . . I just want to make sure you understand how serious this case is being treated. You can't imagine how sorry I am about Detective LeBoeuf's murder. I'm told that we haven't lost one of our own in the Parish for ten years or more, and I damn sure haven't lost anyone. We all suffer from the murder of an officer. We'll catch whoever did this. You have my word on that."

"Is Bobby Troup in charge of the investigation?" Liddell asked.

She scooted her chair closer, almost knee to knee with him. "Do you have a problem with Detective Troup?"

He suddenly regretted asking about Troup. He weighed his response and answered, "He was a good investigator." It was true. Troup *was* a good investigator. He was a horrible policeman and crooked as a dog's hind leg, and he'd slipped out of a murder charge.

But Liddell thought she should know all about the murder charge if she was the one that hired him.

She seemed to relax. "If you remember anything that would help the investigation into Detective LeBoeuf's murder, I would appreciate you passing it on to Detective Troup."

Liddell hadn't told Troup about Bitty's call that had brought him from Evansville. He thought about telling Whiteside now, but something told him not to. At least not yet. "Of course."

Whiteside changed subjects. "If I may ask, what was the purpose of your visit?"

"I'm visiting family. I got in town last night," Liddell said. "Bitty—Detective LeBoeuf—was my partner in the Sheriff's Department for years. I went to say hello this morning and found her dead. Before I could call it in, Officer Barbierre placed me under arrest." *And Tasered me a few times and kicked and slapped me in the head.*

She waited for him to expand on what he'd said. He didn't.

"You're free to go, Mr. Blanchard. You can show yourself out. Sergeant Lucas will take care of you."

Liddell didn't get up. "Let me ask you a question, Chief Whiteside. Do you have any leads yet? I haven't been told anything about the case."

She stood and put her hands on her hips. "You seem to have gotten the wrong idea, *Mister* Blanchard." She stressed the *Mister*, reminding him he was not a detective in Plaquemine. "I'm not going to discuss an ongoing investigation with you. I'm not ordering you to stay in town. But I suggest you get in the car with Detective Murphy and go home. You say you don't know anything and, one cop to another, I believe you." She locked eyes with him. "At least at this moment. But who knows what the next few hours will bring?"

Liddell got the idea. She sounded like the sheriff in an old western movie telling him, "Get out of town by sundown." Normal police procedure dictated he either be held as a "person of interest" or at least ordered not to leave town until he could be properly interviewed. They hadn't even taken his statement.

"I'd like to continue visiting my brother," he said.

"Landry. Correct?"

"That's right," he said.

"Did his daughter come home?"

"No," Liddell said. "And he hasn't heard from the detective working the missing person case. I understand he talked to you."

The look she gave him told Liddell she wasn't impressed with Landry.

"Can you have someone call him? He's very worried, and it's been a few days now," he said.

"It's being looked into," she said, and her demeanor softened. "We'll contact you if we have further questions." She walked behind her desk and resumed cleaning her handgun. Conversation over.

Liddell walked to the door, opened it, shut it again, and walked back to her desk.

"I'm not trying to argue with you, Chief Whiteside. If I were in your place, I'd tell me to stay out of it."

She put the oil-stained cloth down and said, *"But?"*

"Look at it from my point of view, Chief. As a fellow officer, I would like some reassurances Bitty's case will be handled properly." He wanted to add that Evie's being missing was not exactly getting the attention it deserved, but he understood that a lot of missing teenage girls showed up at home in a few days, no worse for wear. They had either run away, then decided to come home when they got cold and hungry, or they were off with a boyfriend and lost track of time as well as their virginity.

Her eyebrows rose, and she stood again. "It's being handled."

"Look, I don't know you, but I've worked with Troup before. And so has Bitty."

"Detective LeBoeuf? The victim?"

"Yes. We call . . . called her Bitty. Troup and Bitty butted heads a few times in the past. I just want to be sure Troup will give this his best effort. He was a good detective at one time, but I'm afraid his judgment might be clouded where Bitty is concerned." *And where I'm concerned too.*

The Chief kept her eyes on his and said, "I know my people, Detective Blanchard. And I know your background. And that of your partner, Jack Murphy. And I know who your brother is. And if I may speak plainly, your brother and your partner are big pains in the ass. They are not going to be a pain in my ass. I'm going against my better judgment letting you leave here."

Liddell closed his mouth, turned, and left the office. He wondered why she wasn't locking him up. He figured that by now Troup had set the stage and put him right in the spotlight. He didn't have a chance to ask Whiteside about Evie. It was obvious she didn't like Landry and he didn't think she would appreciate him insinuating that her department wasn't handling a missing person to his satisfaction. Anything he said now would get him put back in a cell and if that happened he couldn't help anyone. Besides, he had to admit she was right about Landry being a pain in the ass. Landry had once called the previous mayor "a frog on a wart's ass."

Sgt. Lucas was waiting for him in the detective's office.

Chapter Nine

After he got his property, Liddell had declined the offer of a ride from Sergeant Lucas. He was toxic, and he didn't want to get her in trouble. He left the police station holding a large manila tie-envelope in one hand and his shoes and socks in the other. He had checked the contents with the Property Room clerk and run into several problems.

First, his Glock .45 wasn't with his property. He was told that Troup had it sent to the State Police Laboratory to be run through the Wildfire program. Wildfire is a Federal ballistics program where guns used in or suspected of use in crimes had ballistics information collected and stored in a database to be compared with outstanding cases. Liddell hadn't seen any evidence of a gunshot at Bitty's place. Troup shouldn't have sent his gun to the lab unless he suspected it had been used in a crime. It should have been returned with Liddell's property. Did this mean that Bitty was shot? Liddell didn't know because no one would talk to him.

Second, the Property Room clerk didn't know where Liddell's backup .45 was. If Liddell's car had been towed—which it had—the car should have been searched and an inventory made of items of value. This was a protection for the police department, the officer, and the tow operator, so that the car owner wouldn't claim a theft from his vehicle. The car owner was given a copy of the inventory, but Liddell had never been given one. If Troup had seized his duty weapon and sent it to the lab, why didn't he take the .45 that Liddell had in a holster under the seat? According to the clerk that .45 hadn't been listed with his property or sent to the lab.

Last of all, his iPhone wasn't with his property. He'd seen Barbie give the phone to Troup at Bitty's and watched Troup illegally search it. He didn't see if Troup gave it back to Barbie.

He considered going back inside to use a landline to call Jack and Marcie, but he didn't want to get in a shitting match with some jerk just to use their phone. Chief Whiteside had warned him about pushing his luck.

The clerk had handed him his shoes and duty holster and transferred the remainder of his property into a large manila envelope. He sat down on the concrete steps in front of the police station and pulled his belt out of the envelope and ran it through the loops on his slacks. He put his wedding ring on, checked his badge case and paper money again, and pulled his socks on. He laced his shoes and put them on. He was still leaning over and tying the laces when a horn honked on the street. He stood and turned and saw a brown Crown Vic setting at the curb with the passenger door open.

"I've never been so glad to see your ugly mug, pod'na," Liddell said and slid into the front seat. "Took you long enough."

"Blame Mississippi for that," Jack said. "I was stopped by a female State Trooper for doing one ten in a seventy. She gave me a ticket and an escort to the Louisiana state line, where I had to do the speed limit. She said Louisiana might not give me a hand."

"She wasn't lying, pod'na. Our Troopers might lock you up for reckless endangerment." Liddell tossed the empty envelope in the back of the car. "We need to get my car and I'll tell you everything I know on the way."

Jack put the car in gear and checked his rearview mirror. A black-and-white police car sat just inches from his back bumper with its headlights off. Someone was in the driver's seat, but it was eleven p.m. and dark and all he could tell was that the driver was wearing a uniform. The face was in shadow.

"Are we getting an escort to your car?"

"That's Barbie," Liddell said.

"Barbie?"

"Yeah. Officer Barbierre. He's the asshole that arrested me." He made a circular motion beside his head with his finger. "He's not all there. And he's a sadist."

Jack's nose wrinkled. "Jesus, Bigfoot. You stink," he said, and powered all the windows down. Hot air came in like a blast furnace. "We need to get you some clothes."

"I know," Liddell said. "I've got vomit all over me, and the drunk in my cell smelled like a dead skunk. I've got a change of clothes at Landry's, and I can get a shower there."

The emergency lights of the police car came on behind them and reflected around inside of the Crown Vic like a disco ball.

"Is he wanting me to pull over? I'm already parked at the curb," Jack said and checked the rearview mirror. The police car's headlights switched off and the dome light came on. Jack was able to see the driver was young with blond hair worn in a severe crew cut, spiked in front. Barbie was smiling, but he was showing a few too many teeth, like an attack dog with a target in sight.

"He's smiling. The jerk," Liddell said disgustedly.

"Maybe he's looking for a date," Jack said.

"Just drive," Liddell said. "This guy doesn't play by any rules."

"And I do?" Jack asked.

"You just shoot people that need it, so you're just a teensy bit antisocial compared to that psycho back there."

Barbie made no move to exit the police vehicle. He pulled close to the back of the Crown Vic just short of bumping it. No traffic moved on the street at this hour. Jack used his left turn signal before pulling out, and the police car stayed right on their bumper. Jack tried to ignore being tailgated, but he wasn't good at patience. "If that's Barbie, I'd hate to see Ken," he said.

Liddell chuckled and said, "Turn right at the second light."

"Your holster is empty, Bigfoot," Jack said. "Did you forget your gun, or is that a fashion statement?"

"They kept my daddy Glock and the extra ammo. The property officer said my backup gun must still be in my car."

"Captain Franklin told me that your old partner was murdered and you found her, but he didn't know much more. I hope I'm not being insensitive. You don't have to talk about it if you don't want to," Jack said.

Liddell leaned back and stared at Jack. "Who the hell are you and what have you done with Jack?" he asked.

"Bite me, Bigfoot. I can be sensitive. I have a full range of emotions that you haven't seen."

"You're right, pod'na. You're the most sensitive man I know."

"Let's not get carried away," Jack said.

Liddell took a breath and said, "They haven't told me squat. Zip. I went to Bitty's and saw the back door had been kicked in. I went in and found her butchered on the kitchen table. She was eviscerated. Her face was smashed, hacked to shreds, and some kind of symbol was drawn on the wall in blood. And, no, I don't mind talking about it. In fact, it's a relief to finally talk to someone about it. I want to know who killed her and why."

Jack thought about it and said, "Did you see a weapon?"

"No. But I didn't have a chance to check out the rest of the house. When I saw her on the table like that I went in the backyard and threw up. Next thing I know I'm getting Tasered by Barbie."

"If they're keeping your gun, they must think a gun was used."

"After Barbie Tasered, handcuffed, and forced me back into the house, Bobby Troup shows up and more or less accuses me of the murder. Bobby Troup is the detective supposedly working this case. Barbie takes me to lockup, where I sat in a cell until the Chief of police told me I'm free to go, but not to get involved. She hinted that I could still be arrested as a material witness."

"That's messed up." Jack had heard Liddell talk about Bitty many times and he knew how much he cared for her.

"I've got a history with Troup. Bitty did too."

Jack turned on his right signal as he approached the red light and watched the police car in his rearview mirror. Facing them on the other side of the intersection was a new charcoal Dodge Challenger with dark tinted windows. A tall, skinny man with a long face like a horse stood in the street beside the car. He had on a too-loose black suit and dress shoes. He was going bald on top, and had a white fringe that was long and pulled back in a ponytail. Jack put him somewhere in his fifties. The man took a long drag on a cigarette but never took his eyes off them. He dropped the cigarette and crushed it with the toe of his shoe, still without taking his eyes from them. His ill-fitting dark suit was reminiscent of a prop for an undertaker in a horror movie. The man's gaze passed over Jack and locked on Liddell.

Jack asked, "Friend of yours?"

"That's Bobby Troup," Liddell said. "He's the investigator. Like

I said, Bitty and me had some issues with Troup way back when. He was with Iberville Parish Sheriff's Department longer than either of us until he got fired. Now, somehow, he's a Plaquemine detective."

"He's the one that kept you locked up all day?"

"Yeah, that's him. Officer Barbierre is his mini-me-wannabe."

The light changed from red to green, and as Jack turned the corner Troup made a gun with his forefinger and thumb, pointed the make-believe gun at Liddell, and dropped his thumb.

"Did you see what that asshole . . . ?" Jack pulled over to the shoulder and was unlatching his seat belt, but Liddell put a hand on his arm.

"Let it go, pod'na. He's not worth it. He'd put us both in jail on some trumped-up shit."

"Maybe he won't have to trump it up," Jack said, and looked behind them. He saw Troup get back in the car. Jack drove on and saw Barbie was staying with them. "What did you do to this guy anyway? Troup I mean," Jack said.

"We, Bitty and me, had a hand in an investigation that eventually got him fired," Liddell said.

"Oh. You never told me about that," Jack said.

"Well, we didn't exactly get him fired, but our testimony at a grand jury hearing almost got him charged with murder."

"Did you say murder?"

"Yeah. Troup and another detective—Doyle Doohan was his name—were the Sheriff's Department Vice Unit. They worked on the side for some mobbed-up guy, jacking up small-time gamblers and shutting down the competition. Of course no one could prove anything. One night Troup shot a guy dead. He and Doohan claimed it was self-defense, but Bitty and me were first to the scene and it didn't look right. The dead guy had a machete in his hand and four bullet holes in him."

"Sounds like a good shoot to me," Jack said.

"Bitty knew the dead guy and knew he was left handed. Even though the guy had fallen down a flight of stairs after Troup shot him, the machete was still in his right hand. The coroner said he died immediately. One bullet severed his aorta, and one took out half his brains."

"Okay, so not so good," Jack said.

"Troup, his partner, and a prostitute were the witnesses, and the prostitute was so hopped up on heroin she didn't know who she was or what year it was."

"So how did he walk away from that?" Jack asked.

"Same old story," Liddell said. "The district attorney was running for reelection and he didn't need the stink or was on the mob's payroll. The Grand Jury only hears what the D.A. wants them to hear, so they voted not to file charges. The D.A used that to refuse the case, citing not enough evidence to convict. Our Sheriff fought with the D.A., but that went nowhere. The Sheriff fired him and Doohan anyway on the grounds that Troup and Doohan didn't follow standard operating procedures. They didn't call dispatch to say they were going to the victim's house, so no one knew where they were until the guy was dead and an ambulance was called."

"So Troup is a dirty cop that might have gotten away with murder, and now he's a detective with Plaquemine PD," Jack said.

Red and blue lights lit up the inside of the Crown Vic. Barbie was pulling them over. Jack stopped on the side of the road. Barbie drove alongside them and angled in front of their car. Bright headlights came up behind them and the Dodge Challenger was on their bumper.

"Is he insane?" Jack asked, and kept his hands on the steering wheel where they could be seen. Liddell also put his hands up on the dash.

Barbie exited the police car and took up a position by the trunk with his handgun out and pointed at them. Jack heard a car door shut and feet crunching on the grit at the side of the road. Bobby Troup rested a hand on the doorframe and leaned down, looking at Jack.

"Who have we got here, Barbie?" Troup said.

"Looks like some dangerous assholes," Barbie said and grinned, but the gun didn't waver.

"Did I say you could leave your cell, Blanchard?" Troup asked.

Jack stared at him. He could pull his Glock and blow the mortician's face off, but he wasn't sure he could get Barbie. He thought about what the Mississippi State Trooper had told him about the police here. He believed her now.

Troup put both hands on the doorframe and squatted down, staring at Jack now. "So this is Jack Murphy," he said in a mocking tone. His suit coat was open and the gun in his shoulder holster hung loosely in Jack's face. He saw Jack looking at it, and his mouth set in a tight line. Jack expected him to say something corny, like "Go ahead and try it" or "Do you feel lucky, punk?" He didn't.

"You know who we are. Are you sure you want to do this?" Jack asked Troup.

Troup rose up enough to say to Barbie, "He wants to know if we want to do this."

"Like the Energizer Bunny," Barbie said, and the gun pointed at Jack's face. Jack didn't quite get Barbie's remark, but he could feel an electric tension building as if something very bad was about to happen.

"Did you know your buddy here is a cop killer?" Troup asked Jack. "He's a piece of shit I should have wiped off the sole of my shoe."

Jack said, "I think we're all killers here. Except for your little buddy over there anyway."

Troup sucked at his front teeth and cast a glance at Barbie "Barbie's okay. He's loyal. True blue. A cop's cop." He lowered his voice and said, "He's a little aggressive, so if I was you I would watch my mouth."

Jack smiled. This was kind of fun, but he had places to go and people to see. "So, now you showed us yours, and I'm impressed with your tactics. Can we go?"

Troup laughed. "I heard about you. I thought you'd be bigger. More menacing."

Jack answered, "I've heard about you too. I thought you'd be smarter. Smell better."

Troup laughed out loud and said to Barbie, "He thinks we're stupid and smell bad," to which Barbie gritted his teeth and slammed a gloved fist into the palm of the other hand.

Troup leaned in the window and said, "Hey, I'm just messing with you." His hand went inside his suit jacket and Jack's hand went to the grip of his own .45. Troup froze and said, "I'm not going to pull a gun on you. Take it easy. I'm just reaching inside my coat pocket for property that belongs to your buddy." He pulled a cell phone out of his pocket and tossed it toward Liddell. "You forgot to pick this up." The phone landed on the floor at Liddell's feet. Troup slapped on the door frame and said, "You boys have a good night and a safe drive back to Indiana." Troup and Barbie went to their cars and drove away.

Liddell retrieved the iPhone from the floor and examined it. The screen was crushed. Grit and small rocks were ground into the rubber casing and plastic.

"Bastard stomped it," Liddell said.

"He's the Alpha male," Jack said. "You're lucky he didn't pee on it."

Liddell snorted. "I thought you'd be smarter? Did you really say that?"

"Did Barbie say Energizer Bunny? What the hell does that mean?" Jack said.

"I'm almost embarrassed that I let that idiot arrest me." Liddell was still looking at his phone.

"How far to this impound lot?" Jack asked. He was anxious to get Liddell's car and get the smell out of the Crown Vic. They were on River Road headed west. It was two-lane and without streetlights. The smell of something dead and rotting overshadowed the smell of vomit. "What's that smell?"

"Oil, gas, fish. Bart's is just down the road."

The sign for Bart's Towing came up on their right, and Jack pulled into a gravel area in front of a wood sided one-room house/business. The building was dark, and a CLOSED sign hung on the door.

"Doesn't look like anyone's home," Jack said.

"We'll have to come back in the morning. There's a number you can call to get someone out here. But it goes to the police station, and I don't think the police will call anyone for us."

They drove to a Krystal's in Baton Rouge and loaded up on four-for-a-dollar burgers, fries, and black coffee.

"I promised Marcie and Katie I would call as soon as I got here. Katie's staying at your place," Jack said.

Liddell held his hand out for Jack's iPhone. "I'll do it."

Jack watched Liddell put away ten Krystal burgers and two large orders of fries and talk to Marcie at the same time. When Liddell was through talking, he handed the phone to Jack, saying, "Katie wants to talk to you."

Jack pushed his unfinished Krystal Burgers, fries, and milkshake across to Liddell and talked to Katie. He made a cross-your-heart-and-hope-to-die promise to call in the morning, told her he loved her, and hung up.

Jack and Liddell sat in the Crown Vic outside Krystal's and talked.

"I'm not sure why Bitty called," Liddell said. "She didn't seem to want to talk about it on the phone. She asked if I had some vacation time coming. I called last night and this morning but she never answered. I should have known something was wrong." He looked over at Jack. "Maybe if—"

Jack interrupted him. "Maybe what? You couldn't have known. There's nothing you could have done, Bigfoot. Did she sound worried?"

"Yeah. She did a little. But she didn't sound scared. Of course, Bitty wasn't scared of much. I wish she had talked to me."

Jack started the engine and turned on the air-conditioning.

"She was mutilated. No one should die like that." Liddell took a deep breath, and his jaw clenched. "Troup is keeping everything from me. Chief Whiteside isn't treating me like I'm a suspect, but she wouldn't tell me anything either. I don't know what the hell is going on. If Troup wantd to frame me for this, he's had the whole day to plant evidence."

"What do you want to do?" Jack asked, but he knew the answer.

"I've been warned twice now not to interfere. By the Police Chief and now Troup. But to be fair, if we were back in Evansville they wouldn't want me sticking my nose in either."

Jack didn't tell him what Captain Franklin had said. "You didn't answer my question, Bigfoot."

"You should go back to Evansville, pod'na. You don't need this kind of trouble," Liddell said.

Jack ignored him and asked, "So what's our next move?"

Liddell said, "My brother says Evie hasn't been home for a couple of days. I told you I have a niece, right?"

"How old is she?" Jack asked.

"Evie's fourteen. And before you ask, she isn't the type of kid to give her dad any problems. He's worried, and frankly I am too. When I saw Bitty this morning, I was going to ask her if she would have her friend help find Evie. Bitty's friend, her ex-life partner I should say, is the Missing Persons detective for the Sheriff's Department."

"Well, I guess we should stick around and ask some questions. We need to find your niece, Evie. Right?"

"Thanks for sticking with me, pod'na."

"Where else am I going to go? The Captain sent me to get you. He didn't say bring you back against your will."

"We'll have to avoid Troup. He's likely to find a charge to put on me. On us. But I'm not going anywhere until I get some answers," Liddell said.

"Me neither," Jack said.

Chapter Ten

Papa sat in his office at the mansion and looked at the built-in bookcase that lined one wall. It was filled with hundreds of leatherbound books, some rare and valuable. He had read none of them, but they had given him enjoyment and a sense of accomplishment that he could own such things. They gave him little enjoyment now.

He had been assured the Indiana cop's arrest was an open-and-shut deal, but things had gotten even more screwed up than they were. He had no choice but to call the investors, and they were more than just unhappy. If he had to close this operation down, a lot of money would be lost by a lot of people. Plus he had two dozen workers who would have to be silenced. It would be—messy. To say the least.

And there was the possible involvement of the federal authorities. He didn't know how much the woman had told the detective from Indiana. And he didn't know how much that one had told his brother. The brother was already looking for his daughter. It was a matter of time before he came there looking for her. And now another detective was in town. It was the perfect operation. And it was unraveling. He knew he should just disappear. But the money . . .

Ten miles south of Grand Isle, Louisiana, in the mouth of Baritaria Bay, a 117-foot yacht flying the Cayman Islands flag was anchored, and a smaller craft sped away into the darkness. The U.S. Coast Guard randomly patrolled these waters looking for drug runners, weapons dealers, and human traffickers, among other things. The men on the small craft were prepared. They each had Florida driver's licenses and various credit cards and Louisiana fishing licenses to support the story they were on vacation. Additionally, they had two cabins reserved at Bayside Marina Resort on Grand Isle. Two Suburbans had been rented and were waiting for them at the Marina should a trip to Plaquemine become necessary.

The concrete room was no more than four walls, a low ceiling, and floor. Air was piped in and circulated by two ceiling vents with metal bars set into the concrete. Evie knew it was hot outside, but down here the air was always cool.

A stainless-steel toilet/sink combination was bolted to the floor in one corner. Eight small pallets were arranged on the floor. Each was covered with a thin foam mattress and blanket, and on each was a sleeping child. Four young girls had occupied the room when she was brought to this room three days ago. An armed man had taken three of the girls out over the last two days. They didn't come back. Yesterday another girl and two very young boys—the oldest boy was eleven—replaced the missing girls. It was always the same man who came for them, and she'd heard another man in the hall outside the door call him Luke. Luke, the man she had come to think of as "the warden," was short and stocky and old. He had to be at least forty, and he never spoke to them.

Twice a day they would be rounded up by other men and taken to a room with steel picnic tables and a kitchen. On their march down the long hallways, the overhead lights would come on in front of them and go off behind them. She couldn't complain about the food because the tables would be loaded with piles of bacon and sausages, trays of homemade bread and blackberry jam, and pitchers of orange juice and milk.

After breakfast, they were made to clean the dishes and wash the tables. When they were done, several other armed men—different men—took each of them to do chores.

This morning she had been taken down a hallway to a room where she saw blood on the floor and walls. A piece of rope was hanging from a chair that set in a puddle of blood. She was given a bucket of water and rags and a black plastic garbage bag. She had picked up bullet casings, and the room smelled like burnt gunpowder. She knew what that smelled like because her father had taught her to shoot, and it smelled like that.

She had cleaned up the blood, put the bloody rags and rope fragments into a black plastic garbage bag, and taken it into the hallway, where she was ordered to clean up more blood. Bile had risen in her throat, but her guard told her if she threw up he would beat her.

That had been a long time ago, and she had just picked at the food on her plate when they were taken for the second meal of the day. She heard footsteps and laughing outside in the hall. She stared at the door and prepared herself. She would be taken soon. It was her turn. But the noise faded and all she heard was the sobbing of the little ones.

She lay back on the lumpy foam mattress, hands under her head, staring up into the dark, and thought about last night. The woman who opened their door last night was bloody and naked, but she'd promised to come back with help. She hadn't come back. Evie wondered if the blood and bits of scalp she'd cleaned up this morning were from the woman.

She closed her eyes, and tried to imagine that above her were the constellations, and she could see a shooting star streak across the horizon. At night, at home, she would climb out her window onto the roof and lay just like this. She knew all the stars and constellations and would wonder if people lived on them. There had to be some life out there. Had to. Otherwise the world was just one big cosmic joke. She wished she were at home, on the roof, looking at the real stars right now.

But like her father would say, "If wishes was fishes, none of us would starve." He had a saying for everything. Sometimes she didn't understand his point, but she did now. Wishing wasn't going to get the job done. The woman was gone or dead. Help wasn't going to come. If there was any chance for her to be saved, her father would have already found her. But how could he find her when she herself didn't know where she was?

He would watch the stars with her sometimes. That's where she'd learned all that stuff. And she would ask him if her momma was up there among the stars. He would always say, "It's just you and me, Evie. And that's enough for me, kid." He would put his arm around her shoulders and hug her close and kiss the top of her head.

"Oh, Daddy. What have I done? I'm so, so sorry. Please come and get me." Tears wet her cheeks, and she lay on her side and hugged herself until she slept.

Chapter Eleven

When Jack awakened the next morning he'd been dreaming about Katie and his father, Jake Murphy. In the dream Jake was happy that Jack and Katie were back together, but he was trying to tell Jack something important. Like most dreams, after you wake, the feeling was still there, but the words and meaning drifted off into tendrils of nothingness. Maybe his dad was trying to tell him not to mess up his chance with Katie. Maybe he was telling him where the family gold was hidden. Who knew?

Landry had let Jack sleep in Evie's room, and because he had left Evansville with literally the clothes on his back, he hadn't brought a shaving kit. He used the hand soap by the sink to shower with. It was either that or herbal body wash that smelled like lemonade. The body wash promised luxurious soft skin all day long, but he didn't want to smell like lemonade. There was a toothbrush and tooth-paste in a glass. He used some of the toothpaste and brushed his teeth with his finger, rinsed, spat, and made sure the sink bowl was clean.

He dressed in the clean clothes Landry had loaned him. The khaki work pants and khaki button-up shirt didn't go with his bur-gundy loafers, but he was grateful that they fit at all. Landry wasn't as big as Liddell. He made a mental note to buy a pair of jeans, box-ers, and a couple of shirts if the case kept them here very long.

He hadn't been able to sleep. He was that way when he drove long distances. With the death of Liddell's friend and the niece missing, he would need to get his head on straight. He'd never met any of these folks, and as this was his first time in Louisiana, he had a lot of catching up to do.

With a murder, you start outside the scene and work your way in to the body. Asking questions like, "What's the neighborhood like, where was the body found, how could it have gotten there, what is around here, where are windows, people, cars, surveillance cameras, postmen, newspapers, dogs?" Everyone and everything were potential witnesses or held some scrap of evidence. Not so with a missing-person case.

With a missing-person case, you went to the last place the person was seen: their room, their house, their neighbors, their friends, their work, school, haunts, hangouts. You worked the case outward to get a picture of the missing person's routine, their life and likes and dislikes and tastes, and maybe from there, who they were targeted by.

Last night Landry had told him about Evie. Landry was a little rough around the edges compared to Bigfoot, but he was a good guy, and it was obvious that he doted on his daughter.

Jack surveyed Evie's room. When he'd come in here last night her bed was made up, at least by the standards of a fourteen-year-old girl. A pair of shorts was laid over the back of a chair, and no clothes on the floor. He opened the closet and saw the clothing was on hangers or folded on the upper shelf. Her shoes were paired and lined up against the back of the closet. If he checked out her dresser, he was sure he would find it the same. She was organized for a teenager. On the back of the door was a bulletin board with ribbons, and lots of pictures. In the pictures, she progressively aged from an infant to a child to a young adult. One picture was taken with her arm around Landry's shoulder and she was sticking her tongue out at the camera. The look on her face was one of pure joy.

Liddell had told him about the Voodoo talismans and stuff that Landry had found in a box in Evie's room. Even though her mother, Sally, was the source of the Voodoo stuff, it didn't fit with the girl he was seeing here. This girl was too neat. She liked to have fun, but she was levelheaded too. She would be the one taking charge of groups at school, or organizing an outing, not fodder for a mindless cult.

Landry had mentioned someone named Marie Laveau last night and Jack had asked if he knew where she lived. He suggested they start there looking for Evie. Bigfoot and Landry had had a good laugh at that. Marie Laveau, as it turned out, is like Elvis. Queen of the Voodoo Prom. Seducer of Souls. Beetlejuice of the Ball. Dead but not gone.

He didn't know much about Voodoo, except what he'd seen in movies and TV, but he couldn't see this girl being involved in any of that. No way. He promised himself that he'd do everything in his power to get her home safe.

He folded his dirty clothes and had a sudden twinge at the thought of wearing someone else's underwear. That would be number one on his clothes-buying list. He tried to be quiet and carried the clothes downstairs hoping he'd find coffee makings, but Landry was already up and making a pot of coffee in the kitchen.

It was dark outside, and he could feel a cool breeze coming through the open window. He'd never get used to this kind of life where windows were left open all night, doors were left unlocked, keys were sometimes left on the visor in a car or truck, and everyone carried a gun. But, maybe it was good weapons and not good fences that made good neighbors. They were doing something right here because the crime rate involving weapons was lower here than in most other states, including Indiana. Jack had asked, "Do you get an assault rifle when you get your marriage license?"

Liddell was asleep on the couch, snoring like a tree limb shredder. Jack had been so wiped out last night that when Landry suggested he go to bed, he hadn't given a thought as to where Liddell would sleep. Jack tiptoed past the couch and went in the kitchen, where Landry was lighting the burners on the gas stove with a wooden match. Landry was a surprise. He was two years older than Liddell, a head shorter, and a hundred pounds lighter. He looked strong enough to wrestle a bear and make it cry uncle. Landry's skin was as tough and dark as leather, and the muscles corded in his arms were like coils of wire. His neck was thick, his fists like mallets, and Jack had never seen such intense eyes. They were the color of an angry ocean.

"Just push his big ass off the couch," Landry said.

"He had a tough day yesterday," Jack said.

"I'm serious. Roll him off on the floor," Landry said.

"I'm up," Liddell said and came trudging into the kitchen. He had bed-hair, and one side of his face was smooshed up and red from the couch pillow.

"Maybe we should stay in Baton Rouge or somewhere out of this jurisdiction if we're still here tonight," Jack said.

Landry dropped bacon in an iron skillet and said, "What's wrong with this place?"

Liddell reached for the coffeepot, and Landry admonished him. "I'm getting it. Sit down."

Jack sat and across from Liddell. He said, "I appreciate you putting us up last night, Landry, but I really think it would be best if we stay somewhere else while we look into all of this. These people are really messed up, and I don't want to bring it to your door."

Landry laughed and said, "You hear that, baby brother? He doesn't want to bring trouble here."

Liddell put a hand on Jack's arm and said, "Landry thrives on confrontation. Even animals avoid him. Mom and Dad moved a couple of times while he was at school, but he kept finding us."

Landry pointed with a spatula. "You tell people that because you were adopted. That's right. Mom found him in a garbage can in the State Park. They made the mistake of feeding him and look what happened?"

"I think he's got you there, Bigfoot," Jack said, and Landry winked.

Liddell looked at the empty table and said, "Are you going to feed us or talk us to death?"

Two mugs of dark coffee were set in front of them, and Landry spooned a generous amount of sorghum into Jack's. A dash of Tabasco sauce was added, and Landry said, "Stir it up. That's real Creole coffee. Best you'll ever get." Liddell was already stirring his.

Jack stirred the thick liquid and took a sip. *That's pretty good.* He added a couple more shakes of hot sauce.

Landry spooned sorghum on top of the sizzling bacon, ground black pepper onto it, added some other ingredients, and started a skillet of scrambled eggs. When the eggs were finished, he scooped generous portions onto three plates, added a pile of bacon, sprinkled grated Parmesan cheese on the eggs, and served them.

As they ate, Landry said, "Cops need guns like cows need tits." He reached in his back pocket and pulled out a blued-steel semiautomatic handgun and put it on the table next to Liddell with two loaded clips. "Walther PPK .380. Same thing James Bond carries." He went back to eating as if guns on the table were part of the meal.

Jack's eyebrows rose. "Are we supposed to shoot the bacon, or are you expecting a war?"

Liddell said, "It would be a short war. Landry's got every kind of weapon known to man around here. Big Jim—that's our daddy—was a collector. Our grandfather was a collector too. We have everything from muzzle loaders to FNFAL 5.56 assault rifles to Bushmaster AR15s, pistols, bowie knives, hunting knives, you name it."

"The war is over. The South lost," Jack reminded them.

"If we'd have had a couple thousand AR15s, things might have turned out different," Landry said.

Jack decided to change the subject. "This is interesting bacon, Landry. Is it Creole too?"

"Pork," Landry said and chuckled.

Liddell said, "They call it Million Dollar Bacon. You take thick sliced bacon, cayenne pepper, ground black pepper, brown sugar, and red-pepper flakes. Landry substitutes sorghum for maple syrup."

"Whatever it's named, it tastes like a million dollars," Jack said. "You need to turn your house into a restaurant, Landry. You could call it Biscuits and Bullets."

Landry turned serious. "Bring Evie home, you hear me."

Liddell drove the Crown Vic toward the impound lot. It was still dark outside, but Liddell assured him the lot would be open. They rode in silence part of the way before Liddell said, "Evie is a good girl. I don't think she would just take off and hurt Landry like that."

"I believe you, Bigfoot. But she's fifteen years old."

"Fourteen," Liddell corrected. "She'll be fifteen in two weeks."

"Okay. Fourteen. Let me play devil's advocate. Does Landry spend much time with her?"

Liddell hesitated before answering. "Landry's been a single dad since Evie was eleven months old. He and Evie lived with our parents for several years. My mom took care of Evie while the men worked. When our parents passed on, Landry was on his own. Evie was about ten. He had the house, a job that very few men retire from—alive at least—and he had Evie. He worships the ground that girl walks on."

"I only brought it up because, if we're going to find her, we need to think like detectives, not like an uncle and a friend. Get me?"

"I don't know if I can do that, pod'na." Liddell tightened his grip on the steering wheel and increased their speed. Traffic was almost nonexistent on the two-lane.

Jack had to remember he wasn't in Kansas anymore. What worked in Evansville didn't necessarily translate to this place, and Liddell had been gone for about five years. Liddell had even remarked that things had changed.

"We need a plan." Jack said.

"I have a few things in mind."

"Me too," Jack said. *Shoot Barbie, then make Troup talk. Or vice versa.*

"I still can't figure out why Whiteside would hire Troup," Liddell said.

"How'd she get the job here?" Jack asked.

"Landry said the old chief retired or quit and the City Council picked her. Landry thought he heard she was a detective with New Orleans PD."

Jack asked, "Isn't there any oversight over who she hires or fires?"

Liddell said, "The Chief of Police pretty well has a free hand. You know how that works with small towns."

Jack thought about a small town near Evansville with a similar population and law-enforcement setup. The City Council went through town marshals like shit through a goose.

The impound lot was even sorrier looking during daylight hours. The office was a wood frame farmhouse that had seen better days. A buzzer announced their presence as they entered, but no one was behind the counter. Jack opened and shut the door five or six times, and the buzzing continued until a froggy voice yelled from the back. "Just hold your water!"

The office floor was so dirty and littered that rats would go somewhere else for fear of catching a disease. The Formica countertop was covered in circular coffee stains and cigarette burns on the edges. He could see the impound lot through the windows to his right, and most of the cars were wrecked or missing something: like a motor, wheels, doors, trunks, and hatch lids. He could see the top of Marcie's cobalt blue Prius setting up next to the window.

A toilet flushed and a woman came to the counter wiping her hands on paper towels that she tossed on the floor. The woman's eyes passed over Liddell and locked on Jack's. A smile spread across her face, and she said, "What can I do for you, darlin'?"

Jack might have been flattered, but the woman was a twin for Ned Beatty from the movie *Deliverance*. He could almost hear the dueling banjos playing in the background.

"My friend wants to pick up his car," Jack said.

"It was brought in yesterday by Plaquemine PD. They said it would be released, no charge," Liddell said.

"That what they told you?" She pulled a ledger from under the counter, flipped pages. "What kind of car d'ju say it is?"

"It's a blue 2015 Prius," Liddell said. He pointed out the window. "It's right there."

"Yep. Sittin' right there." She found the keys and held them up, but when Liddell reached for them, she said, "Eighty-five dollars."

Jack said, "When I spoke to Chief Whiteside, she said there would not be a charge to get the car released. Maybe you should call her." He hadn't spoken to Chief Whiteside, but she wouldn't know that.

"The Chief, huh?" She handed the keys to Jack and said, "There you go, darlin'."

"Thank you very much, ma'am," Jack said.

They waited outside while she unlocked the padlock and swung the gate open. Liddell went to the Prius and squeezed himself in, turned the ignition, and powered the windows down. The inside of the car was hot as hell. The steering wheel burnt his hands as he drove out of the lot. The car bumped and banged over the pitted gravel lot and he stopped it just outside the gates. The woman shut and locked the gates behind him and scampered back inside.

Liddell opened the glove box and the center console. Next he reached under the driver's seat and came up with an empty leather holster in his hand. "My backup piece is gone. My camera is missing, and all my stuff is pulled out on the floor."

Jack pointed to the right side of the car and said, "You've got two flat tires too."

Liddell got out and walked around the car. Both tires had been slashed. The car had a knob tire for a spare. Before Jack could stop him, Liddell marched back into the office and Jack could hear him yelling. The woman who could be a stand-in for Ned Beatty was croaking just as loud. Liddell came out red in the face. Jack couldn't remember the last time he'd seen Bigfoot this mad.

"She showed me a little sign on the wall that says they aren't responsible for lost or stolen or damaged items. She said the police must have taken my things, but the police didn't have an inventory sheet either."

Jack heard the office door lock and the OPEN sign was flipped to say CLOSED.

"Your call, Bigfoot," Jack said.

"I would call the police, but I think they would just do more damage to the car. Let me use your phone." Liddell pulled a plastic card from his wallet and showed Jack. "Triple A. I'll have them tow it to a Toyota dealership in Baton Rouge. I get the service for free, so might as well use it."

"I think we should call a policeman out here. The camera and phone are one thing, but a missing gun is serious," Jack said.

Chapter Twelve

Jack and Liddell had waited in the air-conditioned Crown Vic for almost an hour before a young officer came and took the stolen report. The officer didn't bother talking to the impound-lot lady and barely spoke to them. The looks he kept giving Liddell made it clear that he didn't want to be there talking to a cop killer. AAA showed up while the officer was taking the report and gave Jack the address where they would take the Prius. Jack gave them his cell number, and the car was hauled off on a flatbed.

Liddell called the property room, and the clerk said the gun from Liddell's car had most likely been sent off to the Feds with his duty weapon. When he pressed the man to verify that, he was assured it was with the Feds. The missing camera was a mystery.

Liddell demanded a copy of the complete inventory of property taken from his person and his car. "I want to know everything of mine that was seized. You can give it to your Chief to hold for me. If I don't get it, I'm getting an attorney. Do you understand?" The clerk had seemed disinterested.

Now they were on a road that paralleled Interstate 10. It was more of a path than a road made of hard-packed dirt with deep ruts where heavy rain had scored it. A few times they'd had to go off road to get around a particularly deep wash.

Liddell said, "We're coming to a cattle guard just up ahead. I'll get out and check it. Sometimes pieces of metal come loose, and we don't need another flat." He drove through a narrow opening in the brush, and Jack could see cows grazing on a hillside. A steep ditch ran for as far as the eye could see north and south and was bordered on the far side by a barbed-wire fence. A ramshackle house could be seen in the distance, and visible behind the house were the metal roofs of other buildings.

Liddell stopped, got out, and examined the cattle guard, also called a "vehicle pass," made from heavy metal bars set into the road. Barbed-wire fence was strung out on each side of the opening.

Liddell came back to the car, and Jack rolled the passenger window down.

"The gaps between the bars are wide enough for livestock's legs to fall through," Liddell explained. "Keeps the livestock in and allows vehicles to come and go."

"So, get back in and let's go," Jack said and powered the window back up.

Liddell stood looking toward the house. After several minutes, Jack lowered the window again. "What's up, Bigfoot?"

Liddell came to the window and said, "I forgot to tell you that Cotton claims he's three-fourths Cherokee and three-fourths Haitian. He says he's purebred Creole too."

"So, we're waiting, why?" Jack asked.

"I want to give him a few minutes to see us before we go up to the house. Gives him time to get dressed or hide stuff he doesn't want us to see."

"How do we know when it's okay?" Jack asked.

"He'll let us know."

"That's just great," Jack said. He put the window back up and turned the a/c on high blast.

Liddell got back in the car. "Cotton Walters was with the Sheriff's Department. He retired a long time back, but he used to do the Missing Persons cases. He owns all the land you see around you, all the way over to the Mississippi River."

Jack watched the front door of the house open. An arm came out and motioned impatiently to come ahead.

"Anything else you want to tell me about this guy?" Jack asked.

"Cotton was kind of forced to retire. He claimed to see his ancestors' spirits. Other spirits too. He was paranoid back when I knew him, and I suspect he's gotten worse, but he always liked Bitty. He would let her visit him and no one else. And he's got guns all over the place."

"He's crazy and has guns all over the place, and this is where we're going to get a lead?"

"We won't have a problem, Jack. I promise. Oh. And he's into Voodoo big-time," Liddell said.

"Voodoo. Well I guess that makes sense if he sees spirits. It does tie in with the symbol you saw on Bitty's wall and the Voodoo stuff Landry showed us. You think he'll tell us anything worth hearing?"

"I do. It was the Voodoo stuff that ended his career with the Sheriff's Department. He didn't show up for work for a couple of days and didn't answer his phone, so the Sheriff sent a couple of deputies out here to check on his welfare. They didn't wait at the cattle guard like we just did. They just drove up to the door, big as you please, and Cotton shot their SUV all to hell. No one was hurt. He claimed the spirits had sent him a warning that they were coming to kill him."

"And he's not in prison? Or a nuthouse?"

"He was arrested and all of his guns were seized, but the judge let him go. His defense was that the deputies hadn't identified themselves, and he had a right to protect his property. It didn't matter that the deputies had just gotten out of the car when he shot at them. The judge said no one was hurt, and he knew if Cotton wanted them dead, they'd be dead. Case closed. The PD held onto his guns but eventually had to give them back."

Jack said, "Do you think we should call him first? Tell him who we are and why we're here."

"Wouldn't matter," Liddell said.

Jack asked, "Do you think he recognized you?"

"Never met him," Liddell answered.

Liddell stopped twenty yards away from the house, and they got out and walked toward the house.

The storm door was unlocked, and the inside door was standing open. Liddell opened the storm door and they entered a kitchen. The kitchen was just as Jack had imagined. The cabinets were covered with a patina of grease from years of cooking. The countertops were weathered plywood. The sink had last been cleaned during the Civil War. No one was in the kitchen.

"Cotton," Liddell called.

The sound of a gun being cocked was his answer.

Liddell raised his hands and said, "It's Liddell Blanchard. I was Bitty's partner."

Still no answer, but Liddell didn't put his hands down. "This is my partner, Detective Jack Murphy, from Evansville Police Department." To Jack, he said, "Put your gun away."

Jack didn't even realize he'd drawn his gun. He holstered his .45, but he wasn't about to raise his hands. "We just want to talk," Jack said.

"He's a cop," said a voice from directly behind them.

Cotton had somehow gotten behind them and was standing in the doorway with a lever action rifle. The barrel was pressed against Jack's spine.

"Yes, I'm a cop. My badge case is in my back pocket."

Liddell said, "We've never met, but Bitty talked about you all the time. She said you ran the Missing Persons Unit at the Sheriff's Department. We just want to talk. I've got some bad news concerning Bitty."

The rifle came out of Jack's back and pointed to the floor.

"Can I put my hands down now?" Liddell said.

"You go ahead, but I don't know this guy. How do I know he ain't here to kill me? They been trying long enough. But they ain't got me yet. Never will."

"My name's Jack Murphy," Jack said over his shoulder. "Pleased to meet you."

The rifle came up again, and Jack said, "Look. There's no need for anyone to get hurt. You don't want to talk to us, we'll be happy to leave. You don't shoot me, I won't shoot you. Okay?"

"Speaks his mind, don't he?" Cotton said, and walked past them into the kitchen.

Retired Sheriff's Detective Cotton Walters was pushing eighty, but his arms were huge, and his jaw was a block of iron. He was black as night, and his white eyes shone behind thick eyeglasses like full moons seen through magnifying glasses. His graying hair was in one long braid that ran down his back. An antique lever-action rifle was in his hands.

"You come about Bitty," Cotton said. "I already know she dead. Anyone know you're here?"

"We didn't tell anyone," Liddell said.

Cotton leaned the rifle against a cabinet and went to the sink. He ran some water into a saucepan and put it on a hot-plate burner.

"They drink coffee in Indiana, don't they?"

"We do," Jack said. "I wouldn't mind a cup."

Cotton dumped half a bag of ground coffee into the pan, stuck the lid on, and said, "Well, let's get down to it. What'chu want to know?"

Cotton was full of information but most of it was "I heard" or "Someone said" or "It's obvious" when *it* wasn't obvious at all. If Cotton hadn't been a retired detective, Jack would have been tempted to walk away. In fact, Jack had all but tuned the old coot out when he heard him say something about Marie Laveau. That was a name Landry had mentioned.

"Would you repeat that last part?" Jack said and sat forward.

"I said Marie Laveau isn't who she claims. For one thing, that's not even her real name. I got a friend in New Orleans that tol' me this woman was working the street until she got arrested for prostitution and drug trafficking. And another friend tol' me she was involved with some pretty big players. He wouldn't tell me who these big players were because he was afraid. And another friend told me a Voodoo practitioner was in Plaquemine. I didn't believe it because nine tenths of Iberville Parish has always been Catholic. This friend tol' me to stay clear of her and her friend."

"What's her friend's name?" Jack asked.

"No one knows his real name. He claims he's Papa Legba."

Liddell and Jack shared a look, and Liddell asked the question on both of their minds. "Was Bitty interested in Marie or Papa?"

"She sho' was. I tried to tell her to leave it alone, but you know how she was. Like an alligator. Grab onto something and drag it around the bottom."

Jack said, "We can get back to Marie and that, but we have another thing to ask you about. Liddell's niece is missing."

"Evie," Liddell said. "She's fourteen years old."

"Don't know nothing 'bout that," Cotton said.

Jack said, "Well, she had a gris-gris bag and some other Voodoo items. Did Bitty mention anything about missing children?"

"Not that I can recollect," Cotton said. "You should talk to Bitty's friend about that."

"What friend?" Jack asked.

"Detective Parnell. She with the sheriffs."

"We'll talk to her when she gets back in town," Liddell said.

"She ain't out of town," Cotton said. "Seen her in town yesterday. She working."

Liddell said to Jack, "Troup told me she was in Hawaii."

"Okay, let's get back to Marie and her friend. What can you tell us about these two?" Jack asked.

Cotton pulled a folding chair up to the card table that served as his kitchen furniture, and motioned for them to do the same. When they were all seated he said, "Papa Legba is a Loa, a Houngan; that's like a priest that presides over rituals. He is the passage from this world to the next. Papa has the power to bring the dead back or send a soul to the underworld forever."

"You mean like zombies?" Jack asked.

Cotton said, "No. They're still alive, but not in control of their body. Papa can make them do what he wants."

Cotton got up and opened a drawer under the sink. He pulled out a pencil stub and a scrap of paper and drew. He pushed the drawing across to Jack. "Papa Legba."

"So what about Marie Laveau?" Jack asked.

Cotton drew on the back of the paper. "Avizan. That's who Marie represents," Cotton said.

Cotton said, "The real Marie Laveau lived in the 1800s. She was a Loa called Avizan and a mamba, or priestess. She is the Loa for healing, love, and religious ceremonies like initiations in the Voudon. The real Marie was in New Orleans, and people would bring her gifts of yams, plantain, palm fronds, and sugarcane syrup in exchange for a blessing of some sort. She was a force for good and not evil.

"Papa is a gatekeeper. You need him and Azivan together during rituals."

"Cotton, I don't understand how this could have led to Bitty's murder," Liddell said. "Do you think Marie or Papa killed her?" Liddell had lived in Louisiana, and so he'd heard talk of Voodoo, and he'd heard some of these names, but he'd never been interested. He hadn't known about Sally's involvement with Voodoo.

"Voodoo isn't usually a problem, but if Bitty was asking about it she must have thought something big was going on. Big people involved." His face clouded, and his expression turned dark. "You don't mess with shit like that. I shouldn't even be talking to you two. You sure no one followed you," he said, and took his rifle back to the window. He seemed to be watching something outside in the distance.

"I told you that no one followed us, Cotton," Liddell said. "Come and sit down."

Cotton opened the drawer again and this time came out with a spotter scope and trained it out the window. "Damn. It's gone."

Jack got up and went to the window. "What's gone?" Jack could see the barbwire fencing, and behind that a short field and some stunted trees. Beyond that he thought he could make out traffic.

"Is that Highway 1?" Jack asked, but Cotton waved him away and continued to watch. He lowered the scope and put it back on the shelf. "Gone," he said.

Jack dismissed this as paranoia or the onset of dementia. "You said there are big people involved, Cotton. What do you think these big people are involved in? You were a cop. What would you call it?" Jack asked.

Cotton sat down again, one hand on the rifle. "Just wait a sec," Cotton said and went into the room from where he'd brought the chairs. When he came back, he was carrying a small dark-colored leather purse or bag. It was roughly stitched around the edges, and had a leather drawstring at the top where a couple of feathers peeked out. The feathers were speckled with something reddish black.

"Is that the same thing Landry showed us, Bigfoot?" Jack asked.

"I don't think there was a symbol sewn into the one Landry showed us."

"It's called a gris-gris," Cotton said. "It's a spell bag. It can be good or bad spells depending on what's inside, and what it's intended to do."

"Okay," Jack said.

Cotton continued. "This one here," he held up the bag, "this one is a warning." He turned it over, and Jack could see a symbol

stitched into the material with red and black thread. The symbol resembled a trident with two bars crossing the shaft.

"Okay," Jack said again. He wasn't afraid of leather bags, especially small ones with speckled feathers.

"The Divine Messenger," Cotton said in a soft voice. "It means
I've been warned. I'm not sure what I've been doing, but whatever
it was has definitely pissed someone off."

Jack saw the way Liddell was staring at the amulet. "What?"

Liddell said, "I think this is the same symbol that was drawn in
blood at Bitty's."

Cotton had nothing further to tell them about Bitty, but as they
left he said, "I got her killed. I should'nt'a tol' her nothin'. My fault.
All my fault."

Jack turned and saw Cotton pick up the scope and watch out the
grimy window again.

Chapter Thirteen

Papa Legba entered the plantation church, his bent frame leaning on a cane. White dreadlocks were heavily beaded with bones of all shapes and colors that framed the white painted face with dark circles around the eyes. Unlike the traditional clothing of Papa Legba he wore a purple alb—a sacramental vestment associated with Catholic priests during a Mass—tied at the waist with hemp. Canted on his head, he wore a battered top hat with a red feather stuck in the white hatband. He walked with a shuffle to the door on the left of the intricate altar and entered a small room where six hand-chosen female acolytes set cross-legged in a semicircle around Mamba.

Mamba's head was covered with a bright red scarf tied behind her neck. She wore a one-piece faded blue dress, the color of which was threaded with gold and silver. In the space between her and the acolytes were the elemental ingredients needed to make gris-gris amulets. A clay bowl of water, an incense stick representing air, a dish of graveyard dirt, and a stub of lit candle for fire. At each girl's feet were small squares of leather, bright-colored shards of bone fragments and colored glass, threads, and pieces of parchment with sigils drawn on them in magic ink.

Mamba gazed at Papa Legba while the acolytes bowed their heads, not allowing their eyes to wander toward the god of the underworld.

"Tomorrow," Mamba said to her group of acolytes who were all female, all under the age of fifteen, all beautiful with faces glowing in the presence of their Mamba. They wore expressions of the blessed as they rose and filed past Papa Legba, each one crossing themselves and kissing the back of his offered hand as they exited quietly.

Papa waited until the last footstep echoed and the doors to the church closed with a bang. His slumped figure straightened up to his six-foot, ten-inch frame.

"We need to talk," he said.

"How is she?" Mamba asked.

Papa turned his face away, and his jaw clamped tight. "We have a problem," he said and turned back toward her.

Mamba uncrossed her legs, and he helped her up from the floor. She tugged at the hem of her dress and smoothed the wrinkles. "Does it have anything to do with the drawing Luke asked me for?"

Papa considered his answer. He wasn't sure how much she knew about last night, or how much he could tell her. She had changed since they created this business. When Papa had found her she was skin and bones, living in a crack house, spreading her legs for anyone who would keep her high.

Papa removed her from there because he saw something special in her. Something he could develop. He cleaned her up, she put on some weight, and he saw just how beautiful she was. He was the one who had turned her from Sally the crack whore into Marie Laveau, Voodoo Queen of New Orleans. She went from being a whore to running whores. Business had been prosperous for both of them.

After Katrina hit New Orleans, he, like so many others, watched his business wash away. But he and Sally had come to the attention of some very powerful people. Prostitution wasn't the only business making a comeback in New Orleans after the floods.

With the backing of investors Papa Legba and Marie Laveau had moved here. She knew the town, knew the people—or so she said—and had connections with law enforcement. She could guarantee they would not be interfered with, and so he had proposed Plaquemine to the investors. Now it was all going to hell right in front of his eyes. All the careful and tedious planning, making the right friends, buying the right people, turning the heads of those who weren't friends, starting slowly and growing the business. All threatened by one female cop. She was dead now, but she was like the Hydra. Where one head was cut off, two more grew. And all Sally could ask was how her daughter was doing.

But now was not a time for recrimination. Now, more than ever, he needed his partner to mind the shop and keep her mouth shut. She was good at what she did; recruiting, turning young girls and boys against their guardians, bringing them to a better place where the promise of a blessed and plentiful life appealed to their child-like minds.

"I want my daughter to know who I am," she said, dropping all pretense and persona of Mamba.

"She's alive. She's healthy. She's eating well, being treated well."

Sally visibly relaxed. "I want to see her."

Papa's anger flared. "You stupid bitch. We're here because you neglected to tell me you had a daughter here. *You* brought her into this. She's here because I had to keep her safe—for your sake. I've done everything I can. Now you have to do your part and let me do mine."

Sally was undeterred. "I want to see her," she said, taking him by the arm. "I need to see her."

Papa pulled his arm away and walked to the door, but she said to his back, "If you don't let me see my daughter, I'm going to . . ." She didn't finish the sentence.

"I'm going to do you a favor. Because we been together so long, I didn't hear what you said. You're a good partner when you're clean." He met her eyes and asked, "You are clean?"

Sally cocked her head. "Do I look wasted? I'm just pissed off. We've been here six months and I haven't seen her except from a distance. I didn't ask her to come to this place. She did that on her own. She must have sensed I was here. How else would she have known to come here?"

"How else indeed," Papa said.

"She didn't know who I was. You could have just left her alone. I was happy just to see how she's grown. To know she was okay. I wasn't going to tell her. I'm warning you, Lincoln. She is not for sale. When this blows over . . ."

Papa bit his anger back. "I'm sorry I was angry with you. But she's had a better life than either one of us. You know that's true."

Sally cast her gaze at the floor.

"I admit I made a mistake taking your daughter, but we can't af-ford to attract attention right now. We've got to keep this together a little longer. Ok? When we get to a place where we can walk away, we'll run for the hills. You and me and your daughter too." He'd said it with a straight face. He didn't know how the investors figured out that Evelyn Blanchard was Sally's daughter. He himself hadn't found out until they told him. They were worried she would become a distraction, a complication.

Loving had a price tag. But he didn't love anyone. Had no one. When this was over, Sally and her daughter would be casualties along with everyone else. The investors were known for their "scorched earth" policy. He still had a value to them. He would get his money and set up somewhere else. He would find another Marie.

Chapter Fourteen

Jack parked on the street outside the Iberville Parish Sheriff Department, a nice one-story building surrounded by modest homes in the Historic District. Cotton had told them he found the gris-gris tied to his fence after Bitty's last visit. He didn't see anyone leave it or he would have shown them the grave. Jack believed him.

Jack didn't believe in magic or coincidence. He believed in Mr. Glock. *Murphy's Law says: never bring a sissy little bag to a gunfight.* But if the same Voodoo drawing had been left at Cotton's and Bitty's, it couldn't be a coincidence. He would have been concerned for Cotton's safety, but the old buzzard was well armed and more than willing to defend himself.

"Why didn't we come here first, Bigfoot?" Jack asked as they walked between parked brown and tan uniform cars and SUVs toward the door marked SHERIFF.

Liddell put a hand on the heavy glass-and-steel door. "Landry told me there's a new sheriff."

"A problem?" Jack asked. He knew Liddell wasn't the kind of man to make enemies.

Liddell said, "Sheriffs are elected just like in Evansville. This one came from Jacksonville, Florida. I've no idea what he can, or will, tell us."

"So let's skip over him and talk to some of the other deputies you know," Jack suggested.

"Things work different here, pod'na. The chain of command is never broken. These are smaller law enforcement agencies for one thing. That means smaller staff, smaller budgets, less equipment, more reliance on state or federal resources. You couldn't get away with calling someone Double Dick down here."

"You're implying they wouldn't like me," Jack said.

"Maybe I should do all the talking," Liddell said.

The receptionist was a male civilian. His name tag read Jon Dempsey. They introduced themselves, and Dempsey said, "Y'all have been the topic of conversation around here." Here came out as *he'yah*. "The Sheriff's been trying to call you. I'll tell him you're here."

Dempsey punched a button on his desk phone and asked, "You know where his office is? He's expecting you."

Jack took out his cell phone. "Looks like you're good to go, Bigfoot. I'll let you talk to him. I need to call Katie."

"I'll meet you outside," Liddell said, and walked through the office and down a hallway.

Jack went back outside and dialed Katie.

"Jack," Katie answered. "I've been worried."

He felt his face redden. He should have kept her updated, but by the time they got to Landry's house last night it was late and he was done in. "Sorry I didn't call last night."

"Or this morning," Katie said.

He guessed he was still getting used to being back together with Katie. Living with someone had different rules than living alone. When you lived alone, you didn't have to hang clothes up, say where you were going or when you'd be back, worry about the time, or for that matter, even what day it was. But living alone also meant losing a connection to someone beside you. He'd rather go to bed and wake up every day next to Katie than have any of the "freedoms" he might be giving up.

"We're at the Sheriff's Department," Jack said. "Liddell's talking to the new sheriff."

"Jack, I know Liddell told Marcie he was okay last night, but I want to hear it from you. Is he really okay? Are you okay?"

Jack told her everything that he knew, leaving out the parts about being threatened by local law enforcement and having a rifle pointed at him. She already knew that Bitty had been killed and the part about Liddell being held for questioning, but he hadn't told her about Liddell's niece, Evie. She listened and didn't ask questions until he was through. In other words, she was a good example of a detective's wife. When it was her turn, she asked questions about the things he'd held back, and like any good husband, he'd lied.

It was Jack's turn again, and he'd asked about her and about Marcie. She assured him they were fine except for not knowing what was going on.

"I'm with Marcie," Katie said.

He didn't have to guess what they were doing. She and Marcie were shopping for cute shoes, getting manicures, pedicures, or having a late breakfast. His guess was confirmed when he heard someone in the background say, "Would you care for some more coffee?" Sometimes they shook it up and got their hair done together.

He said, "Tell Marcie her man says hello and he loves her very much and he'll be home as soon as he can."

"Did he say all that?"

"No. But he's thinking it," Jack said.

"When *will* you be home?" she asked.

He didn't know. He said, "When this is over, I guess." She was a cop's wife. She knew he would do anything for Liddell, and he hoped she knew that didn't detract from his loyalty or love of her, but he also knew she'd had to ask the question.

"Be careful, Jack," she said, and those few words made him fall in love with her all over again.

"I'm always careful. That's why you never knocked me up, Muffin." It was a joke they shared.

"I'm going to be serious for a minute. There's something you need to know before you and Liddell get into something dangerous."

Jack waited, wondering what she meant. Was Double Dick raising a "hue and cry," arming the peasants with torches and pitchforks? He knew he should have called Captain Franklin last night to get permission to stay in Louisiana. But what was he going to say? "Captain, I still haven't shot anyone or violated anyone's rights. I think I'll stay a while and make the trip worth it." She was quiet. That was worrisome.

He heard her excuse herself from the table, and she said, "Wait a minute. I'm going outside." She came back on the line and said, "Your remark about being knocked up made me realize I should tell you. I probably shouldn't say anything. I promised Marcie that I would keep this to myself until you both came back."

Jack blurted out, "What are you saying? You promised Marcie what?"

In an excited whisper, Katie said, "She's pregnant. Marcie's pregnant, Jack!"

He was speechless. A million thoughts went through his mind. He was ecstatic for Bigfoot and Marcie, of course, but he was shocked and falling down a rabbit hole into a past that he'd tried to put behind him. He remembered how happy he'd been that he was going to be a father. How he'd planned everything, and how his world had revolved around the idea of a baby. That plan didn't take into account a miscarriage and a divorce.

He didn't trust himself to say anything because he didn't want to ruin Katie's obvious joy over Marcie's good fortune.

"Say something, Jack," Katie said.

He found some words. "I won't tell him a thing. And I promise to bring him home safe."

"And I want you to come home safe, Jack. I love you, you know. I don't know what I would . . ." her words trailed off.

"And you will never know, Muffin. I'll get us both home. Just promise me one thing."

"Anything," she said.

"Promise me you'll never let Cinderella sleep in our room again," he said, and she laughed. He could imagine her smile and it warmed him, made him stronger for what was to come. "I'm still throwing up in my throat a little."

"Hey, Jack. Sorry to interrupt, but I want you to meet some people," Liddell said, coming out of the Sheriff's Department doors.

Jack held a finger up. He said to Katie, "I'll get this done. You tell Marcie to quit worrying. If it gets dangerous I'll handcuff him and bring him home in the trunk of my car."

"Thank you. And don't forget, Marcie doesn't know I told you."

"Understood," Jack said, and followed Liddell inside.

Sheriff Bo Guidry met Jack in the doorway of his office and invited him in.

"Would you like something to drink, Detective?" Bo asked. "I'm afraid all we have is water and soft drinks. I understand from your partner here that you're a Glenmorangie man. I'm a Glenlivet man myself, but I'll forgive you."

Jack accepted the man's strong handshake. Bo Guidry was in

his sixties, but fit and with jet-black hair that belied his age. His freshly pressed uniform shirt displayed a chest full of commendation ribbons. His nails were perfectly manicured, but his hands were calloused, like those of a bricklayer or carpenter.

"Detective Blanchard has been telling me a little about this case, and I'm ashamed to admit it, but, like I told him, my office was shut out of the investigation by the PD. Apparently Bitty was killed at her home. That's just inside city limits and not my jurisdiction, so they aren't obligated to tell me squat. But Liddell tells me that you all have been kept in the dark as well. Is that right?"

It wasn't asked like a question. "Yes sir," Jack said, remembering his promise to Katie to be respectful. Besides, he was warming to this guy.

"Elizabeth—Bitty is—was—one of mine. I understand Chief Whiteside's hesitance in letting us help with the investigation, but I won't tolerate my department being disrespected. If they think someone in my department was involved in the killing, Whiteside should have come to me."

Guidry didn't invite them to have a seat, so Jack figured they wouldn't be in his office long. He wondered what the sheriff was leading up to. He didn't have to wait long. Sheriff Guidry was a direct man.

"I found out Liddell here was released into your custody last night and I tried to call him. No answer. So I called your Chief of Police—Pope, right?—and he said he hadn't heard from either of you. But he gave me your number, Murphy, and I couldn't reach you either. One of you should have damned well called me last night."

Jack could feel his face getting warm. "Sheriff, you're right. We should have thought to call you. Now that you mention it, I did see an unknown number come up on the phone late last night and didn't answer."

Guidry gave Jack a hard look and said, "Apology accepted. But you will give us your number and any other contact information before you leave this building."

"Okay," Jack said though he hadn't apologized and technically he didn't have to give them shit, and the sheriff should know that. Guidry wasn't in on the investigation, and the murder took place within the city's jurisdiction, not to mention Jack didn't work for him and wasn't under arrest. But Jack would rather have Guidry and the Sheriff's Department as friends. They already had enough enemies.

"Second," Guidry said. "You found the body, Liddell. That gives them the right to hold you as a suspect long enough to ascertain you did, or did not, kill my investigator. But you're telling me they didn't read you Miranda, or ask you any questions, even though they held you in a jail cell for half a day. Am I right?"

"True," Liddell said.

"And Bobby Troup arrested you," Guidry said. "I'm told he used to work here. As a detective, no less. Heard nothing but bad things about him. So the third thing I wanted to tell you gentlemen is that you need to watch your asses. Troup is bad news. From what I hear he's a liar and got a mean streak a mile wide. He pretty much does what he wants—to hell with the law or police procedure. You boys stay away from him."

"I know Whiteside wouldn't talk to you about the murder, but you seem to hear a lot. Can you tell us anything about what happened?" Jack asked.

"I'll do better than that," Guidry said. "I called the District Attorney's office and let them know how important this case is, what with Bitty being one of my detectives. The D.A. is a personal friend of mine. He offered to bring the State Police in, but I talked him out of that, and he agreed to sanction our office 'assisting' with the investigation. The Plaquemine PD is still the primary on the case, and anything we find we're supposed to turn over to them." He said this last as a promise waiting to be broken. "Chief Whiteside has been notified this morning that she has a partner, and I don't have to tell you—she wasn't too happy. Called me an interfering old goat."

Neither Jack nor Liddell said anything to that. Obviously Guidry didn't have any love for Whiteside, or Troup for that matter.

"I'm telling you all of this because I'm going to use my authority as Sheriff of this Parish to hire the two of you as consultants on this investigation. If you agree, you will answer only to me. No one else. You will not talk to the media or to any other law enforcement agency or release any information regarding this investigation to anyone without my specific permission. If you find anything, you will give it to me and me alone. You will not identify yourselves as deputies for this department, but you can say you are assisting us with our investigation." Guidry asked, "Is that agreeable?"

"Do we get mileage?" Jack asked, and Guidry laughed.

"I heard you were a smartass, Murphy. Your Chief knows what I'm offering, and he said I had the right guys for the job. He also said you were in hot water when you get home. Said someone named Dick wants your asses." He looked at Liddell and then at Jack. "He wasn't making me the butt of a joke, was he?"

"No, Sheriff. Chief Pope doesn't have a sense of humor," Jack said. He didn't give a dick what Dick was planning. Right now he wanted to ask about practical concerns, like carrying guns. For example, what if they had to shoot someone? More than once? But maybe now wasn't the best time.

Liddell said, "I'll get a temporary cell phone and give you the number, Sheriff."

Guidry took a cell phone out of his pocket and handed it to Liddell. "I already got you one, courtesy of the Narcotics Unit. The number is taped to the back and it has my number programmed in it."

Jack said, "Now that we're 'consultants,' I guess we should tell you that we've talked to one person today. He suggested we talk to Bitty's ex-partner."

"Parnell. Dusty Parnell. I'll arrange for her to meet with you two in a little bit. She's out on a missing-person case right now."

"I was led to believe she was in Hawaii," Liddell said.

"She's not been on a vacation for six months." Guidry's expression went stiff and he said, "Bitty was—how do I put this—she and Dusty were sort of an item."

Liddell said, "I knew Bitty was lesbian. Parnell was living with her last I knew. Something happen there?"

Guidry seemed relieved that he didn't have to broach that subject, the world being politically correct as it was. He said, "They split a couple of months ago. I offered to move one of them to a different shift, but they seemed to be okay with working together. Damned hard when they work in the same office, same shift, and had already weathered out the macho bullshit they had to put up with from these guys."

"Does Parnell know about Bitty?" Liddell asked.

"Hell, everyone around here knows by now."

Jack didn't understand. If Parnell was as close to Bitty as he'd heard, why was she working today? He assumed they must have had one hell of a falling-out for Parnell to be so unfeeling. But he'd learned through experience that every person handled grief in their own way.

"Meantime," Guidry said, "you boys should go talk to one of our retired detectives. Cotton Walters. He and Bitty were pretty tight. Detective Parnell actually took his job when he retired. Missing Persons. He was good at it."

Jack noticed Guidry didn't give Parnell the same praise.

"Thanks, Sheriff," Liddell said. "I know where he lives." Neither of them told Guidry they had talked to Cotton Walters earlier.

"You leave your numbers with Jon and be sure to keep me updated. I want to know if a gnat takes a piss, you read me?"

"Gnats. Piss," Jack said. "Understood."

"Chief Pope's got his hands full with you. You'd better be as good as he says, boys."

Outside, Jack stopped Liddell at the car and said, "Do gnats piss?"

Liddell responded with, "Does the Pope shit in the woods?"

"I talked to Katie and everything is fine there, Bigfoot. They were having a late breakfast. Marcie said to tell you to come home soon and the usual."

"I need to call her today."

"What's stopping you? I'm sure the sheriff wouldn't mind you using the phone he gave you to call your wife."

"Oh yeah," Liddell said and took the phone out of his pocket.

"Hold up there, Bigfoot. We have to decide where we're going next."

"The sheriff is supposed to have Detective Parnell call us as soon as she's got a minute. Let me drive, and I'll take us by Plaquemine's version of Donut Bank."

Jack couldn't turn down an offer like that. They drove into a run-down part of town where the houses had room enough between them to squeeze through. *Can you spell fire hazard?* Some of the houses were missing, with only foundations to show where they once stood.

They came to an area where the homes had been converted into small one-owner businesses: a salon here, a tire-repair shop, and one with a carport turned hand-car-wash. Tiny sidewalk cafés had multiplied like rabbits.

"Donuts, pod'na. Right down the street. The best you ever tasted. I promise. And the coffee is great."

Liddell had to wait for another car to leave before they could park outside a place called Mama JuJu's. The shotgun-style house set on a stained cinderblock foundation. The walls were white vinyl siding. A mural of a giant glazed donut was painted on the side wall and one on the picture window. Built on the side with the donut was a railed wood deck with a handicap ramp. The deck was full of people eating themselves into a sugar coma.

"This is Mama JuJu's," Liddell said. "She's been here since I was a kid. Katrina didn't put her out of business because the community wouldn't allow it. All the work you see was done with volunteer labor and material. Mama JuJu's is like a historical landmark."

The woman Jack assumed to be the owner turned out to be a white woman in her thirties, and very shapely underneath a knee-length white apron sporting an embroidered donut on the left chest area where policemen wore their badges. She saw Liddell come in and hurried over, giving him a hug. She was tiny and it was like watching a child hug a redwood.

"How's yo' mama?" Liddell asked her, to which she responded, "Who's your daddy," and they bantered back and forth.

Jack found a table while they were catching up. The tables were small and round, and the legs were just about to come off. The chairs were painted in pastels with colored specks to imitate sprinkles on icing. The tabletop was hand-painted to look like a big donut. Stenciled inside the donut hole were the words "Mama JuJu's."

Liddell came back, and the chair groaned under his weight but held him. The woman came to their table with two steaming mugs of coffee and a tray piled high with king-size glazed donuts.

"Jack, I want you to meet Mama JuJu," Liddell said. "We went to grade school, high school, and college together. She got her MBA and I got you," Liddell said with a chuckle.

She slapped at him with the towel and wiped her hand before taking Jack's hand. "My real name is not Mama JuJu." She shook his hand. "Denise. Any friend of Liddell's is always welcome."

"Glad to meet you, Denise. I was beginning to think he didn't have any friends," Jack said, and Denise laughed.

"Do you want something to eat? This one will eat all of these by himself."

"I'm fine. He's eating for two," Jack said and pointed at Liddell's stomach.

"He's eating for five."

"Hey," Liddell said, "I resemble that remark."

A bell rang on the counter, and Denise hurried away.

Liddell inhaled a donut and said, "Denise is the granddaughter of the original owner. I forget her name, but she was called Mama JuJu by the locals. The Creole believed she could cure illnesses, bless people, and stuff. The Creole are a combination of French, Blacks, Indians, Spanish, Caribbean, Acadian, South Americans, Chinese, Russian, German, and the list goes on. The term Creole covers any ethnicity that was born in Louisiana during the French or Spanish era. They consider themselves royalty among the Cajuns."

"Blanchard. Is that Creole?" Jack asked.

"Cajun. My family roots go back to Nova Scotia. The Acadians were called Cajuns. Still are."

Liddell's phone rang. It was Sheriff Guidry. He'd arranged a meeting with Parnell at her house. The address wasn't far.

Chapter Fifteen

Liddell drove back to Main Street and headed west, where they entered a stretch of road with cypress trees on one side and massive Southern live oak trees with branches sweeping across the ground on the other. Jack could smell the Mississippi. He imagined Bigfoot piloting an airboat through this and how his world must have changed, trading this for the flat, populated, concrete jungle of Evansville.

"Dusty's house is in Bayou Goula, about twenty minutes away. It's unlike anywhere in Indiana."

"Reminds me of Oak Meadows Country Club," Jack said. "Minus the trees and the Mississippi River and the yuppies."

"If I remember Dusty's house correctly, it sets on a twelve-acre lake. Bitty and I used to fish in that lake. Trout, crappie, catfish, you name it. Of course, Dusty didn't own the house when I was fishing here. I wonder what she paid for this place."

Liddell's phone rang. IBERVILLE SHERIFFS DEPARTMENT showed in the display. He answered, and it was the young man working the desk.

"Hey. This is Dempsey. I just got a call from Dusty. She's going to be a few minutes, but said to make yourself at home. The back door is open."

Jack heard the last part of the conversation. "Her door is open?" In Evansville the people who leave their doors open are overinsured. Jack had a cable over his hot tub, with a padlock and alarm on the door of his river cabin.

Liddell turned on a gravel road that went through more of the sprawling oaks, some with a trunk diameter of at least four feet, and the low-hanging limbs were draped with Spanish moss. They emerged into a field of wildflowers as far as the eye could see, with a two-story antebellum house smack in the middle.

Jack couldn't help but think of Katie. She would love this. Maybe he would bring her back on a short vacation. They could do a plantation tour. Liddell had told him about one mansion that was reputed to be haunted—and another that had turned into a five-star hotel with a restaurant.

Squared shrubs encircled a rose garden that was the showpiece of the crushed brown-stone circular drive. The crushed stone made loud popping sounds under the tires. Liddell stopped in front of the house.

"She lives here?" Jack asked. "With twelve acres of woods and a lake? In Indiana, a property like this would cost at least five million."

Liddell turned the engine off, leaned the seat back, crossed his arms, and closed his eyes.

"She said we could make ourselves at home. Are we going in?" Jack asked. He wanted to see the inside.

Without opening his eyes, Liddell said, "You can if you want. Not me. Last time I did that I ended up spending the day in a jail cell."

A white Land Rover bearing SHERIFF decals came down the gravel road and pulled in behind them.

They exited their vehicles, and Liddell made the introductions. "Dusty, this is Detective Jack Murphy from Evansville, Indiana. Jack, Dusty."

Dusty shook hands with Jack but gave Liddell a hug. She was average height with an athletic build that was enhanced by the painted-on blue jeans that were tucked into the tops of Western boots. She wore a tight-fitting short-sleeve uniform top and was packing heat up there as well as the .45 on her gun belt. He guessed her age as late forties. She smiled. That she had heard the news of her former life partner's death showed in the redness of her eyes.

"How you doing, Liddell," she said and rubbed the backs of her hands across her eyes. "The door was unlocked. Come on inside. It's like a furnace out here."

Jack and Liddell followed her down a pebble path leading to a side door. At the back of the house was a large aluminum carport over a raised concrete pad. The concrete and the carport were new, as were the two dirt bikes and Harley-Davidson motorcycle parked there. One of the dirt bikes was covered with mud, but the Harley was spit-shined, and the sun glinting off its surface was blinding. They followed her into a room Jack assumed was the kitchen. One entire wall of the kitchen was taken up with a stone wood-burning fireplace. The fireplace opening was large enough for a man to walk into without touching the sides or roof. A hardwood table that seated eight faced the fireplace. Everything in the kitchen came out of a *Better Homes and Garden* magazine. Dusty put a teakettle on the gas stove and turned a burner on. "Have a seat, and I'll make coffee."

Jack and Liddell sat in heavy wooden chairs at the conference-room-sized table across from each other. Liddell pulled a chair out beside him for Dusty.

"I've got instant," she said.

Jack didn't want coffee again, and he hated instant, but he said, "Thank you, Detective Parnell."

"Dusty, all right? I hate being called Detective Parnell except by dirtbags."

"I'm not a dirtbag, so Dusty it is," Jack said.

She stood with her back to them while the kettle heated, took three mugs from a cabinet, filled them with hot water, and set them on the table. Next came a tray with spoons, sugar, cream, and a jar of Folgers instant coffee. "You can add your own coffee. I like mine strong," she said.

Her leather gun belt creaked as she sat in a chair next to Liddell.

"New leather," she explained. "Like wearing new shoes. You got to break it in. Today's the day."

Liddell and Jack waited for Dusty to broach the subject of Bitty's murder. Aside from the red eyes, Jack hadn't seen any real emotion. She didn't say anything and wasn't asking questions, so maybe she already had some answers. He hoped she would share that with them and make it worth his choking down instant coffee.

"I'm sorry about Bitty. If there's anything I can do while I'm—" Liddell said.

Dusty cut his sentence short. "Thank you. I'm okay. Well, as okay as I can be."

Jack said, "We've talked to Sheriff Guidry and—"

"He called me," she said before he could finish. "He said he asked you two to help with the investigation. That's very unusual. I'm not even sure it's legal. And with Liddell being her old partner, that might constitute a conflict of interest. But I guess that's on Sheriff Guidry. Not my call."

Jack exchanged a look with Liddell. "That's part of the reason we're here," Liddell said. "You and Bitty were tight. And we can't seem to get any information from the PD."

She blew across the top of her mug and took a careful sip. "I don't know how much help I'll be," she said. "Does your partner know about—you know?" she asked Liddell.

"Do I know that you and Bitty were a romantic item? Yes," Jack answered. "That means you know more about her than anyone."

"You would think so," Dusty answered. "Liddell can tell you. She played her cards close. She didn't talk about her work much." Dusty gave a short unamused laugh and said, "Oh yeah, she'd complain about the brass, or some particular asshole she was taking down, but she didn't go into details."

Liddell clasped his hands on top of the table. Without any expression, he said, "Yeah. I guess she could be like that."

Dusty stared out the door looking toward the dirt bikes and the Harley. Jack could imagine her wanting to be anywhere away from here.

She asked, "What do you want to know?"

"How long ago did you two separate?" Jack asked, and she didn't appear to take it personally.

"Four months ago," she said. "We weren't having any particular problems. We just decided to go our separate ways." She scoffed as if she'd just thought of something funny. "Maybe if we *were* having problems it would have been better. Maybe I could have understood."

"So she's the one that suggested it?" Jack asked.

"It wasn't like that," she hurriedly said. "I told you it was a mutual decision." She put her mug down and crossed her arms, eyeing him. "Is this an interrogation, Detective Murphy?"

Jack smiled. "When my wife calls me *Detective Murphy,* I know I've pissed her off."

She laughed and said, "I'm sorry. I don't know what I was thinking. I'd be asking the same questions if I was in your shoes. I just wasn't expecting it, that's all."

"And I apologize if I came across wrong. I'm glad you understand," Jack said. "You're a detective, so why don't we just talk? That'll be easier for both of us, and there won't be any guns involved." He smiled at her.

She asked Liddell, "Is he like this at home? Wow!" She took a breath, let it out, and said, "Okay. You probably want to know if she and I had a fight. No, we didn't. We never fought, and what I meant before was that not fighting was part of the problem. We had grown apart, and it seemed we didn't care enough to even disagree. But fighting? No."

"Forgive me for asking personal questions, but was she seeing someone else?"

Dusty gave a short laugh that Jack recognized as a defense mechanism. If you can laugh about it, it doesn't hurt as bad. You see cops standing around at crime scenes, smiling or telling each other jokes, and it's easy to mistake this defense as callousness. Cops can't afford to fall apart at every death they go to.

"No. At least not that I knew of," Dusty said, and added, "Did anyone hate her or want her dead? No. Everyone loved her." She picked up a napkin from the table and dabbed at her eyes. "That girl had some pretty hairy cases. Put away some really bad guys. Dangerous guys, you know. One or two of them might have meant her harm. But what they did to her would take a sick mind. Someone with no feeling. Whoever did that to her was in a rage, or a psychopath. It would have to be someone big and strong. She was a tough cookie."

"Do you know how she was killed?" Jack asked, hoping she knew more than they did.

The question surprised her. "You don't know how she was killed?"

Jack said, "I'm just trying to see what you know." He knew what Liddell had told him. The crime scene was off limits to them, and it seemed even Sheriff Guidry didn't know any of the details.

Dusty eyed him. "I've heard what everyone else has heard. They're keeping a lid on this. But you know how rumors are. I heard everything from she was shot, to she was stabbed, to she was eviscerated and dismembered." She touched Liddell's hand. "You found her. You would know."

"Yeah, I found her," Liddell said and squeezed her hand. "Before I could call it in, a guy named Barbierre Tasered me."

"Barbie, huh?" She snorted, and her mouth turned down at the corners in distaste. "That figures. He shouldn't be allowed to carry that thing, much less a gun. He's about—no, he *is* crazy. Well, let me tell you about Barbie. He wants to be a detective. He sucks up to Troup like Troup is a lollipop. Once he gets sicced on you, he can't be pulled off. He's crazy and sadistic."

"You said a person in a rage or a psychopath. Do you know someone like that?" Jack asked.

She thought about it. "Barbie. You think it was Barbie?"

"Do you think Barbie is capable of doing that?" Jack asked.

"He's capable, I guess, but he wouldn't have any reason. I mean she wasn't any threat to him."

"Troup?" Jack asked as if an afterthought.

"Troup. Huh. Funny you should mention him."

"Funny how?" Jack asked.

Dusty took a sip of her coffee and made a face. "My doctor is on my ass about too much caffeine." She went to the sink and poured hers out. "You guys need a warm-up?"

Both men declined and Jack asked again, "Funny how?"

Dusty took a drink from the faucet and sat again. "Troup was one of ours. I mean with the Iberville Sheriff. Liddell should tell you about him."

"He did," Jack said.

Dusty continued. "Well, she and Troup had issues in the past. Liddell got on his bad side too. The Sheriff's Department was investigating Troup for murdering a bookie. I think he blamed her and Liddell for getting fired."

"I know all that," Jack said.

Dusty said. "Don't you see? Troup had a reason to kill her."

"That happened almost eight years ago, Dusty," Liddell said.

"They say revenge is a dish best served cold," she said.

"What about Doyle Doohan? Troup's partner in crime. Whatever happened to him, anyway?" Liddell asked.

Jack and Liddell sat quietly, waiting for her to continue.

She said, "I heard Troup's the detective working this. I haven't heard anything about Doyle. He probably hates you as much as Troup, but Bitty said he was kind of a doofus, wasn't he?"

"You're right about Doyle, and about Troup. He is working the case," Liddell confirmed.

"Troup's Whiteside's pet. I mean *Chief of Police Whiteside.* She's so full of herself it isn't funny. Why would she hire him in the first place? Couldn't be for his personality or looks." Dusty rubbed the back of her neck and said, "Barbie was the first to show up at the scene of the murder. Right? Barbie would do almost anything to get Troup's approval. He's like Robocop on meth."

What she was saying made sense, and they didn't have a better suspect. If either Barbie or Troup killed Bitty, the other one was in a position to cover it up.

"What if Barbie knew she was dead before you got there?" Dusty mused. "He could have killed her and was anxious for her body to be found? I mean, he was on duty. It would give him an alibi if he were working. I don't think that's even his beat to work."

She twisted her coffee cup in a circle and raised an eyebrow questioningly.

Liddell said. "We had a case like that didn't we, Jack?"

Jack remembered the case. A married cop killed his girlfriend because she threatened to expose the affair. He bludgeoned her to death and bludgeoned her dog to death when it tried to defend her. The asshole poured gasoline on them and set them on fire. But the fire didn't catch because he had shut the door to the bedroom, and the flames blew themselves out. The cop waited all night to hear a fire department dispatch but when none came, he returned to the house and set the fire again. This time he was successful. Good detective work caught him, and he was tried and convicted. He did all of this while he was on duty. He'd even faked some car stops to have a dispatch record for an alibi.

And something Liddell had told him stuck in his mind. The killer cop in Indiana referred to himself as Robocop. Liddell had told him that Barbierre acted like Robocop. Now Dusty said the same thing. *Coincidence?*

"Have Barbie and Bitty had any interaction? Recently? In the past?" Jack asked.

"Do you mean were they friends?" Dusty asked. "I don't know. She's kept her personal life to herself since we broke up."

Liddell said, "Bitty was outspoken. Did she think Barbie was an ass-kisser too?"

"It's common knowledge. Barbie doesn't exactly hide his admiration."

Jack asked the question Liddell hadn't brought up, and so far, Dusty hadn't mentioned. "Was Bitty involved with Voodoo?"

This time Dusty was caught off guard. Her mouth tightened into a straight line and her eyebrows rose. "Voodoo? You mean like the walking dead and spells and that kind of shit?"

"Voodoo symbols have come up in the investigation a couple of times," Jack said. With Evie. On the wall at Bitty's. And again at Cotton's. Cotton said Bitty had been asking questions about Voodoo. Maybe she was investigating some Voodoo fanatics. Someone was sending a message that they didn't want the attention, or they were making it look like it was Voodoo related.

Dusty said, "Katrina did more than wipe out some businesses and homes. It washed away civilized behavior too. You've heard the stories about cops deserting New Orleans, or stealing whatever they wanted. Rapes, murders, and robberies were commonplace. And not just in New Orleans. Look around and you see signs of it everywhere. Graffiti on garages, school walls, sidewalks sometimes. Probably just kids though. I don't think anyone here really truly believes in that crap."

She seemed to weigh her next words before she spoke. "If you're asking did she believe in Voodoo, or practice it, I would have to say no. She wasn't wired that way. Don't get me wrong. She wasn't an atheist or anything. She believed in a higher power. But she mostly believed in herself. She wasn't one to ask for blessings, or love potions, or zombies, any of that hocus pocus."

"So, you didn't know anything about the Voodoo symbols in Bitty's house?"

Dusty gave him a cautious look. "I heard some rumors, but I thought that's all it was. You know how cops like to talk." She asked Liddell, "Was there stuff there?"

Liddell held his hands up. "I don't want to be one of those rumor sources, Dusty. I'm hoping you won't tell anyone we talked to you. We're trying to fly under the radar."

"Sure," she said. "But if you need another partner helping out, I'm willing."

Jack said, "Thanks. We'll let you know."

"I'm serious," she said. "You have to trust someone. And I can get a lot of information that you can't get. Liddell hasn't worked here for ages. People won't talk to him as easily as they will to me. And they won't talk to an outsider."

She was right about that. He had no reason not to trust her. Still, he'd have to keep an eye on her.

"Okay," Jack said. He wrote his cell-phone number on a napkin and gave it to her.

"I just ask one favor of you," Dusty said. "Don't tell the Sheriff or anyone that I'm helping you. The other cops will feel more comfortable talking around me if they don't feel like they're being grilled. Liddell, you know some of these guys believe you killed her, don't you?"

"Point taken," Jack said. She was right about that, too.

"I'm just saying you should be careful who you talk to," she said to Liddell.

"One more thing, Dusty," Liddell said. "Have you heard my niece is missing?"

"Your brother Landry has been making himself a pain in the ass with the PD. Nothing has come across my desk yet, but I heard talk. Figured she'd come back because Landry had quieted down. Sorry for being blunt," she said and spread her hands.

"No offense taken," Liddell said. "He speaks his mind."

"Her name is Evelyn, right?" Dusty asked.

"She goes by Evie. She's fourteen. I don't have a picture with me, but I'll send you one if you can help out with that too. Landry said the PD took a report, but they haven't entered her into the system. Cotton said we should talk to you."

"Those lazy assholes," Dusty said. "I can make the report. Tell Landry to call me."

"So, Bitty didn't mention Evie?" Jack asked.

"I told you. We haven't talked for a good while. Besides, Bitty never talked about what she was working on. I guess if she was looking for a missing kid she would have asked me, but she didn't."

They went out the side door, and Jack took in the surroundings. "This is some place you have here."

She smiled. "Three hundred acres. Twelve-acre lake. I had to put some money into improvements, but look at it. It's my dream. When I retire, I'll never leave. Have groceries and everything I need delivered."

"That's every cop's dream, isn't it?" Jack said. "One thing I forgot to ask. When was the last time you talked to Bitty? A week, a month?"

"It's been a while," she said.

"How long of a while?" Jack pressed.

"A couple of weeks at least." Tears welled in Dusty's eyes, and she turned her face away. "I can't believe she's gone."

"Okay. I'm sorry if I caused you any grief this morning. Call us if you hear anything," Jack said, and he and Liddell left.

As they were driving down the gravel road, Jack asked Liddell, "How well do you know Parnell?"

Liddell stopped at the intersection with Highway 1, and asked, "What's on your mind, pod'na?"

"I just wondered how she could afford a place like that. Three hundred acres, a big house and a lake. The house alone probably goes half a mil. And did you see the motorcycle and dirt bikes? It must cost a fortune to keep the grounds up. If she didn't inherit a lot of money, I'm curious where it came from."

"I don't know if she comes from money," Liddell said. "You know there's a lot of old money down here. Oil, cotton, sugarcane, you name it. She could have a fortune stashed away, but if she does I didn't hear about it from Bitty. In fact, Bitty had kind of insinuated that Dusty *had* to move in with her. She didn't come right out and say that, but it's the impression she gave, you know? Maybe I'm way off base."

"Did Bitty ever mention Dusty being loaded? Or for that matter, why Dusty would move into Bitty's house and not the other way around?"

"I never asked about it," Liddell said. "Not my business. At least not then."

"Did they get along?" Jack asked.

"They seemed to be happy. No big fights that I can remember or that Bitty told me about. You know. Typical domestic stuff."

"Did Dusty ever cheat on her?" Jack asked, and this time Liddell almost stopped the car.

"She never let on if Dusty did," Liddell said. "We should have asked. But Dusty probably would have denied it. I mean, how many cheating spouses or partners admit something like that?"

"I'm just thinking out loud here, Bigfoot. You know these people better than I do. But I thought it was strange that she never once said Bitty's name. It was always 'she' or 'that girl' or 'her.' That's a way of distancing yourself from the victim. And she was evasive, answering a question with a question. I have the feeling she's holding back on us. And how the hell did she know that you found her early that morning?"

"Police grapevine?" Liddell suggested.

It was a possible explanation.

"And she didn't seem too interested in Evie's disappearance. I mean she is the Missing Persons detective. She'd heard that Landry was raising Cain with PPD, so when she didn't see a bulletin why didn't she call Landry or PPD and look into it?"

"Maybe she has the Larry Jansen disease," Liddell said.

Larry Jansen was a rumpled-trench-coat-wearing wannabe-Columbo who was the Missing Persons detective for the Evansville Police Department. He was slovenly, lazy, and corrupt. His idea of finding a missing person was to wait for them to come home and call him. If anything, Jansen should be listed as a missing person. He was hardly ever seen around police headquarters.

Liddell turned left on Highway 1 and headed west. "Let's eat. I can't think when I'm hungry."

Jack laughed. "In that case, I'm surprised you ever think."

Chapter Sixteen

The Plaquemine Police Department cruiser pulled in front of the Crown Vic and slammed on its brakes. Another PPD cruiser came up from behind and pulled almost against their bumper. The officer behind them got out of his car and stood at the back-passenger side of the Crown Vic. The officer in front walked toward the driver's door, hand on his sidearm and a serious look on his face. He made a circular motion with his hand indicating Liddell should roll down the window. Liddell powered down his window.

The officer leaned in the window and said, "The Chief wants you two in her office."

Liddell kept his hands in plain view on the steering wheel. Jack had seen the police cars in the side mirror and stuck his Glock .45 under his leg.

Liddell smiled at the officer and said, "We were just on our way to eat. You can join us and we'll go see the Chief."

The officer didn't return the smile. His hand remained on his gun. "You can either drive there, or come with us."

"We'll follow you," Jack said.

"Good choice," the officer said. "You stay behind Pete. And I'll be right behind you."

"The whole way," Jack finished the officer's sentence under his breath.

"Did you say something, sweetheart?" the officer asked.

"I said, let's do this."

The officer went back to his car and made a U-turn. The car behind them backed up doing the same. Liddell pulled off the side of the road and turned around on the dirt shoulder to follow.

"The whole way?" Liddell said. "Do you want one of these ya-hoos blowing our shit away?"

"I had you covered," Jack said, and retrieved the gun from under his leg. "Besides, if they were really going to do something they would have just run us off the road and shot our car up. These guys are more like Buford T. Justice in *Smokey and the Bandit.*"

Liddell said, "I wonder what she wants now?"

"Someone must have seen us going to or leaving Cotton's place," Jack said.

"I'm really getting sick of this."

"Let's see what she has to say, Bigfoot. What have we got to lose? We're working for the Sheriff, and he told us she was going to have a shit fit."

They were directed to park in front of the police station, and an-other officer came down the steps and ushered them into the Chief's office. Jack knew that as far as any of them were concerned, Liddell was a cop killer and a traitor to his badge.

Chief Anna Whiteside sat behind her desk. She was dressed in blue jeans and a blue T-shirt with a PPD badge silkscreened on the left chest. She motioned for the officer to leave. Her dark eyes moved from Jack to Liddell and back to Jack.

"So you're Jack Murphy," she said.

He was surprised that she was attractive. Not that a female offi-cer couldn't be attractive. But most upper brass he'd ever known were ragged around the edges from climbing through the ranks and getting some of the stupid rubbed on them along the way.

"You got me," he said. "Have I done something wrong?"

She said, "Why would you think that? Have you done some-thing wrong, Detective Murphy?"

"When you're called to the principal's office you're in trouble. But if you just wanted to meet me you could have called. I would have been happy to stop by. I know this place called Mama JuJu's and—"

She silenced Jack with a look. She opened a desk drawer and took out a plastic evidence bag with a gun inside and set the bag on the desk.

"That's my backup piece," Liddell said. "It was in my car when it was towed."

"This is *your* weapon."

"That's what I said. It's my weapon. Where did you find it?" Liddell asked.

Jack had a sick feeling. He said, "I was with him when he tried to pick up his car today and . . ."

"I don't want to hear anything out of you, Detective Murphy. In fact, if you say another word I'll have you removed from my office."

Liddell sat down in one of the chairs. "That's my backup gun. I tried to pick up my car from the impound lot this morning and the tires had been slashed. My backup gun and my personal camera were missing from my car."

"They were missing?" Her expression said this was the most ridiculous lie she's ever heard.

"That's what I just said."

"A gun and a camera were missing from your personal vehicle and you didn't report it to the police," Whiteside said.

Liddell tried not to show his annoyance and anger. "I called your property guy this morning. He said my gun—that gun—was sent to the lab for ballistics. So, no, I didn't make a police report."

Jack said, "Chief, I if may . . ."

"No you may not. I'm warning you for the last time, Detective. Your chief may think you're hot shit, but you're in my city now. This isn't the Wild West, and you can't be a cowboy here."

Jack's fists tightened but he sat down and kept his mouth shut.

She continued. "Yeah. I read up on you after I heard you were here to get Mr. Blanchard. You've had some exciting times in Evansville. Would you say you're capable of killing to protect the ones you love?"

"Where are you going with this, Chief Whiteside?" Jack asked.

"I'm just thinking out loud, Detective. I'm thinking that you and Mr. Blanchard have been partners for quite a while, and partners are willing to put themselves at great risk for each other. Great enough risk to kill someone. That is, if they thought that someone was going to harm their partner, that is."

Liddell said, "I told you why I didn't report the gun missing. Your property clerk said it had been sent to the lab with my duty weapon."

She was quiet for a beat, then said, "Well, as you can see, your gun is not at the lab. It's here. On my desk. In an evidence bag. I don't know anything about a camera, but you can bet I'll look into it."

"That gun hasn't been fired for weeks. Check it, and I want it back. And I want my camera. And I want my tires fixed."

"Is that all?" she asked.

"No," Liddell said. "I want to know what the hell is going on. Why do you have my gun?"

Instead of answering him, she asked a question of her own. "What were you and Detective Murphy doing at Cotton Walters's today?"

Jack answered for him. "We have been asked to run a parallel investigation into the death of Elizabeth LeBoeuf."

"This request came from Sheriff Guidry?"

Jack didn't answer. It was a rhetorical question. She was playing cat and mouse with them and he had a suspicion why. He hoped he was wrong.

"Let me ask so you understand the question. Were you asked by Sheriff Guidry to conduct a parallel investigation, with this department, looking into the death of Elizabeth LeBoeuf?"

"I guess I didn't understand the question, Chief. The answer is yes. Sheriff Guidry hired us and we were told your department had primary jurisdiction. That was why we were talking to Mr. Walters. He was a friend of Bitty's," Jack said.

"Was?"

Jack was getting tired of her repeating everything back to him as a question. "Yes, *was*. She's dead, so he *was* a friend of hers. Past tense. Am I not speaking English here?"

"So, Mr. Blanchard admits this is his gun. And states it has not been fired for several weeks. And you admit you were both at Cotton's house this morning. Have I got that straight?"

"He's *Detective* Blanchard if you want to be correct. But yeah."

She smiled like the cat that ate the canary. "Cotton Walters was found dead an hour ago."

Jack was stunned. They had talked to the old man just hours ago. Jack thought Cotton was paranoid or crazy or both, but there's an old saying: "You're not paranoid if they really are out to get you."

"How?" Jack asked. "When?"

"I want to know why you went to Cotton Walters's house," she said.

Jack watched her face. No one had searched them for weapons before they were ushered into her office. They hadn't been read Miranda or handcuffed. But he figured he'd better ask. "Are we under arrest?"

"You're not under arrest," she said to Liddell. "Or you either, Detective Murphy." She stood and walked to the window, looking down in the street, absently pulling at one ear lobe. "Although I have enough circumstantial evidence to hold you both for investigation, I'm not going to do it. If, that is, you cooperate with me."

"So what do you want to know?" Jack asked.

"I want everything. Starting with the truth about why you are in Plaquemine, Detective Blanchard."

Chapter Seventeen

Evie didn't hear anyone come down the hall, and when the door opened it startled her. The woman standing in the lit doorway was tiny and barefoot. Her skin was brown and perfectly contrasted with the long white silky dress. The woman's hair was tucked under a white cloth skullcap, what the kids at school called a doo-rag. She might be Chinese or Korean or something because her friend at school, Amy, was Korean and this woman had the same shape face and dark eyes. Those eyes were fixed on her.

"Come with me," the woman said.

Evie walked to the doorway. She turned and could see the other children were asleep or pretending to be.

"Where are we going?" Evie asked.

"Come," the woman said and motioned for Evie to come to her.

Evie stepped into the hallway and asked, "Who are you? Where are we going?"

"My name is Ubaid," she said with an accent that Evie couldn't place. The woman pronounced the name "ooh-bed."

"That doesn't sound Korean," Evie said, and the woman smiled.

"That's because I'm not Korean," Ubaid said in a quiet voice. "I'm Egyptian. A Muslim."

"I'm pleased to meet you, Ubaid," Evie said. She wasn't pleased, not pleased at all. But her father taught her to be polite. Especially with older people, and Ubaid was older, in her thirties at least. "I've never met anyone from Egypt. Or a Muslim either. I don't think I have."

Ubaid made a slight bow, and bade Evie walk in front of her down the hall. "Please don't speak. You understand?"

Evie said she understood. They were in a hallway she didn't

think she'd seen before, but then everything in this underground maze was concrete hallways and steel doors and motion-activated lights. They came to a set of stairs leading up, and Ubaid stopped.

"Please," Ubaid said and directed Evie go up the stairs.

At the top of the stairs a set of steel doors were straight ahead and another steel door was to their right. This one was open and led into a brightly lit hall with wood-paneled walls, a real ceiling, and tiled floor. She had felt the air warm as she came up the stairs, but now it was more than warm. She imagined that on the other side of the paneled walls was the outside, and it was daytime, and the sun was shining.

They reached a door and Ubaid opened it. The mouthwatering smell of fresh baked bread and baked ham hit her. Down below it always smelled mildewy, or damp, except for where they ate the meals.

"Where are we going?" she whispered to Ubaid.

"Somewhere nice," Ubaid said.

Evie walked through the doorway into a large kitchen. The kind they had at her school, but not as big. Two people were working in the kitchen. One at the oven and one washing dishes. Neither of them paid them any attention. She was taken to a set of wooden stairs leading up. This was a house. A huge house.

At the top of the stairs was a room, like a suite at a fancy hotel, the kind she saw in magazines that her father didn't like her to read. A bed sat against the far wall, next to a tall window whose curtains were tightly closed. She could just see a seam of light down the sides of the curtains. The bed was massive. Someone would have to use a step stool to get on top of it, and it was big enough to get lost in. She thought it was the nicest bed she'd ever seen. Not anything like the lumpy, smelly pad in her downstairs room.

Ubaid shut the door and locked it with a gold-colored skeleton key that hung from her wrist. She opened two sets of folding doors, and Evie's eyes lit up. It was a dressing room. A dressing room like she had always imagined celebrities owning. Dresses and evening gowns and shoes of every kind and color hung on rods and filled shelves on both sides of the opening, and at the back was a mirror as big as one wall in her bathroom at home. To one side of the mirror was a dressing table with lit glass balls shining down on an array of perfumes and lotions and makeup.

Ubaid touched her shoulder and she jumped. Ubaid said, "Take your shower now. Go in there." She pointed to an open door in an alcove. "Take as long of a shower as you want. When you come out, we'll fix you up. Okay?"

"You bet!" Evie said and hurried to the shower.

They sky was black to the west, and it was coming their way. If it were as bad as she imagined it would flood the streets. But the Chief didn't care if it was a hurricane coming. Her orders were to say on the street and patrol. She reminded them about the screwup during Katrina, and said people needed to know the cops were the authority and not thugs. But Barbierre dreaded storms. They had scared him since he was a teenager. His roof had been blown off one time, and he felt like he was being sucked out of the house. He didn't like that helpless feeling.

Officer Barbierre exited his patrol vehicle, repositioned his gun, and tugged at the notch of his ballistic vest that had an annoying habit of riding up when he sat down. It was rubbing his neck raw. But, as his instructor at the police academy had told him, "Better raw than dead." He'd heard stories of guys who didn't wear them getting popped. Some crippled for life. Most dead. And detectives were the worst of the lot. They dressed sloppy, and some of them still carried revolvers. Detective Troup would never go for that. Troup was a cop's cop.

He gazed up and down the street of dilapidated homes and rubbish-strewn lots and gutters full of trash and fast-food wrappers and could feel the sickness that was growing in his city. The people that lived down here didn't care about anything. Themselves. Their property. Even the law. Laws were for breaking. If you ate a McBurger you just threw the wrapper in the street. For God's sake, don't walk ten feet and put it in a trash container. In fact, they got their jollies down here by setting trash containers on fire and watching the emergency vehicles come.

But he had to keep all that to himself because it wasn't "politically correct" to say anything. God forbid he should have an opinion. He hated these people, and they hated him, but they were too chicken shit to face him down. Let them try.

He noticed a black male standing in the alleyway between two condemned houses. The guy was just looking at him.

"What do you want?" Barbie yelled across the street, and the man tucked tail and slunk off. Just like the rest of the rat bastards down here. Someone had given him the finger—once. The guy was without a finger now. Barbie had beaten an Internal Affairs investigation over that incident because Detective Troup had helped him, but after that he'd checked a Taser out of the armory. No one else had complained.

He crossed the street and walked between the houses where he'd run the creep off. No one was around. He was confident no one would mess with his police car, but he hated being out of sight of it. He gazed up at the sky. The clouds were pregnant with rain, and the wind was picking up.

He hurried around to the back of the house just as the sky opened and a deluge of rain came down. Luckily the door was unlocked. He stamped the water off his feet and pinched the water out of his eyes with a finger and thumb. He shut the door, and the room went dark. He squinted his eyes but he couldn't see jack-shit. He reached for the flashlight on his gun belt and a voice said from the darkness, "That won't be necessary, Officer Barbierre. Come into the front room."

Barbie did as instructed, and it was even darker in that room. "I can't see you," Barbie said, trying to locate the voice.

"That's the point."

Barbie thought for a second and said, "Oh yeah. I get it. We shouldn't be seen together."

"You're going to make a fine detective," the voice said.

"I did everything you said." He squinted into the darkness. He didn't like being at a disadvantage. They were somewhere to his left.

"Does anyone know you were coming here?"

Barbie felt water trickling down his forehead, mixing with sweat and stinging his eyes. "No one still alive," he said with a laugh and wiped at his eyes with the backs of his hands.

"And the car?"

Barbie grinned, because that part was fun as hell. "Both tires. I wish I could've seen his face."

The voice didn't respond, so Barbie hurriedly said, "All I want out of this is a chance to prove myself. I've done everything you've asked. And I'm willing to do more, but I've got to know if I'm getting what I want when this is over."

The voice came from a different location. Closer. "You've proven yourself. We'll take care of you."

"I need to know if I'm getting . . ." Barbierre managed to say before he noticed a red dot moving up the front of his shirt.

He reached for his weapon and heard a soft sound as something struck his neck. It felt like a bee sting. But it wasn't a bee sting, because his arms wouldn't move and he couldn't feel his hands. The numbness spread quickly, and his legs wouldn't hold him. He fell to the floor, but he didn't pass out. He could see and hear everything.

He lay on the floor and watched as boots and legs materialized out of the dark.

Chapter Eighteen

Luke Perry watched the woman named Ubaid and the teenager go up the stairs. Ubaid was hot, but—he hated himself for the thought—the teen was hotter. Papa'd get a good price for that one. Of course, Luke wasn't supposed to know what was going on with these children, but he wasn't ignorant. He'd seen Marie recruit her "acolytes" and bring them to the mansion for their final initiation rites. All the acolytes were hot too. But Luke didn't benefit. Papa had him out cruising the bus stations in New Orleans and Baton Rouge, picking up runaway boys that were never over the age of twelve or under the age of eight. He hadn't picked up any younger than twelve yet. Luke knew where these boys were going to end up. They'd be sold just like the girls. It made him sick that the boys would be used for sex too. He wasn't supposed to know, but he wasn't ignorant like Papa thought.

He felt sorry for them. He had two younger brothers himself, Levi and Leonard. Levi was thirteen, much younger than Luke. Leonard, who preferred to be called Len, was ten. Len was a fighter. He had the heart of a lion, his momma always said, because when he was born he came out squalling and twisting and punching, not to mention the mane of dark hair that ran down his neck and feathered out on his back. Luke tried not to think of his brothers when he was sent on these "shopping trips" by Papa, but it was hard not to. He hadn't seen them for quite a while.

The boys he found for Papa were brought right to the plantation. They were stuck in with the girls after a doctor checked them out. Head lice and fleas were a problem with the runaway boys. Luke had had to fumigate his van after picking up a couple of boys from the bus station in Baton Rouge. One of them had fleas so bad he could see them popping around like popcorn on the van's floor.

He followed at a distance and watched Ubaid and the girl disappear into a room on the second floor. Both of them made his loins feel weak. He heard the door lock click and went to report in to Papa.

Luke thought about that woman cop that had been snooping around. Killing a cop was always a mistake. And he didn't agree with Papa killing the guy who shot her. But he guessed it sent a strong message to the other guards.

He'd worked for Papa a long time. He trusted Papa. But trust or not, Luke had thought about cutting out sometimes. He didn't like what he was doing, and he was starting to feel guilty, ashamed. He hadn't minded the killing of that woman, but kids were something else.

Jack listened to Liddell narrate his movements since he'd arrived in town, but he had one eye on the blackness moving in from the west, a part of him looking for signs of tornadoes, or was it hurricanes down here? In any case, he'd experienced a few of these storms in Evansville, and they were scary as hell. He'd been on an indoor firing range one time and it sounded like a locomotive was traveling across the roof. It passed after a few minutes, and when he'd gone outside debris was blown all over the street, roofs were gone, walls had collapsed, and trees had fallen on power lines. But his car and the firing-range building were untouched. The tornado had been one of the worst Evansville had ever experienced. It cut a winding path through the city and had flattened almost every tree in Garvin Park.

He zoned back in on the conversation when Whiteside interrupted to ask a question addressed to him.

"So you were at the impound lot when your partner discovered his gun and camera were missing?" Whiteside asked.

"Yes," Jack said.

She sat, looking out the window as calm as you please, and Jack couldn't help but admire her relaxed attitude toward impending disaster.

"We talked to Cotton because I knew he was a friend of Bitty's,"

Liddell said. "I thought she might have talked to him. We were there about twenty or thirty minutes and told him the same thing we've told you so far. I take it you've had some experience with Cotton before now?"

Whiteside took a deep breath. "I've gone out there myself. Maybe a year or so ago. He had the place locked up like he was expecting Armageddon. The Four Horsemen couldn't get on his property without him knowing."

Liddell gave Chief Whiteside a serious look and asked, "If that's the case, and we went through that today, so we know it to be true, how did someone get in his house and shoot him?"

"So you're saying Cotton let his killer in?" She tapped her fingers on the desktop as if debating something with herself. "There are some things I haven't told you. I shouldn't, but you're going to hear it on the grapevine sooner than later."

Jack tried to get a read on her. He didn't see any indication she was lying. But she was an administrator, so she had to have a master's degree in lying.

Lightning flashed outside and preceding the cannon rolls of thunder, the skies split open, throwing buckets of rain at the office windows. The effect added an ominous touch to what she told them.

"Cotton was killed just like Bitty," Whiteside said, and waited to let this sink in before continuing. "They were both shot in the face. The coroner ruled both deaths as due to massive brain trauma caused by a gunshot wound. The bullet was found at Cotton's, and it matches your backup .45. We never found a bullet at Detective LeBoeuf's, but the Coroner advised she was shot with a large caliber, or a rifle. We don't think she was shot at her house because of the lack of blood, tissue, and other things you expect to find at a scene. We believe she was killed at an as-of-yet-unknown location, and her body was transported there just like you thought. I guess you've seen more murders than me or my guys."

Whiteside put a hand on the evidence bag with the gun. "Cotton was shot in the face point-blank like Detective LeBoeuf. His face wasn't disfigured like hers, but he was eviscerated in a similar fashion. Just like her."

"Was he killed where he was found?" Jack asked.

"Cotton, unlike LeBoeuf, was killed in his house. In the room where he kept most of his guns."

"His armory," Jack said, looking at Liddell. "The killer must have been someone he trusted," Jack said, remembering the reception he and Liddell had gotten.

"I can't imagine anyone getting the drop on him," Liddell added.

Whiteside absentmindedly turned the evidence bag around on the desktop. "The killer smashed LeBeouf's face. I'm thinking it was to hide the gunshot. So why not Cotton? Symbols were drawn on the walls in blood at both scenes. You didn't know this, but a symbol was carved into the flesh of LeBeouf's stomach. We didn't see it until the autopsy because she'd been gutted. They found it when they sewed her up. Nothing like that on Cotton's body."

"What kind of symbol did you find on Cotton's wall?" Liddell asked.

Whiteside hesitated and Jack assumed she was going to tell another lie. She didn't.

"It was a Voodoo symbol for death," Whiteside said. "That's what Troup says, anyway. He thinks the scene was staged to distract us, make us think it had something to do with a cult. He thinks both of the murders were staged. I agree. Troup says the symbols come from Haitian Voodoo. I did some research. Symbols drawn in blood on the victim's property are a warning. In New Orleans, we found a dead gang member with symbols cut into his flesh, *and* he was beheaded as a warning to a rival gang. But this isn't about gangs. We don't have that kind of trouble here."

Jack didn't think any of this involved gangs. Gangs didn't as a rule go after cops. They knew the response would be swift and harsh. The only gang he knew of that would take a chance like this was MS-13, a gang from El Salvador. They were known to behead their victims, but they didn't carve Voodoo symbols. The heads were the warning.

Jack said, "Do you have results on the blood evidence from Bitty's murder?" Jack asked.

"I was getting to that," she said. "The bloody boot prints on the door and around the table matched Detective LeBoeuf's blood. As did the drawing on the wall. We recovered some latent fingerprints and we've identified hers. There were several others we haven't identified as of yet. We're running them through AFIS."

AFIS stood for Automated Fingerprint Identification System and was maintained by the FBI. It contained millions of fingerprints taken from crime scenes, victims, applicants for gun permits, and suspects from all over the United States. It also included fingerprints of the military and law enforcement. It didn't contain the fingerprints of ordinary civilians or politicians unless they had been arrested or murdered.

"The latent prints on the gun at Cotton's house were yours, Liddell, and another set was on it too. When I tell you who they belong to, you'll understand why I had you brought in the way I did."

She put the gun back in her desk drawer. "The prints belong to one of my officers. Officer Barbierre."

"So why isn't Barbie here?" Jack asked.

"Officer Barbierre is missing," she said. "He isn't answering his radio or his phone."

"You still think he's not the one that stole my backup gun?" Liddell asked.

"I'll ask him when I find him," Whiteside said.

Jack said, "Maybe he doesn't want to be found. If you found Liddell's gun at Cotton's house, it means that Barbierre had it at one time. That alone makes him a suspect."

She said, "A suspect, yes. The killer, no. We still have to run ballistics on that gun and Liddell's duty weapon. Maybe Officer Barbierre's prints are on the gun from his search of your car," she said to Liddell. "You said the property sergeant told you it had been put in evidence."

He held a hand up and said, "I already checked with the sergeant, and he said he didn't remember seeing that gun. I checked the property sheet myself, and it wasn't listed."

"Are you thinking someone besides Barbie stole Liddell's backup gun? The property sergeant would be the only other likely suspect since Liddell's gun wasn't listed on the property sheet." Jack said, thinking Cotton's murder seemed open and shut.

Whiteside said, "Look. The gun might have been inadvertently left off the property inventory. Or maybe it was left in the car by Barbierre and was stolen at the impound lot. I don't know, and as long as I have questions I'm going to wait until we locate Officer Barbierre."

"If he's that incompetent, you should fire him," Jack said, and asked, "Who's working Cotton's case?"

"Don't go there," Whiteside said.

"It's Bobby Troup, isn't it?" Liddell asked.

"Detective Troup is assigned to Cotton's case since he's working a similar murder," she said. "End of discussion."

"Does Barbie's cell phone have GPS tracking?" Liddell asked. The EPD had issued cell phones to Motor Patrol officers and all were equipped with GPS tracking programs. Motor Patrol officers hated them, for obvious reasons, but they could see the benefit. The detective's office had not been issued those phones yet, but it was coming.

Whiteside's jaw dropped. "What a great idea. Why didn't I think of that?" she asked sarcastically. "That's the first thing we checked. It must be turned off completely or damaged."

A patrolman stuck his head in the Chief's door. "We found Barbie's car, Chief."

Chapter Nineteen

Liddell drove and they followed Chief Whiteside to where Barbie's car had been found. Jack thought about what Liddell had told him yesterday. Liddell said Troup didn't know that Bitty and Parnell no longer lived together. Troup wanted Liddell to believe that Parnell was on vacation in Hawaii, but when they talked to Sheriff Guidry, he hadn't said anything about Parnell having been on vacation. In fact, he said she was on a missing person case and he was going to arrange for them to talk to her. *He hadn't thought to ask.* And maybe Troup was just trying to confuse Liddell to try and trip him up. He had meant to ask the Chief if they had found Cotton's or Bitty's cell phones. *Another thing he'd missed.*

But he came back to Barbie's quick appearance at Bitty's house. Liddell said he'd been at Bitty's two or three minutes, tops. He was inside less than a minute. Troup was the reason Barbie was lying. In fact, the one thing all of these murders had in common so far was Bobby Troup.

Troup hated Bitty. Liddell would make a perfect scapegoat, but how did Troup know that Liddell was going to be at Bitty's? How did Barbierre arrive so quickly? Were they waiting at Bitty's house? Had Troup or Barbie already found the body and something to indicate Liddell was coming? Did one of those two leave the note for Liddell under Landry's door to lure Liddell to Bitty's house?

"Do you still have the note from Bitty that Landry found under the door?" Jack asked.

Liddell groaned. "They emptied my pockets during the booking at lockup. I don't think it was in the property envelope when they gave it back."

"You still have the property envelope?"

"I threw it in the backseat," Liddell said.

Jack felt the floorboards behind them and found the big envelope under the driver's seat. Jack held the envelope open and saw a piece of paper stuck to the inside. He pulled it loose, and it had purple sticky stuff on the edge. "You must have had jelly on your fingers, Yogi," he said to Liddell. "Your constant eating is paying off."

He unfolded the note. He wasn't worried about fingerprints because everyone that could be a suspect had already handled it. It read:

DON'T CALL
COME OVER

It was written in large letters, and not signed. Liddell had told him about the note yesterday but Jack hadn't asked to see it, because it didn't seem important at the time.

"Is this Bitty's handwriting?" Jack asked, holding the note up.

Liddell didn't even have to look. "I don't think so. I just assumed it was her. Very few people knew I was coming, and no one but Landry knew I was going to her house that morning."

"Did she have an answering machine, or voice mail, or did you message her, anything like that?"

"Well, yeah, I called, but I didn't leave a message. We didn't text."

Jack thought about it. "When I put a contact name and number in my phone, their name comes up when they call me. If Bitty had your contact in her phone, whoever killed her might have gotten it. But I guess, they wouldn't know you were a policeman unless they knew you."

"Which leads us back to Troup," Liddell said.

"Whiteside said Barbie's phone was found on the east side in a Dumpster. We're headed west." Liddell pointed out.

"She said his phone had been wiped. I wonder if she's getting a subpoena for the phone carrier to get a list of calls made? We need to ask the Chief if they found Bitty's cell phone. If they didn't, we need to see if the Sheriff's Department issues them, and if they have the GPS tracking."

"I'll bet Whiteside didn't think of that," Liddell said.

"Or the Sheriff for that matter. Or at least he didn't say anything about it."

Liddell took out the phone the Sheriff gave him. "I guess we should report in." He handed the phone to Jack.

Jack called the number programmed into the phone. Sheriff Guidry answered it.

The neighborhood they were heading into was poor at first and downright dilapidated the farther they went. They drove past entire blocks where houses had either been burned to the ground or were condemned. Jack could see the big red CONDEMNED notices plastered to the doors or front walls.

"This looks like a war zone," Liddell said.

About a block ahead, Jack could see two black-and-white patrol cars waiting at the curb. Chief Whiteside pulled her car into a yard, and a uniformed officer approached her. She motioned for Jack and Liddell to join them.

"This is Officer Rahm," Chief Whiteside said.

They shook hands, and Rahm said, "I spotted the car here but there's no sign of Barbie, I mean Officer Barbierre."

"Where is he?" Whiteside asked Rahm. "Where's Officer Barbierre?"

Rahm looked confused. "Dispatch only said to find his car, Chief. I asked what was up and they didn't know. Is Barbie in trouble? Did someone steal his car?"

"Can I talk to you for a second, Chief?" Jack asked and took Whiteside aside while Liddell talked to Rahm.

"I know you don't want to think Barbie is behind all this. He's your officer and you want to give him the benefit of the doubt. But he's missing. If he didn't kill Cotton he's being set up. Just like Liddell. But if Barbie is the one that shot Cotton he might be dangerous. I don't think your officers know what they're facing. Even if he didn't shoot Cotton, his phone was wiped and dumped in one part of town and his car abandoned here. We have a cop killer on the loose. Your people need to be prepared."

"I know what the hell I'm doing," she said, and lowered her voice and octave or two. "Okay. I've never had one of my people go crazy before. And if he's doing this, he's gone crazy. If it's someone else that's targeting cops we better damn well be sure before we cause a panic. I don't want innocent people shot."

Jack felt sorry for her. She was in a tough spot for sure. And if the public caught wind—and they would as soon as she put something out on the radio—it would make a bad situation even worse. But to do nothing wasn't an option. He hoped she would see that for herself.

"I've got to make a call," she said, and walked away punching buttons on her cell phone.

Jack could hear her talking to someone, hang up, and dial another number. The second time she got a little cranky with whoever was on the receiving end.

She came back and said, "I'll have dispatch call each officer individually and tell them to find Barbie and use caution. I had to call the Town Manager. That asshole was more worried about his job than the fact that we have all these murders and an officer missing who might be on a killing spree."

"Did dispatch tell you what his last run involved, or where he was?" Jack asked.

"He made a missing person run early this morning, and that's it."

"A missing person?"

"Yeah. A girl. Fourteen, black female, lives about a mile from here. Why?" she asked.

"Have you had a lot of missing persons recently? Specifically, young girls?"

"This is Louisiana, Murphy. Kids go missing here all the time. They run off to California or Nashville to become stars or get hooked up with drug dealers. Nine times out of ten, they show up a few days later, hungry and dirty, but no worse for the wear."

"I'm asking because Liddell's brother, Landry, has been trying to report his daughter missing for several days. Her name is Evelyn. Evie. She's fifteen."

"Yes, yes. Look, I'm sorry for his worry, but I need to stay focused on this case right now," Whiteside said.

"I'm telling you this for a reason, Chief Whiteside," Jack said. "Landry found some Voodoo things in Evie's room after she went missing."

She watched him. "Are you suggesting that these killings are linked to Landry's missing daughter?"

"I'm not suggesting anything. I'm pointing out that there is a common element. There have been Voodoo symbols at both murder scenes, and Landry's daughter was involved with Voodoo somehow. What about the other missing kids? Were they involved in any way with Voodoo? If they were, we may have a lead."

"Is this how you work at home? Jumping to conclusions? Accusing someone based on one commonality? We don't do that here. We need evidence, and you don't have anything to back up that cockeyed theory." She walked away, saying over her shoulder, "Please tell me you don't believe we have a cult killer. Or that it's a policeman cult killer."

He knew it was a stretch, but thinking about it, the killings and Evie's disappearance could be connected. Whiteside herself had researched the symbols drawn at the scenes. Why would she be so against the idea it could be a lead?

Liddell was being set up for the murder, but Whiteside just lets him go. She doesn't explain why he isn't a suspect. She orders him not to get involved in the investigation. Liddell said no one knew he was coming to Plaquemine. That's where all this falls apart except for the note. Someone, knowing Bitty was already dead, wanted Liddell to come to her house. Troup. He could have manipulated Barbie into watching for Liddell to arrive at Bitty's, waited just long enough to take Liddell down hard.

It was possible, but like Whiteside said, he had no proof.

So far Voodoo, Troup, and maybe Barbie were the things in common in all of the cases. He would bet a case of Scotch that if the Chief checked out the other missing girls' cases she would find Voodoo was a factor in all of them. Or at least the missing girls had dabbled in it. But she had already dismissed the idea of Voodoo being a factor.

He said, "If you don't need us here, Chief, I think I'll take my partner and go eat."

"I don't need you," she said flatly.

"C'mon, Bigfoot. Show me this place you were raving on about a while ago."

As they walked to their car, Jack heard Whiteside turn on Officer Rahm, giving him nine kinds of hell, and he felt sorry for the guy. Rahm had only done what he was told to do, but he was a convenient target for the Chief's anger. Jack could relate to that kind of pettiness. He was always ground zero for Double Dick's wrath.

Liddell said, "Hey, do you want to drive this time? Maybe we won't get pulled over again."

"You're doing okay," Jack said. When they got in the car, he bounced his ideas off Liddell.

"It's still a mystery to me how Barbie or Troup could have gotten to Bitty's so fast yesterday. The Chief didn't even tell us who called the police." Jack buckled in and cranked the a/c on high. "To be honest, I don't think she even knows. Troup is running this show, and she's afraid of him or he's holding something over her head."

"Or she's just an idjit, podnah. Rank doesn't always mean smart."

She seemed plenty intelligent to Jack. She also seemed to be keeping a lot of secrets. "Where to next?"

"Let's eat," Liddell said.

"Okay. But afterwards let's have another go at Parnell," Jack suggested. "She glossed over the missing person stuff. I want to know how many kids are missing, how old they are, where, when, and all that stuff. We may have to talk to all the parents. I don't think PPD has done squat along those lines."

"Do you think Evie's being missing and the murders are connected?" Liddell asked.

"We won't know that until we know."

"Is that a Murphy-ism?" Liddell turned back onto Highway 1 and punched it.

"Grasshopper, shut trap and drive please."

Chapter Twenty

Fewer than thirty true antebellum plantation mansions had survived between the 1800s and today. All were uninhabited now except the Nottoway Plantation in White Castle, a tiny burg ten miles east of Plaquemine as the crow flies. The once-abundant crops of sugarcane were gone, but the mansion had been turned into a successful resort with a five-star restaurant.

Liddell turned left at the one intersection in White Castle. The road was lined with hackberry trees whose limbs were filled with leaves and small red berries. On the other side of the hackberry trees were rows of sugarcane. The sugarcane plants were packed tighter and the rows wider than the cornfields Jack was familiar with at home.

Liddell drove another half-mile into a generous parking area filled to capacity, and to the turnaround at the end of the road. He stopped in the turnaround and pointed out Jack's window. "That's the Mississippi."

They found a parking space near the entrance where a car was just leaving.

"Welcome to the Nottoway," Liddell said.

Jack did a 360 and said, "I never thought I would see something this big in a little backwater place like this."

"This ain't nothing, pod'na. Wait till you see the rest of the grounds."

They had to go through the gatehouse-slash-gift shop to get to the restaurant, which was downstairs in the mansion. The air-conditioning in the gatehouse was a shock after the sweltering heat and 90 percent humidity outside.

Except for a small circular reception counter, the remainder of the floor space was laid out with racks and tables and display counters and shelves filled with clothing articles, jewelry, postcards, antique and modern looking tea sets, and local gift items like fleur-de-lis wall hangings, Nottoway mugs with a stencil of the mansion, prepackaged spices for Cajun recipes, recipe books, historical books, and other typical detritus you find in a gift shop. It was doing brisk business for a place that was all but hidden from the main road.

Jack followed Liddell through the store and out the other side. Liddell was right. The view of the mansion and grounds was breathtaking. A pristine lawn the size of two or three football fields was decorated with statues and flower gardens that led to an enormous water fountain in front of the massive antebellum mansion. It was like a scene from *Gone with the Wind*, and he could imagine Southern belles strolling arm in arm with men in tuxes and top hats, carrying silver-tipped canes.

"This is the little eating joint you were talking about? Do I have to sell a kidney to eat here?"

"They have Scotch," Liddell said. "I'm buying. Want one?"

"I'd be crazy not to."

Liddell led the way into the dining room. The seating was spread out along what used to be an outside porch, twenty-foot wide by one-hundred-foot long, semi-circular in shape. Tables covered in white cloths faced the windows with a view across the breathtaking grounds of fountains and gardens.

Only two tables were vacant, and a hostess seated them, asking for drink orders.

Jack ordered a double Scotch, Glenmorangie, neat. Liddell ordered two large pumpkin spice shakes. The hostess hurried off to get the drinks.

Master Chef David Reyes came to the table with a plate of cream-filled beignets and set it in front of Liddell. He said, "I will decide what you eat in my restaurant." Reyes told them the special and said, "But I have something even more special for you."

"Won't matter. It all tastes like hog-slop," Liddell said.

Jack watched the chef's expression turn dark and his eyes narrow. "Since when did you even taste the food? You suck it down like a Hoover. Don't worry, I won't charge you."

"Charge me? Are you kidding? The smell in here would run off a starving dog."

Jack's Scotch came, and the hostess waited while he took a sip. "My Scotch is excellent," he said. She beamed at him. He half expected her to leave the bottle wrapped in a cloth napkin, but she hurried away.

"I apologize for my partner," Jack said to the chef. "He was raised by yetis." To Liddell he said, "What the hell is wrong with you?"

Reyes smiled and said, "I heard he was hatched like an alligator but meaner and nastier."

"Bite me, Reyes," Liddell said and stood and they hugged.

To Jack, Reyes said. "We've known each other a long time. He used to eat here daily—and complain. He never paid."

Jack had checked the menu prices and thought he knew why Bigfoot never paid. You *would* have to sell a kidney to afford this place. "I'm Jack Murphy." He stood and shook hands with Reyes.

"David," Reyes said. "I'm the cook."

"Cook? He's being modest," Liddell said. "He's a master chef. Like New York or San Francisco good. He should open his own place."

"How long are you going to be in town?" Reyes asked.

"Not sure." Liddell said.

Reyes's expression turned somber. "I heard about Bitty. I'm sorry. I know how tight you two were. She was special."

"She was that," Liddell said.

Jack asked, "Did Bitty eat here?"

"Yes. She came in pretty often with Detective Parnell." He gave Liddell a questioning look.

Liddell said, "He knows about Bitty and Parnell."

Reyes continued. "I haven't seen them together for a while. You know they split up months ago."

Liddell asked, "When's the last time either of them were in?"

Reyes didn't hesitate. "Last time together, maybe two weeks ago. Bitty ate here a few days ago. I asked her how Parnell was, and she got quiet. I had an idea they'd had a fight. Anyway, I kept watching for her to come back. I'm so sorry about Bitty. If I can do anything . . ." his words trailed off.

Jack and Liddell traded a look, and Liddell said, "David, can we get a couple of burgers to go. Quick like?"

"Sure," he said and left.

"Let's go see Dusty," Liddell said.

Reyes brought a sack full of food. "I made some extra. Don't stay away so long."

Jack downed his Scotch and said to Liddell, "You're driving."

Liddell was on Highway 1 heading toward Detective Parnell's house when he saw a Plaquemine Police car running Code 3, emergency lights and siren, coming toward them.

The Plaquemine police car drove right past them, slammed on the brakes, and did a perfect one-eighty. Jack could hear the patrol car's engine spool up as the driver poured on the gas to catch them.

"What the hell?" Jack uttered, and Liddell eased the Crown Vic onto the shoulder.

The car stopped behind them. A uniformed officer got out and walked up to the driver's side, motioning for Liddell to roll the window down. Jack recognized Officer Rahm, the officer who had found Barbie's car.

Rahm squatted down and Jack could see his face was pale. "Chief Whiteside wants you to come back."

"Back where?" Liddell asked.

Officer Rahm didn't seem to hear him. "Barbie. He . . ." Rahm leaned close to the window. "He's dead. Chief Whiteside wants you back—back where we found his police car."

"Lead the way," Jack said, and the officer ran back to his car, peeled out, and veered around them.

Liddell caught up with Officer Rahm as they entered the city and Rahm led them through backstreets and stopped in front of a house roped off with yellow-and-black crime scene tape.

Chief Anna Whiteside stood in the yard, her head down while she wrote in a reporter's notebook, the kind a lot of cops carry. She watched the detectives approach, and before they could get to the sidewalk she stopped them.

"You boys have brought nothing but trouble to this town," she said. Her neck and cheeks were splotchy, and sweat stained her collar and ran down her shirt. She shoved the notepad in her back pocket. "Where the hell have you been?"

Jack said, "Why don't you tell us what's got you so pissed off? Officer Rahm said you found Barbie dead?"

Instead of answering she jerked a thumb over her shoulder and turned toward the house. Jack and Liddell followed.

"Isn't this the same street where Barbie's car was found?" Jack asked.

"Yeah. About right where we parked, pod'na."

Whiteside walked to the left of the house and Jack could see they had taped off a large area down the sides and back of the house as well as the front. That was encouraging. They slid under the caution tape and approached the back door. It was standing wide open and Jack could see someone decked out in a white Tyvek suit, minus the hood. The Chief snapped on latex gloves and handed a pair each to Jack and Liddell.

"Booties?" Liddell asked. Whiteside gave him an angry look.

"No need. My boys found him while I was back at the office, contacting every agency I could think of to put word out and arrange a search. By the time they notified me, everyone and their dog had traipsed through here. I'm still trying to find out if anyone touched anything, but I'm not holding out any hope. I swear to God, working with men is like being a playground monitor. Give me a bunch of women officers any day. They don't tend to lie and they at least know not to screw up the scene of a death. Murder or not."

Jack could argue one point with her. He knew a female detective who tended to lie. One who was part of the investigation. And someone who had jumped to the top of the suspect list. Dusty Parnell wasn't someone who could be trusted or believed. But he needed to focus here and now on Barbie. Being dead doesn't make one less of a suspect. It just makes one easier to find.

Chief Whiteside tracked mud inside from the still-wet yard, if you could call a mud pit that was strewn with plastic bottles and broken glass a yard.

"Give us the room, Tommy," Whiteside said to one of the crime scene techs. He snapped another picture before rising to his feet, and she added, "I mean now."

The tech scurried out of the door, and Whiteside shut it. Portable floodlights had been set up in the room, and a power cord ran under the door to a police van. Whiteside unplugged the cord to the lights and the room was black. She waited a few seconds for them to get the point and plugged the light back in.

"That's what it was like in here. Officer Rahm did a house-to-house search after we found Barbierre's police car. Rahm got to this side of the street last. When he opened the door, he saw Officer Barbierre hanging from a ceiling beam. Rahm says he entered to check for life, secured the scene, and called dispatch for additional units. Dispatch called everyone, including the coroner, but the one person they didn't call was yours truly. Damn it all to hell!"

Jack asked, "Did he come in the same door we did?"

"He came in the front door. How do you think he saw the body?"

Jack asked, "Is the body already with the coroner?" The room they'd entered was a kitchen at one time, now gutted by scavengers who would sell anything that could be ripped up or stripped out of the walls. Most of the drywall was knocked out, and any floor coverings had been carted off. Think of an army of ants taking a conquered beetle apart.

Whiteside walked out of the room and Jack thought she wasn't going to answer him, until she said, "In here."

Jack and Liddell walked into the next room and stood beside the Chief, looking up at the purplish-red swollen face of Officer Barbierre. His eyes and cheeks bulged, his swollen tongue filling his mouth, and he was hanging by his neck from an exposed ceiling beam. Lying on its side near his feet was a child's wooden chair with one leg missing. He was still wearing his gun belt and duty weapon, and all of his equipment seemed to be in its correct place and on his belt. Even his expensive sunglasses were in his pocket.

Jack saw the rope was yellow nylon and heavy enough to tow a vehicle.

"That's the type of rope we carry for water rescue, among other things. It's super strong and doesn't take up much room in your trunk." Whiteside yelled for the crime scene tech. The young man stuck his head in the back door but didn't come in. "Check Officer Barbierre's trunk to see if his rope is missing. You know. The yellow rope."

Jack yelled after the young man before the door closed again, "You can leave that door open."

Jack wiped sweat out of his eyes but more poured in. Even with the door open the temperature inside was at least one hundred. Jack guessed Barbie's weight at around two hundred pounds, give or take ten or fifteen pounds. Barbie was almost as tall as the yeti, maybe six-five. The house was an older one, maybe from the fifties housing boom when the soldiers came home from World War II. Ceilings were built taller in the fifties. Air-conditioning was for the rich. For the poor, it was window fans, screens, open doors in summer; fireplace, gas stove, extra clothes in winter.

"I don't think he hanged himself, Chief," Jack said.

She swung around, hands on hips to face him. "What are you saying? It's an obvious suicide."

Liddell walked over to the child's chair, knelt, and saw it had already been dusted for fingerprints. He could see some of the black powder on the floor beneath it. "May I?" he asked Whiteside.

Whiteside yelled for the tech. He popped his head in again. She said, "Are you done with that little chair in here?"

"What?" the tech said. "You mean the chair with the broken leg?"

"Do you see another chair in here?" she yelled, and added, "moron."

"Yes, ma'am. I mean yes, Chief. I mean I'm done processing the chair. The one with the broken leg."

Liddell set the chair up on the three legs. The broken one was bent under it like an injured wing. The chair was one of those wooden ones for five- or six-year-olds, painted pink, with the stencil of some kitty cat on the back. The seat didn't appear to be wide enough for two size-thirteen boots, and not strong enough to handle the weight of a man Barbie's size.

Whiteside kept her hands on her hips and leaned closer to examine the chair. She straightened up and yelled for the tech once more. The tech stuck his head in, and this time she motioned for him to come to her. When he did, she pointed to the chair.

"Did you get any impressions of any kind off the seat of that chair?" she asked.

The young tech pulled a notebook from inside his Tyvek suit.

There wasn't jack-shit furniture or other items to process in this little house, so Jack couldn't imagine why the tech would have to consult his notes.

The young tech flipped to the first page and read, "One wooden chair. Measurements sixteen inches in height, depth, that's front to back, is . . ."

Before Whiteside exploded, Jack interrupted and said, "I think we just need to know if you found any usable fingerprints or shoe impressions. Was someone standing on the seat? Did they pick it up to move it?"

The tech didn't need to consult his notebook to answer those questions. "No, sir. The seat and arms are covered in dust. It's my opinion the chair has been laying just like we found it for quite a while. It hasn't been touched today, if that's what you mean."

Jack asked, "And did you take impressions of Officer Barbierre's boot soles?"

The tech said, "Size-thirteen Wolverine brand. They look new. No breaks or cuts in the lug soles, nothing stuck between the lugs like gravel etcetera."

"In your opinion would those boots have even fit together on the seat of that chair?" Jack asked, and the tech smiled.

"No, sir. The boot prints on the chair are five point five inches wide at the sole. That's eleven inches total if he was standing at attention, feet together." When he said this he deliberately turned his back to the hanging body. A squeamish look was on his face. "I don't think—" he said, and was interrupted by Chief Whiteside.

"That'll be all, Kurtis. Wait outside until I need you."

"Yes, ma'am. I mean Chief Whiteside," he said and scurried back through the door.

"Okay. So he didn't use the chair seat to stand on. He could have stood on its side, and the leg broke and he hung. It still isn't anything but a suicide."

"What convinced you?" Jack asked to be fair.

"Isn't it obvious?" she asked. "Barbierre killed Detective LeBoeuf and tried to pin it on Blanchard. When he found that you two were investigating the case he got nervous. He must have followed you to Cotton's. When you left, maybe he tried to get Cotton to tell him what you talked about. Barbierre shot him and tried to make it look like the same type of murder as Detective LeBoeuf's. He had access to the gun that was stolen from your car."

Jack and Liddell were silent. She had a point. Cotton didn't seem like someone you could threaten.

"Don't you see?" Whiteside said. "When I let you go Barbierre got scared that we were going to start looking at him. He'd stolen your gun and maybe the camera. Maybe he thought you had taken pictures at LeBoeuf's house. According to you he arrived at the scene a minute after you got there, but maybe he didn't know how long you'd been there. He lied to Troup about you being in the house when he caught you. He may have had a romantic interest in LeBoeuf and she rejected him. Things got out of hand. He killed her and tried to cover it up. When you showed up he saw an opportunity to pin it on you."

"Some of that makes sense, Chief," Jack said. "But it still doesn't explain why he would kill himself. You yourself said we have no evidence that he killed her. Barbie, excuse me, Officer Barbierre would have known that. So why kill himself?"

"Guilt," she said. "He didn't want to get caught," she said. "He was proud, arrogant. Barbierre thought of himself as a one-man police department. But he admired Bobby Troup. With Troup investigating the LeBoeuf and Walters cases Barbierre knew it was just a matter of time before he got caught. Shame, guilt, fear of humiliation, fear of prison. Take your pick."

Jack felt sorry for her. She was the Chief of Police, and so the buck would stop with her whether Barbie was a killer who had committed suicide or if he'd just committed suicide or if persons unknown had killed him. Any way you went about it, this wouldn't look good for her or her department. If the killer struck again it would also kill her career.

He wanted Barbie to be the killer, but her theory was weak on motive. A detective had to look at everything from a defense attorney's point of view. A detective had to determine what was exculpatory, or that which proves innocence, as well as inculpatory, or that which proves guilt. You follow the evidence, but with an eye on how the resulting case would play out in a court of law and to a jury. And Jack could see a big piece of exculpatory evidence.

"I suppose you don't want me to tell you about the rope," Jack said.

Whiteside put her hands on her hips and got in Jack's face. "I don't want you to tell me anything, mister. You're done here. Not another word. Get out of my crime scene. And as a matter of fact, you and your partner get the hell out of Dodge, ASAP."

Liddell took Jack's arm and pulled him toward the door. Outside the house they ran into the crime-scene tech that Whiteside had run off.

"Can I talk to you for a second," the tech said. He led them around the side of the house and introduced himself. "I'm Kurtis, Kurtis Dempsey. My brother is with the Sheriff's Department. He said he met you."

"Yeah. Jon right?" Liddell said.

Kurtis cast a nervous glance toward the back of the house.

"The Chief was a little hard on you in there, Kurtis," Jack said.

"She's okay, I guess," he said. "But she's dead wrong about Barbie killing himself."

Jack said, "Why do you say that, Kurtis?"

Kurtis swallowed, looked around, and said, "When you guys came up, I was collecting this." He showed Jack two evidence bags.

One bag contained dirt mixed with something white, the consistency of baking soda. The other contained strips of something like bamboo or shoots of grass.

"What is this?" Jack asked.

The tech lowered his voice but he was obviously excited. "I found this on the floor in the kitchen. And there was more of it on the floor near Barbie's body."

"Do you know what it is?" Jack asked.

"Its soil and some plants and chips of paint. I think the white stuff is a fertilizer. The pieces of plant look like sugarcane. The chips of green paint might have come from farm machinery, like John Deere stuff. I think this stuff came from a sugarcane field. It hasn't been in here long."

"Did you check Barbie's boots?" Jack asked.

"Yeah. They had some grit on the bottom, but none of this stuff. And this didn't come from the ground around here. I can tell you that for a fact."

Jack appreciated the information, but he asked, "Why aren't you giving this to your Chief?"

The tech shot an angry look toward the back of the house. "Because she won't look at it. You heard her. She's made her mind up this is a suicide. And it might disappear before it goes to the lab."

Kurtis took a business card out and wrote on the back. "My work and personal cell number if you need anything else," he said and handed the card to Liddell.

Chapter Twenty-one

Evie came out of the shower to find her clothes missing and Ubaid holding open a thick pink robe.

"Wear this, and we'll do something with that hair," Ubaid said and smiled.

Evie slipped into the robe and pushed long dark locks of wet hair from her face. She asked Ubaid, "Where are my clothes?" Her clothes weren't much, and they smelled bad, but they were all she had.

"You have clothes laid out on the bed. But now we are going to do something with your hair."

Evie cooperated with Ubaid drying her hair, pulling it back from her face and braiding it, but she didn't want new clothes or to look beautiful. She just wanted to go home. She was mad at herself for getting mixed up in this. She had only wanted to find out about her mother. They had promised to tell her. They had lied.

Something trilled. Ubaid took a cell phone from a pocket. She stepped out of the room, and Evie could hear her talking softly. Ubaid came back in the room and her whole demeanor had changed. Nothing about her was smiling now. When she spoke, she sounded reserved, flat, the smile forced. "Beautiful. Just beautiful. Now we put on some makeup and do something about those clothes."

Evie turned to Ubaid. "My dad doesn't let me wear makeup."

"Just a little to bring out your eyes," Ubaid said. "You've worn makeup before, haven't you?"

Evie hadn't. She sat at the small makeup table and allowed Ubaid to apply eye shadow and lip gloss.

Ubaid examined Evie's reflection in the mirror. She patted the long braid that ran down Evie's back and smiled. "Now for clothes."

"Ubaid. Can I ask something?"

Ubaid's smile faltered. "Yes. But let's get some clothes on you first."

Evie let Ubaid help her slip into the beautiful blue gown that was laid out on the bed. She had shaved her legs during her shower and had been unable to resist a dab of the perfume set on a glass shelf beside the vanity. Ubaid led Evie to the floor-length mirror and Evie could hardly believe the reflection was hers. She looked like a grownup woman. Felt like one. The feeling was both thrilling and terrifying.

"Why are you doing this?" she asked Ubaid.

Ubaid said, "I must—" but was interrupted by a soft knock at the door.

Papa sat on the purple velour seat of the heirloom chair as the girl across from him sat on the side of the bed, feet barely touching the floor, wearing a $2,000 silk evening gown. A pair of expensive high heels, silk and the same color as her dress, lay on the floor where she had kicked them off. Papa knew her as Evelyn Blanchard, but he had given her a new name. A new name for a new life. He was waiting patiently for her to repeat it back to him.

She held her arms across her chest and deliberately didn't look at him. Even mad she was beautiful.

Papa had one chance, one showing, to get the investors' attention. They would come in two days to view, and if they liked, they could "sample" the goods. If the investors rejected her, she would need to be disposed of. It was a business decision. He had been nice to her up to now, but he would have to be curt. If she didn't change her attitude, if she continued to sulk, she wouldn't like what would happen next.

"Your name is an important part of your new life. Your past is inconsequential. You will have the best clothes, the best food, attend fine parties, and make important and rich friends. But you must accept your new name. You must forget Evelyn Blanchard ever existed. Do you understand?"

She was mad, but he could see she was more frightened. Her will was bending to his demands.

"Jacqueline. My name is Jacqueline," she said, and a tear ran down one cheek.

Papa's deep laugh startled her, and she came off the bed so fast she almost fell.

"Jacqueline. That's your name. It's a good name. A refined name. And you will be a refined young lady. We will teach you, Ubaid and I. And you must strive to learn. Much depends on it. Your life and your father's life depend on you now."

She refused to look at him and tears flowed freely.

"Smile," he ordered.

She forced a smile through the tears.

Satisfied, for now, that she would cooperate, he got to his feet and patted her on the head. He was incredibly big. He wore a purple silk suit with wide lapels, lighter colored purple pants, and even his shoes were purple. His head was bald or she thought he would have purple hair as well. He walked with a cane made of very dark wood with a silver handle in the shape of a skeleton.

He stopped at the door and gave Ubaid instructions. Evie/Jacqueline was to be put in a new room. Given new clothes. And watched. He shut the door behind himself and Evie could feel the floor move under her feet with his heavy steps in the hall.

While Papa had been present, Ubaid stood motionless, eyes cast down, moving when Papa directed her to do something, like move a strand of hair that had fallen over Evie's ear or change some jewelry—a necklace, a ring, a bracelet.

Now her voice had taken on a forceful tone, one that demanded if not obedience, compliance. She took Evie into the dressing room and helped her remove the expensive jewelry, placing each piece on a silver tray. She put the tray in a wall safe and closed and locked it. Next came the silk evening gown, leaving Evie wearing her skivvies only.

"Where are my clothes?" Evie asked Ubaid.

"You will find appropriate clothing in the drawers of that dresser." She pointed to a low dresser/bench at the back of the dressing room.

Evie opened one drawer after another and found jeans, a multi-colored tie-dyed T-shirt, and sandals. She dressed quickly and asked, "Am I going back to the room?" She didn't want to go back to that dank, depressing room after being here, being able to take a long hot shower with sweet-smelling shampoo and body wash. She had to admit that she felt grown up wearing the gown and jewelry and being made a fuss over, but it was scary too.

Ubaid took her by the arm. "We must hurry. Do not speak."

"You didn't tell me why I'm here," Evie said.

"You know why," Ubaid said softly. "Don't ask more questions of me, child."

At the bottom of the stairs she was led down a different hallway where Ubaid stopped and knocked on a door.

"Come," Papa's deep voice came from inside.

Ubaid led Evie in and stood her in front of Papa, who was sitting at a massive desk. Behind his desk were three large windows with the blinds closed and the curtains blocking what light might filter through.

"You are to be honored tomorrow evening," Papa said.

Evie didn't understand. Had she won an award of some kind? Was she being presented to the President? Or was this weirdo going to try something with her? If he thought he could he had another think coming. He was bigger, but she knew where a man's weak spots were. Her father had taught her that much when he thought she was getting to the age she could date. Not that he would let her date yet.

She stepped forward, facing Papa. "What's going to happen to the other girls?" she asked. "Where are you taking them? What's going to happen to me? Are you a kidnapper?"

He laughed that deep laugh of his with a twinkle in his eye.

"The buyers will love her," Papa said. "You've done well, Ubaid. Very well indeed."

Papa put his hands out and held her at arms' length. He looked her up and down, nodding approval, his eyes stopping at places that made her face fill with heat.

"Take her to her room," Papa said.

Without speaking, Ubaid took Evie by the arm and led her away.

Ubaid led Evie down two sets of stairs into what had to be a basement, but unlike basements Evie had ever seen. This one had painted walls with chair rails, and wood paneled ceilings and carpeted floors. Definitely not the concrete prison she'd come from. They stopped at a wooden door with a keypad lock. Ubaid entered a code, and Evie heard the locking mechanism whir. Several doors lay ahead, and Ubaid opened one of these and led Evie inside.

"This is your room now," Ubaid said.

Evie checked out her new accommodations, which took about three minutes. A rollaway bed with a mattress sat in one corner. The bedding appeared clean, and the room didn't smell of sweat and fear. The door to a bathroom stood open, and she could see a sink and a toilet and a shower stall. She turned to ask Ubaid a question but she was gone and the door was shut. She heard a lock turn.

She went to the bed, lay back on the mattress, and stared at the ceiling until the lights blinked out. She waved a hand and the lights came back on. If she turned over in her sleep she wondered if the lights would come on. But at least she had lights.

She lay still and thought and the lights blinked out again. She hadn't wanted to believe it, but she would never be found here. She'd read about stuff like this on the Internet. White slavery, that's what it was called. They would kidnap women, children, sometimes men and boys, and sell them on the black market.

She was going to be sold. *A sex slave.* And she hadn't even kissed a boy. Jamie Thibadeaux didn't count, because he had kissed her first, and Jamie Thibadeaux's breath stank.

She closed her eyes and tried not to be scared. This was crazy. All she had wanted to do was to meet her birth mother. She'd always been curious about her and had never seen a photo or a letter or anything personal until she found the box in her closet. Her father had gotten rid of all her mothers' things before she was even old enough to have questions. She knew he didn't do it to hurt her. He did it because he was hurt. And he didn't want her to get hurt.

In that shoebox, she'd found pictures and other things that she later found out were amulets. She knew her father wouldn't have owned stuff like that, so it must have belonged to her mother. She'd looked the amulets up on the Internet and learned about gris-gris and Voodoo dolls and spells and chants and rituals. Was her mother involved with Voodoo? She didn't know then, but she had heard of a place where she could find out more. That was how she found the plantation and Marie Laveau. Marie was nice to her. Marie had promised to tell her things about her real mother. And then she had been taken to the concrete room where she'd spent the last four days.

In her mind she conjured up the pictures she had found in the shoebox. In a couple of the pictures she had recognized her father, alone, fishing on the end of a pier, or making crazy faces into the camera. But there was one picture that showed a woman holding a newborn. She had examined the woman's face and compared her own in the mirror. They were different, but similar. They had the same eyes and high cheekbones. She'd always thought her shoulders were too wide for her body, but they were identical to those of the woman in the photo. Her grandmother had once told her that her mother was Creole, and her mother's side of the family was part French and part Choctaw. That accounted for the high cheekbones. In the photo her mother had long, thick black hair, with a braid down almost to her waist. Her father said that her mother was gone, but he'd never said if she was alive or where she might be. She had never believed her mother was dead. Her mother had simply left her behind. She needed to know why? Where had she gone? Did she ever think about her daughter? Did her mother ever love her?

Her last thought before drifting off to sleep was that she still hadn't found her mother, and now she was going to lose her father too. If she didn't cooperate, they would hurt him. If she did cooperate, she would never see him again.

Chapter Twenty-two

Liddell drove on autopilot as he talked to Marcie on Jack's cell phone. He was holding it away from his ear, and Jack could hear enough to know Marcie was giving a rundown of everything she and Katie had been doing for the last two days. Liddell ended the conversation by assuring his wife that he and Jack were in no danger and would be wrapping this up soon.

"You're very confident in our detecting abilities, Bigfoot," Jack said.

"I am. We now know that dirt and debris from a sugarcane field was left on the floor in a condemned house where a policeman was found hanged. How much more do we need, pod'na?"

Jack smiled. "You're right. Let's shoot someone and head home."

"Maybe even several someones," Liddell suggested, and handed the phone back to Jack.

"Should I call Sheriff Guidry and tell him we have this case wrapped up?"

Liddell said, "Not until we find Evie, pod'na. I promised Landry. And if she is with some boy I'm going to turn him into a eunuch."

"Cotton was crazy, but he was a good cop," Liddell said pensively. "He'd talked to Bitty about missing girls even before Evie disappeared."

"And don't forget Reyes, the chef," Jack said. "Reyes said Parnell and Bitty had been in several times after they broke up. Parnell outright lied to us."

"I wonder what they fought about?" Liddell said. "Do you think it was about something personal, or about a case Bitty was working on?"

"Would Bitty have told Parnell you were coming?" Jack asked.

"Yeah. I wish Bitty had told me what was going on."

"You said she didn't want to say anything on the telephone. Was it because she was just trying to make you curious enough to drive twelve hours to find out? Or did she believe that she was close enough to something that she was being watched?"

"I think she would have told me," Liddell said. "Who knows what Troup found at the scene that we don't know about? He was so busy trying to screw me I don't know what he might do to any evidence. His boy, Barbie, stole my gun. I'll bet ballistics comes back proving my backup gun killed Cotton. Barbie's fingerprints were on the gun, but why was he stupid enough to leave it there with his fingerprints on it?"

"Good question."

They sat quiet for a few miles before turning onto the lane that led to Parnell's house.

"Stop," Jack said, and the car stopped. "Do you think we can get in Bitty's house?"

"Maybe," Liddell said.

"Well, let's go see what we can see," Jack said.

Liddell made a three-point turn to avoid driving over sugarcane.

"I'll go in by myself," Jack said. Liddell maybe didn't want to see where his friend was butchered again.

"I'm okay," Liddell said. "I know where her hidey-holes are. Maybe we'll find something that Troup or CSU didn't."

Jack thought about Kurtis Dempsey. Kurtis was thorough. Nothing else would be found. But maybe just walking through it would help before they interviewed anyone else.

"Bitty's house is about five miles from here. But we might have a little problem when we get there."

"Problem?" Jack asked.

"Old Lady Martin. She's about a hundred and eleventy years old but she still has eyes and ears like a hawk. She has to be the one that called the police on me if we're wrong about Barbie watching the house."

"You can charm her, Bigfoot. Besides, we're still working for the Sheriff and have every right to be in there."

Liddell snorted. "Charm, yeah right."

"Well, if that doesn't work you can eat her."

"Not even a snack, pod'na. Too bony and tough."

"If Troup shows up, we can shoot him and blame it on the old lady," Jack said and this got a laugh out of his partner.

When they parked in front of Bitty's house, there were no police cars, no crime scene tape, and no neighbors outside.

Jack said, "In Evansville a murder like this would have brought out street vendors, news crews, admission booths, kiddie rides, and a few ambulance-chasing lawyers and political hacks to work the crowd."

Liddell grinned for the first time. "It's good to have you here, pod'na. I missed your sarcasm and positive take on human nature."

"Let's talk to the old woman," Jack said and popped his door open.

Liddell sat still. "I know we kind of talked about this, but what are we going to say to her? We don't have any authority to be asking questions, and I'm almost sure she's the one that called the cops on me."

"We don't tell her anything, Bigfoot," Jack said confidently. "We look like cops." He leaned back and studied Liddell, and said, "Well, at least *I look like a cop*. I'll tell her you're a yeti ride-along. If cops come, it sure as hell won't be Barbie again. You say you think you left your gun around here somewhere and you need it back."

Liddell scoffed and got out on his side.

Jack said over the top of the car, "You can say your mother gave that gun to you, and it's all you have left to remember her by. Work up some tears."

"Bite me," Liddell said.

Jack's gaze was fixed somewhere over Liddell's shoulder, and he said, "I think I saw the curtains by the door move." He reached back inside the car and took several pairs of latex gloves from the console and stuck them in a pocket. "I'd say we've lost the element of surprise."

They walked up on the porch of Bitty's next-door neighbor and Liddell knocked.

"Mrs. Martin. It's Detectives Blanchard and Murphy, ma'am."

Jack added, "Sheriff Guidry sent us." It wasn't a big lie.

A voice said from behind the door. "I saw the big one get arrested yesterday."

Liddell said, "The officer didn't know me, that's all. It all got worked out. We just need to ask you a few questions, ma'am."

She didn't unlatch the door, and Jack whispered in Liddell's ear. "She's probably calling the Sheriff or the police."

The door opened and an elderly woman stood in the doorway and said, "I am not calling the police. I just needed to get decent." She was wearing a well-worn nightgown that reached to her ankles. Under it her breasts sagged almost to her waist and her stomach pooched out. A fluff of white hair floated atop her head like a cloud.

She showed them into what was a parlor in the old days. The room was pristine, with clear plastic covers on the couch and love seat, but none on the easy chair.

"I'll make coffee," she said and moved away with a swiftness Jack didn't attribute to someone her age. She had to be ninety years old at least.

"Thank you, ma'am," Jack said in a low voice after she left the room, but she didn't respond.

She came back wearing a housedress that was as worn-out as the nightgown but thankfully not showing as much. She carried a tray with a coffeepot, sugar bowl, a tiny pitcher of cream, and a plastic jar of honey molded into the shape of a bear. Next to all of this was a plate of homemade beignets.

Jack waited for her to sit and everyone to make their coffee. He did the majority of talking since Liddell's mouth stayed busy with the beignets. Within ten minutes he learned the life history of Mrs. Jean Martin. He'd interviewed elderly people and found they needed more time to warm up than kids. Kids wanted you to get right to the point, anxious to get back to their texting or Tweeting or whatever the hell they did instead of interacting socially.

She must have found Jack's interest appropriate because she changed to the subject of Bitty. Jack had asked about Dusty Parnell. She said she hadn't seen Parnell at Bitty's for several months now. She had some other unflattering remarks, all having to do with "living in sin." She told them that no one from the police had talked to her yet, and she made a few derisive remarks about the way this was handled because those guys on *CSI: Miami* were better.

Liddell had finished off the beignets and Jack had run out of questions, so they excused themselves and Mrs. Martin showed them out.

Jack waited until he thought they were out of bionic earshot and said, "She's a very competent witness, Bigfoot. They should have talked to her. She even remembered you and Bitty were partners. I believe her that she didn't call the police or that they didn't even try to talk to her."

Jack took the gloves from his pocket and they both pulled a pair on before approaching Bitty's house. Any crime scene tape or a coroner's seal had been removed. Jack tried the door and it opened. He pulled it shut without entering. "Let's go to the back. You can show me what you did when you got here."

They walked down the west side of Bitty's. It was on a corner lot with a farm field of sugarcane across the way. Hydrangea plants with blue and white blooms grew thick along the side of the house. A wood privacy fence stretched from the back of the house to the alley. They went to the back, and Jack saw Bitty's orange Camaro.

"Did she have a department-issued car?" Jack asked.

"Everyone in the Sheriff's Department does. Or did. Whiteside didn't say anything about her department car being missing, or she may not have known. It doesn't appear the PD and Sheriff's Department are on speaking terms."

Jack tried the driver's door and it was unlocked. "Was she in the habit of leaving everything open like this?"

"Would you?"

They searched everything in the car but didn't see a release button for the trunk.

"I wonder where the keys are?" Jack said.

Liddell used a small folding knife on his key ring and pushed it in the lock. He twisted it and the trunk popped open. "Bitty never got that fixed, I guess."

They opened the trunk lid and found the usual assortment of trunk junk: road flares, a blanket, and so on, but it was in total disarray. Jack stooped and felt around the lip of the inside opening. He pulled his hand back and had a strand of dark hair with a piece of skin attached.

Jack held it up to the light and Liddell said, "It could be Bitty's.

We'll give it to Sheriff Guidry. I wonder why PPD didn't find it? Maybe they didn't even search her car."

"We need to ask our new crime scene friend. He should know or be able to find out what they searched. The Coroner should have samples. Maybe we can get a comparison done."

"Do you trust Kurtis?" Liddell asked.

"As much as I do anyone, so far."

The liner and carpeting in the trunk was a dark fiber. There were roundish stains from motor oil or some type of greasy equipment. It would have been nearly impossible to check for blood without proper test equipment. They closed the doors and trunk.

"Okay," Jack said. "Walk me through what you remember."

Liddell said, "I parked right here beside the Camaro. She was supposed to be here. I mean I had the note. I assumed she was here."

Liddell recreated his movements, including finding the smear of blood on the back gate latch, seeing the drag marks, and finding the back door kicked in.

They walked toward the back door and Liddell pointed out a couple of paper dots in the grass. The dots were about the size of the head of a nail. A Taser can be used two ways. As a shock device by placing the two probes in contact with the person's skin. Or by discharging barbed probes—darts—from a cartridge that is powered by CO_2. When a Taser cartridge fires darts, the CO_2 gas expels dozens of tiny paper dots that are packed around the darts.

"From Barbie's Taser?" Jack asked.

"Yeah."

Jack saw the boot print on the back door and the splintered wood and missing dead bolt. He used his iPhone to take pictures of the damage and boot print. "Troup left the door unsecured." The last officer or detective to leave the scene should make sure the scene is secured so no one would enter and contaminate it. "What the hell? With this kind of case you'd think they would still have someone guarding the crime scene."

Jack saw Mrs. Martin peering out of the window on the other side of the fence. He waved. The face disappeared, and the curtains shut.

Liddell pushed the back door open. "This is the kitchen. The table is on the right. That's where I saw her."

"Just to be clear, you said you came inside?"

"Yes." Liddell walked into the room and stopped. "I was about right here when I saw her body on the table. At first I didn't want to believe it was Bitty. I probably should have come in and checked the rest of the house to be sure the killer wasn't still here. I was so shook I went outside to call the police. I was fishing my phone out when I got sick. I was throwing up when Barbie lit me up with a Taser."

"And then he handcuffed you and took you back inside?" Jack asked, shaking his head in disbelief.

"Yeah. He walked me through the kitchen to the front room—over there—and set me down on the sofa," Liddell said.

The doorway between the kitchen and front room was wide. Jack could see the sofa. Liddell wouldn't be able to see the kitchen table from the sofa. A small blessing.

"Barbie had me sitting there less than five minutes before Troup showed up. I'm telling you, pod'na, they got here *too* quick. Then I was hustled off to the police station. The whole thing took about ten to fifteen minutes."

Jack mulled this over. It was very efficient work for Barbie and Troup considering how badly they handled the scene after they arrived. He looked around the kitchen and could immediately see that there was too little blood for the murder Liddell had described. The removal of the body had left smears and streaks of blood on the tabletop. On the floor were bloody boot prints but only a small amount of blood, droplets except for what had been tracked around the kitchen. On the kitchen wall behind the table a bloody symbol was drawn on the wall. *The Divine Messenger.* It was a simple drawing that any child could have made depicting a three-pointed trident with two bars crossing the staff. Except this one was finger painted in blood that had dried to a muddy brown.

"Were there that many boot tracks there?" Jack asked.

"I don't know," Liddell answered. "I'm sure they were some, but who knows what Troup and his people messed up in here." He pointed to a cigarette butt crushed out on the floor in the doorway to the front room. "Troup's idea of not contaminating a crime scene."

Liddell pointed to the finger painting on the wall. "That's the same symbol that Cotton showed us. The Divine Messenger."

The ceiling above the table showed "cast-off" blood spatters.

These were called "cast-off" patterns because they were the result of blood being slung off the blade when it was drawn upward or backward from the blow. Jack wasn't a crime scene technician, and he wasn't an expert in blood-spatter analysis, but he'd seen his share of blood at crime scenes. The size, shape, and distribution of the blood on the ceiling suggested a long-bladed knife, like a machete. He didn't see anything to suggest a struggle had taken place in here.

"She didn't fight her killer. She was unconscious or already dead when this stuff was done," Jack said flatly.

"Staged," Liddell said.

"That's what I'm thinking," Jack said and took his phone out of his pocket. "I wish we had some pictures to . . ." He broke off and looked at Liddell. "Sorry to be insensitive, Bigfoot."

"I was thinking the same thing," Liddell said.

Jack zoomed in on the blood on the ceiling and took close-up pictures. He repeated this with the symbol on the wall and the bloody boot prints.

"I wish we had our own crime scene unit here," Liddell said.

"That's a great idea, Bigfoot," Jack said, and punched in a number on his cell phone.

"You're serious? You think the Chief will let them come here?"

"Are you crazy?" Jack said. The phone was answered.

Liddell listened to Jack's side of the call, which was mostly uh-huh's, and yeah's before he got down to why he'd called.

"Listen, Tony. I'm sending you some pictures from my phone. Can you look at them and give me an opinion? I don't have a ruler or anything I can use for a scale. Can you just give me your impression and get back with me pretty quick?"

Jack listened some more and said, "Yeah. I'll send them now." He handed the phone to Liddell and said, "Can you figure out how to put him on hold and send the pictures I just took?"

Liddell took the phone and said, "Tony, can you call me back on FaceTime? Okay." He hung up and said to Jack, "I sent the pictures, but we can show him the scene live." The phone trilled in his hand and Liddell touched the screen. Sergeant Walker's face filled the phone screen.

"Show me what you've got," Walker said.

Liddell handed the phone to Jack and said, "I'm going back out-side, pod'na."

Jack watched him go. He turned back to the phone. "I'll start at the back door, Tony. Remember this has already been stepped on by their Crime Scene guys."

"Gotcha," Walker said.

Jack showed Walker the boot print on the outside of the door first, and the splintered wood and missing dead bolt. He was glad he started there because Walker's keen eye picked up something both Jack and Liddell had missed.

"Can you give me a close-up of the steps?" Walker asked. "And then I'll want to see the door again."

Jack put the phone on speaker and did as asked, holding the phone inches away from a place on the concrete step where Walker directed him. He did the same thing for the door, but not of the boot print. He trained the phone's camera on the area around the brass kick plate on the bottom of the door.

"You've got some drops of blood on the steps," Walker said. "And there is a smudge of blood on the kick plate. It looks like someone used the toe of a shoe or boot to push the door."

Not positive proof that Liddell's friend was carried inside. Not even positive proof that she was alive or dead when that happened.

Jack then took Walker slowly over the ground he and Liddell had just covered in the kitchen, the boot prints in blood on the floor, the smudges and streaks on top of the table, the symbol on the wall, ending with the cast-off blood patterns on the ceiling.

"I could be more of a help if I was there, but I think you're right about the murder not happening in the kitchen. For one thing there's not enough blood. For another, if they tested the outside walk and steps for blood they would find more drops of it."

Jack asked, "Does that tell us that she was alive or dead when she was brought here? There's nothing to indicate she put up a struggle. Bigfoot knew her and said if she was conscious there would have been one hell of a fight."

"What I'm seeing makes me think she was dead. The cast-off patterns on the ceiling would be more pronounced if she was alive or newly dead when that was done. And you're right. Those were made by some kind of long-bladed knife. I would guess a machete."

"What about the boot prints around the table? Any chance you can match them to the one on the door?"

"I couldn't even guess with what you've showed me, Jack. If I had access to the scene and all day to try and separate the prints out—maybe I could make an educated guess. Sorry."

Jack thanked Walker and found Liddell standing in the alley beside Bitty's car.

"Do you want to go through the rest of the house with me?" Jack asked.

He told Liddell about Walker's thoughts on the scene while they went back inside. Jack and Liddell walked through the remainder of the house, looking under couch cushions, in drawers, under mattresses, in closets, refrigerators, and even dumped the ice trays in the sink. They found nothing.

"She had a laptop computer," Liddell said. "I didn't see a computer or any computer stuff."

"Neither did I," Jack said. "Maybe Troup collected all of that."

They walked out the front door under the watchful eye of Mrs. Martin, who was once again standing in her doorway, and went to their car. The trip hadn't been wasted entirely. The blood spatters had given them some indication of the way she was mutilated, but according to the coroner—or from what the Chief had told them the coroner said—she had died from a single gunshot in the face. A large caliber. The PD had not found evidence of a gun being fired. What they did have was hair and possibly tissue found in the trunk of Bitty's Camaro.

They walked back to the Crown Vic, and Liddell said, "Walker was right. She was killed somewhere else. They used her car to bring her here and stage this. That means another car and maybe a couple of guys. I can't believe Mrs. Martin didn't see or hear anything."

"Even the nosy have to sleep," Jack offered.

"I wonder why Chief Whiteside didn't know any of this?"

Jack said, "Who says she doesn't know? She's appointed by a mayor, so she must lie like a politician. It's part of the job description."

They got in the car. Liddell was driving. "Parnell's?" he asked.

"Yes. She's got some 'splainin' to do."

*   *   *

Liddell turned off Highway 1 onto the lane leading to Dusty Parnell's. As he did, Jack caught a movement out of the corner of his eye, and when he turned he saw just the back end of a dark-colored sedan disappearing down Highway 1.

"Did you see something?" Liddell asked.

"No. Nothing. Let's talk to Parnell."

Liddell turned onto the gravel road lined with the massive oaks and the fields of wildflowers and stopped in the circular drive in front of the two-story house. Parnell's Land Rover was there in the circular drive. They walked around the side, and the Harley and one of the dirt bikes were under the carport, but one was missing. Jack heard a motor winding up and soon Dusty pulled the dirt bike into the carport. She took her helmet off and shook out her hair.

"I wondered when you'd be back," she said.

They were sitting in a cavernous front room, in front of a huge set of picture windows. Dusty sat on one of the three couches, next to Liddell, and Jack was on an oversized ottoman. She'd skipped the offer of coffee this time, and seemed to be at peace with some big decision.

"I guess you know I wasn't quite honest with you earlier," she said.

Jack and Liddell were quiet. Silence was a great tool in interviewing. It pushed the interviewee into filling in the empty space. Dusty Parnell was a detective, but she was no different when it came to this.

"I heard you went to eat at the Nottoway, so I figure Reyes told you about me and Bitty being in there a little while back."

"Who told you that?" Liddell asked.

She kept her eyes on Jack, with quick glances in Liddell's direction as she hesitated.

"I guess I might as well tell you," she said. "We were broke up, but still seeing each other. I mean, hell, we worked in the same office almost every day. It was hard . . ." Her voice trailed off.

Jack wanted to know why she hadn't answered Liddell's question, but he wasn't going to interrupt. So he waited her out.

"Look, I know this makes me look bad. I mean, I lied to you

about not seeing her for several weeks." She clasped her hands in her lap like she didn't know what to do with them. "We had a fight. Okay? We were fighting."

Her eyes were on Jack while she said, "It wasn't anything that could be related to her murder. People don't always get along, you know. We had good days, and we had bad ones like everyone else."

"So what were you fighting about?" Liddell asked.

"Honestly. It was nothing. I mean, it was something stupid. Like most fights, I guess."

"Is that what you argued about at the restaurant? Reyes said you were mad." It wasn't exactly what Reyes said. Reyes said he had a "suspicion" they had been arguing. Dusty's hesitance to answer told Jack it was true.

"Was Bitty seeing someone else? Is that what the fight was about?" Liddell asked.

It was just a guess, but she gave Liddell a challenging look and said, "I know I'm not getting any younger, but I keep in shape and all that. I don't look bad for my age. Why would you ask me that?"

"You still haven't told us how you knew we were at the Nottoway restaurant. Did Reyes call you?" He knew that wasn't true, but he needed to push her a little. People said all kinds of things when they were under stress.

She didn't say anything. She just sat, unblinking.

Jack said, "You're a detective, Dusty. You know that even little things make a difference in an investigation like this. Are you going to help us out or yank us around?"

She sat up straighter, and her face turned to stone. "I don't like what you're insinuating, Detective Murphy. You have no authority here. I don't have to talk to you."

Liddell put a hand on her arm and said, "You don't have to talk to us, Dusty. But someone will be asking these questions. Sheriff Guidry asked us to help look into this, but we don't have to tell him everything. Not if we think it's purely of a personal nature and has no bearing on the case."

She seemed to be thinking it over, and come to a conclusion. "Get out of my house." She didn't say it in anger, but there was a note of finality. There would be no discussion.

The men stood and showed themselves out the side door. They walked past the carport and Jack saw something in the treads of the dirt bike Dusty had rode up on. He bent down and scraped some of it out of the tread and into the palm just as Dusty came out the door. He stuck his hand in his pocket.

"Nice bike," Jack said, and she just stood there with her arms crossed.

When they got in their car, Liddell asked, "What did you find?"

Jack brought his hand out of his pocket and pulled a tissue from the console. He brushed the material from his palm into the tissue and Liddell saw it was blackish with fibrous material embedded in it. It was still moist.

Jack called the number they'd been given by Kurtis Dempsey, the crime scene tech. He was off duty but agreed to meet them at a family-owned business in Plaquemine called A Slice of Heaven.

Chapter Twenty-three

They found Kurtis sitting in a booth where he could watch the front door. He smiled nervously as they joined him.

"Figured Liddell would remember this place," he said. "It's to die for."

The waitress, a sixty-something, hard-looking woman, came to the booth and said, "What d'ya want?"

Kurtis said, "Bring us one of them cherry pies, Tooty. And coffee for everyone. Put it on my tab."

Tooty wore a pink-and-white waitress outfit that resembled a hospital candy striper's dress. Her thick hose ran from just below her knee to the top of her dirty-white Dr. Scholl's.

She said, "You ain't got no tab, Kurtis."

Kurtis said, "Well, start me one, Tooty. I've been coming here every day for nearly four years."

Tooty just scoffed and walked away. She came right back with three mugs and a steel carafe of coffee. She set the mugs down, and Jack put a hand over the top of his.

"None for me. I'm trying to quit."

She must have thought that was the funniest thing she'd ever heard in her life, because her mouth almost twisted into a smile. "I guess you won't be needing cream," she said and walked away.

Kurtis braced forward with hands on the edge of the chipped Formica table top and asked, "So what are we doing, fellas?"

Jack pulled out the tissue, put it on the table and spread it open. Kurtis said, "Yeah. That's the stuff. Where'd you get it? You want me to check it out for you?"

Jack handed him the two small envelopes of dirt Kurtis had given them earlier. "I was hoping that you would."

Tooty came back and was holding a glass cobbler with green kitchen mitts. She set it on the table. It was made like a pie with a top crust, but was at least three inches deep like a cobbler. Kurtis stuffed the tissue and envelopes in his shirt pocket and his tongue ran around his mouth like a kid in a commercial, but to his credit, the pie/cobbler was just this side of heaven. Jack talked while Liddell and Kurtis inhaled pie.

"We found something else today," Jack said. "But first I need to know if you can keep this between us for now. If you have to report it to your department, I understand, but I'm hoping you'll wait a while." He already knew Kurtis wasn't prone to share what he thought would disappear.

Kurtis swallowed and watched the front. Satisfied they weren't being overheard he said, "Depends."

"On what?" Jack asked. Shit! This wasn't going the way he had thought it would. If Kurtis grew a conscience now, Jack had just given him most of their evidence. And Chief Whiteside or Troup would soon be coming for the rest.

"Depends on you paying for this pie," Kurtis said with a wicked grin. "Gotcha."

Jack took out his phone and pulled up the pictures he'd taken at Bitty's. "Kurtis, do you know anything about Voodoo?"

"No. There's some of them fanatic people around here, but I don't associate with that stuff," Kurtis said.

"Okay, but you do know about blood-spatter analysis?" Jack asked.

Kurtis studied Jack and said, "Yeah. I know that stuff. Why?"

"I'm going to send you some pictures we took earlier, but you have to promise me you won't tell anyone or show anyone. I just want your best guess as to what type of weapon was used, and if you think the victim was dead or alive when these spatters were made. Okay?"

"I'll try," Kurtis said.

"You'll try? Or you can do what I asked?"

"I meant I'd try to answer your questions. I won't tell a soul. I have never even seen this stuff."

Jack handed the phone to Liddell, who sent the pictures to Kurtis. Jack insisted on paying and had made a friend for life.

Back in their car, Jack said to Liddell, "Chief Whiteside sounds like a tough boss. She seems competent enough, but she keeps getting in her own way."

"She's new," Liddell said. "Maybe she feels like she has to prove herself."

"Maybe she's just a bitch."

"That too." Liddell put the key in the ignition. "Where to next, pod'na?"

Jack checked the car clock. It was almost 8 P.M. "I'm going to make a call. Why don't you call Sheriff Guidry and catch him up. But don't mention Kurtis. I don't want to get the boy in trouble."

"Who you calling?" Liddell asked.

"Angelina."

Angelina Garcia began her career as the IT person for the Evansville Police Department and had proven herself valuable in digging up—read that hacking—information using computers and her connections in the cyber world. She had first come to Jack's attention a few years back when he was chasing a serial killer who was staging his murders as nursery rhymes. At that time, she had been assigned as a data analyst to the Vice Unit but after working with Jack and Liddell she was frequently requested by other units.

She got engaged to Mark Crowley, the Sheriff of Daviess County, semiretired, and moved into Mark's cabin on Patoka Lake. She was now a consultant for the Evansville Police Department and several other agencies.

"What do you want her to do?" Liddell asked.

"I don't know yet."

He dialed her cell phone and it went right to voice mail.

Liddell had better luck and was engaged in a conversation with Sheriff Guidry, who must be an expert in the investigative technique of laying down bullshit. Liddell laid out their day, and skillfully told parts of the truth about the possibility of blood evidence at Bitty's that didn't jibe with what they were being told by PPD.

Liddell handed the phone to Jack and Sheriff Guidry waded in. "How did the talk with Dusty go? Did she give you any shit?"

Jack hesitated to answer, and Guidry said, "I called her right after you left, and she admitted she'd not been honest with you. In my book, lying is lying. There aren't any degrees of being a damn liar. When do you want to talk to her again? I can make her come in to headquarters."

Jack could hug this guy, but he didn't know how to explain that even if she told the truth now he wouldn't know if she was lying again. "If she's willing to talk, we'll go to her," Jack said.

"You don't need me there?" Guidry asked.

"I appreciate the offer, Sheriff, but I like to work alone. I'm saddled with this yeti, so I let him come along."

Guidry laughed and said, "He is a big'un. I'll tell Dusty to make herself available. You have her cell phone number?" Jack said he did. "Call me if she gives you any more shit. She's on thin ice with me, and she knows it."

Jack thanked the Sheriff and hung up. Liddell, who had overheard most of the call, said, "Well, I hope we don't have to read her Miranda rights to her. If that isn't a coerced statement I don't know what is. We going to talk to her tonight?"

Jack could feel the coffee jitters, and the acid factory in his stomach was working overtime. "I feel like I've been rode hard and not put away," he said. "Let's get Dusty first thing in the morning when we're fresh. Let her sweat it out all night." She'd had time to think about what she was going to tell them next. It was a better tactic to come at a liar sideways instead of head-on. They'd just show up early and catch her half asleep.

"So where to now?" Liddell asked.

"I need some sleep and some Scotch. In reverse order," Jack said.

By the time they got back to Landry's house, Angelina called.

"Hey," Jack said.

"Horses eat hay," Angelina answered. "Given the late hour, I guess you didn't call to talk about my upcoming wedding that you promised to attend with Katie. You crossed your heart and hoped to die, Jack." Without taking a breath, she said, "Hey, you and Katie are still together, aren't you? If you broke up again, I'll have my soon-to-be husband beat your ass."

Jack had to raise his voice to get her attention. "Angelina! Dial it back a little."

"Tell her hi," Liddell said from the kitchen, where he was preparing a snack of skillet-fried donuts.

"Is that Liddell? Is he okay? Are you coming home soon? Mark told me what happened."

Jack wasn't surprised that word of Liddell's dilemma had already spread to adjacent counties at home. Police departments were like ant colonies.

He didn't know which question to answer so he answered them all. "Yes, Liddell is good. Yes, Katie and I are together, and plan to make the wedding. No, I don't know when we will get home. And yes, I called about something other than all the above."

"I'll shut up," she said.

That'll be the day. "I need some help with a few names." He gave her the names.

"What do you want to know?" she asked when she'd written them all down.

He could already hear her keyboard clacking in the background. "I don't know," he said. "Anything you can give me, I guess."

"Leave it to me, Jack. When do you need this?"

"Last week," he said and heard her snort. "We're groping in the dark."

"Tell her about the missing girls," Liddell said.

"I heard him," Angelina said. "What missing girls? Never mind. I'll put that on the list."

Jack gave her Evelyn Blanchard to add to the missing persons.

"Got it. If there's anything, I'll let you know. Is that it? 'Cause Mark is naked. I think he needs my services more than you do."

"That's too much information, Angelina. Oh. Tell Mark extramarital sex is prohibited in the sheriff's manual."

"Yeah, right."

He heard her telling Mark what Jack said just before the connection was broken.

"Want some donuts?" Liddell asked, bringing a platter of them to the table. They were still so hot the powdered sugar he'd sprinkled on top was melting.

"Do they go with Scotch?" Jack asked, and Landry came down the stairs.

Landry said, "Yes, Scotch is the recommended pairing for donuts," and opened a bottle of fifty-year-old Ardbeg.

They moved to the front porch with their drinks. Liddell had a beer. The heat had died to a tolerable level, and the smell of the

Mississippi was in the air. Watching Liddell eat donuts and drink beer reminded Jack of the new breakfast cereal he'd discovered. Guinness poured over Rice Krispies. Beer-eal. The breakfast of champions.

"Thanks for what you're doing," Landry said to Jack. "And for having your friend at home help out. She must be good at what she does."

"She needed something to do," Jack said. "And she's the best in the world at squeezing every drop of information out of every computer system."

"I know it's late," Landry said, "but what can I do to help you guys?"

Jack said, "Just be available if Evie calls or tries to get in touch with you. If she comes home, you want to be here." He didn't have to suggest Landry take off work. And he knew it must be maddening for him to stay by the phone and do nothing when his child was out there somewhere, maybe needing his help, maybe hurt, maybe worse.

Landry asked a question that Jack wasn't prepared for. "Do you think these murders have anything to do with Evie going missing?"

Jack and Liddell exchanged a look. Jack said, "We aren't ruling it out."

"Excuse me a minute, but I have to get rid of some of this beer and get some more," Liddell said and went inside.

"Liddell told me that you and your wife just got back together," Landry said.

"Ex-wife," Jack said, and thought about how that sounded. "Yeah, we maybe got it right this time around."

Landry picked up a twig from the ground. He broke off small pieces and threw them into the dark.

"Liddell told me a little about your ex-wife, too. Sally, right?" Jack said.

Landry tossed the twig into the yard. "She left me and Evie a long time ago. What kind of woman could do that? I mean I ain't much to look at, and I'm not ever going to be rich, and this house and land is all I've got—besides Evie, that is. But to leave your daughter like that, without a word. And leaving me to wonder if she was kidnapped or killed or . . ." His words trailed off, like his thoughts had dried up.

Jack didn't know what to say, so he changed the subject. "What was it like growing up here?"

Landry seemed relieved to talk about something else. "You mean growing up with a human waste disposal for a brother?"

Jack smiled. "Yeah. He has a healthy appetite."

"And he gossips like an old woman," Landry said, and they both laughed.

"Landry, just out of curiosity. Could she have had contact with any of the dead people?" Jack asked.

"No. Not any of the people you named," Landry answered.

Jack pulled up a photo on his cell phone and showed it to Landry. "This symbol was on the wall at Bitty's house near where the body was found. We were told it was a warning of some kind. Cotton Walters called it the sign of the Divine Messenger. Bitty was killed somewhere else and her body was transported to her house. We're not sure who this is warning since the symbol was drawn after she was murdered."

Landry held Jack's phone and asked, "Was this at Cotton's place too?"

"How'd you know there were symbols drawn at that scene?" Jack asked. He hadn't told Landry much about Cotton's murder.

"You wouldn't have shown me this picture otherwise, for starters," Landry said.

Jack had to remind himself he was talking to a detective's brother. "Does it mean anything to you?" Jack asked.

"It does. But from a long time back."

"How long back?" Jack asked.

"I told you Sally, Evie's mother, was into Voodoo. Well, I've seen that symbol before. It's a sign of death. The Four Horsemen of the Apocalypse kind of stuff. Indians believe that owls are messengers of death. Well, back in high school, if Sally was mad at someone she'd draw that symbol on their locker. She said it was a curse."

Jack continued to study the picture on his phone. "Cotton said it was the symbol of the Divine Messenger."

"I'm not into this stuff, Jack. I'd be guessing if I said anything else. Besides, that was a long time ago. At least fifteen years. And I haven't seen anything like it since high school."

"Your guess is the best I have right now, Landry," Jack said.

Landry said, "I'm assuming that it's a warning. Warning you not to mess around with whoever is drawing it. So far it's gotten a lot of people, wouldn't you say?"

Jack had to agree with that assessment, but he didn't believe in the supernatural. He believed these deaths were related, but the Voodoo was just a red herring. A feint.

Liddell came out of the house with a fresh beer and set it down on the porch.

He was sitting down when they heard a gunshot and the glass in the storm door shattered.

All three men scrambled in different directions. Landry ran and dove behind the Crown Vic. Liddell and Jack ran for Landry's pickup truck and crouched behind the tires. Another shot rang out, and the front tire of Landry's truck went flat. Jack took a quick peek around the back of the truck and a bullet buzzed by his ear and buried in the front of Landry's house. Another shot hit the hood of Landry's truck.

Jack had his gun out and was yelling at Landry, pointing out the direction the shots were coming from and asking Landry what was behind there. He didn't want to shoot up a house on the other side, or hit anyone. The drawback to being a policeman is that you don't always have the luxury of trading bullets with a bad guy. They don't have to care where their bullets go.

Jack peeked again and caught a brief flash of light from the copse of cottonwoods. Jack ducked back again but there was no sound.

Jack and Liddell held their fire, but Landry produced a semi-automatic pistol and ran toward the woods expending an entire magazine of ammunition. The shooting stopped.

Officer Rahm sat at Landry's table filling in a report form. His eyes were red, and Jack could smell alcohol on his breath. Rahm said, "So you didn't see if someone was shooting at you."

"They were shooting at us from the tree line, and it's dark." Liddell pointed toward the river. "The house lights were on, and we were sitting on the porch. They could see us."

"So, I thought you said you were standing when the first shot was fired?" he asked Liddell.

"I had just come outside. I was bending over to pick up my beer," Liddell answered.

"So, you all have been drinking," Rahm stated. No one answered. "So. You think they were shooting at you?"

Jack couldn't believe what he'd just heard. Not only did this idiot start every sentence with "so" but he was accusing them of making a false police report.

"Whoever it was almost hit Liddell—twice," Jack said. "They hit the truck, flattened a tire, shot out the door glass, and hit the house. You think that was an accident? You can see the bullet holes."

Rahm lifted his eyes from the clipboard, pen poised over the paper, and said, "People hunt along the river at night. Sometimes they're just shooting at rats. Shooting cans. That kind of stuff. Maybe that's all this is."

"We look like rats to you?" Landry asked.

Jack put a hand on Landry's shoulder and could feel the muscles in his arms and back vibrating. Jack asked Rahm, "You moonlighting? I thought you were on day shift." Rahm was the officer who had found Barbie's car, and the one who found Barbie's body to his obvious detriment.

Rahm pushed the clipboard across the table for Liddell to sign. He said, "I thought so too. And yet, here I am. Why is it every time I see you guys I'm on someone's shit list?"

Landry signed the report and Rahm stood. "I'll let you know if I find anything, but my gut feeling is someone was shooting at rats."

When he left, Liddell said, "If we checked Rahm's car, I wonder if we'd find a recently fired rifle?"

Jack didn't think Rahm was the shooter. He did think he was being an asshole, but his attitude seemed to be about being reassigned to night shift. PPD officers had had quite enough of Jack Murphy and the Blanchard brothers.

Landry pulled a curtain down in the kitchen and flipped off the light.

Liddell said, "I'm sorry we brought this to your house."

Landry made a dismissive wave of his hand. "I hate to give that asshole any credit, but he's right about people shooting down there along the river in the last few years. It's not the first time a bullet has struck this house. But those shots were aimed at Liddell. Not me. Not Jack." He spoke to Liddell. "So who'd you piss off bad enough to shoot your ass?"

Jack wondered why Chief Anna Whiteside hadn't made an appearance, but he didn't want to make the situation worse by calling her. Their being shot at was a low-priority run, because Rahm had shown up alone and didn't bother to check the area where the shots had come from. Whiteside would say it was another suicide attempt.

It was a fitful night sleep for Jack. He had a dream about Bobby and Eddie Solazzo. In his dream Bobby and Eddie had assault rifles and had him pinned down in an alley. Jack tried to shoot back, but every time he pulled the trigger on his Glock, the bullets would go about two feet and fall to the ground. Bobby had laughed, and out of the corner of his eye Jack watched a blade slash down and he could feel it cut into the flesh beside his ear, gouging through bone, and continue slicing down across his neck. In the dream, Jack saw Bobby standing over him grinning as he plunged the bowie knife into his chest.

Jack had jerked awake, covered in sweat and feeling like he'd run ten miles. It wasn't the first time he'd had the dream. In real life Bobby *had* cut him from his face to his chest with a bowie knife. But Jack had blown Bobby away, and in real life his gun had fired perfectly. Later he'd killed Eddie, who was on a murder spree trying to avenge his brother. The brothers were both badasses. Both crazy. And both dead.

The details of the dream didn't change much each time. Sometimes Jack was the one with the knife. Sometimes he shot Bobby before being cut, but Bobby would never fall down, and they would get in a struggle. Sometimes, when he had this dream, he'd have to get up and change his T-shirt and shorts and lay back down on a damp pillow and mattress. The shrink he'd been ordered to see told him these dreams were called night terrors. He'd told her they always ended well, with him killing the bad guys. She'd come back by saying something chilling. "It's not the bad guys you're killing in your sleep, Detective. You're killing the things about you that you think are bad." He thought she was full of shit.

He felt sorry for Landry. First his daughter goes missing and he can't get any help from the people who are supposed to help. Liddell comes to help and gets arrested for a murder he didn't commit. To boot, Landry's house and truck get shot up, and he's accused of making it up. *Real nice.*

Jack came downstairs. He'd been given Evie's room to sleep in, and it was a nice room, but he felt like he smelled like teenage perfume. Liddell was already up, and Landry was making breakfast.

"I was beginning to think you'd been hit last night and were dead," Liddell said.

"I knew he wasn't dead," Landry said. "He sounds like a chainsaw. Just like you."

Jack poured some coffee and sat down listening to the two brothers bicker. They were different in a lot of ways, but both had toughness to them. He was getting to like Landry.

"I was thinking," Liddell said. "Those shots came close, but no one is that bad with a rifle around here."

"He's right," Landry said.

Jack had been thinking the same thing. Liddell was a big target. Like hitting the side of a barn.

"Regardless, we need to move into a hotel or motel," Jack said.

Landry said, "Bullshit! Last night was supposed to scare you off. They won't come back. They know we'll shoot back. Big Jim always said, 'Never run from a bully.'"

Chapter Twenty-four

They set out before the sun was up. Landry agreed to stay home, while Jack and Liddell walked toward the woods where the shots had come from. It was farther away than it appeared to be last night. The sun was still a glint on the horizon when they got to the trees. Jack stopped and turned back toward the house to judge the distance. Three shots at three hundred yards. The shooter was good.

"I saw a light somewhere in here," Jack said. "May have been a penlight, or they were smoking."

If crime scene techs were here, this area would be marked off in a grid and every inch searched. It was just the two of them now. They would do the best they could. Jack had just about given up searching after thirty minutes, but his shoe kicked up something small and white. Jack took a little pocketknife out, opened the blade, and stuck it in the filter of a cigarette butt.

"Hasn't been there very long," Liddell said.

Jack and Liddell got down on hands and knees and ran their hands through the grass. They found five more butts, all the same brand, and an assortment of bullet casings, .22s, .45s, and .223s. The .22s were long-rifle shells and could be used in either a pistol or a rifle. The .45s were from a semiautomatic handgun. The .223s were from a rifle. He'd found exactly three of them. Varmint rifle or an assault rifle.

Jack took pictures with his iPhone and collected the butts and shell casings, putting them in the pockets of the work shirt he'd borrowed from Landry.

"Hey look," Liddell said. "Here's a business card." He read from an imaginary card, "Troup's Exterminators. We Kill Anything."

"Very funny, Bigfoot," Jack said and looked all around. "So how did the shooter get in here and out again without us seeing a vehicle?" And that raised another question. The shooter was standing back in the woods long enough to smoke a bunch of cigarettes. Did the shooter know the police wouldn't be coming and so didn't worry about the length of time? Or was the shooter a policeman?

Liddell pointed farther into the woods. "There's a dirt road back there a hundred yards or so. It runs parallel to the river. We have a fishing cabin back that direction."

"Fishing cabin?" Jack asked.

Liddell made a sweeping motion with his arm. "This was all crops at one time. Big Jim leased it out. Landry doesn't do that. He doesn't like having close neighbors, or people just coming onto the property."

"How much property does Landry have here?" Jack asked.

"Part of this is mine. Landry has the house and twelve acres. He takes care of the day-to-day business."

"What day-to-day business?" Jack asked.

"Blanchard Landing," Liddell said with a grin. "That's why there's a dirt road running behind the trees. It goes along the river about a mile or so and ends at the fishing camp. We have a cabin there."

"So you're a land baron?"

"It's no big deal," Liddell said. "Two or three shanties and a cabin. A little boat ramp. Cleaning station to dress the fish. He rents the spots out by the week."

"And that's why he doesn't lease out the land to farmers?"

"Yeah, part of the reason," Liddell said. "He's had offers to buy all this, but we won't sell. It's been in the Blanchard family for several generations."

Jack said, "You never answered my question back there. How much property do you two have here?"

"We have three sections now. This part along the river and a couple of sections that was cotton. In the old days, Blanchards owned twelve sections."

"Pretend I don't know shit about land and tell me how many acres that is?"

Liddell laughed. "I finally found something that Jack Murphy isn't an expert on."

"Yeah, well there weren't many farmers in my ancestry. Mostly horse thieves, murderers, and cops. Sometimes all three at once."

"A section is one square mile," Liddell said.

"You own three square miles!"

Liddell said, "Yeah. Someday I hope to have children, you know? I'll have something to pass on to them."

"That would be something, wouldn't it," Jack said, and again imagined a baby Bigfoot. A boy. Definitely a boy. Covered in hair. Eating an elk.

Landry was waiting on the porch when they got back. "Find anything?"

"Yeah," Jack said and they went back inside. "I need some sandwich bags if you have any."

Landry dug in a cabinet drawer and set some on the table. Jack dumped his pocket onto the table and took his knife out again. He put each shell casing in its own bag, knowing that it was probably too late to be cautious. *Better late than never.*

Landry picked up one of the bags and examined the shells. "Two-twenty-threes," he said.

Liddell said, "It's still early, so we're going to see Dusty Parnell. You going to be okay here?"

Landry tilted his head. "Do I look like I can't take care of myself?"

"I was just being polite, you jerk," Liddell said.

"Asshole," Landry jabbed back.

"Give me the keys," Jack said and off they went.

Chapter Twenty-five

They had decided not to call Dusty before coming out. If she wasn't home they'd track her down. Sheriff Guidry had told them that Dusty had taken the morning off. Jack pulled into the circle drive in front of the house and he could see movement on the side of the house nearest the carport.

"C'mon, Bigfoot. Someone's over there." Jack said and hurried to the house with Liddell close behind.

He saw someone wearing all black running from the back of the house. Jack drew his weapon and pushed up against the house, peeking around the corner. No one was there, but he knew he'd seen someone. He called out in a loud voice, "Police. Come out with empty hands," and remembered he wasn't the police here. But he sure as hell wasn't going to be shot either.

Liddell moved up close to him, also hugging the wall. "What is it?"

"I'm not sure. Someone darted toward the carport when we pulled up. I don't think it's Parnell. They were wearing black."

"I'll go around the other side," Liddell said and moved off.

Jack felt uneasy about this. What if she had a gardener? Or a visitor? He yelled, "Detective Parnell. It's Liddell and Jack Murphy. Say something." Nothing. He gripped the .45 and eased around the corner. To reach the carport he would have to expose himself, but there was no going back.

He made it to the carport when he heard an engine roar to life in the woods behind the house. The engine wound up, and Jack ran to the far side of the carport just in time to see someone in black clothes and a black helmet heading away fast.

"They're getting away," he yelled.

"Who's getting away?"

Jack turned to find Dusty Parnell standing in her doorway in full uniform. The motorcycle engine was already a distant sound. Dusty's motorcycle and both dirt bikes were parked under the carport.

"Someone was messing around out here when we pulled up," Jack said, feeling a little foolish. "We thought they were trying to steal your bikes," he lied.

"My nephew just left on his dirt bike. My brother lives on the other side of the lake. Do you want me to call him back over here so you can interrogate him?" She pointed at the gun in Jack's hand and said, "You must have scared him to death. Put that away."

Jack slipped the .45 back into his holster.

Liddell came running up. "What's going on?"

"Ask the gunslinger," Dusty said and smirked. "Coffee?" She walked into the house and left the door open for them.

Jack and Liddell followed after her. It was in the nineties outside, and her air-conditioning was running full bore.

Dusty said, "Leave the door open. My nephew is a pothead and he stinks the place up." She held her hands up and joked, "It's not my weed, officer. I'm holding it for a friend." It was a universal joke among cops. When someone was caught with pot, they always said it belonged to someone else.

Jack and Liddell stood at the kitchen table and waited while she heated coffee on the stove.

"If you were trying to surprise me, you should try being quieter next time. I heard you coming down the gravel."

Jack hated to admit it, but he'd been the one caught off-guard. "We should have called," he said, and it sounded lame even to him.

She poured hot water into a couple of mugs and set the instant freeze-dried stuff on the table with spoons.

"Thanks," Jack said, even though he was already up to his eyes in coffee.

She handed a mug to Liddell and said, "Living room, kitchen, or am I summoned to the sheriff's office?"

Her smart-ass remarks were getting under his skin. "The table here is fine," he said. "Let's start with you telling us the truth." He and Liddell took seats but she stood, arms across her chest, giving him a look that said, "I don't have to tell you shit."

Jack waited her out, and she let out a loud sigh and sat down. "Thanks for getting me in trouble," she said.

Jack shot back, "We didn't talk to him. He must have guessed. He must know you better than you think."

She twisted her coffee mug in a slow circular motion on the table, looking down, which was never a good sign. Just her eyes lifted, and she said, "Bitty was seeing someone else."

"That's what you were fighting about?" Liddell asked.

She stared at her coffee. "She was seeing another cop." Her jaw set, and she shifted in her chair. "This is severely screwed up, ain't it?"

"So Bitty was seeing another woman?" Jack asked.

Dusty's face came up and she said with a sarcastic smile, "Did I say it was a woman?"

"Are you saying Bitty was bisexual?" Liddell asked. "We were partners a long time. I would have known."

Dusty gave a dry laugh and said, "Well, you're not a very good detective, are you? But I guess you're not alone. She had me fooled too."

"Who was it? Who was Bitty seeing?" Jack asked. He didn't know if he was buying all of this, but if she'd thought this up out of the blue, it was a doozy.

What she told them was even more of a doozy.

Liddell leaned forward, big hands gripping the table edge. "She was dating Barbie? Barbie?"

Dusty didn't take her eyes off Liddell. She didn't elaborate. She didn't say anything.

"I'm asking you how you know she was seeing Barbie. Simple question, Dusty," Liddell said.

"Oh. I didn't know that was a question. Yes. She was seeing Barbie. It'd been going on for a couple of months. We—she and I— were talking about getting back together. We used to live together at one time. But after we broke up, I moved into this place. I'm rattling around in here all by my lonesome.

"When she told me she wanted to move in here with me, I believed her. And the whole time she's cheating on me with that piece of shit Barbie. And before you ask, the answer is yes. She told me. But she told me after I put all the pieces together."

"What pieces are those?" Jack asked.

Dusty took a breath. "Pieces. Stuff like Barbie always hanging around the station talking to her. Or sitting in her car in the parking lot. They'd *run into each other* when we were out together," she said sarcastically and held fingers up on each hand making quotation marks in the air. "Oh, please! Like I'm that stupid.

"They would sit in Barbie's car, giggling like schoolgirls. I asked her what that was all about and she told me to mind to my own business. I never saw Barbie with a woman and so I wondered if he was . . . you know. So anyway, I asked her point-blank if they were doing it. She didn't answer that question. I mean, if they weren't doing anything why wouldn't she deny it? So I took her to Nottoway thinking she'd open up. I didn't want us to end. But when we were at Nottoway, I got mad and accused her of dating Barbie behind my back and she admitted it. She laughed in my face and said she left me because I bored her to tears."

Dusty went to the sink and stood with her back to them. She said, "So, that's what I didn't tell you about. I lied about a stupid argument with the only woman I'll ever love." She wrapped her arms around her front and stood that way for what seemed like a long time.

Jack thought she might be crying or trying to make herself cry. So far she'd done nothing but lie.

She said, "I never even got to say good-bye. All I'll remember is how mean I was to her. How . . . boring." Her shoulders shuddered and the tears came.

Jack didn't have the reaction to this that Dusty may have hoped. He'd seen women—and men—cry as a way of deflecting suspicion. Most innocent people were in shock at someone's death. They were unable to cry. Or they would break down and need to sit or be comforted. Dusty fell in the category of liars. He was sure this was an act, and looking at the expression on Liddell's face, his partner thought so too. Murphy rule number one for dealing with crying liars: *Let them cry until they can't keep it up. The next thing they say or do is the closest they will come to being honest.*

While she was still going at it, Jack thought about the possibilities this raised. If Dusty was even being truthful about Bitty dating Barbie, it changed everything. Maybe Barbie set all of this up. It would explain how Barbie found out that Liddell was coming to town to see Bitty. It might have been Barbie who left the note at Landry's. Barbie might have killed her, knowing Liddell was coming. But was Barbie shrewd enough to get Troup involved? Was he playing Troup? From what Liddell and others said, Barbie was just a step above an idiot. Was Barbie set up for Cotton's murder? By whom? Dusty? If so, was she strong enough to haul Barbie's weight that high off the floor with a rope? She appeared to be strong, but not strong enough to lift that much deadweight. Not by herself anyway.

Dusty lasted longer than most. The tears turned to sniffles, and she splashed cold water on her face before she turned around. The tears looked real, but Jack had learned to do that trick himself. It helped sometimes when you wanted to make your suspect feel remorseful enough to admit the truth. He'd learned it from girls he'd dated who could cry at the drop of a hat.

Jack's expression was unreadable as he asked her to sit down. She did. He said, "I'm going to ask you this one more time." He let that sink in. "If you lie, or don't answer, I *will* go to Sheriff Guidry and he'll have your . . ." He had been going to say "balls." "You'll be on his shit list forever."

She sat up straight and said, "Shoot."

Looking a person in the eyes was supposed to be an indicator of truthfulness. But she knew this.

Jack asked, "How did you know we were at the Nottoway before we came to see you yesterday?" All he wanted was one honest answer; something to judge all the rest of her crap against.

She laughed and said, "Is that it? That's your big question?" She leaned forward for emphasis like a good interrogator. "It's simple, Einstein. I was out that way and saw you guys pull in there. And I know David Reyes. I'll bet he couldn't wait to gossip about me. I don't have dash-cam video to prove that, so you'll have to take my word."

"One more question," Jack said.

She sat back and waited. She was good at this. In fact, she seemed to think she was on the moral high ground. She was the one being wronged by everyone. That, or she had convinced herself of her virtue enough to take on the role of victim.

"Where were you last night?" he asked.

The question took her by surprise. Her jaw almost came unhinged, and she drew in a deep breath and let it out. "You're not going to pin that shit on me!" she said. "I'll let the proper authorities search my house. Hell, they can search anything they want, and they won't find a damn thing."

"What are we trying to pin on you, Dusty?" Jack asked.

"You can play dumb all you want. I heard the run come out last night. Rahm was dispatched to a 'shots fired' at Landry's house. He told the dispatcher that bullets had hit the house, but he put it down to someone shooting along the river and didn't know the house was up there. If you think I had something to do with it, you can go piss up a rope. You have no authority here."

She jabbed her finger in Liddell's direction. "And you. You're something else. You come here like you're my friend, one of us, but you think we're hicks and that you're some big-shot cop. And I'll tell you something else. And this goes for both of you. No one wants you here. No one appreciates you asking questions and sticking your noses into things that are none of your business. I have half a mind to sue the Sheriff for sexual harassment. Maybe I'll sue your asses. Your department too."

Jack wasn't deterred by the threat of a lawsuit. "You're deflecting my question by using anger. That's Detective 101 stuff. Tell us the truth for once. The truth will set you free."

Jack turned onto Highway 1 in the direction of Plaquemine. Dusty had responded to his last remark by throwing them out of her house. He wanted to think that her demeanor made her look guilty, but in truth, if someone from another state came to his house and accused him of a crime the accuser wouldn't have lasted as long as Jack did.

This case needed all of his skill and resources, but he didn't know his way around, was unfamiliar with Louisiana law, and couldn't use their crime scene people. Except for Kurtis and Jon Dempsey, he and Liddell were getting the runaround.

Maybe Dusty was right about the other cops not wanting them messing around in this case. Maybe some of them believed Liddell had something to do with all of this, or was the killer. Maybe some of them just felt like Jack and Liddell had brought a curse down on their heads. He tried to imagine what he would feel like if the situation were reversed, but that didn't work because he couldn't think like these people.

"Do you believe Dusty? I mean about Bitty and Barbie?" Liddell asked for the third time in as many minutes.

Jack hadn't answered because he was thinking. Liddell had been Bitty's partner. Partners knew more about each other than their wives or best friends. But he hadn't known that Liddell was a land baron or that he owned a fishing camp. And it still pissed him off a little that Liddell had never invited him down here to fish the Mississippi. But something about Dusty didn't seem right. Maybe it was because she was always threatening them. Or maybe it was because she always had a pat answer for everything, or if she didn't, she would make threats. And Dusty was a bitch.

"I think Dusty was right about one thing, Bigfoot. She has half a mind."

"Sheriff's Department next?" Liddell asked.

"Yeah. I think we need to see what Bitty was working on. And what Dusty is hiding. Maybe there's something on their computers or in a file. While we're at it, we might want to see if Dempsey can dig into what Barbie was doing in that part of town." He wouldn't have to get a search warrant to go through the computers on Dusty's or Bitty's desk because they were the property of the Sheriff's Department. All he would need is permission from Guidry.

Liddell said, "I don't know. Dempsey is already sticking his neck out. Maybe the Sheriff can do some digging for us."

"I just had a thought. Why haven't the Feds been called?" Jack asked.

"We don't want that. Do we?"

"No. We don't. But they have almost unlimited access to labs and other things the PD doesn't. Maybe they should be informed. If nothing else, it would light a fire under the Chief."

They both knew that if the FBI got involved it would pretty much end any cooperation Whiteside might show them. But they also knew that someone had to trump Troup's hold on the Chief. Troup had pretty much kept his distance from them since this began, and had a tight grip on any case information.

"If I was Troup, I would be all over us," Jack said. "He hasn't even tried to talk to us. Except for trying to intimidate us. What's he playing at?"

Liddell tapped Jack on the arm. "Look over there."

They were just coming into Plaquemine and saw the Dodge Challenger parked in a no-parking zone. Troup stood in the street and flagged them down.

Liddell said, "Speak of the devil," and Jack pulled to the curb behind Troup's car.

Troup was wearing the exact same outfit he'd had on the first time Jack had seen him. He resembled a mortician, or a walking corpse, with a cigarette dangling from his thin lips.

Troup walked to Jack's window and sucked down half of the cigarette before he leaned down. "What do you two think you're doing?" he asked.

Jack smiled. "You do realize those things will kill you."

"Nothing can kill me," Troup said. "You two, however . . ." he trailed off without finishing.

Jack said, "If you don't have anything constructive to say I'm going to drive off and get back to pissing you off."

Troup stubbed the cigarette out on Jack's door and flicked the butt into the street. The entire time his eyes were on Jack. It was a challenge from a crazy man.

"Has anyone ever accused you of being too negative? You should look on the positive side. When we solve these murders, you'll have time to pick out different color suits. Maybe go to a gym."

Troup sucked his front teeth and grinned. "I got two words for you, *detectives*. Kurtis Dempsey."

Jack drove past Troup, being careful not to touch him with the car and giving him cause to arrest him for assault on a police officer.

Chapter Twenty-six

Jack parked in a visitor parking spot outside the Sheriff's Office. Jon Dempsey met them at the door and led them down a hallway to an interview room with a brown door placard that said, IN USE.

"He's in there," Jon said, and left them.

Liddell opened the door and they went inside. Kurtis Dempsey sat in a corner away from the door, hands fidgeting with a stack of papers in his lap. Sheriff Guidry sat at the interview table, head down over some paperwork. "What kept you?"

There were two empty seats at the table and they took them. Jack said, "Sorry. We didn't know you were expecting us."

Guidry yelled, "Dempsey!"

Kurtis's head shot up and the papers in his lap tumbled to the floor.

"I meant the other Dempsey," Guidry said.

"Sorry," Kurtis said and gathered the papers. He put them back into some semblance of order and sat down again.

The door opened and Jon Dempsey stuck his head in. "Sheriff."

"I told you I wanted to talk to these guys an hour ago," Guidry said.

"Yes, sir," Jon said. "But you told me never mind. You said you'd call them yourself."

"I did?"

"Yes sir."

Guidry pretended to study the papers again. "That's all. They're here now, aren't they?"

"Yes, sir. I'll be just outside if you need me," Jon said, and shut the door to the room.

The Sheriff read through the paperwork while the others waited. No one wanted to speak first. Sheriff Guidry turned the last page facedown on the table and drew a deep breath in through his nose before looking up.

"Do you gentlemen know what the term FUBAR means?" he asked, with a deliberate smile.

They waited again.

"Well, that's what this is now. Fucked up beyond all recognition. A circle jerk without a pivot man," Guidry said, and he was on a roll using an array of colloquial terminology commonly used by military and police personnel to describe a screwed-up situation.

When Guidry was finished with his colorful dissertation of what had happened to the investigation, Jack addressed Kurtis. "We just saw Bobby Troup." Jack didn't think the young man's complexion could get any paler, but it did.

"I got caught," Kurtis said.

Guidry said, "Of course he got caught. You sent this kid in to do your snooping, and now he's going to lose his job." Kurtis flinched at the mention of losing his job. "Hell, I'd fire him if he worked for me. But he don't."

Jack had had enough of Guidry's sharp tongue. "If you want to take your anger out on me, do so. But if you say another word to this policeman, I'll punch you in the face." Jack hated to see someone berated by everyone. It was possible that Troup had caught Kurtis looking into things for them. Troup wanted them to think Kurtis had been busted, was selling them out.

Guidry's mouth snapped shut, and Jack could see color creeping into his cheeks.

"I apologize, Sheriff Guidry," Jack said. "It's been a stressful day, and I don't think this is the time for us to argue amongst ourselves. Or worry about what other agencies are or are not doing. Someone is killing policemen. Liddell and I are doing what we can to find them. And Kurtis here offered to help even though he knew it was a risk. If Whiteside doesn't recognize a good officer, that's her problem."

Kurtis shot Jack a grateful look, but his hands were still clenched on the stack of papers.

Guidry seemed to calm down. He said, "Sorry if I was insensitive. I'm just mad about my detective's death. And I guess I'm worried about this kid here too. No one wants to see a kid run into the street and get hit by a Mack truck."

Kurtis said glumly, "I'm going to be suspended pending a review by the City Safety Board. Chief Whiteside is the head of the Safety Board, so it's going to happen. But I'll do what I can to help you guys until that happens."

Guidry said, "If that bitch fires you, I'll give you a job here. I can see why Barbie would hang himself."

Jack said, "Speaking of hanging. We don't think Officer Barbierre's death was a suicide."

Guidry's eyebrows rose.

Jack described what he knew about Cotton Walters's murder, and Barbie's hanging. He told Guidry about their talks with Detective Parnell. He ended with Troup flagging them down and making unveiled threats.

Guidry's range of expressions changed like a Rubik's Cube, but settled on a wicked grin at the mention of Bobby Troup.

Jack asked, "Did I say something funny?"

"You boys don't worry yourselves about Troup. I got something for him."

Liddell asked straight-faced, "Does it involve two alligators, a rope, and a concrete block walking into a bar?" Even nervous Kurtis had to smile.

Guidry slapped a hand on the table and said, "By God, you're a hoot, Blanchard. Ain't he a hoot? You should come back and work for me."

Before Liddell could jump ship, Jack asked, "I take it you have something for us, and that's why you called?"

"You go first, young man," Guidry said to Kurtis. "I mean Officer Dempsey," he added, and shot a look at Jack.

Kurtis stood and approached the table. "If I may," he said and laid the thick stack of papers on the table. "This is what I could find for you." He ruffled the papers with a thumb, stopping periodically to tell them what he had in the pile.

When he was done, Jack was thinking that if PPD fired Kurtis he'd try to get the Evansville Police Department to recruit him. Kurtis and Sergeant Walker working together would kick some crime scene butt.

Kurtis had brought printouts of dispatch logs—calls for service—covering the last two months. The majority of Barbie's police activities were self-initiated, meaning Barbie had called dispatch to report things like traffic stops, checking a suspicious person, or finding lost property, etc.

Liddell flipped through the pages and asked Kurtis, "Are there pages missing?"

"No sir," Kurtis said.

"What is it, Bigfoot?" Jack asked.

Liddell handed the sheets to Jack and said, "There's no dispatch record of Barbie being sent to Bitty's. He didn't tell dispatch he was out of the car there, or that he was bringing in a prisoner."

Jack flipped the pages of the log. "There doesn't seem to be any time missing." The dispatch log notation that Liddell was talking about was for *Edward-54*. Jack assumed that was Barbie's radio number. Barbie had said, "*I'll be 10-19 with one prisoner for lockup.*" That was at o-seven-o-three hours, and it gave an arrival time of about twenty minutes later.

Jack laid the log sheets back on the table. "I see where Crime Scene was requested to go to Bitty's address, but I don't see where a detective was dispatched. How did Troup get there?"

Kurtis raised his shoulders and said, "Those are the logs I got from dispatch. Maybe Barbie just happened to be around there. He and Troup are tight. He might have called Troup on the cell phone."

Liddell spoke up. "Barbie works the east side of town, doesn't he?" Bitty's was on the west side.

Kurtis offered, "Barbie didn't particularly pay attention to sectors. That's why we called him Robocop."

Jack perused the log. Barbie showed no activity both before and after locking Liddell up. Nothing. Jack flipped to the date and time Troup and Barbie had stopped them the night Liddell was released. Nothing. Barbie hadn't let dispatch know he was out of the car where his body was found. Jack wanted to question Officer Rahm as to why he had begun his search for Barbie in that particular neighborhood, but that kind of question would stir up more shit.

Kurtis had also checked the soil and fiber material.

"I took it to LSU. That's Louisiana State University," Kurtis said for Jack's sake. "The white stuff in the dirt is sulfometuron methyl. It's an herbicide, but it also makes the plants mature and ripen faster."

"What kind of plants?" Jack asked.

"He's talking about sugarcane, pod'na," Liddell said.

"The fiber and dirt is stuff you'll find just about everywhere on farmland."

Jack asked, "Can you pinpoint where any of this came from?"

Kurtis glared at him as if he hadn't been listening. "That's what I'm telling you," he said. "Most of it is crop dusted in early August. But this was applied as a liquid."

"How does that help us, Kurtis?" Jack asked.

Guidry spoke up. "It means we can narrow down where these chemicals were bought, when, and by who. If we know who, it might point to one particular area."

Kurtis said, "That is correct, but we have the problem of who had this stuff on their boots. I checked Officer Barbierre's boots and they had mud from outside the house and other grit. But Barbierre's boots didn't drag this chemical inside."

"Too bad we can't check Parnell's boots," Liddell said. "She was wearing an identical brand of boot to Barbie's when we spoke to her this morning. In fact, she has sugarcane growing on her property."

"Half the officers in the Parish wear the same brand boot. Either Browning or Wolverine," Guidry said. "I don't mean to rain on your parade, but have you noticed what's grown around here?"

Kurtis perked up. "But if we can narrow it down to one or two plantations and cross-reference that with runs made by officers, we can at least get a list of suspects." To the Sheriff, he said, "That is, if you guys still think the killer might be law enforcement."

Guidry said, "It's a start, Kurtis. Good thinking. Get with your brother and see what you guys can come up with."

Jack was going to ask about the boot print found on Bitty's back door, but Kurtis hadn't worked that scene and hadn't brought it up, so he wouldn't have that information. And now they couldn't get it. "Before we get ahead of ourselves, I have another question for Kurtis," Jack said.

"I didn't forget, Detective Murphy. I have a friend at the State Lab who's working on the hair evidence you gave me. He'll do it on the QT unless the shit hits the fan. If that happens he said he'll throw me under the bus like any good friend would do."

Guidry's hands bunched and un-bunched. "The head of the State Lab is awful friendly with Chief Whiteside. Maybe some distant relative."

That reminded Jack of a not-quite-politically-correct joke he'd heard around the police station. *If you get divorced in Kentucky, are you still brother and sister?* Of course Kentucky could be replaced by any state in the South if you lived in the North.

Liddell said, "Speaking of relatives, Sheriff, can you find out if Dusty has a relative living across the lake from her house?"

"I'll ask Jon to look," Kurtis offered and left the room.

Guidry's eyebrows rose. "Important?"

"Just a question," Liddell said.

Jon Dempsey came back with Kurtis. Jon said, "One of you asked if Detective Parnell has a relative across the lake from her residence, but she doesn't have any family. She has no siblings, and her mother and father are both deceased. If one of her parents was married before and she has stepsiblings, it isn't in her personnel files. I can try to find out if it's important."

"So, she lied again," Jack said.

Liddell explained, "Someone took off through the back on a dirt bike when we got to Dusty's this morning. She said it was her nephew that lived across the lake."

Guidry said, "Damned woman. I won't tolerate liars. I told her that."

To Jon Dempsey, he said, "Get Parnell in here. And I mean *right now.* And this time if I tell you that I'll do it—ignore me."

Jon left and Kurtis took a seat.

"Any idea who we might've seen leaving her house?" Jack asked Guidry.

"Not a damn clue," Guidry said. "Maybe it was a girlfriend."

"Would she have lied to us about that?" Jack asked. "She told us she's a lesbian. Why hide?"

"Damned if I know. It seems I don't know Detective Parnell quite as well as I thought I did. I can tell you this though. This shit is going to come to an end." Guidry had made a fist on top of the table and spread the fingers, placing the palm down. "I'll squash her like a bug. The truth will set you free," he said and snorted. "Well, dishonesty will get you fired."

Jon came back, knocked, and stuck his head in the door. "She's not answering her phone, Sheriff Guidry."

"Try the damn radio," Guidry said.

"She's not answering her radio either, Sheriff. Dispatch has been trying to reach her. They have a missing person. She's not responding."

Guidry slammed a hand on the table. "Well shit fire and save the matches!"

Before Jack and Liddell left they asked Sheriff Guidry for permission to go through Bitty's desk and locker and computer. Guidry added Dusty's things to that and told Jon to get them anything they asked for.

Jack was going through desk drawers while Liddell tried to get into Bitty's computer.

"Password protected," Liddell said. Jon shrugged.

"Call Angelina," Jack suggested.

Liddell called Angelina and she walked him through it, but each folder was encrypted. She walked him through the process of sending it all to her. When the files were on their way, Angelina said, "I'm sorry about your friend. I didn't get to ask before, but how are you doing?"

"I'm fine, Angelina. Just fine. Never better."

"Liar," she said. "What's it like being back home?"

"Well, I've been arrested, abused, Tasered, and shot at and threatened by the police. I'd say it's been a full experience," he said half-jokingly. "To be honest, I think I've missed it here and missed my brother. But with all that's going on I haven't had time to take it all in. A lot has changed."

"Tasered? Shot at?"

"It's a long story," he said. "On top of this, my fourteen-year-old niece is missing. I think the reason I'm not in jail is everyone is afraid of Jack. He's like Superman."

"Bullets bounce off him," she said.

"Kryptonite fears him."

"And he'd like you to get back to work," Jack said in the background.

"Let me talk to him," Angelina said, and Liddell handed Jack the phone.

Jack took the phone. "He doesn't need any encouragement, Angelina."

"I just wanted to tell you some of the stuff I found," she said.

Jack had known Angelina long enough to tell when something was bothering her. He hoped there wasn't trouble in paradise. Maybe she was arguing with the soon-to-be hubby? If something was wrong, she'd tell him when she was ready.

Jack said, "Let me get a piece of paper. My memory is not getting better with age."

That got a chuckle out of her. "Yeah. You talk like you're an old-timer but you have a mind like a computer, Jack. You just don't know how to operate it."

Now it was his turn to laugh. She was happy, so whatever was bugging her wasn't too bad.

He took out his notebook and pen. "Go," he said, and she did.

Chapter Twenty-seven

The Crown Vic hurtled down Highway 1. Liddell had a hand on the dash and one gripping the armrest. "I never thought I'd say this, but slow the hell down, pod'na."

Jack could feel adrenaline pumping through his body. His heart beat a steady rhythm, but his hands and arms felt like they could crush a rock. Nevertheless, he forced himself to ease up on the gas. He was down to twenty above the posted speed limit when a Sheriff's SUV hurtled past them.

"Guidry?" Jack asked. They had come by so fast he hadn't seen who was driving.

"Who else?" Liddell answered. "You might as well catch up to him. The state he's in, he'll kick her door down and screw all this up." He tried to imitate Guidry's voice and said, "Shit fire and save the matches, fellas."

Jack had been thinking about doing the same thing at Dusty's place. He knew in his cop's mind that Liddell was right. Still, the adrenaline rush was intoxicating. Addictive. And he knew he'd never quit this job. Never be anything else. He loved Katie, and he knew she worried, but this is what he was born for. Bigfoot too.

Jack had a more sobering thought. He had made a solemn promise to both women that he would keep Liddell out of danger. But nothing about any of this was safe, smooth sailing, easy peasy. But he'd promised.

Screw that. He stomped the gas and caught up with Guidry as the SUV turned onto Dusty's road. Jack wouldn't want to be in Dusty's shoes when Guidry caught up with her. There wouldn't be enough left to put in jail.

He hoped Guidry wouldn't go charging in and give the store

away. He still needed some answers and didn't think they had enough to make an arrest. Not yet. On the other hand, if they didn't do something and another murder occurred it would be on them.

"Remind me, Bigfoot. Dusty told us she and Bitty were planning to move into Dusty's house, right?"

"Yep," Liddell said.

"And she couldn't have a nephew, right?"

"Yep."

"Angelina told me that Dusty's house and land were up for sale months back, so she lied about them moving in together," Jack said. "How could she be stupid enough to think we'd never find out? And don't just say 'Yep' again. Help me out here."

"Do you make Dusty for all of this?" Liddell asked.

"Well, according to her she was mad at Bitty for two-timing her. We've seen people murdered for less."

Liddell agreed. It was a fact. "What else did Angelina say?"

Jack went on autopilot as he drove and related to Liddell the information Angelina had gathered on Barbierre, Troup, Dusty, and Bitty. She was unable to locate anything on Chief Anna Whiteside.

Barbierre was ex-military, but his MOS—method of service— was a clerk typist. He got an honorable discharge and went to work at a string of private security jobs. At different times he was a bank guard, bouncer, garbage collector, back to bouncer, and on to Plaquemine PD. He had two thousand three hundred and thirteen dollars in the bank, and there were no suspicious deposits or withdrawals. He was just what he appeared to be. A brownnose that liked to carry a gun. Not to mention a Taser cowboy.

Barbie had opportunity and willingness to kill Bitty and Cotton, but being willing to kill and pulling the trigger were two different things. Barbie was sadistic and a number-one A-hole, but Jack figured him more of a braggart and sadist than a killer. Barbie's motive to have done these killings would be his desire to gain Troup's approval.

On to Bobby Troup. Angelina told him pretty much what he already knew about Bobby Troup. Troup worked for the New Orleans PD for a year before coming to work for the Iberville Parish Sheriff. She found some newspaper articles about his being brought before the grand jury for the killing of the bookie. The Grand Jury returned a No Bill, which meant they didn't recommend charges be filed. The District Attorney didn't file charges, and Troup walked. However, the old Sheriff fired him. There was no mention of Liddell or Bitty in any of the news articles. Troup dropped from sight, literally. Angelina checked Social Security records and there was nothing to indicate employment. Six months ago he went to work for the Plaquemine PD.

Troup would have had the opportunity to kill Bitty and Cotton and hang Barbie, making it look like a suicide. Liddell said Bobby Troup had killed a bookie and involved his old partner, Doyle Doohan, in a cover-up. Troup and Doyle were fired and disgraced. So Troup had a motive. He wanted to get revenge on Bitty and Liddell. Cotton may have been collateral damage. Troup didn't know what Cotton had told them when they visited. Cotton thought he'd seen a car setting on the road, watching the house while they talked. Of course, Cotton was paranoid, so there may not have been a car. But why would Troup want Barbie dead? If Barbie was involved in Troup's trying to pin Bitty's murder on Liddell, Troup might be tying up a loose end. Or maybe Barbie was pressuring Troup to get him a detective position. Bitty's and Cotton's murders were connected. Jack could feel it in his gut. And it was somehow tied to Evie's disappearance. Landry said she hadn't run away. He believed Landry. Parnell had said Bitty hadn't talked to her about any missing children. Parnell was a known liar.

Angelina told him about Dusty last, but what she found was quite interesting. Dusty left home when she was sixteen and used an assumed name to join the Navy. Angelina had contacts in unusual places. A case they'd worked a while back required some sealed military records and Angelina had a friend who was a programmer for the Department of Defense. This time she had called an Army recruiter friend who owed her a favor. She had run all the above past him and he came up with the tidbit about Dusty joining the Navy under an assumed name. She hadn't known that was even possible—neither had Jack—but according to Angelina's friend it's not unheard of. The name that Dusty used was Jane Smith. Very original. Hard to track.

Angelina said she'd found nothing on Jane Smith except for her separation from the Navy ten years ago. That coincided with Dusty joining up with the Iberville Parish Sheriff's Department, now using her real name, Dusty Parnell. But Angelina had a thought and

Googled Dusty Parnell's address and found an online real estate posting by Jane Smith. The property was up for sale by owner. Jane Smith.

Like Troup, Dusty had the opportunity to kill Bitty, Cotton, and Barbie. She had the best and oldest motive in the world, jealousy. There is an old saying, "Hell hath no fury like a woman scorned." Dusty seemed angry enough that Bitty was cheating on her with Barbie that she would have reason to kill them both. And now, Angelina said Dusty had her house and property for sale long before she and Bitty broke up. It was still listed for sale under the assumed name of Jane Smith. So she had lied about her and Bitty's plans of getting back together and living in Dusty's house.

Coupled with Dusty's other lies, it was enough to bring her in for some serious questioning, and Jack needed Sheriff Guidry for that task. He didn't want to zero in on Dusty, but unfortunately three of the people he'd like to talk to were dead.

He didn't know how the Sheriff had been able to obtain a search warrant for Dusty's house, but he wasn't going to look a gift horse in the mouth. Guidry hadn't told anyone about the warrant to avoid anyone calling Dusty, but Jon had typed up the Affidavit of Probable Cause to obtain the warrant, so it was probably a safe bet that Kurtis knew about it as well.

Jack hadn't been given a copy of the search warrant and didn't know the particulars of what they were searching for, but he knew he would be looking for a machete and a .223 rifle.

They had turned down the gravel road leading to Dusty's when the Sheriff braked hard, his arm came out of the window, the hand pointing over the hood in the direction of thick black smoke roiling into the air.

Chapter Twenty-eight

Sheriff Guidry pulled off the road well back from Dusty's house and Jack pulled in behind him. They got out of the vehicles and stood watching as flames shot into the air and sirens wailed in the distance. The three men walked down the drive to get as close as the heat would allow. A SUV was burning so intensely it scorched the vegetation that grew within fifty feet around it. Flames shot out of the house windows, and the roof was smoking, ready to go. Jack tried to move to a place where he could see the carport side of the house, but the heat was too intense. There was no activity near the house, and there wouldn't be with such a fire. He approached Sheriff Guidry and was forced to hold up an arm to shield his face from the extreme heat.

"Can you find out who called this in?" Jack asked him.

Guidry seemed frozen to the spot, and Jack had to repeat himself before the Sheriff got on his portable radio and asked dispatch for the information. Dispatch said something, but Jack couldn't hear it over the roar.

Guidry said, "It came from a cell number. Dispatch is trying to trace the number but so far no luck."

"They didn't give a name?" Jack asked.

"I would've told you if they did," Guidry said. He walked back to his SUV with Jack and Liddell in tow. Guidry watched the road. "Damn it all. What the hell is holding up the fire department?"

Jack empathized with the Sheriff. Dusty's house would be a total loss and anything of value inside would be gone. House fires can reach eleven to twelve hundred degrees, depending on the material and the cause of the fire. Steel melts or deforms at about eight hundred degrees. If Dusty had a gun safe that was rated for temperatures reaching seventeen hundred degrees, there would still be a chance that if the fire burned long enough and hot enough, it wouldn't survive. So much for the .223 rifle or the machete. Even if they found one or both, the fire had erased any evidentiary value.

A pumper and two engines passed them on the lane, braving the heat. Jack watched the firemen drop off the trucks and go to work putting on equipment and laying out hose. He was just thinking that one pumper truck wasn't going to get the job done, as a second engine drove through the cane field, skirting the house, heading toward the lake. That they were attacking the flames from two sides would help contain it, maybe keep it from causing a wildfire.

Jack approached the Sheriff again. "Sheriff Guidry, can you have someone check Dusty's phone records? I take it her issued cell phone records would be accessible by one of your people without a warrant?"

"Damn it all," Guidry said. "I should have done that already. Give me a second." He got on his cell phone and talked to someone, hung up, and said, "She hasn't used it for a while. My detective said no calls have been made from it for several weeks. She's received a bunch of calls, but most of them were from dispatch. A couple of calls were made to it from numbers that weren't from dispatch, but they were all under a minute long. We're trying to trace the callers now."

She was screening calls, answering the ones she had to, and maybe calling the others back from another phone.

"She must have another phone," Jack said. "One you don't know about."

"Yeah." Guidry said.

"There's nothing we can do here, Sheriff. I think we'll take off," Jack said, but if Guidry heard he didn't respond.

They got in the Crown Vic, and Liddell drove to the intersection and parked on the side of the road.

"This fire was pretty convenient," Liddell said.

He had given the .223 shells and a couple of cigarette butts they'd found that morning to Kurtis. The shell casings were of no value now unless they found a rifle somewhere else. Like in Troup's trunk. They weren't going to get a search warrant for Troup's car or home. Kurtis and Jon were going back to the woods across from Landry's house to search for evidence Jack or Liddell had missed.

Jack called Kurtis Dempsey's cell phone. "Found anything?"

Kurtis filled him in. "We've still got a bit to cover here, but so far we've found thirteen various shell casings, a folding knife, and some used condoms."

"And?"

"We found two more .223 brass casings that look pretty new. Tell Liddell his brother is out here with us. He's got good eyes."

Jack said, "I'll pass that on. How soon can you run a check on the .223s? Three of the casings should match the same gun. Those will be the shots that were fired at us."

"I can't send them to ballistics but Jon might be able to. He can put a rush on it if he uses the Sheriff's name," Kurtis said.

Jack had forgotten that Kurtis was on super-secret probation. What he was now doing, searching for evidence, could get him fired by Chief Whiteside.

"How long?" Jack asked again and could hear Kurtis let out a breath.

"No quicker than tomorrow," he said. "But . . ."

"But what?"

"Well. Me and Jon know a guy. He used to work for the lab. He's pretty sharp and he has some of his own equipment. He could give us a yes or no. It wouldn't hold up in a court of law, but . . ."

"Call him, and call me back," Jack said. "We're just leaving Dusty's house. No joy there. The house was on fire, and it doesn't look like we'll find anything useful."

"No shit!" Kurtis said, and Jack heard Kurtis passing this on to Jon and Jon saying "shit!"

"Call me when you find something," Jack said and disconnected. Jack said to Liddell, "They found two more .223 casings."

"They're going to find a bunch of shell casings down there. People plink along the river all the time, but not that close to Landry's. He's been known to return fire sometimes. Don't worry, he just shoots in the air."

Jack was angry that Officer Rahm hadn't conducted any kind of search. Rahm was probably a good officer but low morale was like a virus.

"The Sheriff will call us," Liddell said. "Let's go see where Barbie lived. Maybe his neighbors can tell us if he had a girlfriend."

Jack's phone rang. It was Sergeant Walker.

"Tony. Got anything for me?"

"I've gone through the pictures you sent of Bitty's house and the ones Officer Dempsey sent of the hanging scene. You're right about both of them, or at least that's my unofficial opinion. The blood patterns aren't consistent with what you would find if someone was hacked to death. But I can't be any more specific. Sorry.

"But the hanging wasn't a suicide. Unless this guy had arms six feet long, he couldn't have accomplished that. I couldn't be certain from looking at the photos, but it didn't look like he put up any struggle. Someone that hangs themselves will sometimes change their mind or go into survival mode at the last instant and grab at the rope. There will be some scratches on the neck around the rope, skin under the fingernails, that kind of thing. I don't know if they examined Barbie's fingernails, but I didn't see any evidence of him trying to get the rope loose. You might want to check toxicology on him."

Jack thought about that. "You think he was drugged?"

"I'm not there. You'll have to ask the Coroner," Walker said.

Jack thanked him and hung up. The phone rang in his hand. Jack answered, "Forget something, Tony?"

The line was silent for a beat, then Kurtis Dempsey said, "It's me. The guy I know is willing to look at the shell casings. Landry dug some of the bullets out of the house, so he can compare the shells to those. If you want him to take a look at the ballistics involving Cotton's or Bitty's murders, Troup has all that stuff."

"I don't know if a rifle was used on Bitty or Cotton," Jack said. "The Chief never told us what they have collected. She showed us Liddell's backup .45 and said it was found at Cotton's house," Jack said.

"Officer Barbierre was wearing a .45," Kurtis said. "I collected it, but it hadn't been fired. I'll take the bullets you found at Landry's to my guy. But I have to get to work before the Chief changes her mind."

"You're not suspended?" Jack was almost surprised. He thought it had been a done deal listening to Kurtis this morning.

"I got a call from the Chief after I talked to you. She wants me to come back to work."

"Good for you, Kurtis," Jack said. "Thanks for working on this and keeping it mum." He ended the call and was about to pocket the phone when it rang again. It was Angelina this time.

"I'm popular this morning," he said.

"What?"

"Never mind. Do you have something for us?"

"Yeah. You driving?" she asked.

Jack told her he wasn't.

"I tried to get something on Anna Karenina," she said.

"Anna Whiteside," Jack corrected her.

"Whatever," Angelina said. "The woman is a ghost. I thought I found something with New Orleans PD, but it wasn't her. Unless the woman you have there is seventy-two years old. I found birth records for an Anna Whiteside, age five when she died. What the hell have you gotten into?"

Jack wasn't sure. He said, "If I told you, I'd have to kill you," and that earned him a chuckle. "I've got another request. Can you get an address for Barbie?"

He heard her type, listened, and repeated the address back to her. Liddell said, "I know where that is."

Jack thanked Angelina and disconnected.

Barbie had lived in an upscale condo community just inside the city limits. A sign above the brick and stone entry declared LAFITTE ESTATES.

"I wouldn't want to be the people that live near the entrance to this place," Liddell said. "One way in and one way out, with maybe a hundred homes squeezed into a few square blocks. Traffic will be a bear getting out in the morning and coming back in the evening."

"Angelina said Barbie owns a charcoal-colored Dodge Challenger," Jack said but didn't see the Challenger on the street or in the driveway of Barbie's condo. "Just like Troup drives."

A coroner's seal was affixed to the door of Barbie's condo and yellow crime scene tape closed off the small porch.

"Barbie didn't die here. So why is his domicile off limits?" Liddell remarked.

"We shouldn't break a coroner's seal," Jack said. "But we can talk to the neighbors."

"And then we break in, right?" Liddell asked.

"What do you think I am, a burglar?"

"Yep," Liddell said.

They knocked on doors where cars were parked in the driveways, or where other neighbors thought someone might be home. No one had ever seen Barbie bring a woman home. In fact, they didn't think he liked women. Or at least that's what one single mother said. She was a knockout, and she said Barbie never even checked her out. Jack had replied, "He was a very eager policeman. It wasn't you, believe me." She had said, "Why, thank you," and smiled in such a way that Jack almost felt his face redden. Jack had said, "We're married." Liddell had chimed in, "But not to each other," and she giggled some more.

They learned one thing of interest, however. One of the residents had seen Barbie get into a Sheriff SUV late at night. It was about a week ago now, and they couldn't see who was driving.

"No one seems to know Barbie is dead," Liddell said.

"What the hell do they think the crime scene tape is for? Halloween?"

"In my neighborhood everyone knows everybody and every move you make," Liddell said.

"In my neighborhood everyone acts standoffish now that I'm back home with Katie," Jack remarked. "It's like they have taken sides. And a lot of them are families I've known since I was a child."

"You're still a child, pod'na. Have a backyard BBQ and invite the neighborhood. Hell, invite me."

Jack didn't care if the neighbors liked him or not. But he didn't like getting stared at by the old women, or *tsk*ed at by the old men. He sure as hell wasn't going to feed them.

They went back to their car. Jack said, "No point in going in his place. It's already been searched, so I'm betting anything we need has already been taken. The crime scene tape is just to let us know Troup was there."

They got back in their car, and Jack called Guidry while Liddell drove.

The phone was answered. "Guidry."

Jack asked, "Find anything, Sheriff?"

"They don't have the fire all put out yet. It may take a while to start going through the debris looking for a body."

Jack told Guidry about Kurtis being taken off suspension. He didn't tell him about Kurtis taking shell casings to an outside expert because doing so violated rules of evidence, and he didn't want to create problems for Kurtis in case he needed to take Guidry up on the job offer. What the Sheriff didn't know wouldn't come back to bite him during elections.

Guidry said, "I put out an APB on Dusty. Just in case she's not a crispy critter. What if she's not involved like we think and the killer has struck again?"

What if she's not? "I understand, Sheriff. We'll keep digging. It's all we can do right now. We just went by Barbie's place, and it's roped off with crime scene tape. His car is gone too."

"I'll get my guys to put a bulletin out on his car. I don't suppose you have the plate number? Of course you don't. I'll get it and let you know. Why are we looking for Barbie's car anyway?"

"Dusty made a connection between him and Bitty. His fingerprints are . . ." Jack said before Guidry interrupted.

"Got it. I'll let you know."

The line went dead, and Jack said, "The sheriff is having second thoughts about Dusty being the doer."

"Are you?"

"Until they identify her body, I'm going to keep plugging. She changes her name when it suits her. Who knows what happened out there? She might have set the fire to cover her tracks. Maybe we're looking for Jane Smith now."

Jack's phone rang. It was Kurtis.

"Detective Murphy, I think I may have something."

Kurtis was back in uniform and waiting for them in a squad car outside A Slice of Heaven. Liddell pulled up alongside Kurtis, and Jack rolled his window down. Kurtis didn't look nervous. He was excited.

"I think I'm in good with the Chief again," he said and smiled.

"Tell us what you have for us," Jack said.

"Follow me," Kurtis said and put the car in gear.

Liddell had driven Code 3 when he heard where they were to meet, and he acted disappointed that they weren't going to meet inside.

"Why don't you just tell us here?" Jack asked.

"I'll let the Chief explain," Kurtis said. "She said to ask you to come to her office. And I'm supposed to say please. So please?"

"Why didn't she just call us? Why meet here?" Jack asked. He was a little wary of this complete change of attitude.

"That was my idea," Kurtis said. "I thought you guys wouldn't come to the police station direct because of what's already flowed under the bridge."

Jack deciphered Kurtis's meaning and agreed to follow him to meet the Chief.

"You're gonna love this," Kurtis said.

Jack tried to stay on Kurtis's tail as the police car ran, lights and siren, through several red lights and stop signs before stopping in front of the police station. They parked, and Kurtis led the way through the station. Without knocking, he opened the Chief's door and showed them inside.

Chief Whiteside stood in front of her desk. She was resplendent in her full uniform, badge, ribbons, and stars on her collar, polished gun belt, and spit-shined shoes. A female George Patton.

She smiled and said to the men, "Come in. Have a seat."

To Kurtis she said, "Have someone bring coffee."

Jack said, "None for me. I'm trying to quit."

Her smile faltered. "Shut the door, Kurtis. No, wait. Tell whoever's out there to keep everyone away from my door. I want you back here."

Kurtis went out and came right back and shut the door behind himself. "The outer office is empty, Chief," he said and walked to the window behind the desk.

Jack thought Kurtis was still nervous and wanted to tell him the worst was over and to relax. But maybe it wasn't over. Whiteside sat on the edge of her desk facing them.

"Look. We got off to a bad start," she said. "I'm not always easy to work with. I know. I've been told. And I see the looks on my people's faces. But I'm not a bad cop. Or a bad Chief. I have reasons for everything I do."

Jack didn't know if a response was asked for, so he listened. He watched the expression on Liddell's face and couldn't tell if he was angry or happy. Whiteside hadn't exactly apologized for Liddell's treatment. But she didn't seem the type to roll over and give up her belly like a submissive dog.

"I've examined what Kurtis found," she said.

"Okay," Jack said. He hoped she didn't have everything.

"I rushed to judgment," she said. "I wanted this to be over. My troops were demoralized enough when Detective LeBoeuf was murdered, and they were led to believe another policeman had killed her. Liddell should never have been brought in like he was. I blame Barbierre and Troup for that."

"I accept your apology," Liddell said.

"I'm not apologizing. Just explaining," she said, and took a deep breath. "I'm sorry. I'm still touchy. I apologize. As Chief I'm where the buck stops."

"We understand. Who wouldn't be touchy after all of this?" Jack said. "What can we do to help?"

"Well, Kurtis told me you found soil samples at the place where Barbie was found."

Kurtis gave Jack a sheepish look.

Jack said, "He did? I mean we did find samples." Apparently Kurtis had lied to Whiteside, but Jack didn't know why. "We gave the samples to Kurtis to see if he could tell us where they came from. I hope we didn't overreach, Chief."

"Did he tell you I caught him going through our files? Or that I found out he's been running dispatch logs without authority?"

Jack acted shocked.

She continued. "Well, he did, and I was going to suspend him. But when I went through the logs I could tell he was on to something." She appeared pleased, reached in a drawer, and put a stack of papers on top of her desk. "When you boil all this down it tells you something. Know what this is?"

"No," Jack said, thinking that Kurtis hadn't told her he'd made copies. Another lie for Kurtis.

"For one thing, Detective Troup and Officer Barbierre didn't use proper radio procedure. They know better. I've already had a talk with Detective Troup and warned him in the strongest way that this is unacceptable."

Jack didn't know what to say, so he just tried to look like he was listening.

The Chief took a few pages from the stack of papers and handed them to Jack. It was full of scientific terms and all Greek to him. Jack saw the words "sulfometuron methyl" and figured this was the soil sample result.

Jack held the papers where Liddell could see them.

She said, "As you can see, this report tells us that whoever left that soil on the floor had been in a sugarcane field. I had the State Department of Agriculture confirm the results. We can assume that the soil hadn't been in that house very long. And Kurtis assures me he found no such soil or fiber in the treads of Barbierre's boots or on his clothing."

Jack was disappointed. He'd hoped she had done more with these samples than Kurtis. But he wondered where she got the samples. He had his answer when he saw Kurtis's face turn red.

Kurtis said, "I gave Chief Whiteside the samples you guys collected at the scene. But don't worry. I put it in a report that I'd collected the samples. I mean, we were all there at the same time. And I saw the stuff and all. I just didn't get around to collecting it yet. And since you guys are policemen I didn't figure it would hurt if I took them from you."

Whiteside was looking away while Kurtis talked. Jack could see she didn't believe a word Kurtis was saying, but she didn't give a rat's ass who collected it. All she wanted was this case to be closed.

"The State Department of Agriculture have samples of soil from all over the state. And they have a list of every chemical that is used on crops. They were able to narrow the samples down to two places, and both are outside this Parish. They are nearer Baton Rouge. So the murderer might not be one of our cops after all. I don't think Officer Barbierre killed Cotton Walters. Or Detective LeBoeuf. I don't think he committed suicide. Gentlemen, I think we have a serial killer on our hands."

Jack was stunned at the level of denial the Chief was capable of. First it was Barbie who killed Cotton and killed himself in a fit of conscience. Now it's a serial killer from Baton Rouge. As long as it's not one of hers, like Troup, or a local cop, like Dusty, she's happy as a clam.

Jack said, "I don't understand why you want us to know all of this. Look, I appreciate you telling us that you no longer think we're interfering morons, but I still get the feeling that you don't like us being here. So what is it that you want from us?"

Whiteside leaned back in her chair and cocked an eye at him. "I'm going to let that one pass. In fact, I'm going to let all of your smart remarks pass as long as I get you to agree to help us out. I need your help finding whoever is killing cops."

"Why would we help you now?" Jack asked. "We're doing pretty good without you."

"I'll tell you why. Blanchard needs to clear his name. You need the closure of catching Detective LeBoeuf's killer. And you have a pretty good reputation of catching serial killers. Not many cops have ever dealt with that level of crime. I'll put all my resources into finding Evelyn Blanchard, and I'll even look into the shooting out at Landry's place last night. If you will work for me."

Jack and Liddell exchanged a look.

"What do you say?" she asked.

"I'm thinking," Jack said.

Whiteside stood and put her hands on her hips. "Look. I don't need this. If this leaks to the news media we'll have every Tom and Harry dick in town. If we catch them quick, I think I can keep it down."

Jack said, "You know the harder you try to keep something like this quiet, the more the news media will make of it. And they'll bury you for even trying. We'll work on this, but we have conditions."

"Name it," she said and sat on the edge of the desk again.

"Okay. We get all of the case information. All the cases. Evidence. Dispatch logs. Telephone logs. Everything. You open your personnel records to us. Pay records. Anything we deem important."

"Well, I don't know if . . ." she said, and Jack interrupted her.

"In that case, I don't think we can help you. You said it yourself. We've dealt with these kinds of nut jobs before. You've got to decide, Chief," Jack said with finality.

She stood and put her hand out. "You've got yourselves a deal."

"And we want Kurtis," Jack said. "And no interference. That means Troup stays away."

"I won't take Troup off the cases," she said. "He'll share everything with you, and I hope you'll share with him. Three heads are better than two. And you might as well take Kurtis. He's working for you anyway. Ah hell. He's doing a good job."

Chapter Twenty-nine

Kurtis followed Jack and Liddell outside. "Meet me at the pie place," Kurtis said, smiled, shook hands with both men, and walked away.

When they got in their car, Liddell asked, "What do you think that's about?"

"I think things are not as happy in Happy Valley as the Chief would have us believe. Kurtis told her some big lies, and I think she knows it. But she's a quasi-politician, and her ass is hanging out if she doesn't catch this guy. Or gal," Jack said.

"We'll make Kurtis pick up the check this time. I'm hungry, pod'na."

"When are you not?" Jack put the car in gear, checked the mirrors, signaled, and eased out onto an empty street. He continued checking the mirrors.

"You think someone's following us?"

"I don't know. I don't really care. I just hate to be surprised," Jack said. He wasn't too confident that Chief Whiteside could control Bobby Troup. And Troup was still a suspect.

Jack pulled in front of A Slice of Heaven and left the motor running.

"Did I mention that I was hungry?" Liddell asked.

Jack shut the engine off. "Do me a favor and tell me if you see any unmarked cars or Dodge Challengers."

"Don't you trust Whiteside?" Liddell asked.

"I trust you and me. And Landry."

They went inside and sat in the booth that was the clandestine site of their first meeting with Kurtis.

Tooty was beside the booth before they even got situated in their seats. "You boys want your regular?"

"We've been in here once, Ms. . . . ?" Jack said.

"It's just Tooty," she said, putting pencil to paper. "Everyone calls me Tooty."

"That's an unusual name," Jack remarked and smiled.

"It's my name," Tooty said. "You want something to eat?"

Liddell said, "Yes please. Two big slices of cherry pie and two coffees."

"We got coconut cream, and black coffee. Ran out of creamer. Got sugar."

"I guess give us our regular," Jack said.

She left without writing anything on her order pad.

Liddell leaned in conspiratorially and said, "Do you trust Tooty?"

"Crazy name, crazy unpredictable person," Jack said.

Jack heard a door open in the back of the business. Kurtis slid into the booth opposite them keeping his back to the front door.

"I thought the Chief said we could have you?" Jack asked. "Why all the Secret Squirrel stuff?"

"Because I don't trust her," Kurtis said, pulling a piece of folded white paper from inside his shirt and spreading it out on the table. "She wasn't being truthful with y'all about the ag report."

Jack pulled the paper across and he and Liddell read it. "Kurtis, this is just a bunch of map coordinates, and chemical terms, or whatever."

Tooty came back with a whole pie, three mugs, and a pot of coffee. She set these down and remained standing beside the table.

Jack took two twenty-dollar bills from his wallet and handed the money to Tooty. She took the money and left.

Kurtis watched her leave and after she was gone he said, "I didn't send the samples to the State Ag people. LSU must've done that and faxed over the results. The Chief don't know shit about soil, and I doubt she had enough sense to contact the State Ag people. But anyway, the map coordinates are numbered, most likely to least likely. The first one is near Baton Rouge, like she said. But this one here," he said, putting a finger on a line of print, "this is the Laveau Plantation."

"Laveau?" Liddell said. "I should have remembered it when I heard the name Marie Laveau. Cotton told us Marie is also called Mamba. She is represented by, among other things, sugarcane. That plantation has a mansion, church, five or six shacks, and a cemetery. It's been deserted since I was a kid. We used to take girls to the cemetery. No police patrolled out there, so we could do pretty much what we wanted. I thought that was cool when I was younger."

Kurtis said, "It was unoccupied until about six or eight months ago. Someone bought the plantation from the State. Some long-lost family member. Claims to be a Laveau anyway. Long story. They did a lot of remodeling and construction on the mansion and the buildings. Sugarcane is growing there again."

"Who's responsible for patrolling it? PPD or the Sheriff?" Jack asked.

"Part of it is claimed by the city and part by the Parish, but I don't think it gets regular patrol. At least not now that it has a reputation."

Jack asked, "What kind of reputation?"

"Not a reputation, but more like it's taboo around here. This Parish—hell, most of the State—is Catholic. But there's a group of these fanatics. Voodoo people. They hold secret rituals out there; at the church and maybe even in the old shacks." He laughed and said, "Well, I guess they can't be secret rituals or nobody would know about them. But you know what I mean. Anyway, this Laveau woman is running that. She has some big ol' guy out there running the sugarcane production. Nobody messes with them because they pretty much stay to themselves. I don't recall there ever being a problem there."

Kurtis gave Jack a questioning look. "Why you so interested? Besides the dirt coming from there, I mean. You think something's going on?"

"So who all knows about this plantation, or the Voodoo stuff?"

"It's a big Parish, but there isn't a big population here. I guess everyone that doesn't live in a hole knows about the Voodoo stuff. All the cops know, I guess."

Jack asked a question. "Why is that, Kurtis?"

"Well. I don't know for sure, but I know most of the cops avoid the place on purpose. Maybe they're superstitious. I don't ever have a reason to go out there myself."

Jack followed up with, "Whose beat is it on the PPD side? What officer is responsible for it?" In Evansville, officers are assigned to beats or sectors and that's where they spend the bulk of their time. If something is going on in their beat they know about it, or someone tells them. That's the advantage of having regularly assigned sectors.

Kurtis got a strange look on his face, as if a light had just been turned on. "No one would go out there because the Chief told them to stop running radar. But I heard Barbie's gone out there."

"Why would Chief Whiteside tell them to stop?" Liddell asked.

"I don't know. You'd have to ask her that."

"But we're asking you, Kurtis," Jack said. "You're on our team now. You're allowed to think for yourself."

"Well, if you want my opinion, I'd have to say the plantation people put a stop to it. The plantation people primarily use that road. I'm guessing, but I think a lot of their crew is illegal immigrants. They probably don't have driver's licenses."

Liddell changed the subject. "If Barbie goes around the plantation, what was he doing at Bitty's house? They're not even on the same side of the city."

"Beats me," Kurtis said. "He was a supercop."

Jack finished his coffee. He was ready to get back to work. "Can you check on the ballistics again, Kurtis?"

"Where are you guys going?"

Jack said, "Check the ballistics and call me. I think we'll scout out the plantation."

"I'll call Landry. See if he's heard from Evie," Liddell said.

This was the third time the plantation had come into a conversation, and there were too many coincidences. Jack didn't believe in coincidence. Cotton had said something big was going on and Jack had put the old man's ravings down to paranoia and psychosis. What if Cotton was right? If most cops knew about the plantation and the Voodoo rituals being held out there, it was a good bet Bitty knew about it too. And did any of this connect with Evie being missing? If so, how? Landry had told Liddell he hadn't heard from her. Or the police. Liddell had assured him he was still looking.

Before they left A Slice of Heaven, Jack had asked Tooty about the people living at the Laveau Plantation, and she was a wealth of information. She wasn't much of a talker in general, but she proved to be a gossip ninja.

Tooty told him she'd attended a couple of the "ceremonies" held at the Laveau Plantation church. She said the woman identifying herself as Marie Laveau was very charming and charismatic, and the man, Papa Legba, was beyond hot. Nevertheless, she quit attending the rituals. She felt like Marie Laveau wanted a donation. She didn't give them anything. She didn't go to any church that expected money in return for salvation.

Tooty had gone on to say that thirty to sixty people took part in these rituals, and it was like a nightclub floor, but with different kinds of spirits. She said Marie Laveau was called Mamba. Tooty gave Jack and Liddell a fair description of Marie Laveau and too much information concerning Papa Legba.

Tooty told him the rituals she had attended were held at the church, never the mansion. The setting she described was like Halloween minus the candy. She said it reminded her of the religion where they danced with a snake, and people spoke in gibberish, and lots of smoke and touching and whirling. To Jack it sounded like a Congressional hearing.

Tooty also said that there were lots of girls and boys at these rituals. Jack asked how old, and she shrugged. She wasn't good with ages. She said she'd seen some cops at the rituals too, but they weren't in uniform, so she thought they were there to check the place out. That's another reason she quit going. Her business thrived on policemen.

Jack thanked her, and she held her hand out.

"You pay for his kind of stuff, don't you?" she asked, and he gave her another ten.

Outside he handed Liddell the keys. "You're going to owe me some serious bucks. Let's go see Mamba and Papba."

"Papa, not Papba," Liddell corrected. "Loa to the Underworld. I wonder if Barbie's visiting there right now. The Underworld that is?"

Kurtis was dead on about the road leading to the plantation. It ran off Highway 1 to the north and there were no street signs. The traffic on the street was almost nonexistent to the point Jack wasn't sure they were on the right street until he saw the sugarcane fields.

The fields stretched for what seemed like miles on both sides of the road. They reminded him of the cornfields at home, but with shorter stalks, and more narrow rows that gave a dizzying effect as you drove past. Coming up on their left was a packed gravel road that wound through the cane, and Jack lost sight of it as it disappeared into a stand of giant oak trees. They drove past the turn.

"That led back to the mansion and the old church building. There are a dozen cottages and buildings that at one time were homes for the workers, and supply stores. Most of the buildings had collapsed when I brought dates to the cemetery."

Jack said, "You were such a romantic. I'll bet your dates always wanted to go to a cemetery."

"I've changed, pod'na. I take Marcie to nice places."

"Yeah. Real nice places. Burger King, Donut Bank, Sam's Pizza Shack. She has to be impressed with your style," Jack said, and they laughed.

Liddell slowed and made a right on a dirt road. No sugarcane was planted here, and Jack could see a bend in the Mississippi ahead of them. Liddell pulled onto the side of the road beside a well-worn path, and they got out.

"And this is where me and Landry used to fish." He spread his arms wide.

Jack was impressed. It was at least five hundred yards to the opposite bank, and he could see fishermen in singles and groups, set up along the opposite bank with lines in the water and beers in their hands.

"After we find Evie and catch the bad guys, and if the girls will let us, we need to come down here and fish for a few days," Jack said.

"Yep," Liddell said.

Two shirtless preteens came walking down the path behind them, heading toward the river. Their blue jeans were rolled up to their knees. One wore an Atlanta Braves baseball cap that had seen better days, the other had on a Saints cap bearing an embroidered fleur-de-lis with the word SAINTS embroidered in gold beneath the emblem in case you were stupid. The boys were carrying fishing poles made of bamboo, and one carried a Styrofoam bait bucket.

"Fishing good along here?" Liddell asked.

"We ain't got to fishin' yet," the boy with the Saints cap said. His tone said, "Don't you know nothing?"

"My buddy was fishing here before you were even a gleam in your papa's eye," Jack said. "So show some respect."

"Sorry, Mister," the boy in the Braves cap said. "He's been grouchy ever since the Seahawks lost to the Patriots last year."

"Have not," Saints cap said.

"See what I mean?" Braves cap said with a shrug.

A rabbit ran across the path in front of Jack, faked left, turned right, and disappeared into the high grass.

"Hey, Mister. Turn your left pocket inside out," the boy with the Braves cap said in a whisper.

"Excuse me?" Jack asked, seeing the kid was talking to him.

Saints cap said, "If a rabbit runs across your path you have to walk backwards a couple steps and turn your left pocket inside out."

Braves cap argued, "You don't have to walk backward."

"Do too," Saints cap said earnestly. "An' if you hear a screech owl at night it's a sure sign of death."

The Braves cap was moving up and down enthusiastically. "We heard one last night. I hope something don't get you," he said and pushed Saints cap.

Liddell grinned and said, "If a dog howls and lays flat on his back, that's a sign of death too."

"If your ear is burning, someone's talking bad about you," Jack offered.

Braves cap said, "It has to be the left ear though, Mister. If it's the right ear, they're saying something good about you."

The kid with the Saints cap said, "C'mon, Jitters. We got fishing to do."

"Hold your horses." Braves cap, now known as Jitters, reached in his jeans pocket and handed something to Jack.

Jack examined the object the boy had handed him. It was a dirty, balding in spots, rabbit foot. He watched the kid's face, trying to judge if the kid was having him on. He wasn't.

Jitters said, "I found that in the cemetery over there. It's a left hind foot of a rabbit. That's one powerful talisman. It keeps evil away."

Jack tried to hand the mangy gift back, but Jitters stepped back and said, "You keep it, Mister. It's good luck too. You look like you need it mor'n me."

The two boys went off down the path toward the bank, and Jack held the rabbit's foot out between finger and thumb. "What does it mean when someone give you a rotting animal limb?"

Liddell laughed. "It means he likes you."

After another mile the road tied back into Highway 1. Jack hated to admit it, but Whiteside may have been right to put her officers to better use than watching that road. There didn't seem to be enough traffic to merit even a speed trap, and he could see how the people who worked or lived back in here would feel singled out.

"I guess we can just go to the mansion," Jack said.

"What's our reason for being there?"

"We're with a movie company and scouting locations," Jack said. He took a pair of sunglasses from the visor and slipped them on. "From detective to movie producer with a simple pair of sunglasses."

Liddell said, "I'll be the movie producer. You look more like Jack Murphy trying to look like Tom Cruise."

"Bradley Cooper," Jack said. "And I pull it off."

They made a U-turn and drove back down the road. Jack said, "There's nowhere even to pull off. How the hell did the PPD guys run radar? There's not even a billboard to set behind."

"I'll show you." Liddell turned onto a wide gravel lane. The cane fields opened and the gravel road spread around a squat churchlike structure with an arched door and colored leaded-glass windows. The building had been added on to several times over its history. The most recent addition was made of unpainted plywood with no windows and no outside entry visible. The roof was simple tarpaper that hung over the sides like bangs on a flat head.

"Why would Barbie come back here to see this?" Jack said.

"Not this," Liddell said and drove past the church to an intersecting gravel road. He turned a sudden forty-five degrees to the left and punched the gas.

Almost half a mile in the distance Jack could make out the tiled roof of a structure at least three stories high. As he got closer the cane gave way to sweeping areas of manicured lawn dotted with live oaks and cottonwood trees. They were still a good distance from the mansion when they saw heavy chain-link gates blocking the road. There were red signs on the chain link warning against trespassing. They approached the gates. The signs read, NO TRES-

PASSING and No ENTRY. Two men stepped in front of the gates, both cradling pump shotguns to prove it.

"This wasn't here when I was a kid," Liddell said.

"Yeah," Jack said. The guards were wearing baggy shorts, tank tops, and yellow suede Caterpillar boots. One was light skinned, maybe of Cuban descent, the other wore dreadlocks and was dark skinned. Dreadlocks was maybe nineteen and had a Cubs baseball cap angled on his head. The light skinned one was older. Maybe thirties. He seemed to be the intelligent one. It turned out he was. Jack and Liddell got out and approached the gates, standing almost nose-to-nose with the guards. Dreadlocks' eyes vibrated, but stayed on Liddell.

The light-skinned one relaxed his posture and grip on the shotgun. "Wha'chu want?" he asked, but in a polite, nonthreatening tone.

Jack noticed this one had a portable radio clipped to his waistband. Jack said, "We want to see Papa."

"He no wan' see you," Dreadlocks said, never taking his eyes off Liddell.

"We won't know that until you call him on your radio," Jack said. "I think he'll want to see us."

Dreadlocks grip tightened on the shotgun and Jack could see muscles rippling in his arms.

The older one put a hand on Dreadlocks' arm and pushed the shotgun barrel further toward the ground. He said, "I'm callin' Papa."

The older one walked a few feet away, keeping them in sight, and talked to someone on the radio. Jack couldn't hear the response and noticed an earpiece stuck in the guy's ear. He came back and faced Jack. "He's not here, and we're told not to let anyone in."

Jack stood there another minute and watched Dreadlocks' eyes before he and Liddell got back in their car.

"That kid isn't old enough to have a gun," Liddell said.

"Private property," Jack said. "But you're right. He's looks high on something. You towered over both of them, but he wasn't scared in the least. I think he wanted to start shooting."

Liddell backed up and turned around, careful not to get hung up in the cane field. "Makes you wonder, don't it?" Jack said.

"I've never seen armed guards out here before. Fences, yeah. But those two are not locals, if you ask me. Meth lab?" Liddell suggested.

"Did Bitty work drug cases?"

Liddell said, "No. She steered clear of narcotics cases. She always said if they tried to put her in the Narcotics Unit she'd quit. We'd work homicides involving drugs, and it was part of our job on Water Patrol, but not anything undercover. She said working druggies was like trying to empty the ocean with a teaspoon."

"Let's go see the Sheriff," Jack said, and headed back to Highway 1. As they passed the church building, the front door opened and five youngsters emerged. They were all smiling, and looking over their shoulders at someone who must have been just inside the door. Their expressions were fixed on their faces and they weren't talking to each other. Like they were in another world. Liddell had passed the church and hadn't seen the kids.

If they weren't so young, Jack would have thought their expressions were drug induced. These kids were in the age bracket of ten to fourteen years old as close as he could tell.

"Slow down a little. I want to see something," Jack told Liddell. The car slowed. Jack twisted in his seat, looking back at the church doorway. He saw part of a woman's face looking out at him, then disappearing back inside. He'd only caught a glimpse, but he could tell she was white, age somewhere between thirty and forty years old.

She must have called to the kids, because they stopped, turned around, and went back inside, casting worried glances over their shoulders at Jack's car.

Chapter Thirty

Jack used the phone given to Liddell by Sheriff Guidry and punched 1. The Sheriff answered on the first ring. He was still at Dusty's and wanted them to come to him. They did.

Firefighters were still directing hoses on stubborn hot spots where smoldering coals would reignite even the waterlogged material.

"You want what?" Guidry asked when they pulled him aside. He was in a T-shirt and wearing jeans tucked into knee-high rubber boots covered in ashes. The house was destroyed. The stone chimney stood like a lonely statue, the fields behind it. Part of the side wall had collapsed onto the carport, but that turned out to be a blessing because it somewhat protected the motorcycle and dirt bikes from the flames. Dusty's motorcycle was missing.

"We want you to get a search warrant for the Laveau Plantation and the surrounding buildings and property," Jack said.

"Based on what?" Guidry asked.

Jack told him about their conversation with Chief Anna Whiteside, the information Kurtis Dempsey had given them, and the possible connection with Officer Barbierre.

"One of Barbie's neighbors said he saw a Sheriff's SUV pick Barbie up one night," Jack said. He didn't say that the neighbor couldn't see who was driving. He'd let the sheriff assume who. "The Chief gave the soil samples to the State Agriculture people, and she said they narrowed the soil down to some places near Baton Rouge."

"Too far," Guidry said.

"But when we talked to Kurtis later he showed us the report and said there were map coordinates of the places where the soil could have come from. One of the top two places named was the Laveau Plantation. We asked who patrolled that area and Kurtis said the unofficial order had gone out to leave the Plantation area alone. Barbie was known to patrol near the plantation."

"So, Anna lied to you about where the dirt came from? And Barbie is with the plantation. And Kurtis told you that Anna didn't want her people to patrol there."

Guidry stuck his hands in his pockets and rocked on the balls of his feet. Then he stopped rocking and said, "Sounds to me like Kurtis should get the warrant. He's the one with firsthand knowledge of all of this. He's the one that came up with the State Ag info. He's the one that connected Barbie with the plantation, so we only have his word for it that Anna was holding back on you."

Jack said, "Kurtis gave us all of that, but we went to the plantation and were met with armed guards and a locked gate. I didn't know sugarcane was that valuable." He decided to use everything he had. "And a woman in town said she had attended some rituals at the plantation and crazy stuff was going on."

Guidry laughed out loud. "Tooty, right? A Slice of Heaven?"

"She seemed credible to me," Jack lied.

Guidry smirked and said, "I hate to tell you this, but Tooty isn't quite right in the head. Her parents named her right. She's a tad bit Tooty if you ask me. You can't use that woman as a basis to get a warrant. And the Laveau Plantation is in Plaquemine city. If we try to get a warrant, the judge will want to know why PPD isn't involved. That'll open a new bag of worms, and someone from PPD will be calling the Plantation to warn them we're coming. I'm not saying we can't get a warrant, but it would be better if we had something more solid."

Jack didn't mention the strange behavior of the children at the church. Or that the kids he'd seen were about the same age as Evelyn Blanchard, Liddell's missing niece. The missing person case wasn't positively connected to the murders or to Dusty—yet. And he didn't want to give the Sheriff any more ammunition to shoot his warrant request down. He and Liddell had no authority to request a warrant. They could be used as witnesses to the information used to get the warrant, but he wasn't even sure if they would be allowed to be present when the warrant was served. The Chief, Anna Whiteside, had already determined the soil samples came from Baton Rouge and that they had a serial killer on the loose. She would be no help.

"Do you have any real evidence that a crime has been committed or is being committed on the Laveau Plantation?" Guidry asked.

Jack didn't, but he told him about the two armed guards at the gate of the plantation and how the one was high. "Isn't there some law about guards being armed?" Jack asked Guidry. "One of these guys wasn't twenty-one, and he looked like he was high. Is it a requirement here to be on something to carry a gun? In Indiana even security guards have to go through a training program and be registered with EPD or the Sheriff to carry a weapon." In Indiana, most private security guards carried handcuffs, a baton, and a radio or cell phone, not a shotgun.

Guidry sighed. "I can send someone out there to see who these two yahoos are, but the most we could do is confiscate the shotguns for public safety until we look into the matter. But that still doesn't get us into those buildings. I could get Baton Rouge to fly a chopper over the place, but that wouldn't help unless they have a whole crop of marijuana growing. I think Baton Rouge has enough to do without spending time and money on a guess from two detectives from Indiana."

Jack was out of plausible arguments, and being out of options tended to piss him off. "Okay. What would you suggest?"

"I'm not knocking what you boys are saying. I agree with you that something out there stinks to high heaven. There are a lot of coincidences and I'm not a big fan. If you had something more"— He searched for the word—"*immediate.* If you had something like that, we might get some wiggle room around notifying PPD. Know what I'm saying?"

Jack understood. Plausible deniability. If Jack did a little trespassing and got caught, if anyone got thrown under the bus, it wouldn't be the Sheriff.

To make his point clearer, Guidry said, "Don't get yourselves shot. And don't kill anyone."

*   *   *

The Sheriff had issued a "Be on the Lookout" for Dusty Parnell and her Harley motorcycle, but by that evening neither she nor the motorcycle had turned up. If it was up to Jack he would have put pictures of Dusty and the Harley on all the local channels by now, but he wasn't in charge, and he didn't want to damage an already tenuous relationship by telling Guidry what to do.

He had called Kurtis's cell phone twice already and had left voice mails. It was getting dark when he and Liddell headed back to the fishing cabin. Liddell called his brother to see if he wanted to meet them somewhere close to the house and get an update. Landry insisted they come to the house and eat. His words, "I'm not afraid of no asshole that can't hit someone as big as you."

They pulled up in front of Landry's, and he was waiting for them on the porch with two open beers and a tumbler of Scotch. Jack sat down with his Scotch. He was too tired to worry about being used for target practice again. If Troup had fired the shots at them last night, he was a very good shot and warning them off. If Dusty had shot at them, she was long gone by now, or had burned up in the fire. But for some reason he didn't think she was dead. He hoped she wasn't dead. She had a lot of explaining to do.

Liddell wanted breakfast for dinner. Landry filled two plates with scrambled eggs, bacon, and toast. Jack took his food and went back to the porch, where he could have some privacy on the phone, and called Katie.

"Jack, I'm glad you called. I miss you," she said.

He was glad to hear her voice, and hadn't realized how much he missed her until now. Katie's voice had a calming effect on him. Or three fingers of Scotch had done the trick. He could hear the brothers inside the house giving each other hell. And speaking of hell, Landry looked like he hadn't slept for days.

"I just called to say I love you," Jack said. "I miss you too."

"How is Liddell holding up? Marcie has been staying with me, and she's a wreck. But don't tell Liddell."

"I won't tell him," Jack said. "I thought he called her today. I'll have to kick some yeti butt." Katie laughed, and he said, "What? You don't think I can kick this Cajun's ass?"

"You two would make a good married couple, Jack."

"Nah," Jack said. "He snores, and his feet are hairy."

Katie laughed at his tired humor and he felt tightness in his chest. This was the Katie he had fallen in love with. She hadn't changed. He was the one who had fallen down a rabbit hole after the miscarriage. He didn't think he'd blamed her for losing the baby, but he realized that maybe he had. After all, someone had to be to blame. If it wasn't her, it had to be him. And so he'd punished himself by taking away the only love he had left—Katie.

In his grief he'd buried himself in work and Scotch and the violent world that his anger always seemed to draw to him. When Katie had had enough of his dangerous behavior and his total devotion to his job, she'd asked for the divorce. He remembered at the time he was glad. He'd wanted to push her away and he had.

But, like Katie had told him when they got back together, "The past is the past. We can't change it. We can move forward and try not to make the same mistakes." He had to keep telling himself that he deserved that kind of love.

From inside the house he heard Liddell raising his voice in an imitation of Landry and Landry saying, "I don't talk like that."

Katie said, "You come home in one piece, Jack Murphy. I'm counting on you. And bring Liddell home. I know you're dying to tell him Marcie's news, but I think she would kill you."

He promised to keep mum.

"I need you. Come home soon."

"I love you, Katie. I always have. Always will."

"Just be safe," she said.

"I'm always safe," Jack said.

"And don't get yourself arrested."

"I won't. Don't worry."

He was just putting the phone away when Liddell came out and sat by him.

"Can I use your phone to call home?"

"Marcie is staying with Katie until we get home," Jack said. Before he handed the phone over he said, "I hate to bring this up, but we need to have an idea of a time frame to finish this. You know we can't stay here forever. I'll stay as long as you do. That's a promise. But we have to face the fact that we're alone on this. We don't have any resources. We need to shit or get off the pot, Bigfoot."

Clouds covered the sky, and the moon was a pale orb. Jack sat and stared into the darkness, feeling frustration and sympathy and fear of what they may find even if they were successful at getting into the plantation house.

Liddell drew a .45 Smith & Wesson semiautomatic from his waistband. "Present from Landry. Let's do it."

Chapter Thirty-one

Liddell drove down Highway 1 and turned on the plantation road. A heavy fog blanketed the road and trees and fields, but he'd been here many times as a teenager. He found the creek that ran through the Laveau property. The creek was shallow enough that he could have driven closer to the mansion, but that was before the sugarcane production had been restored. As it was, he was lucky to find a spot big enough where he could hide the Crown Vic. The fog helped.

Before they left Landry's house, Jack borrowed rubber boots and work clothes that had seen better days. His Glock was in a holster on his belt in the small of his back. He had two extra magazines of ammo in his back pocket. Liddell was armed similarly. They had considered taking a riot shotgun from Landry's collection of weapons, but decided that it was too cumbersome for a recon mission. And that was what this was supposed to be. After all, Sheriff Guidry had asked them not to shoot anyone.

Liddell had disabled the overhead light. They got out, quietly closed the car doors, and moved along the creek. The ground was covered in a heavy blanket of fog, and the creek seemed to appear and disappear as they walked.

"I hope we don't run into shotgun-toting guards," Jack said.

"There won't be guards in the cane, not this time of night."

"How deep is this creek?" Jack asked.

"If we have to make a run for it, it won't matter," Liddell said. "This way." Liddell led him away from the creek bed and into the sugarcane. The cane was as tall as Jack, and rows were spaced four or five feet apart. After several hundred yards, they turned south, where they discovered the plants had withered and dried. Liddell stopped them and pointed ahead. Two hundred yards in the distance, Jack could see a glow above the cane field, and the shape of the mansion rose out of the miasma.

"We can get closer," Liddell whispered and hunched over.

He and Jack worked their way to the edge of the cane field and squatted. They could see most of the mansion from where they were, and there were dim lights on in some of the rooms on the second and third floors.

The mansion was monstrous. Jack thought it was almost as big as the Nottoway, but not as fancy. Jack could hear voices and laughter near the house. The voices were accented, sounded Jamaican or from one of the islands. He listened. Men's voices. But he couldn't make out any words, and it didn't help that they were talking over each other and laughing was mixed in. The moon was still hidden in clouds, and the ground was shrouded with thick fog, so he couldn't see anyone or anything moving. A shadow passed in front of a window. On the ground, where he'd heard the men, a cigarette flared to life and burned a bright orange, and was gone. He tried to discern how many voices, and could make out four distinct voices and at least one smoker who was standing away from the rest and hadn't spoken a word.

"There are at least five men," he whispered to Liddell.

"Make that seven." Liddell pointed toward the back of the house, and Jack saw two shapes outlined by a back porch light. The two by the back porch had rifles or long guns slung over their shoulders. Both of them were smoking also.

The driveway that they would have come in by under normal circumstances disappeared into live oaks whose branches stretched an impossible length. What Jack could see of the gravel drive led from the trees and into a circular drive with a fountain in front of the mansion. A narrower gravel road branched off the circular drive and continued along the side of the mansion and passed in front of a concrete structure that resembled a tornado shelter or a fallout shelter.

Two steel doors were set into the concrete, and one of the steel doors was open. A dim light came from the opening and backlit another armed man.

Jack nudged Liddell and pointed to the open door. "That's eight."

An enclosed walkway with a tin roof had been built to the left of the shelter, connecting it with the mansion. A few armed men leaned against the walkway near the back of the mansion.

Liddell duck-walked back a few paces, tugging at Jack's arm. They knelt in the dirt between the rows of plants, and Liddell said, "There's too many, pod'na. Even for you. If they weren't all armed with shotguns, I'd say let's see what they got. But they can lay down a lot of lead with those guns."

"Something must be going on inside that place. Why else would they need that much firepower, and at this time of night? Law-abiding citizens are in bed or passed-out drunk by now," Jack said.

A light came on in front of the mansion, revealing two more men at the corner and leaning against the wall. Both had long guns.

"That's ten," Jack said.

"Not counting whoever turned the light on inside. That makes at least eleven."

"You take the ones outside, and I'll take the one inside that knows how to flip the light switch," Jack whispered.

"What if there's more inside?" Liddell asked.

Jack leaned close to his ear and whispered. "Okay. You take all of them, and I'll cover you from here."

Liddell mouthed the words, "Bite me."

A crunching sound that tires make on gravel came from the trees to their left. Jack and Liddell moved farther back into the cane and got lower to the ground. They watched as a charcoal Dodge Challenger drove past and disappeared behind the concrete shelter.

"Well, I'll be damned," Liddell said in a low voice. "That's Troup. Or it's someone driving Barbie's car."

Liddell rose from his seat and Jack pulled him back down.

"Don't go getting ideas, Bigfoot." Jack cautioned. "If that's Troup, he makes an even dozen. We don't know how many more bozos are around here." He wished they had brought assault rifles, shotguns, grenade launchers, and Iron Man.

Jack could hear the *ding-ding-ding* of a chime announcing the opening of a car door coming from the direction he thought the car might have stopped. One of the guys beside the mansion walked around back.

"Must've gone in through the back," Jack said.

"It was Bobby," Liddell said. "That's his car."

Jack thought so too, but he didn't want to get Liddell worked up. They were there for surveillance, not to get into a gunfight. His knees were beginning to complain of the stress of staying crouched for so long a time, and he could feel a burn running up the back of his thighs and settling in his butt cheeks. He wished he'd brought a lawn chair.

One of the men in the driveway flipped his cigarette into the gravel and barked orders at the others. Three men walked down the gravel drive toward the front gate. The rest headed toward the back of the mansion. The light in the shelter went out, and the door was pulled shut with a bang. Whoever these guys were waiting for had arrived, and they were locking up for the night.

"I'd like to see what's down there," Jack said.

"I'd like to see who Troup's meeting. No wonder he tried to scare us off. No one else around here will stand up to him. He may be the reason the Chief didn't want other policemen hanging around out here."

"I've got an idea," Jack said and sprinted toward the gravel drive. He came back with the smoldering cigarette butt.

"We need a diversion," Jack explained. "I want to see what they're hiding down there. It looks like we can get in that walkway and go to the mansion from the shelter." He reached down and pulled a plant out of the ground. "Does this stuff burn?"

The plant felt brittle, dried out, dead. In fact, most of the plants they'd passed through were dead.

"If we start a fire we don't know where it will spread, pod'na. You sure you want to do this?"

"You heard the Sheriff," Jack said. "We can't get a warrant, and no one else is going to even try. That leaves us with two ways to get inside. Shoot it out with a dozen armed men, or we can lure them out and keep them busy putting a fire out. This stuff is all dead anyway. We'd be doing them a favor."

Liddell pulled up an armload of the plants, and they carried them away from the mansion and piled them up. Jack held the cigarette under a brown leaf, and when it caught he held it to a stalk and blew on it until the embers glowed. He turned the stalk until it was on fire. He pushed this down into the pile of sugarcane plants. The fire dampened and smoked but got its second wind and caught.

Jack and Liddell had made it to the side of the shelter when one of the steel doors slammed open and two men emerged, facing toward the fire. Jack feared the men would see the smoke and put the fire out too soon, so he pulled the Glock and turned it around to use the butt like a club.

Red and orange flames shot thirty feet in the air like an angry fist, and the surrounding plants spread the blaze like a daisy chain. The men yelled, "Fire! Fire!" and ran for the back of the house.

Jack and Liddell headed down the steps and heard alarmed voices outside. They reached the bottom of the concrete steps and were in a hallway with steel doors on their right. The hallway ended at a T that branched to the left and right. All the doors were padlocked. "This isn't a storm shelter," Jack said in a whisper.

"More like a bunker," Liddell suggested.

They stepped into the hallway and lights came on. "Motion sensors," Jack said, thinking that was both good and bad. Good because they had forgotten to bring flashlights. Bad because it telegraphed their movements to anyone who was around the corner.

Jack's rubber boots squeaked with every step. He slid them off and sat them against a wall. "Hopefully, if someone sees them, they'll think they belong down here."

He went back up the steps in his socks and watched the chaos outside. There were at least twenty or more men out there running around with hoses and blankets trying to douse the fire. He pulled the door shut and joined Liddell at the T-intersection. He peeked to the left and right. It was dark, but he could just make out doors on each side in both directions. He wasn't sure how long the motion sensors were set to, but no lights meant no one had come through the hall recently. He didn't see any light coming from the ends of those hallways and hoped that meant they were unoccupied as well. He kept his .45 in his hand just in case.

The turned to the left, and as they went the lights came on. Jack saw padlocks on all the doors. If he'd been able to get a warrant he'd be cutting the locks off right now, but they didn't have one and he couldn't risk the noise of shooting the lock.

"I wonder how big this place is?" Liddell whispered.

"Big enough that we ought to leave a trail of bread crumbs," Jack answered.

They stopped at the end of the hall. Straight ahead was a wooden door with an electronic keypad dead bolt. The right side led to another hall that turned to the left. They bypassed the locked door and went to the end of that hall where it turned right. Jack peeked around the corner and said, "Clear." They went to the right, and as the lights came on, Jack could see doors on both sides of this hallway. Not all were padlocked. Jack held up a hand, and said, "Do you smell that?"

Liddell sniffed the air. "Something. I don't know what."

"Cordite," Jack said. "It's not very strong, but I smell it." Gunshots had been fired in that part of the hallway and not too long ago.

"It's a damn maze down here," Liddell said. "Why would you go to the bother of building this elaborate underground bunker if you weren't up to no good? It's not deep enough to withstand a bomb blast. Are they survivalists? Militia?"

"That would explain a lot of things," Jack said. "So the plantation is a front. Cotton said something big was going on. Would a Voodoo cult go to this much trouble?"

"I can't see that being the case, pod'na. And Troup is involved somehow with three murders. It's got to be more than Voodoo," Liddell said. "I've met some Voodoo practitioners, and they were pretty harmless. Maybe we've run across a Branch Davidian compound like in Waco, Texas."

"Let's see what's behind doors number one, two, and three," Jack said.

Jack held his Glock tight to his body. He put his ear against the door before opening it.

Chapter Thirty-two

Marie Laveau was in her element. The ritual began exactly at midnight on the night of a full moon. Papa had somehow found Haitian drums and believers to play them. The beat was steady and hypnotizing.

The air was filled with mixed smells of incense and sweat and other more unpleasant odors. A dozen believers had come to watch the initiation rites for three of the girls Marie had taught. The three initiates were swaying with eyes closed as if in a trance, while the rest danced to the steady beat of Haitian drums beseeching the Divine Horsemen to imbue the initiates with their power and knowledge. The drums were the real deal; handmade from cottonwood, hollowed out, and painted with the symbols for various Loas, their tops covered with stretched animal hide. The most skilled drummer played the Segon—the largest of the drums—with one hand creating the beat, and with the other hand he struck a half-bell made of hammered iron with a stick for rhythm.

Marie Laveau, the Mamba, the Voodoo Queen, stood in the middle of this spiritual chaos known as the Kanzo, or initiation ceremony, and led the chant. Her hair was covered with the traditional white skullcap with long dark hair spilling over her exposed shoulders. She hitched a white gown up with her hands, exposing tanned legs and bare feet as she spun and undulated to the music.

A behemoth of a man sat in a high-back chair on one side of an altar decorated with candles, hand-carved wooden masks depicting various Loa, statues, silver trinkets, tridents, a gris-gris, weavings and wall hangings, and incense. The man's features could have been chiseled from coal. White ringlets of hair flowed from underneath a plantation hat made of straw; a band circled the crown and was adorned with symbols of the seven loas—the divine horsemen of Haitian Voodoo. A hand the size of a skillet rested on the silver cap of a cane.

Papa Legba sat unmoving, staring into nothing. The only sign he was still in this world was the occasional blink of pale yellow catlike eyes. One would have to be ignorant or foolhardy to glance in his direction, for Papa Legba was blessed by the Loa to act as the gateway between this reality and the spiritual world. He alone had the power to take a person into the underworld. He could cure them of an illness, or he could bring back their hollowed-out husk to do his bidding.

The drum beat and chanting built to a crescendo and came to an abrupt halt, the cue for the handful of initiates to form a half circle and kneel in front of Marie Laveau. Their eyes lowered, arms hanging loosely at their sides. This was the second of three rituals required to bring them into the Vodoun—the Voodoo family—and make them the sèvitè, or "servants of the spirits."

The ceremony ended, and Marie Laveau pressed objects taken from her pockets into eager hands as the congregation filed past her and on to Papa Legba where they kissed his ring before filing out. Their faces wore the secret hope that they had been—or would be—blessed. Marie knew enough about all of them that she provided them with the amulet matching their desire, or for those who were not ready to believe, she pressed a piece of candy in their hand to entice them to return. Among those at the ceremony were seven girls Papa had selected as the next group of initiates. Six of them would be chosen to complete their recruitment.

When the church was empty, Papa Legba opened a door beside the altar. He held it for Marie and followed her into her private office. Papa removed the stole and ceremonial robe and hung them in a large wardrobe next to Marie's ceremonial trappings. In a deep voice befitting his size he said, "Whew! I was burning up out there." He unbuttoned his shirt and flapped the sides. "It must be a hundred degrees."

Marie crossed the room and turned down the thermostat. "It's nice in here, but the air-conditioning doesn't seem to want to keep up with the heat."

The door to the office opened and Luke, Papa's second in command, stuck his head in the room.

"He's here," Luke said and shut the door.

Papa turned to Marie and said, "He can wait."

Marie pulled a Styrofoam cooler from underneath her desk. "I brought this," she said and lifted the lid. It was packed with ice, two crystal tumblers, and a bottle of Laphroaig ten-year-old Scotch.

Papa smiled and removed the hat and the wig of white ringlets and put these on top of the wardrobe. He ran a handkerchief over his face and across his bald head and sat next to her. He filled the glasses with ice and Scotch and handed one to Marie.

"Tell me again why we don't take donations from these fools," Marie said, her bright red lips forming a perfect pout. "And why aren't we charging for these ceremonies and rituals? I'm working my ass off here, and I feel like I took a shower inside my dress." To emphasize this, she opened her gown and pulled her soaked top up, revealing generous breasts. She knew that to Papa those breasts were part of the gold mine that was her body. A body he had mined more than once over the years.

Jack opened the door and when they stepped into the room the lights didn't come on. No motion sensors in this room at least. Jack pointed to the ceiling. "Vent pipe. I wonder if they are in each room. There must be a circulation system somewhere."

The room was empty except for a half dozen wooden pallets stacked in a corner. "Storage room," Jack said, and they stepped back into the hall. Jack was about to shut the door when a door closed somewhere and he heard voices coming toward them. He and Liddell ducked back into the room, and Jack pulled the door almost shut behind them and listened.

The voices were masculine. One was deep, like that of James Earl Jones, with an unmistakable Southern lilt. The other had an accent that Jack associated with the Caribbean. The Caribbean voice said, "The room ready, Papa."

Jack watched through the crack in the door. The hall was empty but he could still hear footsteps in the adjoining hall. The one that led to the dead-bolted door. He moved stealthily and peeked around the corner. Two men, one a giant, bigger even than Liddell, the other no more than five feet tall, round, and he was carrying Jack's rubber boots.

Jack felt a hand touch his shoulder and jumped. It was Bigfoot.

Liddell said, "The big one must be Papa. I wonder if they're going to meet with Troup? Do we go after them or check the other rooms first?"

"They've got Landry's boots. Let's go see what Papa and Troup are saying. We'll come back if we have time, but I don't expect to find anything in the other rooms. We would have found a drug operation by now."

They exited the storage room and hurried after Papa and the other man. At the end of the passage Jack put his ear against the wooden door and could hear muffled voices getting fainter. He tried the door but it was locked.

"There must be another passage to the mansion behind this door. We're going to lose these guys. We should go back upstairs and try the other entrance."

A woman's voice came from behind them. "What's the hurry?"

"Lay your guns on the floor," Dusty ordered. "Or don't."

Liddell stooped down and laid his .45 on the concrete.

"Now you." She pointed the rifle at Jack's midsection.

He figured she has already killed three people. Five wouldn't matter. He reached for the Glock, and she said, "Use your other hand." He pulled the Glock from the holster with just his finger and thumb. Jack gently laid it on the concrete.

"Now kick them over here. One at a time," she said.

Liddell shoved the S&W .45 with his foot, and Jack followed suit. The guns slid just out of her reach.

"Now turn around and keep your hands where I can see them."

They turned their backs and held their hands above their heads.

"It's over, Dusty," Jack said. "The Sheriff is on his way if he's not here already."

"It's not over till the fat lady sings," said a familiar voice, and Sheriff Guidry came through the door in front of them. His gun was pointed at them.

Jack should have been surprised, but everyone in this sewer hole of a town seemed to be dishonest.

"We were set up," Jack said.

"You think you feel used," Dusty said. "My house is a complete loss, and it still didn't stop you two from meddling."

"Dusty, your house was overinsured, so don't cry too much," Guidry added, and Dusty gave a snort that passed as a laugh.

Jack asked, "How did you know we were here?"

Guidry pointed his pistol at Jack's face and said, "I'm going to grant you one last request just to show you how nice I am." Guidry pointed the barrel of the gun down to Jack's sock feet. "Your rubber boots told on you, son. Luke saw them in the hall and knew they don't belong. None of these boys would leave anything that could be stolen. Now shut the hell up. I'm getting tired of all this. I'd just as soon shoot you right here, but Papa wants to ask you some questions. You're lucky it's not me or her asking the questions."

Jack could hear Dusty snicker close behind. Guidry kept his gun trained on them and motioned for them to step back as Dusty picked up their guns. "Turn around and walk toward me," she ordered. She held a hand up, stopping them near of one of the doors, unlocked and open now. "That's far enough. Assume the position, boys," she said.

Jack leaned against the wall and spread his legs, glancing back at Dusty. Two men armed with shotguns came up and covered them. Jack recognized one of the men as Dreadlocks from the front gate, the young one that wanted to shoot first and call Papa later. Not good.

"Face the wall, bozos," Dusty said.

"Why Bitty?" Liddell asked, and the butt of a shotgun buried in his kidney. Liddell's knees buckled but he was a big man. He didn't go down. He asked again, "Why Bitty?"

"Takes a lickin' and keeps on tickin'," Guidry said and laughed at his own joke. "I'll tell you why Bitty. Bitty could have saved herself a whole passel of trouble if she'd a just stopped when I told her to stop. She was digging into a case of a missing teen and next thing you know she's off to the races. She came to me and wanted to go to the papers or television with them. These kids were like pond scum. You scoop 'em up and more just takes their place. Runaways, druggies, abused kids. All the same. You can't fix what ails them. But Bitty wanted to try. She was getting too close, and I knew I couldn't control her."

Human trafficking. That's why Dusty is involved. Jack said, "So you killed her to shut her down."

"You already had your one question, smart ass," Guidry said and struck Jack in the back with his fist.

Jack's eyes teared up from the pain, but he held himself steady and asked another question. "What's Troup getting out of this? Where's he at?"

Dreadlocks clubbed Jack across the head with a shotgun barrel. He felt something warm trickle down into his eyes.

"We'll ask the questions, and you better listen good because there's gonna be a test," Guidry said and chuckled.

The two men with shotguns kept them covered while Dusty and Guidry expertly patted them down, taking everything that could be used for a weapon or escape. Dusty said to the guards, "Lock them up."

Dreadlocks shoved Liddell and Jack into the room and stood in the doorway, giving them his best gangsta look. Jack would have laughed if his head didn't hurt so much.

The door shut, the bolt slid home, and the room was thrown into darkness except for a tiny crack of light at the bottom of the door. Jack could see shadows of movement and hear Dusty saying something he couldn't make out.

"Well, I didn't see that coming," Liddell said.

Jack dragged a hand along the walls, measuring the room. It was about ten foot by ten foot and empty of anything to use for a weapon. He sat down with his back against a wall. Things hadn't gone as planned, but there was still a chance. Landry knew where they were going. If he didn't hear from them soon he'd . . . He'd do what? Report it to the police? To the Sheriff?

Liddell must have been thinking along the same lines. "I wish Landry didn't know where we were going. Both of these assholes know we're staying with him, and if he calls one of them to report us missing he might go missing himself."

"They can't just keep killing people, Bigfoot. Somebody's bound to notice a bunch of people getting dead or disappearing. The news media will be all over it. Our department will look into our disappearance." Jack knew what he was saying was bullshit. Even if the EPD investigated their disappearance, it wouldn't go anywhere because of the corruption here. He thought about the promises he'd made to Katie. If he couldn't find a way out of this, her worst nightmare would come true. And he had to consider a baby Bigfoot growing up without a daddy Bigfoot.

"Chief Whiteside," Jack said. "I wonder where she fits into this. She's been all over the map with this investigation. She's lied and threatened us one minute and wants our help the next. Maybe Troup has some dirt on her. Maybe she's just bipolar. Or maybe she's a partner in whatever the hell is going on here."

"Kurtis and his brother Jon will miss us and rally the cavalry," Liddell said, and then, "Oh, shit! You don't think . . . ?"

Jack thought about Kurtis. "Kurtis doesn't like Troup, or Barbie for that matter. I know he gave us up to Whiteside, but he's still a kid. He still wants to be liked by his boss. He's not jaded like us. I don't think he's involved."

"Yeah but what if?" Liddell said. "When we tried to get a search warrant Guidry said something like we needed Kurtis to get the warrant because he gave us everything we know. Kurtis found the soil samples. You said yourself that you couldn't make heads or tails of that ag report, and Whiteside tells us the samples came from Baton Rouge. It was Kurtis that gave us the Laveau Plantation. And Troup stopped us on the road to let us know he was on to Kurtis. It all fits. What if Troup did that to make us believe Kurtis, so Kurtis could set us up?"

It was a good argument. But Jack felt sorry for Kurtis. Whiteside had treated him like dirt in front of everyone and threatened to suspend him for trying to help with the investigation. He was young and full of passion for police work. Unlike Barbie, he didn't equate police work with brutalizing anyone. And unlike Troup, he wasn't arrogant and bending the law to suit himself. He didn't want to think Kurtis was one of the bad guys. But it was possible. The boy did seem to be nudging them along.

"Anyone that has helped us is in danger," Jack said. "If Kurtis is involved, he's played us. But if he's not, I think he'll be seeing the inside of one of these rooms. Both Troup and Guidry know he's helping us."

They had sat in the dark for what seemed like an hour when Jack heard the bolt sliding open. Jack plastered himself along the side of the door and braced himself for a fight. He wasn't going to make it easy for whoever had come to finish them off.

The door was yanked open, and Landry stood there holding a stainless-steel Desert Eagle .50 caliber handgun.

"Liddell, Jack," Landry called.

Jack stepped out of the darkness with Liddell right behind him. Jack asked, "How in the hell did you get down here?"

"You didn't think I'd let you come out here alone, did you? Besides, Evie might be here."

"What I meant was, how did you get down *here*?"

"There's a cemetery back behind here. Liddell and me used to hang out with other kids there. I knew where you'd park because that's where we always parked. I found your tracks, but I had to circle around because there's a fire out there. Everyone was running helter-skelter. I saw Sheriff Guidry and some woman come in here," Landry said.

"That must have been Dusty," Liddell said.

"This wasn't here when we were teenagers. Must be some kind of bunker, huh?"

"Do you think you can find the way back out?" Jack asked Landry.

"I'm not leaving. I've got to look for my daughter."

"Landry, listen to me . . ." Liddell said and was interrupted when the armed men who had locked them up came out of a room across the hall.

Dreadlocks tried to bring the shotgun barrel down, but Jack grabbed it and shoved it upward. The blast went into the ceiling, raining bits of concrete down on them. Jack followed up by shoving the barrel over the man's head while pulling at the pistol grip and brought the barrel down onto a very surprised face. Hands came up in surrender, and Jack slammed the barrel down again, snapping Dreadlocks' left clavicle. The man doubled over in pain. Jack stepped back and put his weight into it as he drove his knee forward into the upturned face. The man crumpled to the floor.

Jack saw the other man had left a smear of blood on the wall where he slid down it. Landry was relieving the unconscious man of the shotgun while Liddell cradled his hand.

"He's still got a mean punch," Landry said.

"How's the hand?" Jack asked Liddell.

Liddell flexed his fingers and made a fist. "I'm good. It's just been a while, but it felt good."

Landry took the weapon off safe, eased the shotgun's slide back, and checked the chamber. He thumbed the safety to the 'fire' position and handed the shotgun to Liddell. "The safety was still engaged. Damn idiot."

"Someone's bound to have heard that blast. We'd better get moving," Jack said.

Jack had Dreadlocks' shotgun now. He checked both men's pockets for extra twelve-gauge ammo. One had several unspent rounds and the other had nothing but a switchblade knife. Jack handed Liddell half of the ammunition and he pocketed the knife.

"Damn amateurs." Landry said.

Jack and Landry dragged the unconscious men into the room where they had been locked up and bolted the door. "You can stay if you like," he said to Landry.

"So what are we doing?" Landry noticed Jack's sock feet. "You went and lost my boots?"

Liddell squeezed Landry's shoulder. "*We're* going to find Evie, and *we're* going to call the Feds and shut these assholes down."

"So what's the plan?" Landry asked.

Liddell asked, "What's the plan, pod'na?"

"I guess we follow Dusty and Guidry," Jack said. "I don't think they went back through there," he said, pointing to the wooden door. I think I heard them go around the corner. There must be something down there."

They took the hallway to the right, and after about twenty feet it came to a T.

"Split up?" Landry asked.

Jack pointed to the left. "I'll take this one. You and Liddell go that way. If you see someone, shoot them. No more nice guy."

"Damn straight," Landry said. "But I think you should take this big fella. He'll just get in my way."

Liddell said, "Just like when we were kids. You never picked me for your team."

"Like I said, you always got in my way," Landry said.

"Come on," Jack said to Liddell, and they turned left. After a few yards, Jack asked. "You think he'll be okay by himself?"

"I pity anyone that gets in his way," Liddell said.

They hurried to the end of the hall where a big door was cracked open and a light was on inside. Jack nudged the door a little wider and saw it was a cafeteria of sorts. The kitchen had stainless-steel worktables and heavy-duty double sinks and a walk-in refrigerator/freezer. A long serving counter separated the kitchen from the half dozen picnic tables. There were plates of half eaten food, soft drink cans, and coffee mugs on some of the tables. Some of the guards must have been in here when the fire broke out, but the room was empty now.

Just to his left was a heavy wooden door. With the shotgun in one hand, he cracked the door open and peered into a maroon-carpeted space that led to a wide staircase. Next to the staircase was another door.

The staircase was enormous, at least ten feet wide, and ascended to an upper floor. The staircase banisters, as thick as his arm, ran up both sides. The ceilings were thirty feet high, and hanging above the staircase was a massive chandelier whose cut crystals glittered like diamonds.

Jack held the shotgun at the low-ready position and crossed to the door on the back wall. He opened the door, and he heard whispering coming from inside. There was a rustle of movement, and the door shut. He cradled the shotgun across his arm with the safety off, finger beside the trigger guard. He tried the handle again. It was locked. He would have kicked it in, but he was only wearing socks.

"Cover me," he said to Liddell, and as he put his shoulder into the door it was pulled open and he fell into the room. Jack hit the floor and rolled to the side, bringing the shotgun up. The woman was petite with almond-shaped eyes, light brown skin, and wearing a long silk gown. She was frightened out of her mind.

"Is anyone else in here?" Jack asked.

She hesitated. "No one. I'm alone," she said and cast her eyes down to her feet.

Jack rose to one knee, the shotgun sweeping the room from left to right. A rollaway bed and tiny wardrobe comprised the room's furniture. The bathroom door was shut.

Jack motioned at the closed door, and asked, "Who's in there?"

"No one is here. Just me," the woman said.

Jack stood, pointed the shotgun at her, and motioned toward the closed door. "Open the door, and it had better be empty or—no pun intended—you're in deep shit."

The door seemed to open on its own, and a small voice said, "Don't hurt her. I'll come out."

Jack kept the shotgun trained on the woman and watched as a young girl emerged from the bathroom. He judged her age as thirteen or fourteen. She was tanned, long dark hair, thin-ish, wearing old blue jeans and a white T-shirt with DEF LEPPARD printed on the front, barefoot. A pair of dirty tennis shoes at the foot of the bed was about her size. She had one hand hidden behind her. Jack would never again assume a teenage girl wasn't a threat after he'd almost been blown to kingdom come by one a few months back.

"Bring your hands out where I can see them," Jack ordered the girl, and a can of hairspray hit the floor.

The girl edged over to the woman, who put an arm around her shoulders and hugged her, protecting her. They both had been crying, but the girl was giving him a defiant look. The girl shrugged off the woman's arm and stepped forward. "My father will be really mad if you hurt us."

Jack saw the resemblance. "Evie?"

The defiant look on her face faded.

"Your father is here," Jack said. "We've been looking for you. My name is Jack Murphy, I'm your uncle's partner." But he didn't know if she'd heard all of that because she had flung herself across the room and wrapped her arms around him, head buried in his chest.

The woman asked, "You're a policeman?"

"Yeah. Who are you?"

"My name is Ubaid. I'm a prisoner as well. Please help us."

Jack gently lifted Evie's face up to his and cocked his head at the woman named Ubaid. "Is she telling the truth?"

"She's protecting me," Evie said and reburied her face in Jack's chest.

"Liddell is at the end of the hall. We'll find your father and get you out of here," Jack said. "Do either of you know how many men are in the house?"

Ubaid said without hesitation, "About twenty men. And Papa and Marie. I think there are some policemen here as well. Not good policemen like you."

Dusty, Troup, and Guidry. That made at least twenty-three

armed, minus the two they had laid out. Twenty-one was still a for-
midable number to take on with two shotguns and a pistol.

Jack moved to the door with Evie glued to him and checked the
narrow hallway. He spoke to Ubaid. "We need to get you out of
here. My car is near the road over by where the creek comes in. Do
you know where that is?"

"I will show you," Ubaid said.

Evie detached herself and said, "I can't leave. There are a bunch
of little kids here. We can't leave them."

Chapter Thirty-three

Liddell came into the room, and Evie rushed to him, almost bowling the yeti over.

"Uncle It!" she said between sobs, and clung to him for dear life.

Liddell kissed the top of her head and wrapped one bearlike arm around her.

"Your father's been looking for you," Liddell said and brought on a fresh spate of tears. Liddell's eyes had dampened as well.

"Uncle It?" Jack said.

Liddell turned his head toward Jack and mouthed, "Bite me."

"Let's get them and Landry out of here," Jack said.

Jack turned to Liddell. "Evie said there are other children. We need to find them. And Landry. He can get them out of here, but we have unfinished business."

Ubaid said, "I know where the other children are. It's on the other side of the bunker." She described the route they needed to take, and it sounded to Jack like it was the direction Landry had gone.

"Well, let's go," Jack said.

"I'll go first," Liddell said. "Evie, you stay right behind me. You hear me?"

Jack took the rear-guard position, and with the women between them they moved off down the hall toward the bunker.

Liddell stopped before they crossed the hallway that led to the exit. He peeked around the side and saw there were no ceiling lights on. The hall was empty in that direction. Landry had gone down the hall that was straight ahead of them now. That hall turned left at the end. There were lights on at the end.

Jack moved up beside Liddell. "I'll go find Landry and send him after you. You should take Evie and her friend and get out of here."

Liddell looked at Evie and Ubaid. "They'll be safer with us. And I'm not leaving without my brother."

Jack thought he'd say that. He said, "Well, let me go first." Jack was nearing the end of the hall when Landry came around the corner in a rush and they almost collided.

"I found some kids," Landry said, and four young children came from around the corner holding hands.

"Daddy!" Evie said and ran past Liddell and Jack.

"I'm right here, baby," Landry said. He grabbed his daughter, wrapping his arms around her, kissing the top of her head and her cheek, and patting her back, all while muttering how he'd never let her get away from him, and at the same time scolding her for scaring him to death.

Jack counted heads. There were two boys and three girls, all preteens.

"Landry, we need to get out of here. Liddell and me will cover you at the entrance. You get these kids out of here. Can you do that?"

"Where you going to be?" Landry asked.

"We'll be right behind you," Jack lied.

"Right behind you," Liddell said. "Don't wait for us. Go. Get to the house. Better yet, go to the first state police barracks you find. Don't trust any local cops. The Sheriff is in on this. Maybe some police too."

Ubaid put a hand on Jack's arm and said, "I know a better way. If you trust me, I know where a van is behind the mansion. Luke always leaves the keys in it. I've heard him tell other men that the keys are over the visor."

Jack asked Landry, "Are you up for that?"

"Anybody get in our way is going to find out what this feels like," Landry said, holding the Desert Eagle up. "Come on," he said to Ubaid and the kids.

Jack turned Ubaid to face him. "Do you know Bobby Troup?"

Ubaid said without hesitation, "I don't know who that is. But if he's one of them, I would guess they are in the library. That's where Papa will be. And Marie is here too. I saw her before I went to get Evie."

She gave Jack directions, then, along with Landry, she led the group of kids back down the hallway Landry had come from.

After Landry's troop of kids were out of sight, Jack and Liddell followed the directions Ubaid had given them. They passed the room where they had locked up the unconscious guards, and it was quiet and still locked. They made their way back to the wooden door with the electronic keypad lock. Ubaid had given them the code.

Jack punched in the code, and the lock made a whirring noise. Liddell covered the door with a shotgun while Jack pulled it open to reveal a lighted hallway. They entered and moved side by side with the shotguns at the ready until they reached the far end and a stairway. Ubaid told them the stairway would lead up to another door and then into the mansion. The door had the same lock with the same combination.

Jack went up first and punched in the code. The lock whirred. He pushed the door partway open and put his back to the wall to let Liddell cover the opening with a shotgun.

"Looks clear," Liddell said, and Jack pushed the door completely open. Nothing. Not even a sound.

The concrete floors gave way to thick Oriental rugs as they entered the mansion. Along the walls were narrow tables and lamps and vases of flowers and other decorative frippery. Oil paintings depicting fox hunts hung in gilded frames on the walls. A stairway was just ahead.

Ubaid had told them to go up this stairway and at the top there would be two doors on the right that were restrooms, and a set of double doors straight ahead that entered the library. She'd said if anyone was still in the mansion this is the room where they would be.

They made their way to the stairs and up without being challenged. Jack could smell smoke from the fire. He wondered if the mansion was caught in the blaze and found himself hoping it was. These assholes needed burning down.

"I'll take the left side," Jack whispered.

Together they kicked where the doors came together. The wood splintered and the doors flew inward against the walls. Jack and Liddell rushed in the room, shotguns sweeping ahead of them. The walls were indeed lined with rows of books, and in the middle of the room was a large occupied conference table. Sitting on the left side was Sheriff Guidry, Dusty Parnell, and another woman. She looked familiar. On the other side sat the giant black man and a white male with a ruddy complexion in his late fifties.

Jack remembered where he had seen the woman. Hers was the face peering out of the doorway of the church earlier. She was Marie Laveau. Had to be.

The giant appeared calm, unconcerned, as did the man seated next to him. But Guidry and Dusty both exchanged a look and reached for their duty weapons.

Jack fired the shotgun blowing a hole in the middle of the conference table, and worked the slide to eject and chamber another round. "I wouldn't if I were you."

Liddell swept his shotgun from one to the next and said, "Well, I'll be damned," he said.

"What?" Jack asked without taking his eyes off Guidry or Dusty.

Liddell raised the shotgun and pointed the barrel at the woman sitting beside Dusty. He said, "That's my ex-sister-in-law."

"What?"

"That's Sally. Evie's mother."

"Oh, this just keeps getting better," Jack said and took a step toward Guidry "You two bozos," Jack said to Guidry and Dusty. "It doesn't feel so good being on this end of the barrel, does it? Undo your gun belts and drop them on the floor."

No one moved and Jack leaned forward. "I will shoot you. Ask anyone."

"I don't think so," Dusty said, and smiled at him. Neither she nor Guidry made a move.

"She's as crazy as a shithouse rat," Jack said and moved closer. "Dusty, at this distance your head will explode like a melon and get all over everyone."

"Jack," Liddell said.

"Cover me, Bigfoot. I'm going to do some cosmetic surgery on this bitch."

"Jack!" Liddell said, his voice urging Jack to look at him.

"Hello, Detective Murphy," a familiar voice said from behind him and to his right.

Without turning, Jack looked back and saw Kurtis Dempsey standing in the corner, pointing a shotgun at Liddell. He looked the other way, and Jon Dempsey was in that corner, with a shotgun trained on Jack.

"Surprised to see us?" Jon asked.

Kurtis was holding the pump shotgun loosely, as if surrender was the only choice on the table. Jack turned his head and winked at Liddell, and they swung around, Jack to his right, Liddell to the left, pulling the triggers almost simultaneously.

Jack saw Kurtis's face disappear in a mist of blood, fragments of skull, and bits of tissue that peppered the wall behind his head. Kurtis was dead before his body knew it. He was still holding the shotgun when he crumpled to the ground. He didn't have time to see if Jon was still a threat. Jack pumped the slide, chambering another round, and hoping to reacquire Dusty and Guidry—but he was too late.

He and Liddell would have been dead if not for the chaos at the table as five people jockeyed to stand. Guidry was fumbling for his gun and fell against Dusty, causing her shot to go wild. The giant and the unknown man had flipped the table up and over, striking Guidry and Dusty, who were trapped beneath it. Jack blew a hole in the conference table where he thought Guidry or Dusty might be and was rewarded with a pained grunt. He jacked another round into the chamber and yelled, "Throw your guns out."

A gun came out from under the table, but it was pointing in Jack's direction. He quickly took aim and blew the arm off at the elbow.

The giant and Sally had taken advantage of the firefight to flee out of a door hidden behind a bookcase. The unidentified man had fallen backward out of his chair and was pulling himself backward. His hand went under his jacket and Jack pumped the shotgun and pulled the trigger. *Click.*

The man smiled, and pulled a large semiautomatic from under his jacket. He got to his feet and aimed at Liddell. The man said, "Hello, Liddell."

"Doyle?" Liddell said.

"You always were a pain in the ass. Good-bye, Blanchard."

Liddell jerked when he heard the blast, thinking he'd been shot, but an amazing thing happened. A hole appeared in the middle of the man's throat. Another blast and a perfectly round hole appeared in the man's forehead. The man's eyes were fixed on Liddell with a surprised look while he fell sideways, the gun falling from his hand.

Jack turned and saw a black suit, black wing tips, and a dark silk shirt. Bobby Troup held a .45 in one hand and a lit cigarette in the other. Liddell lowered the shotgun he was holding. He'd gotten one shot off when he killed Jon Dempsey and the shotgun jammed. The slide locked up, rendering it useless for anything other than a club.

He thought he was surprised when he saw Sally, but he was wrong. The man that had almost killed him was Doyle Doohan, ex-partner of Bobby Troup.

Chief Whiteside came up behind Troup, her pistol held in a low-ready position. She called back over her shoulder, "We need medics!" She looked around at the carnage and muttered, "And some body bags."

Troup looked at the two detectives and said, "Happy to see me?"

Chapter Thirty-four

Jack and Liddell sat on the back bumper of a Fire Rescue truck while paramedics checked them out at Chief Whiteside's insistence. Dusty and Guidry wouldn't need medical attention. Dusty bled out from her wounds, and Guidry's heart looked like a sieve. A sheriff's deputy was near the entrance to the underground complex, identifying and supervising the removal of live prisoners and dead bodies. Troup was nowhere to be seen. Probably off nursing a fat lip after Liddell had coldcocked him.

Whiteside sat in her police car, door open, alternately talking on her radio and her cell phone. The mansion had sustained some fire damage, but not as much as the fire hoses had inflicted on the interior. The cane fields were another matter. The plantation looked like a five-hundred-pound MOAB—Mother of All Bombs—had flattened everything for a thousand feet. Some charred cane stalks stuck up here and there like a bad haircut in Hell.

Whiteside hooked the radio on the dash of her car and walked to the Fire Rescue truck. "I guess you guys have some questions. Good job, by the way," she said.

Jack couldn't believe the change that had come over her. She wasn't the Jekyll and Hyde that she'd seemed before. This Anna Whiteside was professional, friendly, and complimentary. In the spirit of professionalism, Jack said, "First question. What the . . ." and this was more of a swearing session than a question.

Whiteside gave him a half serious look and said, "That would be my first question too. First, let me introduce myself." She reached a hand out and shook with Jack and Liddell. "U.S. Immigration and Customs Special Agent Anna Whiteside."

Jack gave her an incredulous look. "ICE?" Jack said. "I guess

the Pope is around here somewhere, too. Maybe Troup is the President."

Liddell chimed in, "The Pope is in the woods, pod'na. The Pope
always shits in the woods."

Whiteside laughed. "I guess I should tell you about the operation first, and then I'll answer your questions."

Operation? More like a circus. Even the clowns were here.
"We're all ears," Jack said.

Jack listened to Whiteside's explanation as he watched a seem-
ingly endless parade of State Police officers bringing handcuffed
men to waiting cargo vans and ambulances. He and Liddell had just
been through a small war and somehow came out without a scratch.
It was a first.

Whiteside's phone rang, and she held a finger up and answered.
She listened and said, "Okay. Hold them. I'll be right there."

"I know you hate him, but that was Detective Troup. He's
picked up Sally Blanchard, aka Marie Laveau, and her partner, Lincoln Sutter, otherwise known as Papa Legba. When they escaped, a
couple of my agents followed them to a resort on Grand Isle and
Troup picked them up. We're in the process of rolling one of the
human trafficking rings."

"One?" Jack asked.

"This is only part of an international operation, Detective Murphy. By morning you two will be heroes."

Liddell said, "We just want to get back to our lives. No offense."

"None taken," she said. "Troup has been working undercover for
the FBI and ICE for almost five years now," she said. "You should
know that he was erroneously accused of the murder of a bookie a
few years back. The one you and Elizabeth LeBoeuf worked on.
When the grand jury didn't charge him, he came to us. His ex-
partner, Doyle Doohan, was the real killer. He was already in the
white slavery market before he was fired by the Sheriff's Department. He moved to New Orleans and hooked up with Lincoln and
Sally. They did business in New Orleans, and with Doohan's connections, they came here. He and Sally were old friends. ICE got
wind of it and contacted the Louisiana governor, who pulled some
strings and got me appointed Chief. I hired Troup, and you know
the rest."

"Just so I'm clear, the plantation and the Voodoo was just a front for human trafficking?"

She answered with a smile.

"Who killed Bitty? Did Guidry?" Jack asked.

"I'll answer that, but first let me tell you we have arrested Papa's sidekick. A guy named Luke Perry. He is singing like a bird. He told us that two of Papa's men caught Detective LeBoeuf, or Bitty as you call her, snooping around the bunker. They tortured and questioned her, but she escaped. She killed three of her captors before they caught her again. This time they shot her. Lincoln/Papa was angry that they'd killed her, and he killed two of his own guys. Perry says there are a dozen or more unmarked graves in the cemetery behind this place. Some of them for kids that were kidnapped and were killed for one reason or another."

"And Barbie?" Jack asked.

"Barbie was working for Guidry and Dusty. She was behind him stealing your backup gun from your car and shooting Cotton. She drugged him and then hanged him. I had to pretend I thought it was a suicide. And I had to let you believe Troup was crooked. He tried his best to get you to leave, but lucky for us, you two are hardheaded."

"So Barbie really did kill Cotton," Liddell said.

A State Trooper interrupted to whisper something in Whiteside's ear. She returned to Liddell's question. "Yes. Barbie killed Cotton. He left your backup gun at the scene to frame you. His prints were not on it. Just yours. I lied and said we found Barbie's fingerprints on the gun. You'll get it back, don't worry."

Jack said, "Who are you really? I had you checked out, and my resource couldn't find you under the name Anna Whiteside."

"My name is really Anna Whiteside. I can't tell you any more than that. You'll have to show a little trust. Look, I've got to get going. They just found Bitty's car in the Mississippi River, where Perry said they'd dumped it. I'll answer all your questions tomorrow. Go get some rest. I'll need statements. Tomorrow."

"Can I ask a favor?" Jack said.

"I'll help if I can," Whiteside said.

"Our department is going to chew our asses up and spit us out," Jack said. "Can you tell them we were working for you all this time? I'd like to keep my job."

Whiteside said, "I've already taken care of that. I told your

Chief that you were assisting the FBI and ICE with a sensitive investigation the night you arrived to pick Liddell up. Chief Pope agreed that we could have you. We swore him to secrecy."

Jack had wondered why Pope or Franklin or Double Dick hadn't been calling every five minutes. He figured he was fired. "Thank you for lying on our behalf. There's hope for you yet."

"I have a question," Liddell said. "Did Sally know Evie was her daughter?"

Whiteside said, "According to Luke, Sally was the one that suggested Plaquemine. Doohan was familiar with it, and had Dusty and Guidry on the hook. The traffickers had already spent a fortune on the setup at the plantation when Papa found out about Evie. Sally didn't recruit Evie. The girl found her way here on her own. He didn't think Evie ever recognized Sally. When Papa found out about Evie, he had her locked up and was using her to keep Sally in line. Apparently, Sally was planning to get her daughter and get out of the life. This is all gospel according to Luke, you understand. The others aren't talking."

She smiled and said, "Oh. Call your wives. If you need written excuses, I'll be happy to provide them."

Jack had borrowed another pair of rubber boots, this time from one of the firemen. They were three sizes too big, but it beat the hell out of walking in socks all the way back to their car. He could have asked Whiteside for a ride, but he still didn't trust her. He trusted Liddell, and that's as far as it went.

Jack and Liddell walked through the scorched field, and Liddell said, "I wonder if she'll let us give our statements to the FBI in Evansville? We need to see Landry and Evie to make sure they're okay. And get my car. And then I want to go home."

"Dusty took my phone," Jack said. "We'll have to stop at a pay phone. Whiteside said Landry and Evie are home, and the other kids are being checked out by medics and taken care of. I think we'd better get some shut-eye before we drive twelve hours. Let's ask about the statements tomorrow."

Liddell said, "I haven't been honest with you, pod'na. I got some news I've wanted to share for a couple of days, but there never seemed to be a right time."

Jack stopped and waited.

Liddell grinned. "I'm going to be a daddy."

Epilogue

Jack and Liddell sat in lawn chairs on the back deck of Jack's house. Liddell kept an eye on the smoker with Jack riding shotgun.

Jack upended a Guinness and let the foam run down his throat. "Two pork shoulders, four pounds of ribs, and two whole chickens. Think it'll be enough for the four of us?" he asked.

"The pork shoulders are for Abita Amber Pulled Pork. The chef at the Bourbon House restaurant in New Orleans gave me the recipe. The ribs and chicken are just to balance the meal. And there's potato salad, grilled corn on the cob, green bean casserole, and for dessert I made a bourbon pie."

"What are the rest of us going to eat?" Jack kidded.

"Leftovers," Liddell said.

Liddell was doing all the cooking, so Katie and Marcie lay in the sun on reclining lawn chairs. Liddell had been cooking for the two days they had been home. Whiteside had let them give their statements to the FBI in Evansville, and she was decent enough to have his car shipped home for him so he could ride with Jack. Liddell still had to pay the repair bills and buy two new tires. Typical.

Liddell emptied his own beer and crushed the can in one hand. "Want another?"

"I'd be crazy if I didn't," Jack said and dug in the cooler that set between their lawn chairs.

He and Liddell had given lengthy statements, went through mug-shot books, drew maps, and thought about getting lawyers before the Bureau was finished with them. And they were still going to have to appear in Federal Court in Louisiana sometime in the future to testify to their actions and the discovery of the children. The children were all reunited with their parents or families and/or were referred to Child Protective Services to monitor the effect this had on them. Landry, Evie, and the children may have to appear as well, but Whiteside promised to make it as painless as possible for everyone. All in all, Jack didn't hate her as much as when he'd met her. That was a lie. *Bitch.*

She'd filled in all the blanks before they left Plaquemine. Dusty had driven Barbie's car to the mansion and Guidry was with her. That was the car they thought Troup was in. If this case was a game of Clue, the solution would be, "Colonel Murphy killed Ex-Detective Doohan, Miss Dusty Parnell, and Sheriff Guidry and the Dempsey boys in the library, with the shotgun."

The FBI and Louisiana state troopers had found eleven bodies and counting buried in the ancient cemetery behind the mansion. Everyone had been shot. Luke Perry confessed to his part in the trafficking, murders, and kidnappings and turned state's evidence in exchange for testifying against Sally, Lincoln, and the three Syrians caught by the Coast Guard trying to flee Grand Isle. The yacht was seized, and there were numerous other arrests expected.

She'd cleared up the matter of Barbie killing Cotton with the gun he'd stolen from Liddell's car. Liddell's and no one else's fingerprints were found on the gun. Dusty killed Barbie and made it look like suicide. Barbie was a loose end that needed taken care of.

Dusty really had inherited the property and the house that had burned to the ground. It was heavily insured, just like Guidry had said. She had become suspicious of Bitty when she'd caught Bitty looking through missing person records at the Sheriff's Department. Bitty had made the mistake of trusting Barbie to check missing person records from Plaquemine PD. Whiteside said Dusty would have eliminated Bitty herself, but Papa's bodyguards did it for her.

Sally, aka Marie, had come up with the plan to leave Bitty's desecrated corpse in Bitty's house. Luke Perry had taken the naked body to Bitty's house, hacked her with a machete to hide the bullet wound, and drew the crude Voodoo symbol on the wall to make it look like a Voodoo curse. Sally had given him a drawing to copy from. Luke didn't know anything about the Voodoo symbols at Cotton's house, and the best guess was that Barbie or Dusty or both had been behind that.

Sally and Lincoln were now competing to see who could make

the best deal with the Feds. Sally admitted to most of what they already knew, and said she wasn't going to let them sell Evie. She was planning on "spiriting" her away. Almost a million dollars was recovered from a safe in Lincoln's office. Another fifty thousand was found at the church.

Sheriff Guidry had recruited the Dempsey brothers with the promise of wealth. The brothers were aware that kids were being kidnapped and sold into slavery. Jack wanted to shoot them again.

Ubaid was telling the truth about being sold into slavery by her family. The U.S. State Department granted her sanctuary and she was in the process of starting a new life under the Witness Protection Program.

Like a champion liar, Liddell had acted surprised when Marcie gave him the news that she was pregnant. He'd known for days, because a new secretary at the doctor's office had called the house before he'd gone to Louisiana and spilled the beans. He was a smart man playing dumb, but Jack was still a little pissed at him for not saying anything.

Jack had talked to three people this morning before bringing Katie to the Blanchard backyard BBQ to celebrate Marcie's good news. First he'd called Angelina Garcia and had her check out Anna Whiteside. Suspicion dies hard when you've been lied to consistently. Anyway, Angelina said she'd checked Anna Whiteside out days ago, and had immediately gotten a call from the Justice Department. They threatened her with arrest if she said anything about Whiteside or Troup. She made Jack promise that he and Katie were still coming to the wedding. He promised.

Secondly, Jack had called Anna Whiteside. She told him they had rolled up the trafficking ring as far as they were able to. Interpol was now involved, and they might want to talk to Jack and Liddell. He lied and said he'd be happy to cooperate with our foreign friends. *Screw them.* He'd ended the call by telling her she could thank him and Liddell for making the case for the government to which she'd responded that he was pushing his luck and may be looking at half a dozen murder charges and the violation of civil rights. She'd laughed when she said that, but she was probably lying again. She was very good at lying.

And last of all, Jack had called Sergeant Mattingly about the home invasion burglar case. Mattingly had passed on good news.

The burglar had gone back to Gladys's house for a return engagement. Gladys had gone against Jack's advice and bought a handgun to protect herself. While Jack was in Louisiana, the burglar, named Roland Hay, surprised Gladys while she was coming out of her bathroom. She had surprised him in turn with two .38 caliber slugs in his groin. Case closed. He would live, but he'd had a "mister-ectomy." compliments of Gladys.

Jack finished his second Guinness—or was it his fourth?—and watched the two bikini-clad women lying in the sun, chatting away without a care in the world. He could hardly tell that Marcie was pregnant, but if she were having a boy it wouldn't be long before she would feel his feet kicking and start craving donuts.

He watched Katie say something to Marcie, and both women laughed. Katie put a hand on Marcie's belly and the women laughed again. Marcie reached across and patted Katie's belly and Jack put the beer down. Both women saw the look on Jack's face and giggled.

ACKNOWLEDGMENTS

Of all the writing I've done (this is my fifth thriller) I find the acknowledgments page to be the hardest. Not because I don't like doing this, but because I'm afraid I'll neglect to mention someone important to the work. If I have not mentioned you, I hope I have thanked you and you will forgive my omission.

When I wrote the first book, *The Cruelest Cut*, I questioned whether I would ever be lucky enough to write another. But, here I am, and here you are. My thanks to an outstanding editor, Michaela Hamilton, and Kensington Publishing Corporation's expert staff of marketing, public relations, designers, proofreaders, copyeditors, and—well, I could go on and on naming all the people that work the magic that make these stories available on your eReaders and bookstore shelves. I've visited Kensington several times and inside it resembles the Keebler Cookie factory. Honest.

I need to thank three readers who have tirelessly slogged through my rough drafts of *The Darkest Night* so they could point out my many errors and make this book read-worthy. They are Greg Graham, Sarah Pugh, and Millie Hardy. My gratitude and sympathy to you all. The old saying, "It takes a village to raise an idiot" is very true in my case.

Much of this story takes place in Iberville Parish and Plaquemine, Louisiana, and paints some of the Sheriff and Police Departments in a poor light. Just the opposite is true. The Louisiana part of the series research started in 2010 with a phone call to Sheriff Brent Allain (now retired), who opened many doors for me. It was with the help of Lieutenant Chris Couty, Sheriff Motor Patrol, and Major Johnny Blanchard, Sheriff Water Patrol that the Liddell Blanchard character was created. I also thank the current Sheriff, Brett Stassi, for the cooperation of his office in making this book.

And my thanks to David Reyes, the master chef at the Nottoway Plantation Mansion in this book, for his numerous suggestions concerning Cajun cuisine.

And last, but definitely not least, I want to give my sincere thanks to my friend and a great artist, Deputy Chief of Police Brad Hill.

This novel is a work of fiction and is not intended to reflect negatively on any law enforcement agency. Any resemblance to people, businesses, or agencies is purely coincidental. Having said that, the Nottoway Plantation Mansion is real and an experience of a lifetime. I sincerely hope readers will understand my taking poetic license.

**Don't miss the next exciting Jack Murphy thriller
by ex-cop Rick Reed!**

THE SLOWEST DEATH

Coming soon from Lyrical Underground,
an imprint of
Kensington Publishing Corp.

Turn the page to read an intriguing excerpt . . .

Chapter One

Day 1, 2 A.M.

Moonlight fell through the broken window, casting squares of light like oversized picture frames across a trash-strewn floor. Franco "Sonny" Caparelli regained consciousness. He was naked, lying on his stomach on a freezing floor. The back of his head was cut, and blood had run into his eyes. All he could remember was the driver's-side window caving in toward him, a dark figure, a man, strong hands grabbing him by the head, yanking him through the truck window, a pinch at his neck, and then he was here.

He blinked the blood out of his eyes, but he couldn't seem to move. His face pressed against the floor as his arms were yanked behind his back. He heard ratcheting sounds and felt something tighten around his wrists and ankles. He heard feet shuffling close by, the sound of a zipper, something metallic, a crackling sound he couldn't place.

Although they were completely numb he could wiggle his fingers. He could feel his chest rising with each breath. With great effort he turned his face to the side and lifted it a few inches before something hard shoved his cheek down, grinding his head into the floor like it was a cigarette being put out. Sonny felt his skin tearing, tasted the heel of the boot that was crushing his jaw, splitting his lips.

The grinding stopped and the foot lifted from his face. "Be still," a voice said.

Sonny could see legs with black boots, tightly laced, military-style. Dark pants, neatly creased, bloused into the tops of the pants. A black travel bag set on the floor. The zipper was partially open.

"Who are you?" Sonny asked. His voice seemed to come from

inside a tunnel, from inside his head, somewhere behind his eardrums. His head felt like a balloon that was ready to burst. His mouth was dry and tasted of cloth and dirt.

"Tastes like dirty socks, doesn't it?" the voice asked. "It should. I used your socks to gag you with. If you don't want the gag again behave. The sooner we get this done the sooner we will talk."

Gloved hands snaked a rope around Sonny's neck and threaded it under the restraints.

"Check this out." A boot came down on Sonny's back. At the same time the rope drew tight, drawing Sonny's head toward his ankles, cruelly arching his back, choking him.

Sonny's eyelids fluttered. A roar rose in his ears but subsided as a black curtain drew down. The rope suddenly slackened. Sonny's face slammed into the floor, smashing his nose and driving a tooth through his upper lip. He shuddered as his tortured lungs sucked in air.

"If you do something I don't approve of, I rein you in."

Sonny didn't move or speak.

"Good," the voice said. "You understand the meaning of consequences. Well, at least you do now."

A boot wedged under Sonny's shoulder and shoved him onto his side. He could see a tall figure dressed all in black, standing in front of the broken windows, the bright moonlight hiding face. The voice was a man's. The figure squatted to allow Sonny to see the face of a white man, thirties or forties, black Army fatigue jacket, black cargo pants, black balaclava rolled up like a sock hat pulled down tight over the ears. The man was standing as if he thought— hoped—Sonny would recognize him. He didn't. He had no idea who this crazy son of a bitch was.

"You don't have any idea who I am," the dark man said. "I'm hurt. Well, maybe it's for the best. Not knowing who I am will help you feel what it is to be in the hands of a stranger who hurts you."

Sonny closed his eyes. The rope tightened a bit. "Look at me!" The voice turned menacing. "Study my face. If you close your eyes again you will be experience pain like you've never felt before."

Sonny spat blood on the floor. He looked his captor in the eyes. "Why me?" he asked in a cracking voice. "I don't know you. You're making a big mistake, pal."

A smile spread across the dark man's face. "Shizaru," he said, the voice playful.

"Wha—what?" Sonny asked.

"You've heard of the ancient proverb of 'The Mystic Apes'?" Sonny just stared at him.

"The three wise monkeys? No? Well, I'll enlighten you. Mizaru sees no evil, Kikazaru hears no evil, Iwazaru speaks no evil. The Three Wise Monkeys of the Koshin belief. The monkeys are a code of conduct."

"Screw your monkeys, shithead," Sonny said. "Look, you . . ."

The man took a step back and yanked the rope taut. It dug into Sonny's throat, winched his ankles and head across the cold floor toward his back. Sonny's eyes bulged. A hissing sound escaped around his swelling tongue. His eyes rolled back, his chest heaved, and his face went slack.

"Oh no you don't! We're not finished yet." The man released his hold on the rope and kicked Sonny in the chest. "*Breathe*, damn you!"

Sonny felt ribs break. He sucked in air and coughed uncontrollably. With each spasm droplets of blood spewed from his mouth.

The man knelt beside Sonny, prodding his shoulder until the coughing gradually abated, and the breaths came slow and regular.

"Boy, that was a close call. I thought you'd bought the farm. So, where was I? Oh yes, the Koshin religion." The man shook the rope a few times as a reminder. "Koshin followers believe good behavior brings good health. Bad behavior brings bad health. The first three monkeys are the behaviors you should avoid. If you engage in any of them you will meet the fourth monkey, Shizaru. The punisher. And here I am."

Sonny's eyes widened. He tried to speak but was unable to find any words to say.

"Don't act surprised. You had to know punishment would come for you. Boston or Evansville. You were never out of my sights. Five years, seven months, eleven days. I know you have to remember because I will never forget what was done to her."

Lights flashed across the windows, bathing the room in light creating a scene right out of a murder mystery play. The sound of tires crunching over ice came from outside, but the vehicle never slowed.

Sonny screamed but it was weak, defeated. The light passed and hope fled with it. Sonny stiffened, preparing for what he knew would come.

Instead, the man said, "I'll give you that one. It's human nature to want to live, isn't it? Tell me something, Sonny. Did she beg? The autopsy report said she still alive when she was set on fire. Did she struggle? Of course she did. Bits of nylon were found melted into her skin. Similar to the nylon bindings you're tied with right now. You're helpless. I can do anything I like with you."

Tears ran from the corners of Sonny's eyes and froze on his face. His anger was long gone. His certainty that he would die had taken its place.

"Are those tears of remorse, tears of self-pity, or are they tears of relief? Relief that this is going to be over. No more watching over your shoulder."

He took a small object from a pocket and held in front of Sonny's eyes. It was less than an inch tall. An ivory figurine of a squatting monkey with arms crossed. He set this on the floor in front of Sonny's face. Sonny eyes lifted from the figurine to the man. Every muscle in his body tensed as he struggled with his bindings.

The man reached into another pocket. This time his hand came out with what resembled a pair of brass knuckles, only these were made of shiny black material with metal studs protruding from each knuckle. He slipped the weapon over his gloved fingers, holding it next to Sonny's face. When he tightened his fist the weapon came alive with electricity arcing between the spikes.

The dark man leaned down. His lips touched Sonny's ear almost lovingly. "These are called Zapper-knucks." He straightened. "They're brass knuckles *and* a stun gun combined." He drew his fist back and delivered a vicious blow, driving the spikes deep into the flesh on Sonny's cheek, at the same time squeezing the grip, releasing 950 kilovolts of electricity through Sonny's head.

"Did you really think you could hide from me?" The spikes pressed into Sonny's neck, releasing yet another electric charge. Sonny's body seized. His muscles locked in a spasm as a stuttering sound, "Unh, unh, unnhh, uh, uh," came from deep inside. Drool and spittle flew from Sonny's tortured lips.

The fist came down across Sonny's face again and again, ripping flesh, scraping bone, and infusing each contact with nerve-piercing electricity. When the beating stopped Sonny's eyelids were clamped tightly shut, his mind unable to appreciate that he now lay in his own urine and feces.

A rough hand lifted his chin, dropped it back to the floor. "I know you're still in there somewhere, Sonny." The dark man pulled a folding knife from a clip on his belt. The blade flicked open. The point of the blade dug into Sonny's scalp just above his left ear and dragged downward, slicing through flesh and cartilage and continuing to the bottom of the jaw, where the blade exited with a gush of warm blood. The realization of what had just happened caught up with the pain. Sonny screamed in agony.

"Tell me if I'm hurting you," the dark man said.

Sonny's scream faded, turning into mewling sounds. His body was too exhausted to even shiver from the damage and the cold.

"Scream all you want," the dark man said. "I've heard it helps. Well—maybe not you so much, but it helps me." He shook Sonny's shoulder roughly and slapped the side of his face. "You're not going into shock, are you? No. You're a tough guy. You'll live through this and find me. Won't you? You'll kill me for this. You just keep that thought."

The man stood and took the black bag to a wall, unzipped it completely, and took out coils of thin steel cable, heavy metal eyebolts, and meat hooks whose points had been filed sharp. He busied himself screwing the eyebolts into the wall studs, two of these six feet from the floor and five feet apart, one centered just above these, and two more at knee level.

The dark man said in a mocking tone, "I know what you want to say, Sonny. You don't have to do this. I don't know who you are. You're so very sorry. If I let you go you won't tell. Honest Injun." He nudged Sonny's head with the toe of his boot and said, "But I do have to do this."

He unrolled wire from the cable and cut several pieces into four- to six-foot lengths. While he did this he said conversationally, "Someone inside the DEA was paid to get you a job here. Do you think they know who you really work for? Are they in on it?"

He clamped one end of each cable to an eyebolt in the wall. "I guess that doesn't matter now. But I'll give you a chance to come clean. Tell me who was behind what you did to her? I know who it is, but I want to hear you say it. Who was it, Sonny? Tell me a name, and I'll make this quick."

Sonny laid still, eyes closed, his chest rising and falling faster.

"Time's up. It was Dominic Bertenelli. He's the one that pulled in a favor from his DEA friend?" The man threaded the remaining cables through the eyebolts, took another tool from a cargo pocket, clamped them tight, and yanked on each to test its strength. "Your partner, Sully—what a piece of work that guy is—resigned about the same time as you from Boston PD. He works for Dom now."

Sonny was breathing a little harder after hearing the names. The dark man grabbed Sonny's hair and yanked his face up. "Look at me when I'm talking to you! You're being impolite, and I don't think you can take much more from the Zapper. So tell me something I can cripple Bertenelli's business with."

Sonny opened his eyes. "They're gonna kill you, asshole. No matter what you do to me, they'll do worse to you. I'm not afraid of a piece of shit like you. I spit on your grave," Sonny said and spit blood on the floor.

The man laughed until he was howling with laughter. He got it under control and said, "I applaud your effort to die like a man, even though you stink of fear. Well, I'm touched by your concern for my welfare, but I don't think any of them will be a problem for Shizaru. Most of them are already dead. Bertenelli's wife and kid were the hardest. What with bodyguards and all. But they all get careless. Just like you. I know where everyone is. I know everything about them. I'm saving Bertenelli Senior for last. I want him to suffer like I suffered. I'm taking everything from him. His kid's dead. His wife's dead. His little kingdom will crumble before his eyes."

"You're insane," Sonny said through split lips.

"I sometimes wonder," the dark man said. "I'll ask your girlfriend what she thinks. Is she a screamer?"

ABOUT THE AUTHOR

SERGEANT RICK REED (ret.), author of the Jack Murphy thriller series, is a twenty-plus-year veteran police detective. During his career, he successfully investigated numerous high-profile criminal cases, including a serial killer who claimed thirteen victims before strangling and dismembering his fourteenth and last victim. He recounted that story in his acclaimed true-crime book, *Blood Trail*.

Rick spent his last three years on the force as the commander of the police department's Internal Affairs Section. He has two master's degrees. He currently teaches criminal justice at Volunteer State Community College in Tennessee and writes thrillers. He lives near Nashville with his wife and two furry friends, Lexie and Luthor.

Please visit him on Facebook, Goodreads, or at his website, www.rickreedbooks.com. If you'd like him to speak online for your event, contact him through marketing@kensingtonbooks.com.

A SADISTIC
SEX SLAYER'S
GRISLY DESIRES…

INCLUDES KILLER'S
CONFESSION

Blood
Trail

Steven Walker
and
Rick Reed

THE CRUELEST CUT

"As authentic and scary as thrillers get."
— Nelson DeMille

A JACK MURPHY THRILLER

RICK REED

THE

COLDEST

FEAR

"Reed writes as only a cop can...
impressive and dramatic."
— Nelson DeMille

A JACK MURPHY THRILLER

RICK REED

THE DEEPEST WOUND

"As authentic and scary as thrillers get."
— Nelson DeMille

A JACK MURPHY THRILLER

RICK REED

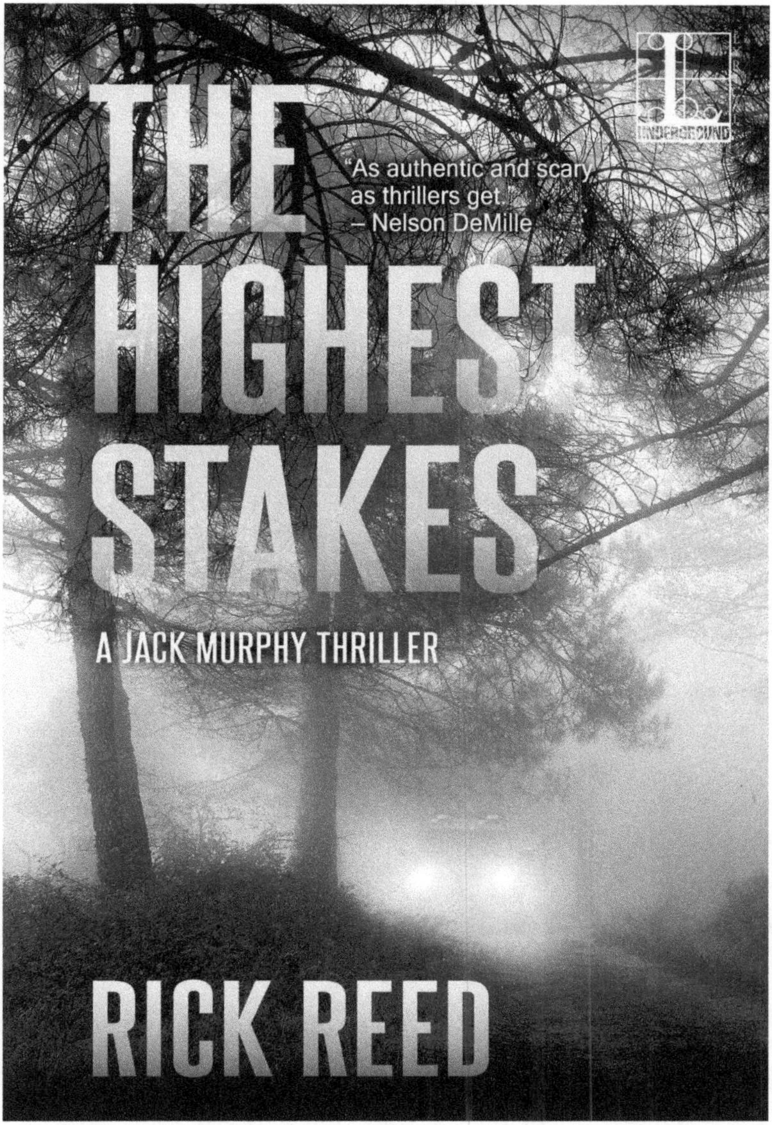
THE HIGHEST STAKES
"As authentic and scary as thrillers get."
– Nelson DeMille
A JACK MURPHY THRILLER
RICK REED
UNDERGROUND

CPSIA information can be obtained
at www.ICGtesting.com
Printed in the USA
BVHW031951291220
596672BV00014B/56